THE
FOURTH
CHILD

ALSO BY JESSICA WINTER

Break in Case of Emergency

THE FOURTH CHILD

A NOVEL

Jessica Winter

HARPER

An Imprint of HarperCollins*Publishers*

THE FOURTH CHILD. Copyright © 2021 by Jessica Winter. All rights reserved. Printed in the United States of America. No part of this book may be used or reproduced in any manner whatsoever without written permission except in the case of brief quotations embodied in critical articles and reviews. For information, address HarperCollins Publishers, 195 Broadway, New York, NY 10007.

HarperCollins books may be purchased for educational, business, or sales promotional use. For information, please email the Special Markets Department at SPsales@harpercollins.com.

FIRST EDITION

Library of Congress Cataloging-in-Publication Data has been applied for.

ISBN 978-0-06-297155-5

21 22 23 24 25   LSC   10 9 8 7 6 5 4 3 2 1

He mooned restlessly about, and daydreamed; then came to Harriet to touch her, or climb on her lap like a smaller child, never appeased or at rest or content. He had not had a mother at the proper time, and that was the trouble, and they all knew it.

Doris Lessing, *The Fifth Child*

THE
FOURTH
CHILD

JANE

She didn't trust easy. If she tried to account for the substance of her life, and of the lives of other people she picked up along the way—other people she made—she might start there.

"Anything that's easy isn't worth doing," her father used to say, and her brothers would snort and snicker. Jane used to think they were laughing only at their father, always aboard his creaky carousel of platitudes. Later she knew they were also laughing at the shape *anything* took on in their minds: the mute curves of a compliant girl. A girl who might be easy; a thing who might be worth doing. This girl had a discernible figure—or pieces of one—but not a face. A swinging ponytail on the Bethune High School basketball court. A tender stripe of flesh above a waistband. Jane herself could be this girl, conceivably, to boys who were not her brothers.

Jane earned three dollars per hour to put the Vine kids to bed and stay in their house until Dr. and Mrs. Vine returned from their Saturday-night bridge game at two or three in the morning. Dr. Vine was an emergency room physician in a perpetual state of convivial jet lag. Mrs. Vine read novels and took naps and crafted delicate silver jewelry in their basement. Sometimes Mrs. Vine would press a trinket into Jane's hand along with the wad of bills at the end of a night. Tiny earrings with the face of a smug cat, or a necklace strung with an ambiguous locket—a pear, a teardrop, a heart. The Vines were lean and tawny, with matching chestnut hair; each stood the same height as the other in their stocking feet. They spoke in low murmuring tones and touched each other frequently and were the first adults Jane ever imagined having sex.

The Vines could not be long for the village of Williamsville, for the suburb of Amherst, for the city of Buffalo, a place that you left if you could, or so Jane's mother always said. "He can't be such hot *S-H-I-T* if he could only get a job in *Buffalo*," her mother replied when Jane said something admiring about Dr. Vine. The Vines were shaping their time in Buffalo as a droll anecdote well before the story was finished. On Saturdays, sleepy and elated with drink, they wandered into their own living room—fly-spotted skylight, floor-to-ceiling oak bookshelves, cherry shag carpet that they never vacuumed—to the sight of Jane awake on their harvest-gold sofa, back straight, eyes red and round, a book to her face. A ghost in their house, swaying like a naked bulb.

"We don't stay awake all night when we're with our kids, and we don't expect you to, either," Dr. Vine said, kindly, the first time Jane babysat for them.

"If you're going to keep watch for predators all night, would you like a rifle?" he asked the second time, also kindly. After that, he stopped mentioning it. The Vines weren't the sort of people to keep guns in their house anyway.

"You don't have to call him *Dr.* Vine if he's not *your* doctor," Jane's mother said.

The Vines' bookshelves provided Jane with the tools of maintaining a silent yet bustling vigilance into the night. Guided by the photographs in a biography of Martha Graham, Jane choreographed tiptoeing dance routines, unidentified grit from the cherry shag accumulating on the balls of her feet. She stood at the older Vine girl's easel, gripping the crayon that mapped out the constellation of radial lines from the cover of *Be Here Now*. She willed herself not to check the cuckoo clock above the fireplace, and when her resolve disintegrated and she finally looked over to see 1:49 a.m., she took a book that felt to her forbidden—a Bukowski, an Anaïs Nin, a *Helter Skelter*—turned to page 149, read that page aloud to herself in a fierce whisper, then attempted to walk across the first floor of the Vines' house, northeast corner to southwest corner, in exactly 149 steps.

She trusted hard. Staying awake was hard. So she did it, she trusted it, Saturday night after Saturday night.

One of these nights, exiting Dr. Vine's car as it idled in her family's driveway, her bones and muscles liquefying under the pressure of sleep deprivation and *Delta of Venus*, Jane slung her hips from side to side as she approached her front stoop. She didn't know why she did it, and she was too tired even to relish the gratification of giving herself over to something perverse. Slinging her hips felt compelled, as compulsive as any of the games she'd played with numbers and words for the previous six hours. She didn't know if Dr. Vine was watching from the car in the driveway. She didn't know what shape she took in his mind. What kind of *anything* was she?

JANE AWOKE A few hours later, Sunday, sweaty and jittery with shame and fatigue. A clammy heat inside her head, her brain rolled up in the Vines' dirty rug. In springtime, her father and brothers, Brian and Mike and Joe, used to skip mass for baseball practice, and in other seasons they skipped mass for football practice or hockey practice or to get a beef on weck at Anderson's Frozen Custard. Now her brothers were all either in or out of college and presumably could do whatever they wished on their Sundays. For Jane, there was no getting out of church. "God will *see* you," their mother said, a warning, and it was tacitly understood that God on a Sunday would see her brothers at the batting cages differently than he would see Jane in bed with a 101-degree fever or vomiting into the bayberry outside the back entrance of Saint Benedict's. Jane's hair was in a ponytail, leaving both hands free to hold the flappy collar of her sailor blouse flat against her chest. Returning inside the church, she paused beside the stoup to dip her hand in the holy water, then ran her wet fingers along her lips and gums. She didn't think anyone noticed, but God would have noticed. It didn't matter whether or not Dr. Vine had watched Jane slinging her hips last night, because God had watched her, and sorrowed for her, she thought. She felt another tremor of shame, for the hubris of thinking she had the power to cause God sorrow.

Saint Benedict's was a bizarre sandstone fortress, no spire, no belfry, no front-facing windows, but it was the church closest to home. Today was April 29, feast day of Saint Catherine of Siena. Jane opened the photocopied pamphlet, tucked inside the Sunday missals, that summarized Catherine's life. As a toddler, Catherine babbled to angels. At age six, she saw Jesus; at age seven, his apostles. She swore off marriage and children long before her beloved older sister Bonaventura died in childbirth. When Catherine's parents urged her to marry Bonaventura's widower, she protested: cutting off all her hair, willing her skin to erupt in a hideous rash, fasting. Her parents relented on the marriage. Her hair grew back; the rash, a full-body stigmata, faded. But Catherine's fasting became a routine, or a pledge: an act of solidarity with the poor. She aspired to survive solely on the wafer and the sip of wine at daily mass.

The pamphlet had an epigraph, a quotation from Catherine. It read: *Build a cell inside your mind from which you can never flee.*

The edges of the pamphlet were wilting between Jane's fingers. Her eyes were gritty and sore. Her mother nudged her to fall in with the voices surrounding them as they stood to recite the Nicene Creed. Jane's lips parted, but the words didn't come.

Build a cell inside your mind from which you can never flee.

Jane knew she had shamed herself the night before, sauntering away from Dr. Vine, because her mind had slipped outside its cell, and her body had swung free of her mind. Fatigue was no excuse— fatigue was to be trusted, not blamed. An underoccupied mind, a mind not pushed to its outer limits, was dangerous: its contents jostling around, causing contusions and swelling. The cell of the mind needed either to be completely full or completely empty. It needed either to be packed tight with problems to be solved, challenges to be met, or it needed to be blown out, scalded bare, by effort, exertion, exhaustion.

A cell needed rules. Jane already had plenty of those. The rule for how many Acts of Contrition she had to silently say before she released her bladder or started a math test or, lying rigid in her bed at night, before she allowed herself to fall asleep. The rule for how many times she had to kneel and cross herself when she passed the little brass crucifix hanging outside her parents' bedroom. The rule for how many times she had to chew each morsel of dinner before she permitted herself to swallow—the number was always a multiple of three, in honor of the Holy Trinity. She had no rules for breakfast, which could be safely skipped so long as Jane dawdled enough getting ready for school before the bus came. Lunch was a brown bag that could be thrown away, the sin of the waste subsumed by the virtue Jane felt in the act of stuffing it between the lips of the garbage can next to her locker, the *ping* of the lid closing shut as clear as the single bell rung at Eucharist.

All Jane needed to keep her mind quiet was to know there was no end in sight. No end to the hunger, the fatigue, the kneeling, the crossing. No end to the nights at the Vines'. The end was the void, terrifying and purposeless.

Build a cell inside your mind

Behind the altar at Saint Benedict's Church, thirty feet high and fifteen feet across, hung a crude wooden bas-relief of Christ on the cross, jagged mourners piled at his feet like kindling. So much of church was staring at a broken and bleeding man as he dies, in real time, week after week, right in front of you. Nobody doing anything about it. Jane didn't know how Jesus had died, exactly— of suffocation or exposure or blood loss or what—and she wanted to ask her mother, but suspected that the question would anger her. She felt the boundaries between herself and the world dissolving. Perhaps Catherine of Siena had felt the same. The church's overhead lights sparking and shorting behind Jane's own eyes. Her dumb wooden hands grafting themselves onto the pews, hardening painfully into the knots and nodules of tree trunks. Her wooden head pitching forward, whirling with hunger and diving for sleep, the weight of it becoming Christ's body atop her own, pinned beneath him on the cross. She gasped, pushing her lungs against the fallen bulk, struggling to free her arms so she could wrap them around him.

"Jane," her mother whispered through clenched teeth. The voice she would use if Jane ever asked her how, exactly, Jesus died. "What is *wrong* with you?"

And Jane smiled, because she knew the answer.

JANE VOLUNTEERED AT the Clearfield Library on Sunday afternoons. Usually she rode her bike there without eating breakfast or lunch. When she hit the downhill section of Klein Road, she stood up on the pedals and felt pleased by the tremble in her thighs. At the library, she sat on the floor toward the back stacks, the Military & War section, next to the cart of returned books she was supposed to be putting on shelves, and reread the authorless *Stories of the Saints*, a slender green hardback whose filigree of pen-and-ink illustrations, suitable for a children's book, belied its graphic content. It was Catherine of Siena in *Stories of the Saints* who imagined herself married to Christ, his foreskin fashioned into her wedding ring. Jane clapped a hand over her mouth when she first read this, looked around to see if anyone was watching, shut the book, reshelved it, tried to forget it. According to legend— *Stories of the Saints* itself seemed half-convinced—Catherine also once sucked pus from a leper's sores.

There was a word in *Stories of the Saints* that was new to Jane: *kenosis*, or emptying out. To become a vessel for God's will, blank and scrubbed, no sustenance, no desire. The saints were saints because they had the gift of imagining themselves onto the cross, into the suffering that was also salvation. The saints were good at this because the saints were insane. This was a blasphemous thought, but it was also true. Frances of Rome burned her genitals with pork grease before sharing a bed with her husband. Teresa of Avila renounced all her companions, choosing exclusive fellowship with her ecstatic visions. When she prayed, she asked other nuns at the convent to hold her down, to keep her from levitating. And all Jane had managed was to get the shakes on her ten-speed.

"Jane?" Mrs. Bellamy, the head librarian, was standing over her. "We need you up front, checking people out."

Mrs. Bellamy's tone was soft, amused. But Jane still felt herself to be in trouble, and worse, in a stupid, trivial trouble, not the important trouble you could get into if you stuck an onion ring from Anderson's Frozen Custard on your finger and proclaimed it the foreskin of God.

"Sorry," Jane mumbled, getting to her feet.

Once, Teresa's prayers summoned an angel, a winsome curly-headed boy. He wielded a golden spear tipped with fire, and he stabbed Teresa again and again with it. Bernini's *Ecstasy of Saint Teresa*, or the splotchy black-and-white photograph of it reproduced in *Stories of the Saints*, depicted the scene. The fabric of Teresa's dress fluttered like a funnel cloud above a mounted cross. A plume of smoke signaled that Teresa and the angel penetrating her were on the verge of disappearing before Jane's eyes. Jane imagined the boy angel squealing with glee each time his blade plunged into Teresa's flesh, in a rhythm.

JANE WANTED TO see the *Ecstasy of Saint Teresa* in person. Her church was a doll's house, but Rome was God's home, where Elizabeth Seton had just been canonized as the first American saint, though Jane's mother wasn't impressed. She was "really just a snooty Anglican, stooping to our level," she said. "Not a real

Catholic." She didn't believe a word of those stories about Mother Seton curing a girl's leukemia.

That was the autumn that the red-haired little Manson girl tried to kill the president and the sun was always low in the sky. Jane's mother warned them about *glare*—when Jane's father took the car out in the morning, when Jane biked to the Vines' house in the late afternoon. Saint Benedict's subsidized an annual fall trip to Rome for high school seniors, and to pay her way, Jane had earned more than enough from babysitting, the cash stored in empty tins from Parkside Candy. Every birthday and Christmas, Jane's mother gave out these tins, filled with fancy sweets. They made a satisfying small *bwip* sound when you squeezed and slid them open. Jane would hand over her sponge candy and saltwater taffy to Brian or Mike or Joe and keep the tins, which had old-fashioned pastel illustrations winding around them: a turn-of-the-century carousel, ladies in petticoats and big wavy hats dancing the maypole. The tins lived in a couple of hatboxes at the back of her closet that also held old birthday cards, her first pair of shoes, her christening dress, the thin garland of honeysuckle and baby's breath she wore at her first communion. The objects inside the box, the box itself, were a chronology of her life that she could hold in her hands, and the antique veneer of the tins enhanced this sense of permanence, like they were heirlooms Jane was handing down to herself, the money inside them the stuff of her future. She felt the most tenderness for her mother when she sat cross-legged in front of this box to count her bills, only to find herself rereading each of the cards, studying the tiny hammocks of her mother's cursive *r*s, the special swoop of the *J* in her *Jane*, pressing a finger to the dried garland. However careless or cruel her mother could be, this was her own squarish cursive, this was the garland she braided herself, and it was only for Jane, youngest of four, the girl she had waited for. Her mother drove to Parkside Candy and picked out the tins. Like Jane did, she put in the work.

But when Jane brought her mother the stack of candy tins piled to their hinges with the ones and fives and occasional tens and a single, spectacular twenty, the money collected from the Vines and the Goslanders and the Felmans and all the other neighborhood families whose children Jane had diapered and spoon-fed and bathed and sang to over years, Jane's mother spent an afternoon in a pique of insult. She took no pride in her daughter's thrift and work ethic; instead she was affronted by Jane's secrecy and her presumption of something earned. Her mother litigated the case with Jane's father.

"Why do you think that money is yours?" her father, once fully briefed, asked Jane. He was wearing his glasses and sitting in his lounger behind a newspaper, like all the cartoon dads in the picture books Jane read to the kids she babysat. "You take my money for the food you eat, the clothes you wear, the bed you sleep in. When you have enough money to pay me back for seventeen years under my roof, whatever is left over, you can have it for your travels."

"Might be enough for a bus to Rochester," Jane's mother said.

"I've worked hard for this," Jane said. "I've been saving for a long time."

"No, but that's the thing, Jane—the idea that you could *save money* is absurd." He turned to the sports section. Jane could see the top of his head. "Be logical. Saved it from what? Saved it from going toward the mortgage for the house you live in? Saved it from going to pay our taxes?"

"Now, if you could bring your brothers to Rome with you, that might be a different story," her mother said.

Her father cracked the spine of the sports section and folded it back. "Now," he asked Jane brightly, "how about those Bills?"

This was the line her father used to declare a conversation over, that it would be tawdry and dark-minded to continue it. The Bills had won their first four games of the season, and the division title was plausible, her father pointed out. O. J. Simpson had run eighty-eight yards in one go, in the game against Pittsburgh. The Juice. O.J. was something good, someone they could all agree on.

Jane knew her father would relent eventually. She could make him. He was a certified public accountant, an orderly and logical man, attentive to numbers, stats, formulae. Watching sports suited him because he seemed to approach it like a monthslong word problem. *On the day of the home game against the Broncos, if O. J. Simpson misses his train out of Syracuse and has to run all the way to Buffalo, what pace per mile would he have to maintain—* Her father struck Jane as a person who had freed himself from interiority, from psychology and foibles and God; he believed in his platitudes, took them literally, and his life was simpler and better for it. He edited out choice wherever possible, a tendency he had in common with Jane. He built his cell. His need for order and logic in his day-to-day life would be thwarted by the fury of Jane and the Rome trip, fury for days, his youngest and most obedient child, the one who helped around the house without complaint or prompting, the one who always agreed. She wept for hours from the moment she arrived home from school in the afternoons, so violently she choked on her own spit. One vessel in her eye broke the surface, then another, each the width and color of the little red string on a Band-Aid. She flung herself against walls and onto linoleum. She bit the backs of her wrists and scratched at her forearms and yanked at her hair.

"Stop *acting*!" Jane's mother shrieked at the height of these fits, fleeing into another room. The admonition further incensed Jane for being correct, because she did feel an actorly distance from her tantrums; she hesitated, measuring arcs and wingspans, before she threw her books against the wall; her fingernails raised red runes on her forearms that flattened and faded after a quick shower. Even in the fullest grip of her saintly convulsions, Jane felt more pity for her mother than righteous, levitating rage. Pity or resentment. How fiercely Jane resented her now, how desperately she wished she could bite down hard enough on her arm to drain the resentment forever, to burst it open with the sweet pain of God. Because God could see all the way inside her mother.

God could also see all the way inside Jane's resentment. Sometimes she thinks he can even now.

SO JANE FOUGHT and cried until her candy tins were handed back to her. First time on an airplane, first time in a hotel. She signed up to room with Elise Davis, pale-freckled and dun-haired, scholarly and sarcastic. Assiduously Catholic. A girl who based her constantly exercised moral judgments on a bedrock of rueful compassion. Jane suspected that her own life would be easier if Elise were her best friend and thus her steadiest influence, if she could mold her opinions and the management of her time solely according to Elise's preferences, even if Jane herself was too high-strung and daydreamy, too often half swooning under the spell of devotion and semistarvation, to lock perfectly into Elise's orbit of scholar-athletes: Christy Torres, who had regional honors in both violin and chess; Sonja Spiegelman, the only girl on the Mathletes team and the only cross-country runner with a shot at qualifying for States; Geeta Banerjee, a varsity gymnast who was already taking premed classes at the local Jesuit college. Jane made straight As, but generic ones, Regents and the occasional AP. It seemed cosmically unfair that Jane was ranked fifth in their class, right behind Geeta, who should have been valedictorian but who had tanked her GPA as a junior when she tried to take calculus and AP Physics a year early, at the same time.

"I don't really know how they calculate the rankings, but you shouldn't be punished for having ambition," Jane remarked to her mother. She was surprised by her ranking and happy with it, and hoped her mother would be, too.

"That Geeta—what *is* she?" Jane's mother asked, not for the first time.

"Geeta is Geeta," Jane replied, as she had before.

"But where is she *from*?" Jane's mother asked.

"She was born at Children's Hospital, like me," Jane replied.

"You *know what I mean*," Jane's mother said. "Where did your other friends land?"

"Elise, Christy, and Sonja went one-two-three," Jane said.

"That Sonja," her mother said. "She is *so Jewish-looking*." She had said this before.

"Whatever that means," Jane replied. As she always did.

"Well, not all of them *look* like it," her mother said. "You don't always *know for sure*."

Jane was puzzled yet again by her own habit of trying to chat with her mother about her friends.

Although Jane often joined Elise's Friday-night homework parties and tagged along to cheer Geeta and Sonja at their competitions, the people with whom Jane spent the most time were children. The children she babysat were why she made it to Rome. The Vine girls, those sweet sparrows. Jane fantasized about living with the Vines, sleeping on the gold couch beneath the skylight. She could be their governess, swooshing around them in hoop skirts, running conjugation drills in multiple European languages.

The children were why she made it to Santa Maria della Vittoria, where the *Ecstasy of Saint Teresa* hung too high in a chapel shrine for Jane to see it closely. Jane logged her disappointment as a minor entry in that day's catalog of saintly pain. She had consumed nothing but water and Coca-Cola for breakfast and lunch. She refused to apply bandages to the blisters mushrooming across her heels, one of which had started to bleed and stick over the miles they covered on foot through the city. Jane looked up at Teresa as she worked her heel against her shoe, the friction turning wet and warm, the corners of her eyes crinkling with virtuous discomfort.

Behind Jane, a boy muttered, "Fairy stuck her with his spear," as another boy laughed.

Colin Chase and Patrick Brennan. Pat. Football players. B+ students. Smart enough, but indifferent to school. Colin tall and horse-faced, shaggy-blond, jaw strong or overbearing depending on the angle. Pat slighter, darker, objectively pretty. Wide-set deer eyes. Elise and the others called them Thing One and Thing Two.

At the Basilica di Santa Maria Maggiore, the *Salus Populi Romani* glittered atop the altar. Mary, Mother of God, was pinched, maybe resentful, gaudy crown perched atop her hooded robe, state-fair baubles hanging from her neck and pinned to her shoulder. Baby Jesus, a skinny homunculus, sat stiff on Mary's lap, peering up at her skeptically. *Are you my mother?* he seemed to wonder, the same question that haunted the just-hatched baby bird in the book that Jane had read a hundred times to Jeanette Vine.

Behind Jane, big blond Thing One muttered to dark pretty Thing Two, "Mary got fucked by God."

Gaat fucked. Gaad. Jane's mother made sure her children were vigilant about the Buffalo accent. "Round your vowels," she commanded them.

Thing Two laughed as Thing One huffed and grunted in an orgasmic imitation of Mary. *"Oh Gaad. Oh Gaaahhd."*

Jane's upper lip kicked. A puff of air escaped her throat. It *was* funny—all of it. The carvings, the sparkles, the incantations, the incense, the spectacle, the *money. Her* money. How many little piles of fives and ones would equal the value of one marble pillar in this place, one square foot of mosaic? Jane's tears dropping on a cheap dumb candy tin as she sobbingly latched it shut, her mother yelling in the vicinity—the whole thing was hilarious.

Jane looked at Elise beside her, who rolled her eyes. For almost laughing at Colin's blasphemy, Jane assigned herself ten Hail Marys and a few smacks to the head the next time she had a bathroom stall to herself.

Sister Tabitha, their catechism teacher, had told them in class that sinful thoughts didn't put your soul in danger, "so long as you don't consent to the thought," she said.

"But how do you consent to a thought?" Alyssa Piotrowski asked without being called on, her hand in the air. Jane felt gratitude toward Alyssa for always posing the questions she was too timid to ask herself. Maybe someday Alyssa would ask Sister Tabitha for Jesus's precise cause of death.

"You consent by taking pleasure in the thought," Sister Tabitha replied. "By not fighting it off with prayer."

"But—the thought is still there," Alyssa said. "Didn't you consent to the thought by thinking it in the first place?"

"Alyssa got raped by her own brain," Thing One said, and Thing Two laughed into his sleeve.

In Vatican City, Michelangelo's *Pietà* presented an optical illusion: vast and solid Mary, curtained knees spread, Jesus' shrunken corpse slung across her lap. Jane squinted at the sculpture, willing Jesus and Mary to change positions, to strike new poses for her mind's camera. She guessed that if the sculpted figures thawed and rose to their full heights, Mary would tower over her son, twice his width.

"Jesus died because Mary sat on him," Thing One said to Thing Two. "Fat cow."

At the Santa Maria del Popolo, Caravaggio's *Conversion on the Way to Damascus* and *Crucifixion of St. Peter* hung facing each other. The apostle Paul, fallen from his horse, his arms outstretched, his dirty legs parted and quivering, his eyes closed against the light of God. Peter at first appeared decrepit, wretched in the hands of his captors and tormentors, but further contemplation revealed him as powerful in his insistence to be nailed to the cross—not just nailed to it but nailed *upside down*, so as not to offend Christ through straight mimicry. Peter was powerful in the pride he took in his degradation, in confronting the desecration of his flesh. His flesh would be seen. It was evidence. His tormentors would look him in the eye.

An odor of old sweat wafted from the canvases. Burlap and hay. The paintings heaved and groaned. Their lights flickered beneath the shadows of shifting bodies. The paintings were alive, animal. They stirred like a sleepy beast who slowly emerges from darkness. The first thing you'd see would be the blinking yellow eyes.

Jane never could have said—she could not say now—what constituted a "religious experience." But if she had to guess, standing right there between the Caravaggios, it was a nauseating little quake of dread and ecstasy. Your throat opens up and you think you might be in love. For a second, it's like the ghost of God is inside you. You can contort yourself however you want to see his face, but he will always elude you.

He is not even looking at you, Jane thought. It existed beyond language, or before it. You had to kill it first, before you could put it into words.

Not for the first time, in another church but far from home, Jane felt the boundaries dissolving. If only for a second, she could flow in and out of her surroundings, take on their colors and compositions without hardening or getting stuck in place; she could absorb and reflect light like a panel of tesserae. She was no longer petrified by the eyes of God. Between the Caravaggios, something opened up in Jane, just then, and it would never close.

Behind Jane, Thing One muttered to Thing Two, "Cara-*fag*-io."

Jane turned away from the paintings and toward the voice. She met Colin's eyes, then Pat's. Colin bucked his big jaw at her and thrust his tongue inside one cheek. Pat stared placidly back at Jane.

The next day, on the Metro, Colin pulled to the edge of his seat across from Jane and Elise and said, to Jane, "Fucking you would be like fucking a rag doll." Beside him, Pat snickered into his collar and looked away.

That's when Jane knew. Knew it was going to happen. Not that day, probably not on this trip—the students' days were too scheduled, too chaperoned, their hotel rooms closely monitored. She hadn't even found the opportunity to smack herself in the head for laughing at the Virgin Mary. But Thing One and Thing Two had discussed and evaluated her as a prospect, and come to a decision, and now, gathered and seated here on the Metro, she was being advised of their decision.

"And you would know, wouldn't you, Colin? You love to play

with your dollies," said Elise, as Jane flushed hot with her shame and her power.

She tried and failed to find a reproduction of the *Ecstasy of Saint Teresa* in Rome. Instead she brought home a print of Caravaggio's *Madonna and Child with Saint Anne*: a buxom, sexy Mary and a naked toddler Jesus stomping decorously on the evil serpent, as Anne, gaunt and ancient, struggles to pretend to admire their work while still remaining upright. Jane also bought a packaged chunk of the Colosseum, about as big as a softball.

"That's not real," her mother told her. "How many hours did you have to babysit to buy *that* hunk of crap?"

Cree-ap. Jane's mother, too, at moments of high dudgeon, could fall prey to the Buffalo accent.

Jane propped up the Caravaggio reproduction on a matboard atop her bedroom dresser, and as she expected, her mother said nothing about it. Surely she objected to it—Mary's bosom, Jesus's penis—but if her mother said a word, she would only be revealing the places where her own dirty mind could go.

JANE FELT PREPARED for the pain. Sonja had done it with Larry Priven over Thanksgiving, much to Elise's restrained dismay; Sonja said the pain was narrowly preferable to a torn ligament. On the thinly carpeted cement floor of Pat's family's freshly drywalled basement, where Pat and Colin and Brad Bender spent off-season afternoons lifting weights and drinking smuggled Budweiser, Jane observed the pain from a distance, her body splayed alongside a kettle ball and a dumbbell rack, but her mind's eye elevated, like Teresa atop her plume of marble, as Pat's courtly ministrations—the tender forehead kisses, the stroking of hair—began to give way to a procedure more autonomic and zoological, something Jane seemed almost incidental to. For an instant, Jane wondered if God was watching, if pain, even in this case, was the presence of God. She bit down on her tongue to punish herself for the thought. God was not so lewd, so prurient. His mind didn't go to those places; he had better things to do.

He is not even looking at you.

Pat was two different people, and Jane liked that, for a long time. When he was sweet, he was so sweet. Mostly when they were alone. Jane loved how much he loved how skinny she was. She loved how easily he could scoop her up and sling her over his shoulder, how he kneaded her rib cage and hip bones with the pads of his fingers, called her String Bean and Mrs. Bones and Fatso and the Buttless Wonder. She loved that he loved how she would order French toast and souvlaki at Stavros's Diner or hot wings at the Anchor Bar, manage a couple of small bites, and smile apologetically as she pushed her plate away, because she *did* love to eat, you see, but she was too dainty and adorable, too easily overwhelmed, too much *his sweet girl*—because when he was sweet, he saw her, too, as sweet—to eat up the world she was hungry for.

"She tries so hard to pack it away," he said to a waitress at Perkins one night, while they were waiting for Colin and Brad to join them, and she nibbled at pancakes already going cold.

If Jane and Pat were with other people, they were usually with his squad of jocks, who found few points of intersection with Elise's coalition of high achievers, although Elise and Christy did find time to sit beside Jane on the bleachers during Pat's home games. With his friends, Pat tended to turn away, irritated, if Jane murmured in his ear; he'd scowl if she spoke to one of his friends in a way he found untoward.

"Why do you have to say *colossal* when you can just say *big*—who are you trying to *impress*?" he asked at Perkins, after Colin and Brad showed up.

And then: "Why do you have to make that *face*?" Her hand went up to her cheek to find out what kind of face she was making.

But just when Jane would begin to grow bored of her own embarrassment and vigilance, when she was ready to retreat from Pat into Elise's sober and mostly chaste world of homework parties and volunteering for bingo night at the senior center, the Saturday nights at the Vines' and the Sunday afternoons in the chirring walnut chairs of the Clearfield Library, he would return to her. He would place her hand in his and gaze at their fingers curled together, tug playfully at her ponytail, press his thumb and forefinger on the nape of her neck or the base of her spine. Right there in front of his friends. He wouldn't do his crossword puzzles in front of his friends, but he would do this. Jane's head tipped back beneath the gravity of his benediction, his tactile declaration of ownership, his pride in what he owned. With his letterman jacket draped over her shoulders, she felt the privilege of being owned, of being wanted exclusively, and the joyous unlikelihood of Pat's choice—that he'd passed over any of the cheerleaders waiting to pair off with him, all yellows and golds with their Farrah-feathered hair and fourteen-karat nameplate necklaces, in favor of *her*, of all people, shy and gangly, tongue-tied and flat-chested Jane.

One time in the basement, Jane apologized for her small breasts.

"Tits are for milking," Pat said, and Jane was moved.

She had accomplished something hard. Pat's intervals of snappishness and indifference were the proof that she'd achieved a hard thing, because turning him sweet was hard. Convincing Pat to love her, and to like her, was hard, and it was work that was never done. She trusted hard.

THE TIME CAME to make the necessary arrangements. A wedding over Labor Day weekend at Saint Mary's, Pat's aunt Diane, the director of the Saint Mary's children's chorus, putting in a word to fit them in. Neither Jane's nor Pat's family was inclined to discuss why the happy event needed to be so hastily planned.

Plenty of other girls who found themselves in the same situation would make a different kind of necessary arrangement.

It's not that she didn't think about it.

It wasn't difficult to get done.

She knew somebody who knew somebody who'd done it. You just had to know who to ask. How to ask. It would be like it never happened. Instead of getting married in September, she could start at the University of Buffalo, with Pat. Geeta and Christy were going to UB, too. Elise off to Vassar, Sonja to the University of Michigan. Jane would be showing by September, probably. But she didn't have to be.

The idea followed her around even after the wedding date was set. The idea was a tall lithe nurse in white linens: paper dressing gown over one arm, one hand beckoning Jane toward a small room with a large chair, a tray of sharp and gleaming instruments beside it. The nurse had a scent Jane couldn't place, not antiseptic, but as wholesome and foreboding as peat and heavy rain. She smelled of wildflowers spattered with freshly dug earth.

Jane turned away from her again and again. She wouldn't look her full in the face.

How do you consent to a thought?

HER MOTHER SLAPPED her when Jane told her she was pregnant. Her mother always lost her nerve just as open palm met cheek. Jane wondered if she'd resent her mother's blows less if they could ever be delivered with conviction.

Her mother's revulsion dissipated, however, once she could pause to consider the prestige of the match, even if it had been sealed under less-than-ideal circumstances. Patrick Brennan Sr. had co-founded Brennan & Menzari, which built dozens of the higher-end Town of Amherst homes, and he'd parlayed his wealth and standing into the chairmanship of the largest local auto dealership. The Brennans managed to be both affluent-for-Williamsville and salt-of-the-earth. They were soft-spoken and churchly, and the six of them lived well within their means in a four-bedroom split-level of Mr. Brennan's own design. They were, Jane's mother said, "the right sort of people," people who "could buy you out if you looked at them funny" yet don't "go begging you to count their money." Her mother could count the Brennans' money without being asked.

Mrs. Brennan, whom Jane could never quite bring herself to call Dee and so rarely called her anything at all, was slight and tanned and usually dressed for the tennis court. She could have probably shared clothes with Jane's mother, but her mother's conspicuous thinness seemed a by-product of perpetual exasperation, while Dee's felt, like everything about her, quietly intentional. She would help get Jane set up in the holly-green clapboard house on Maple Way. Pat's dad was building out the development and others in Williamsville, half-acre lots carved out of forest. The candy tins would be replaced by a checkbook, drawing on a bank account that Pat's parents would control at first. Pat would go to work for the family firm, as had always been expected, while enrolled part-time at UB. Jane could enroll, too, someday. It was the only school she had applied to. She wanted to major in early childhood education. But she would have to wait at least until all the children were in school, because of course there would be more children.

"And then you'll wonder why you ever thought you needed a degree," Mrs. Brennan said cheerily. It was not a dig, not one of her mother's *just you wait*s. It was meant to reassure her that everything would work out fine, and just as it was intended to.

Mrs. Brennan took Jane shopping for furniture, paints, fixtures. Jane deferred so consistently to the older woman's judgment— botanical prints, reproductions of Colonial-era furniture, deep blues and reds and greens—that her participation felt like a formality. One of Jane's few suggestions was to find a frame for *Madonna and Child with Saint Anne*. Another was to place the chunk of the Colosseum on the living room mantelpiece. Jane had not yet removed it from its cardboard packaging.

"You know that's not real, honey," Mrs. Brennan said gently.

"No, it is," Jane said, gripping the box, watching the mantelpiece. They hadn't laid the carpet yet and their voices echoed slightly against the bare white walls. "I bought it right across from the Colosseum site."

"Sweetheart," Mrs. Brennan said, with soft remorse, "they wouldn't just let you bring home a piece of the Colosseum."

"No, it's—see, look at the stamp on the side, it says, CERTIFICADO COME GENUINO." Jane's treasure looked all at once to her like a Happy Meal prize. A sheer plastic square cut into the packaging so you could peek inside at the rock, like the Tonka trucks on the shelves at Kay-Bee Toys. Jane laughed and covered her eyes, and Mrs. Brennan laughed, too.

"I'm a moron," Jane said.

"You are not. Hey, it doesn't even matter if it's real," Mrs. Brennan said. "It's a memory for you, and that means something. For Pat, too. That trip brought you together."

Mrs. Brennan placed the chunk on the mantelpiece, flush against the wall, behind a twin frame holding Jane's and Pat's baby pictures.

When Jane told her friends what she would be doing instead of college, Elise wore a look of stricken compassion. Geeta mentioned that she was learning how to knit, and that she could knit the baby something—booties, she thought, or a cap.

"I can't wait to have kids," Christy said.

"Well, you *can*," Jane said, smiling.

"When I finish my residency," Christy said.

Sonja's brow furled in perplexity. She had gathered enough information from the Human Reproduction section of her old AP Biology textbook to formulate a strict birth control methodology for herself and Larry Priven, one that required neither clinical intervention nor furtive drugstore runs. She had shared her findings with Jane.

"I showed you how to use the calendar," Sonja told Jane. "Remember? I showed you how to count the days."

Jane smiled. "I guess that's why you're the Mathlete and I'm not," she said, and Sonja seized her in a long hug.

For years after, Jane could still summon a physical memory of that hug. Its breathtaking pressure, its frankness. How their friendship had caught them both by surprise. At the time, Jane didn't know if the hug was a reaffirmation of their friendship or a goodbye.

THERE WAS ANOTHER physical imprint from those weeks of celebrations and planning for celebrations, when Jane's future glowed inside her, unseeable and undeniable. A late-summer party at Rhonda Lacey's house, too crowded, Rhonda's parents in Myrtle Beach. The air already cooling, foretelling fall. The Laceys' golden retriever eating pizza and lapping beer on the deck, Brad Bender bellowing in the backyard, snatching cheerleaders one by one by the waist, tossing each over his shoulder like a knapsack as the girl shrieked in laughter or pain or alarm—no one could tell, and no one asked. Pat, plastered, made a blowtorch out of his lighter and Brad's little sister's aerosol hairspray, but he fumbled it and lit his left hand on fire. Maybe whatever he was drinking acted as an accelerant. Pat was screaming, and Brad thought it was the funniest thing he'd ever seen.

"Baby, are you okay?" Jane asked when she found Pat in the Laceys' kitchen, his hand in the sink under cold running water.

"I'm fine," he said. Annoyance bordering on anger, like Jane was the one who had burned him.

Jane leaned over the sink to see. "That looks nasty. Let me ask Rhonda if we can find some ointment, or some Vaseline."

"I'm *fine*. Stop making such a big *deal* out of it," Pat protested, and stamped out of the kitchen, like Jane was going to burn him again. Tomorrow, two of his fingernails would turn black and fall off, the webbing between his thumb and forefinger turned to fatty uncooked bacon.

He'd left the water running. Jane took a Solo cup from a stack on the counter, held it under the water, and switched off the tap.

She turned and leaned back against the Laceys' countertop, sleepy, sipping, as classmates jostled past her in either direction. Colin loomed up in front of her, eyes meandering, tongue swollen with drink. The big jaw looked soft and crumbling. He was built from old paving stones.

"Why don't you drink some bleach, you bitch," he said, stumbling against her. He steadied himself with a hand against her breast, which was small and hard and swollen. "Why don't you shove a coat hanger up your cunt. Why don't you *do us all a fucking favor.*"

His head pitching forward, diving for sleep, pinned her shoulder against the cloudy-yellow tiles on the wall. She thought of pouring her cup of water over his head or kneeing him in the groin. Instead she waited underneath him, head turned from his beery panting, one hand behind her gripping the edge of the countertop, until he slumped away, sliding down the wall in a stupor. She smiled down on him, her profile turned beneath a flattering light toward an invisible eye—Mary beholding a different son, not dead, just drunk and sad. The Solo cup, unspilled, still in her hand. She watched his fallen bulk, crumpled beneath his letterman jacket. She hadn't worn Pat's jacket tonight. Even this early on, the baby kept her warm.

She had practice in loving her enemy. And she knew, too, how painful it could be, to be in love with Pat. It could leave you in pieces on the floor of someone else's house.

EVEN HER FRIENDS who enrolled at UB seemed to be there only for the cheap tuition. They'd leave Buffalo, probably, as soon as they had their degrees. Jane wondered if part of the problem with Buffalo was simply the name: a hirsute, lumbering beast, plodding a flat frost landscape, resigned to its ultimate destiny as ground meat or drive belts or fertilizer. Bilked, buffeted, befuddled, *Buffaloed.* Buffalo was a puffing freight train hauling eternal bad luck, inscribed in the collapse of coal and Bethlehem Steel, the pathos of wingless chickens, the endless blinding nihilist snow. Lake Ontario to their north and Lake Erie to their southwest fogged the lines between water and sky, washing their stars in gray milk when they weren't dumping snow on them for spite. All the historical flashpoints were bad, comically bad. An assassin in Buffalo killed President McKinley. The only president that Buffalo could rightfully claim was Millard Fillmore, muddy dullard, who died there, too. Buffalo had a Frank Lloyd Wright building and they tore it down, in dead of night. Diphtheria in Buffalo killed Mark Twain's baby, his firstborn son, Langdon, at home. They tore that house down, too. Even the name was a blunder: Buffalo, supposedly a garbling of *beau fleuve*, beautiful river, a name that French fur trappers may have used for a local creek, as a joke. No bison ever set foot in Buffalo, except on the jerseys of local sports enthusiasts. The baseball team doubled down on this misapprehension by calling themselves the Buffalo Bisons, although the plural of *bison* was *bison*. The namesake of the football team, hapless but for the splendid O.J., was Buffalo Bill Cody, a man with no ties to the city, who in fact won his nickname for being a prodigious killer of buffalo—his sharpshooting provided meat for the crews building the Kansas Pacific Railroad, thousands of miles southwest. Stacks of dead buffalo, nowhere near Buffalo. To be from Buffalo was to have made a mistake.

Jane gleaned most of this from the Local History section of the Clearfield Library, where she passed the autumn days as her belly grew and the new house sat waiting. Her friends were all in school. Geeta photocopied the syllabi from the UB Intro Early Childhood Development courses for Jane, and Jane looked up the names of all the authors in the Clearfield card catalog. Perhaps because they were English and wrote about children, Jane imagined the names embossed in fussy cursive on the cover of an old storybook: John Bowlby, Mary Ainsworth, D. W. Winnicott, authors of tales about earnest rabbits and doleful bears with terry-cloth fur, tumbling in their bonnets and waistcoats into spots of pastoral mischief. Every backdrop rolling green. Winnicott sounded cuddliest of all: Winnie-cot, a pooh-bear bundled in his crib. Winnicott worked at a hospital called Paddington Green, which was a real place, and wrote a book called *The Piggle*, named for a real girl. The cover of one of Winnicott's books showed a curly-headed toddler in an old-fashioned two-button romper, chubbily working his way down porch steps. The baby of one of the ladies from Jane's candy tins.

Jane was going to have a baby, too, and her whole world would be as gentle and green and terry-cloth soft. Pushing a pram to Paddington Green.

She drew up flash cards: *transitional object, object permanence, strange situation, good enough mother.* She could keep up with her friends at college, remain interesting to them, she really could— she just had to put in the effort. But the books made her dozy the way a bedtime story would. She would end up with her forehead down on a table, the book resting against her belly in her disappearing lap, and if her napping bothered Mrs. Bellamy, she never said so.

THE FATIGUE OF pregnancy was an elaborate prank. There was an exhilaration to it, too, as with the reveal of a prank—the release of the laughter, the endorphin rush of every cell in her body yawning, every fiber stretching to find more oxygen, more energy, for the creature dancing inside her, inhaling the iron in her blood with every somersault. It was almost orgasmic, to be pushed to a limit and then plunge into sleep. It was even better than those nights at the Vines'.

Pregnancy quieted Jane's mind. She slept without sin. Her head did not race with prayers left unsaid. At first, she ate as sparingly as ever, but only out of nausea. Halfway through her pregnancy, she woke up beside Pat at four in the morning—and how strange it was, that after so many assignations in basements, on mudroom floors, crunched and folded in the backs of cars, that overnight she could awaken and raise herself on one elbow beside her husband, this callow and priapic and unconquerable boy *her husband*, in their own house, this pair of children playing at being their own parents, their baby, a girl, Jane knew it was a girl, asleep inside her—and Jane felt a new hunger, not the familiar dizzy emptiness but something new and violent, dirty fingernails scraping and squeezing her innards, clawing her guts toward her pelvic bone. She stumbled in the darkness to the staircase, down into the kitchen, and took a pack of white dinner rolls from the pantry, the inside of her mouth raining with saliva as her teeth clamped down on the spongy, tasteless bread.

Jane became consumed with the idea that if she was hungry, then the baby inside her had to be starving. She could see the baby writhing with hunger, tiny limbs kicking. The baby in a dark liquid prison, unsure if or when her jailer might return with a tray of crusts and brackish water. For years, Jane had seen her want of food as sinful. But now it was a need, and there could be no sin in need.

"You are young, and you can snap back," Dee said, toward the end of Jane's pregnancy. Jane was more comfortable calling her Dee now. It was the Thanksgiving that O.J. rushed for two hundred and seventy-three yards in a single game, made two touchdowns, and the Bills still lost. Early evening, Dee's table cleared, dishwasher humming, all the older siblings dispersed to friends' houses, and Jane had just helped herself to another slice of Dee's pumpkin pie. "You are a lovely girl. It would be such a pity if you *let yourself go*," Dee said.

"Mmm," Jane agreed, licking a dollop of filling off an index finger. She pressed around her lips with her fingers, checking for stray bits of pie crust.

"You know Rhonda Lacey's sister?" Pat asked later that night, back home, Jane putting water on the stove for tea. "Meredith, I think her name is? She's a skinny girl like you—like you *were*—but when she was pregnant it was like she swallowed a bowling ball." He waited and watched her. "Like a snake that's swallowed a mouse! And then right after the baby, she looked the same as before." He waited, watched. "Wearing short skirts and stuff. Tight jeans . . . I guess I thought that's what you'd be like," he said.

"I guess I never paid as much attention to Meredith Lacey as you did," Jane said. Pat's eyes widened in warning, and Jane looked down at the pot, one finger pushing idly at its handle, its lip. She wanted to dunk her hand in the water, to see how close it was to boiling.

"I'm so hungry all the time," she said. "I worry that the baby is hungry, too."

"Yeah, well," Pat said. "That sounds like making excuses."

"The baby can't speak for herself," Jane said. "I have to guess what she needs. Maybe I don't always guess right."

The water simmered. Jane opened a cabinet and took down a box of macaroni and cheese.

"You cannot *possibly* be hungry," Pat said.

"*She* is," Jane said.

"You don't know it's a girl," Pat said. "What if it's a boy?"

"I know her," Jane said, ripping open the box and pouring the elbows into the pot.

PAIN COULD BE trusted. Pain was the presence of God. She told her doctor she didn't want any drugs. She needed to feel what was happening.

"All that hippie natural-birth shit. You read that at the library?" Pat said.

Her best chance for feeling the pain, all of it, was to wait as long as she could before she asked Pat to drive her to the hospital, almost until it was too late. When the contractions started, she locked herself in the upstairs bathroom and ran the taps in the tub until they could no longer camouflage the noise—not a noise she herself was making, not a mechanism of lungs and larynx and vocal cords, but a shifting of plates, mantle roaring through crust, an avalanche somehow sliding upward through her esophagus, a geologic boom of awful movement. Her water broke and kept breaking, pouring out of her fathomless body. She never guessed what she could contain. Seeing her bellowing down the stairs—seeing what she had done, the secret she had kept—Pat was too scared to be angry. The baby was crowning by the time the hospital people got her on a table.

Before she gave birth, Jane imagined pain as a visitation, a localized phenomenon to be accommodated, managed, at times encouraged. She didn't yet know that a person could *become* pain, that a body could become both stimulus and response and explode the higher mind, leaving a dumb howling beast to crawl in its wreckage. There was no thinking-Jane to trust the pain or see God in it. She was tortured, she thought later—the thought was blasphemous—like a saint. The stretching on the rack. The crackling fire. But amid the torture she saw no visions, remembered no prayers. Most saints, after all, did not become mothers. For most—there were exceptions, and it was a sin to think yourself exceptional— it was a disqualifying event. Not for Mother Seton, but again, Jane's own mother said she didn't count.

A groaning beast, a buffalo prone on the plain. Put her out of her misery. If you can bleed out that bad and not die, then you must be an animal.

Thinking-Jane returned to herself on the final push, the baby hurtling out of her body, a meteor, a rocket, a slick, downy aeronautic shell reentering the earth's atmosphere. Jane's insides scorched black, endless as outer space. Her *kenosis*.

"It's a girl," a voice said, a doctor or a nurse.

"I know," Jane said, reaching out with both hands.

It wasn't yet hospital protocol in western New York State at the beginning of 1977 to accede to a mother's request that a newborn be placed immediately into her arms, but Jane wasn't asking. The astonishing baby draped on her chest, swampy and stern, eyes liquid and unblinking, bottomless. Once again there was nothing between them.

THEY NAMED HER Lauren, a laurel, green and fragrant, a wreath for the Christmas just gone past. The ceramic nativity scene at Saint Benedict's was still installed in a side chapel, there until Epiphany: officious wise men in their jewel-toned robes, watchful Joseph, an exuberant angel, beatific Disney livestock. Jane stood dumbfounded by the display, Lauren bundled under her coat, grunting wetly against Jane's collarbone. Beneath her clothes, Jane was soaking through a maxi pad. Mary was draped in puddling porcelain silks, sunk to her knees in pillows of straw, her hands pressed together in prayer toward the swaddled Jesus in the manger. The mother of God had labored on a donkey and then labored in a barn, her body breaking itself open centimeter by centimeter amid hay and shit and cold, an animal among animals. Away in a slop trough, no crib for a bed.

Jane felt a certain kind of way that Christ's suffering on the Cross was exalted, itemized station by station in this same church, an infinity of wood and stone, while Mary's suffering was heated in a kiln and painted in cartoon colors for a children's seasonal diorama. She fumbled around inside the cloudy dome of her postpartum brain for the sound of the feeling, hoping she'd recognize it by touch. Earlier that morning, she told Pat that they needed to buy more diaphragms, or more diamonds, or more *diapers*—that was it. What was the thing she felt? Put out. Pent up. Perturbed! That was it. *Perturbed*, the *er-er-buh* requiring an indignant pursing of lips.

Ringing through her head: *O night when Christ was born / O night divine*

Would Jane's high school English teachers have circled *Christ was born* in red pencil? Was that passive voice? *Mary is the subject and Christ is the object.* She couldn't remember the rules. The cell was empty.

"I love that they add something every year," Dee was saying. "Look at the darling little lambs, right there at the angel's feet."

"Who helped Mary clean herself?" Jane thought, and the thoughts turned into muffled words in the air close by—she could hear them. "Who helped her clean the baby?" It was Jane who was speaking. "Did Mary need stitches? Did they find a spare manger for the afterbirth?"

"Okey-dokey, that's all, folks," Pat was saying as he placed his hands on Jane's shoulders and nudged her toward the exit. The Porky Pig voice he used when he wanted to change the subject, make Jane stop talking. It was Pat's version of her father's *How about those Bills?*

Later, Jane's mother told her that Mary didn't suffer labor pains, because she wasn't a sinner.

That month was *Roots*—there was O.J. sprinting across the screen in loincloth and warrior beads, like Pegasus wings could sprout from his back as he broke from the cold storage of Buffalo— and that month was the blizzard. Midnight in the afternoon, flaying winds, snowdrifts taller than Pat and packed like cement. The roads were unpassable, but the lights and the phone stayed on, the furnace and sump pump chugged away, and so the little house on Maple Way became a moon station, a glowing, lonely pod. Jane and Lauren didn't leave the house for weeks, Jane living off stockpiles of dried pasta and canned beans, Lauren living off Jane. Pat studied and watched a lot of TV in the basement, talked to Colin and Brad on the phone. He was good with the baby. Jane could rely on him for a solid half hour, forty-five minutes at a stretch, of cuddling on the couch or google-eyed play on the carpet, and she could use the time to do laundry.

It was good that the roads were unpassable because nursing the baby agitated Jane's parents. "That's obscene," her father said, fleeing the room, the first and only time he saw the baby at her breast. Until the blizzard interrupted her daily visits, Jane's mother brought with her can after can of Similac—she'd happened to have a coupon for it, and she'd needed to go to the store anyway, she was driving right past, it was *right there*, so why not grab some, you see, she was only trying to *help*, just *let her help*, for goodness' sake, Jane, you have always been so stubborn—and Jane's mother stood in the pantry stacking and restacking the cans, each *smack* a clap of judgment. If Jane gasped or moaned because of a bad latch or a sore nipple, it struck her mother's ear as an echo of her screaming and crying over Rome—her outlandish need for attention, her perverse insistence on *having her way*.

The corners of her mother's lips turned down when Jane told her the baby's name. Her mother's tongue thrust out on the *L* like she was gagging on it. The only Laurens her mother knew of were the two in Jane's year, Goldstein and Cohen.

It occurred to Jane one afternoon as she was changing Lauren's diaper, the snow and wind pounding their dark against the window, that her mother had probably hit her for the last time. To entertain the baby and to pass the hours, Jane narrated even her stray and most fragmentary thoughts. "I am therefore declared unslappable," she told Lauren with a cheery nod, oddly buoyed by the goofy *pa-pa-ba* of the word she had made up, *unslappable*, three brisk little kisses, and she blew a raspberry on the baby's taut round belly. Lauren gurgled appreciatively, all four limbs dancing, looking up at her mother with a surprised pride.

"I'm unperturbed! I'm *unslappable*!" Jane said again, tickling Lauren's ribs and blowing another raspberry, and that was the first time Lauren laughed.

BERNICE IN THE rectory office says they have a backlog of baptisms scheduled," Jane's mother told her in March. "Nothing major. The blizzard threw everyone off. But you don't want to leave it too late."

To let Lauren go unbaptized was to give her an Achilles' heel. A sprinkling of holy water would be a vaccine against the disease of the unclean soul. Jane still prayed every night and at Sunday-morning mass, but her prayers had lost their compulsive charge. She tensed up when she reached the point in her litany when she asked God to watch over Lauren. Her throat tightened with what felt like a lie. She remembered how funny it had all seemed in the church in Rome. Now the joke was stale, but she kept telling it out of habit.

"People get their kids baptized," Pat told Jane. "It's what people do. You're overthinking it."

Jane put Lauren in the eggshell-colored gown that Dee's daughters had worn to their baptisms. It was nicer than her own christening dress had been; its fabric was thicker and softer, the layers of tulle more delicate and numerous. Lauren angled her dribbly chin away from the dress's lace collar, wearing the same quizzical, stoic gaze she'd cast up at Jane after she'd hurtled down from outer space. Her downy hair, still somehow damp. The baby gestured toward one corner of her mouth, her chubby wee hand an elegant comma, as she did when she was hungry. It made Jane think of how Robert De Niro would write in the air in the second *Godfather* movie— graciously refusing a parcel of groceries, persuading his friends of a plan over spaghetti, his voice low and trilling, patient. Jane and Lauren sat down in a pew to eat.

"Not in God's house, Jane!" her mother said as Jane bent over the baby.

"Happy Lauren's christening day, Glenis," Pat said to her mother, shrugging and opening his palms upward.

That same spring, late one afternoon, Jane saw Mrs. Vine in the canned food aisle at Bells market. Lauren round-eyed and drooling in the shopping cart, her face its usual picture of startled delight. Jane in duck boots, an old pair of Pat's jeans, and a maternity coat belted snugly against her still-soft stomach, its hem scarred with dirty snow and road salt. Mrs. Vine had not yielded to sloth during that brutal winter and the sodden, sloppy season that followed: patterned cashmere coat cut to her figure, pants unscathed by sodium chloride, heels high and regal. She moved at precise angles as she chose among cans of green beans, a mission engrossing and humorous. She was a model dropped into an exotic and overlit location for a magazine shoot. Somehow the Vines still lived in Buffalo.

Jane smiled eagerly at Mrs. Vine as they passed each other. Mrs. Vine grinned back and winked as she said, with a conspiratorial note in her voice, "Why, *hello* there," caressing the can of beans, like a jewel thief with her loot, like she was about to press her treasure into Jane's hand, and it occurred to Jane that she had no idea who she was.

AFTER FIRST STEPS but before confident walking, after babbling but before real words, no longer a baby but not yet a toddler, there was a time when Lauren, getting sleepy at dinner, would take Jane's hands, open them palms up, like Pat at her christening, and then rest her little head in them, pressing her cheek against the creases. Then she would return her mother's hands to their rightful owner and get back to the business of getting her mashed potato onto her spoon and making the unpredictable voyage from bowl to lips without spilling. Lauren was equally interested in and pleased by any outcome of this journey.

Jane pressed her own hands together as she watched her child. She felt a crushing panic in moments like this, remorse for the crime she had briefly considered committing. Out of the corner of her eye, she saw the phantom nurse, who probably wore a fond smile, who probably would have convinced her it was all for the best if Jane had even once looked her full in the face. Jane was terrified of something she hadn't done, that could now never be done, as potently as if it could never be undone, as if the nurse could tug her by the arm, press her into a parallel world, white and ceaseless, without Lauren in it. Alone in a pod on the moon. All because

Jane had consented to the thought. It was Jane who had invited this apparition into the nursery, something out of a bad movie, her cold, elegant fingers drumming on the wooden rails of Lauren's crib.

Lauren. Her crooked, crinkly-eyed smile. The honey-and-almond folds of her knees and elbows. The café au lait mark on her hip, the size of Jane's thumbnail; Jane had flipped through an atlas one feverish night, Lauren wheezing in the crook of her arm, and determined that the mark was in the shape of Finland, with particular fidelity to the topography of its eastern border with Russia. The feathery fur on Lauren's shoulders and in the V between her shoulder blades, still lingering there long after her infancy. Toddler Lauren's heartbreaking *byeee-bye* when a door closed that she wished to stay open. Lauren telling an anecdote in her own slushy, temperate language, gesticulating in fluent De Niro, furrowing her brow as she searched for the perfect turn of phrase. In these moments Lauren looked a lot like Sonja, who still called when she was home on break, who still came around.

So did Geeta, but only with Sonja. They were a package deal. Elise would join them or come on her own. Christy faded out, although she was going to UB and still living at home.

The worst was the first year. Geeta and Sonja brought Mylar balloons when they visited Jane after the baby. Nursing Lauren on the couch, her friends cross-legged on the matching overstuffed chairs that Mrs. Brennan had chosen from Kittinger, Jane watched the balloons nudging against the ceiling of the living room, clumsy and aimless blobs, and saw herself as an invalid in a hospital full of false cheer, as if she were recovering from a severe head injury as her friends guided her through some remedial small talk. Part of her rehabilitation. She told them too eagerly about what she was reading, Wordsworth and Winnicott and *Ordinary People*, but she didn't admit that she couldn't pay attention for more than a few pages at a time.

What cannot be taken for granted is the mother's pleasure that goes with the clothing and the bathing of her own baby. If you are there enjoying it all, it is like the sun coming out for the baby. That was Winnicott.

"I'll definitely have to check all those books out," Geeta said finally, and Jane's uterus performed one of its last contractions, letting go a sorrow that she could not name but was nonetheless sitting in front of her.

Enjoy being turned-in and almost in love with yourself, the baby is so nearly a part of you. That also was Winnicott. And it was true that Jane could enjoy this, so long as it was only her and Lauren.

Pat's sister, Marie, ten years older, businesslike in her courteousness and with three small children of her own, always included Jane in her card games and PTA fund-raiser meetings with her friends, all in their late twenties or older, with children who were mostly in school already. But Jane could never entirely learn their repartée of weary disparagement: of their husbands, their children, and the mothers in the group who didn't happen to be present that day. Jane's mother frequently commented on how Marie "carried herself with such grace," like she was a widow or bearing the burden of some unjust opprobrium—or maybe the burden was the fact that Marie looked exactly like Pat and yet, by some abstruse geometry, he was the pretty one. That was the kind of thought that Jane's mother would have.

Her mother often told Jane, "You are so lucky to have Marie." Or, "She gave you a leg up." Or, "She showed you the ropes." Or, "She's been very good to you, really gone out of her way." These were accusations. Her mother's praise of Marie was a euphemism for a darker thought: that Jane had cut corners, received a gift in error, gotten away with something, she had cheated, she had lied, and look, it had all worked out for her anyway, like it always does, this smooth, easy life laid down for her by the work and thoughtfulness and compassion of others.

In the ordinary things you do you are quite naturally doing very important things, and the beauty of it is that you do not have to be clever, and you do not even have to think if you do not want to. Winnicott again.

THREE YEARS WITH Lauren, the idyll of the only child, was so much of what Jane imagined the first months of a romance to be: the hours alone together doing nothing in particular, staring into each other's eyes, laughing at jokes they couldn't have explained to others or even themselves, lolling in grass or snow, kneading each other's flesh, eating off each other's plates. Even Lauren's tantrums, infrequent and easily resolved, could be observed with some degree of detachment. A summer storm through a frosted pane.

Duck, Lauren whispered for *dark,* when she woke in the first inklings of dawn. *Bight,* Lauren whispered for *bright,* when her mother switched on the lamp by her crib. Her little face opening like a flower when she found the names for things.

"That's right, Lauren. It was duck and now it's bight," her mother told her. This was the best time of day, at dawn, before Pat woke, when Jane and Lauren could share secrets about their world and decide, just the two of them, how to name everything in it.

Marie's friends complained about the early starts, the relentless menial labor that multiplied with two and then three children. Pretty much everyone was stopping at three these days. "You've only got the one," they would say. "Just wait—you'll see."

They complained about having to read the same books aloud over and over. For Jane, who could recite *The Snowy Day* and *The Story of Ferdinand* and *Goodnight Moon* by heart, extreme repetition had granted these stories the calming, incantatory quality of the prayers that she no longer felt compelled to say. "Where mouse go?" Lauren asked on every page of *Goodnight Moon,* and Jane intoned the rodent's Stations of the Cross with a lowing reverence. *Mouse on the mantelpiece. Mouse on the drying rack. Mouse near the fire.*

"Where mouse go?" Lauren asked when the book was closed, and Jane was happy to begin again.

WHEN PAT WAS sweet, he was so sweet. But even in the midst of the sweetness, there was the foreshadowing, the menace of when he would not be sweet. The two Pats were always in the room with Jane and Lauren.

The first time Jane thought about running away was the night he snapped a garbage bag in her face when she was holding Lauren, whipping it like a suburban matador as he harangued her about—what? What was it? How could she forget? Something about the cat food, or the cat litter, or the cat. Jane laughed, out of nerves. He crowded her against a wall of the kitchen for laughing and then he taunted her for cowering. He shouted until the baby began to cry—a frightened, staccato cry that Jane had not heard before—and he taunted Jane for letting the baby cry. Lauren had just started holding up her head on her own.

"I will leave you," Jane told Pat. "I will take the baby, and I will get a divorce."

"You would never," he said.

A Saturday in summer, not long after Lauren had started crawling. Jane sensed the stink of incipient anger on Pat as the three of them finished lunch. Proximity to him was dangerous, but packing Lauren into the car for a "shopping run" might be seen as a rebuke. She took Lauren into the backyard with a pitcher of lemonade and a blanket: a storybook scene she hoped Pat might see from the kitchen window, a scene that might calm him, a young mother and her gorgeous baby girl lounging in the low summer sun, discussing the grass, exploring the clouds. He could watch from his house and savor the privilege of what he owned. There was a sinful vanity in this little scheme, the same vanity that poked at the corners of Jane's lips whenever a stranger mistook her for Lauren's big sister. But still: she would set a scene that belonged to Pat, awaiting his benediction.

Jane wondered if her father had ever menaced her mother like this, if his blandness ever turned like Pat's sweetness did. If there was a precedent, if this was normal.

When it was time for Lauren's nap, Jane lifted her off the grass, cuddled in the blanket, to carry her inside. She turned the knob of the back door and, curiously, found it locked; with Lauren on her hip, she walked around to the front of the house to find that door locked, too. She knocked on the door intermittently for an hour, tapped at windows, and otherwise sat on the stone stoop, drowsy Lauren slumped on her lap, thumb in her mouth, Jane hunched over to shield her from the afternoon sun. The *glare* her mother had warned about.

When Pat finally opened the front door, he wore a mask of contemptuous disbelief.

"Why are you out here?" he yelled. Lauren rubbing her cheek against Jane's neck.

The best thing was to enter the house as quietly as possible, put the baby to bed, wait for the menace to dissipate. There was nothing she could say or do to make it better. She was the cause and she would be the effect.

Don't say a word don't react don't say a word don't—

"Because you locked us out of the house, you asshole!" she said.

She was already halfway through the doorway, and the door was slamming against her shoulder, it was slamming against her head, and points of light were behind her eyes and the baby, the baby, the baby is okay, they are outside again, sitting down on the stoop, Lauren is still in her arms, the baby is okay, the baby, the baby is okay.

He hadn't hit her. He hadn't meant to hurt her with the door. He was just angry, that's all. Something came over him. Something had come over her, too! She couldn't help it, and neither could he. He hadn't meant to cause her any pain. Let's be fair about this. She had a part to play, too. It takes two. Why was she so tough on him? Why was she standing there? Right there, right in the way of the door?

Sometimes she wanted so badly for Pat to hit her, with his hands. She had stopped herself in the act of praying for this, and then prayed for forgiveness for wanting this. She wanted this because if he ever laid his hands on her, then she could ask God for forgiveness for taking Lauren from him and running away—then she could justify it. Broken skin or a broken bone—then it would be Pat who had broken the vow.

You would never.

Was God looking now? Could he see that she wasn't provoking Pat's anger, that his anger only fed off itself? Was she provoking Pat's anger by praying for it, or wanting to pray for it? Would God forgive her? What would there be to forgive?

He is not even looking at you.

In the midst of Pat's rages or in their aftermath, Jane took a steadying comfort in discomfort: the near-scalding water she used to sterilize Lauren's bottles; the juice of an orange stinging her cuticles; Lauren's chubby knee digging into her rib cage as they climbed the stairs to her room, Pat's clamor trailing after them, a colander striking the kitchen floor, a cereal bowl cracking open against the wall.

One afternoon as Lauren napped, Jane was on her hands and knees in the living room, picking up toys, when she drew back one arm and smacked it against the wooden foot of the rocking chair. She closed her eyes against the pain, willing it to sustain. She dived into the blood swimming under her skin. She couldn't plan out these opiate bursts of oblivion; they depended in part on surprise. She was grateful for the pain, its dazzling clarity, its sweeping away of everything but itself, and she wanted the pain not to stop but to be smothered and forgotten in more pain. And then the pleasure of it being gone, the pleasure of a pain that goes away.

Discomfort, especially when it breached the borderlines of pain, was clarifying. It was a form of truth. It relieved the damp pressure of the humming in her brain. Jane remembered the call of pain, the seductions of it. She remembered trying to be saintly in her pain. But while Pat's rages were something a saint might endure, saints did not marry. Saints didn't have children. Saints didn't permit men inside them, or babies inside them. Mother Seton didn't count.

She was no saint, Jane told herself over and over again. And he never hit her.

Even before she discovered she was pregnant again, she mourned her solitary romance with Lauren, and she mourned the fantasy she'd been harboring since the night Pat whipped the garbage bag at them: that they could get away. That Jane and Lauren could slip free of the bonds of holy matrimony, local infamy, and the financial and social apparatus that the elder Brennans had built around their son's small sudden family—house, car, budget, gainful employment and college tuition for Pat, the crib, the furniture, the checkbook, the Sunday dinners, the awkward, Marie-facilitated playdates— and run off together, consummate their romance, elope.

The checkbook. Faux leather, a froggy green. Pat gave her cash for her grocery-store runs, and Jane had been setting aside the change, the fives and ones slowly stacking up again. Maybe by now they would fill one and a half of her old candy tins. But she could get the checkbook. Pat kept it in an unlocked drawer, or sometimes left it out on his desk. She could walk into the bank with that checkbook and ask for money. She didn't know how much was in the account. It had to be at least a few thousand dollars, she thought. She could breezily mention to the bank teller that she was buying a used car, or something. She could have a whole story prepared. She wouldn't have to tell the story, wouldn't have to say a thing, it wasn't a clerk's business, but she'd have the story anyway, another small gift to offer herself.

The Monday after the slamming door, Jane went to the faux-Tudor efficiency complex on Evans Road, Lauren in her arms. One-bed, one-bath, wall-to-wall carpeting, black grime behind the toilet. Cash deposit in her purse. *Can't use the coffee maker and the toaster at the same time or you'll blow a fuse. Cute baby you got there. Your husband coming to see the place, too?*

She could do this to herself, but she couldn't do it to Lauren. Jane was the one who had gotten them into this situation. Lauren was not at fault. Jane closed her eyes against the image of Geeta or Elise coming over to the apartment with flowers or a basket of fruit, murmuring, "How nice, how nice." Mylar balloons nudging against the bulges in the ceiling, the flaking plaster. Her mother stopping by with Marie, Marie hyperventilating with false cheer and laughter, her mother lingering in the doorway, refusing to sit down, making a show of not touching anything.

Lauren would not have brothers or sisters. Lauren would never be anyone's sister. She would not know anyone at school who was alone in the way she was. Alone with a crazy mother who'd chewed off her own leg to escape the trap she'd set for a nice boy, a boy who only wanted to do right by her.

"I will leave you," Jane told Pat. "I will take the baby, and I will get a divorce."

"You would never," he said.

She did remember Sonja's birth control math. Pat might get impatient, but he didn't force it. There were other things they could do.

Still, though, it was time. She couldn't leave Lauren alone.

Build a cell inside your mind from which you can never flee.

THEY NAMED THE new baby Patrick John III, or PJ. Just short of a year later, there was Sean.

"Irish twins," Dee said fondly.

"Like rabbits," Jane's mother said darkly.

PJ was fussier than Lauren in his observance of standards and customs: the angle at which Jane offered her breast, the optimal conditions under which he would come to terms with his car seat or stroller or diaper. Sean was as easy and sweet as Lauren had been, only now there were three of them. A memory so crystalline it must have been a composite: the boys side by side on changing blankets on the living room floor, PJ crying himself hoarse, kicking, Sean staring puzzled at his brother from atop a diaper explosion up to his hips, and four-year-old Lauren standing off to one side, chewing her lip, ruminating on some big and mournful decision, and then padding to the opposite side of the room to sit down cross-legged with a book, her back turned to them.

"Lauren?" Jane asked over the din and shit, hearing the helpless tone in her voice. "Are you okay, honey?"

Lauren nodded without turning around.

"Come here, my love," Jane said. "My one and only girl." She wouldn't turn around. They were falling out of love, Jane feared, and this was where it started.

The sweet Pat faded further once one child became two and then three, once the scenes he departed each morning and came home to each night compounded in their noise and mess, as the friends of Marie said that they would. And yet Pat was safest at home: in public, Jane embarrassed him, and the proximity of the children multiplied his embarrassment, turning it more quickly into anger. The five of them clambering out of a booth at Perkins, Jane bending over Sean to unbuckle the strap on his high chair. Pat stepped on her foot, hard, his dried-muddy work boot flat on her open-toed sandal, and she didn't react, of course it was an accident, a grunt of pain escaped her throat, but that was it, she didn't mean anything by it, she wasn't faking it, she kept her smile, she didn't look up, she only hovered over Sean an extra minute, tickling his velvety earlobe with her nose, blowing his hair like dandelion fluff to erase the seething in her ear.

"I didn't *see* you there—why were you standing so close to me?" Pat asked.

Jane teethed Sean's earlobe and he giggled.

"You're like a dog that's always underfoot," he said. Standing so close to her. People in Perkins would start looking at him, and his anger would double for having been witnessed. Jane had made him do it, and Jane had made them look at it. It was what she had wanted to happen. He was sure of this, he *knew* it, he was righteous in his knowledge of her transgressions, her power over his will.

It always felt the same: hands shaking, heart seizing, the metallic taste on her tongue. The sensation of a dank gray blanket thrown over her head. She would have to move through her day and attend to her children with the blanket over her head, and she couldn't complain about or even acknowledge the blanket over her head. The palm of a hand pressing against her forehead. The sinking, sinking. She kissed Sean's soft, perfect cheek, made friendly growling sounds in the sweet folds of his neck. He giggled, and the palm pressed down, down. Her cheek against Sean's, and she was sinking. Her poor baby, having to sink with her. He must know something, must feel himself sinking. She shifted Sean to one hip and hoisted the diaper bag over the opposite shoulder. "I love you," she whispered in Sean's ear, and he giggled again. Maybe Sean didn't want to giggle, Jane thought, maybe he was faking it just like her.

Outside the restaurant, PJ was on Pat's shoulders, pointing and squinting happily at the cars moving up and down Transit Road, Lauren listening attentively as Pat described to her the basic properties of the internal combustion engine. Pat's enthusiasm for the engine and for his children was evident. Lauren looked up at him and took his hand.

THEY USED TO fight all the time, but fighting with Pat was an attempt to win a debate in front of an audience that didn't exist. No one was observing or adjudicating. No one would congratulate Jane for being right, or for being locked out of the house, or for having a body that occupied space. She tried to move through the world like a blessed machine, silvery and shimmering. She tried to move through the world like a light field, all energy and no mass. She tried not to move through the world at all, but aspire instead to the friendly frozen sheen of nativity livestock. Pleasant and bovine. Who could be angry with a cow?

Though Pat's anger would dissipate, for days and weeks at a time, the air was always stagnant with it. Pat could cough, just cough, and Jane would start, and he would notice and accuse her of "performing," and then that would be another two, three days right there.

"Stop *acting*!" her mother would say.

Pat was a roar, a maw, famished for outrage. He still wanted her, even when he hated her. He could still make her come, or rather she could still accomplish that in the midst of him using her body to make himself come. Years after they no longer had to fuck in cars and laundry rooms, it still felt furtive. Something not to talk about, certainly not with each other. How he moved her around, flipped her over, yanked one leg this way and that, pushing and kneading her hips or her ass one centimeter this way or that to attain maximum friction, depth, torque—it used to be funny, flattering, revelatory of all the things she previously hadn't known her body could do. What he could do to her body, what her body could do to his. He was teaching her. That's what she used to think. But who had taught him? And when would it be her turn to teach? And why didn't he ask her? It was too late to ask any of these questions.

SHE WOKE UP one dawn beside him, soaked in her own blood. "Were you even going to *tell* me?" he whisper-yelled at her. She stood silhouetted against the bedroom window as she peeled the sheets off the bed. She thought she was nineteen weeks.

"*Were* you?" he asked.

He could have told himself, had he been paying attention. Marie had figured it out. Lauren had, too. "I see your belly, Mommy," she said, two mornings ago, peeking through the bathroom doorway as Jane emerged from the shower.

"You are far enough along," the doctor said later that morning, "that we have two choices here."

Two ways to get her out. It was a girl. She knew it like she'd known with Lauren. She knew her.

She wanted to tell someone else. She wanted to tell her mother. Not her own mother, but the mother you could tell these things to.

A MONTH LATER, Pat came home with an ice pack down the front of his pants.

"We are done," he said that night in bed. "Three is enough. More than enough."

"It's a sin," Jane said, and he groaned with the effort of turning away from her.

She dreamed she gave birth to a loaf of bread, and when she cut into it, she cut into the baby sleeping inside.

You are far enough along

She tried to put the baby back together as everything crumbled in her hands.

that we have two choices here.

Blood in the bread like a jelly.

She asked God for forgiveness. She knelt on the bathroom floor, door closed and tap running, and tried to explain Pat's position to God, and she chided herself for her presumption. Praying like this, with some special request, like she was calling in to some celestial radio station, felt fraudulent and lonely. Begging for a favor—a vestige of her narcissistic adolescent self. At least as a teenager she prayed every night without fail, and not only when she wanted something.

She reminded herself that such procedures as Pat had undergone were sometimes reversible. When things calmed down, they could talk about it. When Pat had a longer stretch of not being angry. When her nightmares stopped. When the children she did have were a little older. She liked how Pat was with the children, especially as they got old enough for chapter books and Uno games and Underoos. She had to admit that. His gruff there-ness. His love for the children was unremarkable, un-remarked-upon, not worthy of fuss. For him to be demonstrative, to verbalize his love, would be like jumping up and down on the floor and marveling that it didn't cave in. He took a genuine interest in their sports teams, the architecture of their sandcastles and toy train lines. His engagement was not with who the children *were*, their inner lives and friendships and whether or not they liked their homeroom teacher that year—he would not have known their homeroom teacher's name, would not have recognized her if she said hello to him in Bells market, had he ever stepped foot in Bells—but rather in what the children *did*. The children sensed the nature of his interest, identified its authenticity, and reciprocated it. They sought out Pat's opinions. He was the person who explained the world to them.

Still, they knew who he was. If he yelled at Jane, really yelled, they would ask him to stop. Ever since they were tiny, if she went into another room because the fact of her body taking up space was provoking his anger, the children would follow her. Jane sitting on the edge of their bed, Lauren and PJ on either side of her, Sean still inside, Pat looming above all of them. Jane watched as PJ, the only one of her three who was never a thumb sucker, no man of the pacifier, crammed his fingers, one and then two and then three, into his mouth as he stared into space, waiting beside his mother and sister for his father's anger to end.

The business of their father would end, but their mother never would. In subjecting her children to their father, she also sensed her permanence, authority, the eternal fact of herself. Her there-ness. She would always be more immovably there than he was.

Jane cooked and cleaned and drove, drove and cleaned and cooked. She was the primal parent, the chest where they wanted to bury their heads after a scraped knee or a bad dream. Hers was the name they called in the night, if they called at all. Soon enough, they didn't.

At the library, one shelf above *Stories of the Saints*, was a book of fables from the animal world. She flipped through it a lot when she was pregnant with Lauren, when Winnicott's friendly, encouraging sentences started swimming together. The book of fables was really a book of mothers. The panther who only ever has one litter, because her children claw their way out—tearing their first home to shreds, condemning it by escaping it. The bear who gives birth not to babies but to eyeless white heaps of flesh, which she licks and paws into shape and warms into life, their eyes flashing on in the moment of quickening. The tiger who awakens in the night to find her cubs stolen, and she sprints after the kidnapper, who throws down mirrors behind him to confuse her. She has never seen herself before. The tiger mistakes her own reflection for one of her babies; she stops short to wrap herself protectively around the curve of the glass. A pose of sleep and love. She wanted her baby, and she wanted revenge, and she wanted them so wildly that she lost them both.

Imagine, she thought, *looking into your own eyes to find yourself so betrayed. Imagine the moon above you was a mirror. She is your mother, your sister, your child. She looks in the mirror and sees only you.*

AT TIMES, JANE saw another life. They left all three children at his parents' house for Elise Davis's wedding. Elise got married barefoot on the banks of Lake Chautauqua, the reception on the grounds of an old auto baron's mansion. Elise had finished law school and her new husband, Peter, had finished his medical residency, and they were moving to Arlington, Virginia. The weather was perfect. A deck for dancing, strung up with tiny lights at dusk. Colin Chase was there, God knows why, the smiling sociopath, going in for the both-cheeks kiss with Jane like they were fond old classmates from a junior year abroad. Pat was gregarious with various guests, conspicuously so, interrupting, touching first a

wrist and then a bare shoulder blade belonging to Elise's younger
sister, sleeveless in her maid-of-honor dress. Then he disappeared.
Jane found him at the outskirts of the dance floor. The DJ was
playing the Go-Gos' "Our Lips Are Sealed." Three generations
dancing.

"I love this song," Jane said. She loved it because Lauren loved
it, knew every word, and PJ and Sean would always come in on the
title line. *Ah-lips ah see-all!* How she missed the three of them right
now, holding hands in a circle under the tiny lights.

"Let's dance, honey," Jane said. Pat stared straight ahead at an
empty patch of the parquet dance floor.

> *There's a weapon*
> *We must use*
> *In our defense*
> *Silence*

"Oh, come on, let's dance—it's boring just to watch!" Jane said,
touching his arm, smiling too hard, trying too hard.

Pat turned slowly toward her. An evacuated face, the skin hanging looser, as if some animating spirit had been sucked out through
the black-marble hollows of his eyes.

"Oh, I'm *boring*, am I?" he said. A dead face that wanted her
dead. "Am I *boring* you?"

And that was it—she knew that was it. That would be the rest
of the night, the rest of the weekend. How many of Jane's hours,
days, weeks of her life vaporized like this.

"Let's go," he was barking behind Jane a few songs later. She
had finally gotten her chance to speak with Elise, so pretty and
sheepish in her makeup and bone-white garments. "I'm *bored*," he
whined, crowding over her, boozy mouth in Jane's ear, Jane trying
to transmit a mortified apology to her friend with one look as Elise
squeezed her hand in silent understanding.

In the car driving home, flipping radio stations, ignoring the road, running over the speed limit, the car drifting back and forth across lane lines: "I'm so *bored*. This music is *so boring*."

"Pat," she said, as evenly and quietly as possible. "You're going seventy in a forty-five-mile zone."

Pat whacked on the brakes, squealing, Jane lurching forward before the strap of her seat belt locked. He puttered along at thirty for a bit. "You know," he said, "it's just as dangerous to drive under the speed limit as to drive over it."

Even, quiet. "I didn't ask you to drive under the speed limit."

"So if John Law pulls me over I'm going to have to explain to him that you made me drive slow."

"Pat, enough," Jane said. "Just drive the speed limit."

"But driving the speed limit is *so boring*."

Arriving home, he bolted out of the car, slipped through the door to the mudroom, and locked it behind him before Jane could reach the steps. She hadn't brought keys because she wasn't driving, and it wouldn't have mattered if she had—he would have blocked the door with a chair or with his body.

When he unlocked the door an hour later, he asked her, "Isn't it *boring* out here in the garage? You must be so *bored*."

She kept her head low as she edged past him through the door, her arm brushing his, a sickening closeness. She didn't even hate him; she hated herself for wanting him to allow her back inside his house, for moving carefully but quickly in case he changed his mind, for granting him the privilege of ending her punishment. She didn't know what else she could have done but come inside, and she hated herself for that, too. Pat was her whole life, and he could do with her life whatever he wanted.

That wedding was the last time she saw Geeta and Christy and Sonja, the last time she saw Elise. Elise called her as soon as she got home from her honeymoon in Hawaii. She called again and again. The last time, Jane listened as Elise left a message on the answering machine, then rewound the tape as soon as she clicked off, so the next message would tape over it. Elise wrote a letter—sunny, companionable, but ending on a firm plea for a response—that Jane never answered. She had nothing to offer her friend, except the raw material for a sympathy that she didn't want.

But it wasn't as if their friendship were over—Jane told herself this like a prayer, like somebody somewhere could hear it. Their friendship seemed dead but really it was saved, tucked away from where Pat could reach it.

THE CELL INSIDE her mind wasn't empty, and it wasn't full.

Marie and her friends viewed the scars of childbearing as afflictions, indignities. But Jane liked the glossy silverfish streaks across her belly and the small pouch of flesh resting above her pubic hair. These were mementos saved from the first house her babies had lived in, testaments to forbearance. And her breasts were better since the children, actually, a solid B-cup even long after Jane had begun teaching herself again what real hunger felt like. After the last baby broke apart inside her, she felt the old emptiness, and she wanted more of it.

As long as her children were inside her, or drinking from her, and as long as she thought there were more children yet to come, the extra weight she carried was a natural resource, protective and productive. She stood in front of the full-length bedroom mirror and considered her sagging, dimpled stomach and wide round thighs with the same nodding equanimity with which one might assess a grain elevator. She was vast, renewable, in some respects automated. A windmill, the Hoover Dam. She was the Buffalo of olden days: coal and steel and good solid architecture. Hard-used, maybe used-up, but eternal.

But once the children were done, she felt entombed in greasy machinery. Buried alive in bad soil. Not Buffalo but *buffaloed*. She had forgotten herself, and she had forgotten God. Maybe that was why she lost the baby. The old dream that everyone has about finding an extra room in the house, but what Jane found in it were her own living children, disheveled, hollow-eyed with the hunger that should have belonged to her.

She remembered the guilty narcissism of hunger's effects as her old self, or a version of it, began to reassert itself: the bas-relief of hip bone, rib cage, shoulder blade; the clean runner's lines of her legs. A sandwich at lunch became a half sandwich, which became the filling of the half sandwich, which became an untouched half sandwich she would wrap and place in the fridge until such time as it was devoured indiscriminately by one of the three voracious males in her house. She began jogging the mile to Wilson Farms for milk, eggs, tea, and jogging home again with the groceries packed tight in her backpack, taking grim pleasure in the corner of the milk carton digging into the bottom of her spine. She rode her bike the three miles and back to Bells, tying her purchases to the front and back of the bike with bungee cord, a pack mule grunting up and down the shoulders of Transit and Muegel roads. A donkey for Jesus. Her head whirred to the cadence of *he HAW, he HAW, he HAW*, the stress landing on each pump of the pedals.

I've got a mule, her name is Sal
Fifteen miles on the Erie Canal

Jane did Meals on Wheels. She drove developmentally disabled adults to basketball games and pizza parties. She joined the Catholic Charities annual fund-raising drive committee.

She's a good ol' worker and a good ol' pal
Fifteen miles on the Erie Canal

She attended an evening meeting of the Respect Life committee, in a kindergarten classroom in the Saint Benedict's elementary school annex. She slowed down approaching the classroom door and then kept walking, heading instead into the girls' bathroom down the hall, where she locked herself in a stall to pat down her sweaty forehead with toilet paper. She reemerged, approached the classroom again, and again hustled past the door, crossing her arms in front of her and stopping to stare with furious concentration at the kindergartners' artwork lining the walls: family trees cut crookedly out of construction paper and decorated with Magic Marker and pipe cleaners.

"Jane Thirjong?" she heard behind her. She turned to see Mr. Glover, her ninth-grade science teacher at Bethune, always grumpy beneath his bushy white mustache and size-too-big orlon sweaters.

"Oh, hi, Mr. Glover," she said. "It's Jane Brennan now. So nice to see you again."

"It's nice to see you, too," Mr. Glover said as they shook hands. "Would you like to join us? We're just getting started." He seemed kindlier now than he ever had in class. Maybe he only played the part of grouchy old man when he was teaching.

She had already cast and scripted this Respect Life meeting in her head, on the drive over. The committee leader asking each member to stand and offer his or her testimony to the cause: the cousin with Down syndrome, the dream visitation from a child not born. Jane in the role of the teenage mother emeritus, chagrined by her transgressions yet wholesome in her youthful verve, her attractive and moderately prosperous young family, her devotion to children and cause. *Lauren was never just blood and tissue. She was never just an option. She was there from the start.* She could confess to her new friends here about the nurse. She could tell them about consenting to the thought.

I couldn't see Lauren; I didn't know what she looked like. It didn't matter. To be a person of faith, after all, is to believe in things you can't see.

But the meeting had no introductions, no leader to deliver a prologue to Jane's speech. Summer and Charity Huebler were chirpy twin sisters, UB students. Phil and Betty Andrower were older, their children grown and out of the house; Betty volunteered in the rectory office. Mr. Glover's absent wife was incapacitated somehow—multiple sclerosis or Lou Gehrig's disease. They had no children. Jane always felt herself disarmed, at a strange loss, when she met an older woman without children—anxious on the other woman's behalf, as if she needed Jane's assistance filling her time. Jane never would have been able to account for herself alone. The ledgers would not have balanced out.

For one hour, this week and most every week, in a circle of chair-and-desk sets sized for five- and six-year-olds, the Respect Life committee members stuffed envelopes with leaflets designed and printed in a centralized office in Washington, DC. Hale fat fair-skinned babies in grayscale or sepia tones, often sleeping, their images overlaid with calligraphic Biblical quotations.

You knit me in my mother's womb.

You have been my guide since I was first formed.

From my mother's womb you are my God.

Jane used her tongue, not a sponge, to lick the envelopes, and refused Mr. Glover's offers of a can of soda or a cup of water. She wanted to taste ashes, to repent for the thing she hadn't done.

"'You knit me in my mother's womb'—oh, I like that one so much," Betty said. "To think of God busying away with knitting needles." She frowned. "Although—I suppose—the connotations—"

"Like, kind of girly?" Summer Huebler asked.

"No—knitting needles have an—association with how—the terminations—in the old days—"

"Like a *wire hanger*," Charity said darkly, and Summer crossed herself.

"It was Adam who said, 'You knit me in my mother's womb,'" Jane said.

"David wrote the Psalms," Phil said, a reproach.

"He did," Jane said, "but there's an interpretation that he wrote them for Adam—as in, he wrote them in the voice of Adam."

"How do you know that?" Betty asked.

Jane checked Betty's face to make sure she wasn't annoyed. Betty was both voluptuous and petite, her hazel eyes as big in her face as a baby's. It was easy to picture what she looked like as a child, as a younger woman. "I know it by just—reading," Jane said. "I read a lot. You know how it is, your kids get older and they don't need as much of your time, and you fill it however you can . . ." She was trying for a jaunty tone, slightly joking, like one of Marie's friends. Betty smiled. "So yeah, David wrote the Psalms in Adam's voice, maybe," Jane said, "which is interesting because Adam wasn't knit in a mother's womb. Right? Because a few lines later he says he came out of the depths of the earth."

Phil frowned and shook his head. He was jowly but trim, holding on to his summer tan. "*David* wrote the Psalms," Phil said.

"I *know* that," Jane said. She sounded bratty. It was her nerves that were talking. "But how could you be made in a womb and be the first man at the same time? If there was no first woman to give birth to you?"

"Maybe it's a play on words," Betty said. "The depths of the earth like"—she introduced a hammy tremolo—"the *nether-regions.*"

Summer and Charity *ewww*ed. "Disgusting," Phil said.

"A baby in the womb is disgusting?" Betty asked. "Or giving birth to the baby?"

"You're mixing things up," Phil said. "You're twisting things."

Betty was enjoying this, Jane could see. Goofing on her husband by aligning playfully with the young newcomer. She could imagine the couple in their car afterward, Betty tousling Phil's hair in a conciliatory way, Phil trying to keep up a façade of disgruntlement. Speeding back home for some vigorous late-middle-aged make-up sex.

"It's messy, but I'm not sure I would call it disgusting," Jane said. "After all, Mary had a baby."

"Don't bring the blessed Virgin Mary into this!" Phil said.

"Mary *didn't* have a baby?" Jane asked.

"That's why we venerate her," Betty said. "Because she gave birth."

"We venerate her because she's the *mother of God*," Phil said, "and this conversation is over."

"You know," Betty said in a low voice, ostensibly meant for Jane but loud enough for all to hear, "those Presbyterians couldn't give Mary the time of *day*."

"I'm no Presbyterian!" gasped Phil, spitting the word on the floor.

"I didn't say you were, dearest," Betty said.

"It's true that Mary is not in the Bible much," Jane said.

"Maybe that's because she wasn't always pumping herself up!" Betty exclaimed. "She was busy doing women's work, raising the son of God!"

ON FRIDAY AFTERNOONS, Jane cleaned housebound seniors' homes. The work was saintly in its lack of glory, its repetitiveness, its occasional small degradations. Most of her clients had home health aides, or a spouse or nearby relatives, but one man was alone. Mr. Dennison wore cloudy glasses and always the same stained khaki pants, and it took him long minutes to get from his sagging plaid armchair to the front door when Jane rang the bell. He silently offered an apologetic smile, a gracious nod, and then returned to his chair.

October, the sun skulking, the breeze woodsy and lowering, the day closing in. Jane was scrubbing what looked like years-old dog food that she'd found encrusting a corner of Mr. Dennison's mudroom. A sudden stench made her eyes water. Mr. Dennison had shat himself, right there on the plaid. She guided him into the bathroom, silently undressed him, got him into the shower, turned the handle on the window over the tub, pushing it open inch by inch. Got the clothes into the trash. She would have to root around upstairs to find some clean trousers, and maybe call the Goodwill; she would have to call the Department of Sanitation about proper disposal of the chair. The list tabulated in her head, each item a stern jolt of dopamine. It was saintly to be overwhelmed by thankless, invisible work.

As Mr. Dennison painfully exited the shower, one leg and then the other doing an excruciating bend and balance to surmount the lip of the tub, Jane held out a towel to him. She saw a rusty stain in one corner, but it would do. He looked at the outstretched towel and sank to the floor, knees to his chest. Raised gray moles snaking up and around his midsection, his penis, a clean slug, perfectly horizontal on the tile. They hadn't taken off his glasses before he got into the shower. Jane lingered uncertainly over him, then got to her knees beside him, her hand patting his sloping gray shoulder.

"It's all right," she said. "We'll get through this together."

She felt smug in her saintliness and hoped that God would see her acts themselves unobscured by her smugness. As darkness fell outside, though, she accepted that no one could see them at all. No one could hear or smell or judge. They were alone in their suburban pietà.

She raised herself on her knees and nudged him to sling both of his arms over her shoulders. With their foreheads pressed on each other's shoulders, she helped him to his feet.

You were a baby once, she thought, breathing under his weight. *This same body. It was a baby. Go all the way back. Someone held you in their arms.*

PAT AND JANE watched *20/20* on Friday nights. Jane loved Barbara Walters. She loved the fluty music of her voice. She loved her floaty scarves and floaty hair. She loved imagining how Barbara Walters smelled, like hairspray and lilacs and Chanel No. 5. She loved how, whenever Barbara Walters coaxed a penetrating admission from a celebrity she was interviewing, her eyes would narrow in loving judgment: a snapshot of the maternal state itself. She also loved Barbara Walters because her mother hated Barbara Walters. "She puts on airs" and "she sounds retarded" and "thinks she's such hot S-H-I-T"—these were the things she would say. Jane's mother mocked Barbara Walters's interchange of *r*s and *w*s in a manner that even PJ and Sean would find crude. Jane suspected that her mother performed her disgust with Barbara Walters's comportment and voice to displace her actual frustration, which was that she perceived she wasn't allowed to say what she really wanted to say about Barbara Walters, which was that she was an ugly Jew. Jane was always happy if her mother called the house in the evening and she could say, "We're not up to much, just watching Barbara Walters."

Jane hadn't eaten before or after working at Mr. Dennison's house, and she hadn't eaten any of the spaghetti and meatballs she prepared that night for her family. A few bites of the leafy green salad was all. She folded herself into the sofa in front of the television in the living room. Tired and hungry, she stared at the *20/20* logo on the screen. Her peripheral vision darkened, her depth perception shot.

If her mother had called the house, right then, Jane would have told her that she saw Barbara Walters in a vision, just as Saint Bernadette saw an angel in the grotto—a holograph of the Immaculate Conception. Her mother would have heard the conviction in her voice, even as she would deny everything that Jane told her.

In the vision, there were children. Undulating mountains of them, wave upon unceasing wave of them, rocking, rocking. They were naked, their skin scabrous, their dark hair shaved close. Crooked mouths, eyes too far apart, limbs akimbo. Rocking, rocking. They had been abandoned, walled off, warehoused in cages or cribs. They were in a place that never could have existed, and they were here in their living room, one floor below where Jane's children slept at night.

One of them, five of them, would have brought tears, but there were too many to cry for. The vision could only accommodate one child. Jane had to find the one child. Barbara Walters would help find her.

Her. It was a girl. Jane knew it was a girl. She was in the cacophony somewhere. She could be seen. Jane knew it. She would glow with her own light.

Jane felt it, that nauseating little earthquake of dread and ecstasy. In the year that followed, it was as if the ghost of the idea of that girl had been inside her all along. So many times in sleep Jane turned to see the girl's face, but she would always elude her.

Not for the first time, at home sitting next to her husband, Jane felt the boundaries between herself and the world dissolving. She could flow into the images on the television screen. Barbara Walters, backlit by heavenly transmissions, with her childlike consonants and celestial cloud of hair, could take her by the hand and lead her toward the girl. Jane's mother was right, if only about one thing—Barbara Walters wasn't like them, she was from another place, she was beautiful in a way that Jane's mother didn't have the eyes to see, she did have a different first language that neither Jane nor her mother knew, and so Barbara Walters could interpret for Jane here. She could send the message, make the connection. She would gaze upon Jane in loving judgment, hoping and doubting she would come through. Jane had to prove it to her. Something opened up in Jane, just then, and it would never close.

"Did you see that one girl?" Jane asked Pat, turning toward him.

"There were hundreds of them, Jane," Pat said. He was gray and shaken.

"No—you would know the one I mean," she said. "She turned around in the crib and put up her hands. She had a—like, a light around her." Jane paused. "Maybe it was just how the shadows— the camerawork—I don't know what it was. Did you see?"

"I didn't," Pat said. He was looking at her closely, his face open and serious. "You saw something?"

When he was sweet, he was so sweet.

"Not something—someone," Jane said. "I know her. I *know* I know her."

SUNDAY MORNING. A near-sleepless weekend. Not since Sean was a baby had she slept so poorly. She sat stuffing envelopes in a Saint Benedict's classroom with the Respect Life committee. The group was discussing their local leg of the upcoming National Life Chain.

"We can cover more ground if we stand one hundred feet apart," Betty was saying, "but that's not a *chain*. It's more like a *freckling*."

"What do we have against the more graphic signs?" Phil asked. "They grab the attention. If you just keep seeing ABORTION KILLS CHILDREN over and over, you zone out. But a—and I'm sorry to say it, but—a dead baby—"

"Don't, Phil!" Betty groaned beside him.

"Well, that's what we are talking about," Phil said. "Why can't we see what we are talking about?"

"The repetition of a simple, irrefutable message leaves a lasting impression," Mr. Glover said. "Drive the point home over and over, like a great advertising campaign. A more confrontational approach, the graphic imagery—it's more likely to short-circuit an emotional response."

"But don't we want to confront people with the truth?" Phil asked. "Like what Operation Rescue does at clinics."

"Oh-R gets you to think about Oh-R, and a bloody poster gets you to think about a bloody poster," Mr. Glover said. He gestured to a teetering stack of signs propped up under the blackboard. "But these big block letters, spelling out the facts in black and white? There's nothing to think about there but the truth."

"Did anyone see *20/20* on Friday night?" Jane asked. Shaking heads, murmured *No*s.

"Well, I mention it because it was confrontational—like how

you said, Mr. Glover. Richard." She swallowed, still clumsy about using his first name. "It was Barbara Walters." Saying her name soothed her, like her prayers used to do. "Barbara Walters, and it was about children in Romania. Abortion and contraception are against the law in Romania. And the people are very poor. They don't want the children, or they can't take care of them, and the children are put in orphanages run by the state."

"Good for them," Phil said. "Whatever happened to orphanages, anyway?"

"Like *Boys Town*," Betty said. "That movie? With Spencer Tracy?"

"Well, these orphanages are horrendous," Jane said. "The children live like caged animals. Worse than animals. It's unimaginable. You see it, but you can't believe it."

We believe in what we can't see, Jane thought in the silence that followed. "It had an effect on me, although it was hard to watch," she said. "Hard to believe."

"Are you okay, Jane?" Summer and Charity asked almost in unison.

"But I thought—oh, yes, I'm fine, thank you for asking—I thought of this group," Jane said. She kept having to swallow. "I thought of us while I was watching it. Us in the church, and the idea of respecting life, I—I thought there might be something we could do for the children. A fund-raiser, or—I don't know."

"We need to get going, friends," Mr. Glover said. On Sunday mornings, the Respect Life committee attended mass at Saint Benedict's, then walked in a single file, heads bowed, the half mile to the WellWomen clinic to pray the rosary in the parking lot, then another three blocks to Dr. Ben Rosen's private gynecology practice, which he ran out of the first floor of a residential house.

"Or maybe—this is maybe crazy—we could bring some of the children here," Jane said. "Here to live. To Buffalo. Give them a better life here."

Her voice was alone amid the susurrating of papers folded and shuffled, chairs scraping the floor as people got up.

"There could be families who'd be interested in adopting the children," she said.

And then: "I'm interested in adopting the children. Or one of the children." *Interested.* That didn't commit her to anything. She was interested in lots of things.

Betty was still seated and listening. "But, Jane," she said in a confidential tone, "don't you think God has already given you children to look after?"

And Jane smiled, because she knew the answer.

LAUREN

Right before everything changed, events arranged themselves in neat lines. Each of them pulsed with meaning. Right before everything changed, she already wanted to be someone else.

Mom asked many times if Lauren was excited or nervous about starting at Bethune High, about her classes and her new friends, and Lauren didn't bother answering because Mom would ask again the next day, like they hadn't just done this conversation. The town or the village or somebody in charge had redrawn the school zones, and most of Lauren's friends from middle school were branching off to different high schools. Mom worried that Lauren would feel a little lost at Bethune, but the main sensation Lauren felt was relief. When she knew everyone, like she did in middle school, she could rank everyone, including herself, and she had to keep track of which girls were in or out, who was "mad at" or "ignoring" or "in a fight with" or "had a bone to pick with" who, whether it was better to pick sides or stay neutral, how much power Lauren had in the middle of these conflicts, how she should use that power when she had it, and how she could get it back when she didn't. It was a relief to escape all this, and for it to be out of her control. She was excused until further notice from entering a classroom to a row of heads turning slowly toward her, each pair of eyes dark and knowing and *mad at you*. First she would have to figure out why (but "If you don't know, I'm not going to tell you") and then she would have to make up for it somehow (but "If you were really sorry you wouldn't have done it in the first place"). And she was also excused until further notice from being one of the swiveling heads, moving in sync toward their target.

For the most part, Lauren was either the swiveling head or the neutral bystander, not the target. People sometimes told her she was pretty, and maybe that was part of why. She got "heart-shaped face" a lot. Adults said, "You look just like your mother."

"People say certain things to mothers about their daughters, almost out of habit," Mom said. "You look like your dad."

People think you are what you look like. Back in seventh grade, Lauren couldn't figure out what was going on with Renée Zeitler and Kelly Kavanaugh from swim team, who had to be fake friends because their mothers were best friends. Renée was always bursting into tears when she had to spend too much time with Kelly, and Kelly went back and forth between jumping up and down for Renée's approval and totally ignoring her. It was strange. There was something behind it that everyone knew was there but no one could see. But then, coming back from a meet in Batavia, Lauren got a ride with Kelly in the back of Kelly's dad's station wagon, and Lauren thought maybe she had figured it out.

Kelly suggested, whispering, that they "do practice-kissing." "I just *trust* you," Kelly told Lauren, "and if we practice with each other, that means we'll be really good at it when we do it with boys."

"We have to lie down flat," Kelly added, "so my dad doesn't see us." The small of Lauren's back ached in the gap between the reverse-facing seats. Kelly's hand under Lauren's clothes and on her breasts was clumsy but confident. Kelly opened her mouth as wide as it would go and set in motion the suctioning hydraulics of her tongue for the duration of Roxette's "Listen to Your Heart."

Lauren didn't want to be doing this, and she hadn't really agreed to it, but she did find it interesting. She had never kissed anyone on the lips before, except once in a while Mom. She had definitely never kissed anyone with *wetness*, open lips, her senses of taste and sound involved, or had another person's tongue inside her mouth, and when she did think about another person's tongue inside her mouth it was a boy. She did mind that Kelly was doing this, but she didn't mind enough to ask Kelly to stop, or do anything that might draw the attention of Kelly's father up in the driver's seat, and so she waited for it to be over the way she waited for her brothers to stop doing any number of things when she had to share the back seat with them—pinching, kicking, close-shouting, a spitty finger in her ear—while also thinking about how she might get back at them sometime later.

Kelly moaned a little, and it harmonized with the chorus of "Listen to Your Heart."

The following day, during Technology & Business, which used to be called Shop, half the class—the boys—plugged in power sanders across the room from where the other half of the class—the girls—sat down to play Monopoly around a square wooden table riddled with splinters and gouge marks. Lauren stared at Renée, who was fidgeting with the dog player piece. She kept staring after Renée had noticed.

"Renée, it's okay," Lauren finally said. "We all know."

The table fell silent. Eyes flicked around. Renée looked terrified. "What?"

"It's okay," Lauren said, looking away from Renée and swiveling toward Kelly. "*You* haven't done anything wrong, Renée."

Kelly bleated a laugh. She wanted it to sound confused, like she was laughing at a freak blabbering nonsense, but instead it was like she was admitting something. By the end of class, Renée was sobbing as Jamie and Shannon consoled her, Kelly was vomiting in the bathroom, and poor one-eyed Mr. Van Den Leek was hovering near the scene, hesitant to turn his back on the boys carving birdhouses, asking if anyone needed the nurse. Mr. Van Den Leek never knew what to do with the girls, and he never let any of them use the bandsaw.

It was all so easy, Lauren thought now. *It was all too easy.*

That was in the fall. There was another big one in the winter.

On the bus home from the ski club's weekly Saturday-night trip to Kissing Bridge, Lauren shared a seat with Danielle Sheridan. Danielle had gotten breasts and hips and several inches in height all at once. She had a doll's face: perfect-circle eyes, and it was like her freckles were painted on, and her cheeks still had a toddler plumpness. Now her doll's head was sewn on the wrong body. Danielle was turned around in her seat to face Jeff Leidecki and Evan Lewis, who were best friends. Jeff's mini–boom box was playing N.W.A, which was what all the boys were listening to now, and Danielle was standing up on her knees, snaking her shoulders and whipping the yarn of her long doll's hair more or less in time with the guitar sample looping over and over. Lauren turned halfway around in her seat, too, to observe Danielle, flinching away when Danielle's gyrating head swung too close. Jeff and Evan were goading Danielle into saying something mean about Shannon, who was absent that week with the flu. Shannon ate only iceberg lettuce leaves at lunch and could make one stick of gum last the school day: she chewed half of the stick in the morning, the other half in the afternoon.

"C'mon, admit it, Danielle," Jeff said. His googly eyes followed all her movements. "Shannon is not hot. She's just a secret fat chick who diets."

"It's like she tricks people into thinking she's hot," Evan said. "Just *say* it, Danielle."

"Why won't you just say it," Jeff said.

These boys hadn't really talked to Danielle before, not like this. They were paying her lots of attention and tempting her with more attention if she would just bad-mouth her friend. They wanted to make a trade, a deal.

"Shannon's ass is so loose," Jeff said, "that when she farts there's no sound, there's no friction—"

"Because *SO MUCH PIZZA*!" Evan and Jeff finished together, and they fell all over each other in hysterics. Their science class had just done a unit on friction and how it is influenced by the three forces of SMP: surface, motion, and pressure. The mnemonic device that Mr. Philbin used to remember this trio was *So Much Pizza.*

Evan was wiping his eyes, trying to recover. "Oh God, so much fucking pizza," he said.

They were losing interest in Danielle. Evan rewound the N.W.A song to the beginning and shouted along with every word. It was like they were playing a video game that seemed just dangerous enough to be exciting—*what if their parents heard?* Jeff shouted all the n-words in these songs, and Evan sort of gulped them down.

"I love this song!" Danielle said over the music. She wanted them to believe her. There was nowhere she could possibly have heard this song before. She bounced up and down on her knees like a much younger kid.

"Isn't it so great when Shannon isn't around?" Jeff asked Danielle. The same tone Mom used to ask about Lauren's day.

"Yeah," Danielle said, grinding her hips against the back of the seat. "And her butt does look kinda big in those blue pants she wears all the time."

They got you, Lauren thought, and turned to face forward again, as Jeff and Evan brayed. Everyone was getting what they wanted tonight. As the bus pulled into the school parking lot, Danielle was sitting on the edge of the seat across from Evan and Jeff, her knee pressed into Jeff's groin. Danielle didn't say goodbye to Lauren as she filed off the bus with Jeff, walking too close to him.

The next afternoon, Dad was cleaning out the garage, and Mom was at what PJ and Sean called Dead Babies Club. Lauren and her brothers were in the den trying to re-create the University of Texas at Austin's routine from the National Collegiate Cheerleading Championships, which Sean had mistakenly recorded on the VCR instead of pro wrestling. PJ and Sean were surprisingly good at high kicks and scissor kicks, and they made a decent two-man stack. A half hour into rehearsal, everyone's muscles flagging, Lauren took a knee to the eye socket.

"Oh, crap, I'm sorry, I'm sorry!" Sean gasped as PJ high-kicked and applauded.

Lauren sat on the carpet, heel of one hand to her eye. "Please don't tell Mom and Dad," Sean begged. Lauren nodded—Sean hadn't meant to harm her. She hid in her room during suppertime, saying she had a stomachache, passing the time with a pile of *Time* magazines and an ice pack. Before he went to bed, Sean sneaked her a Nestlé Crunch and a bag of frozen peas. When her mother came in to check on her, Lauren pretended to be asleep. The next morning, the swelling had subsided, leaving behind a purplish-black crescent.

"Lauren, honey, what happened to your eye?" Mom asked at breakfast.

Lauren, still sleepy, tapped beneath her eye dreamily. "Oh, this—"

Dad looked up from the crossword. "Is that from whatever pandemonium was going on in the den yesterday afternoon?" he asked, and Sean spilled his milk all over the table. PJ ducked his head and giggled.

Mom stared at PJ, then stood up. "Sean, sweetie, that's okay," she said, grabbing some paper towels off the counter. "Just try to be more careful. Lauren, what happened?"

"Answer your mother, Lauren," Dad said. "How'd you get that shiner?"

Lauren was surprised with herself that she had prepared nothing for this question she'd known was coming, and she was equally surprised at how easily the lie came to her.

"Danielle Sheridan was dancing around on ski bus like a crazy person on Saturday night," Lauren said. "She bumped into me. Knocked her head right into me."

Sean was staring at his milk dripping off the rounded edge of the table. "Dum-dum, wipe it up!" PJ said.

"Sean, my love, can you help?" Mom asked, handing him a dishrag. "Lauren, why would Danielle do such a thing?"

The lie came so easily to Lauren because it could have so easily happened the way she said it did. Go back in time. Move Danielle one inch to the right. Tilt Lauren's head an inch to the left. Play the song a little louder. Why not? Who was looking? Who was keeping track?

"She didn't *mean* to do it," Lauren said, staring at Sean. "She was just being a total idiot."

"Danielle Sheridan *is* a total idiot," PJ said, pulling a face at Sean as Sean mopped his place mat. "She'll knee you in the face as soon as she'd look at you. Right, Sean?"

"Danielle *kneed you in the face*?" Mom asked Lauren, incredulous.

"No!" Lauren said. "Don't listen to PJ. He wasn't there. She was just, you know, messing around."

"Should Mom call this girl Danielle's mother?" Dad asked.

"No, no, I'm fine, it was an accident," Lauren said as Mom came close to peer at the bruise. "Don't do anything, *please* don't call anyone. Promise, Mom."

"I promise. It almost looks like a birthmark," Mom said, caressing Lauren's cheek. "There's something beautiful about it."

"Oh my God," Lauren said, and ducked under Mom and out of her chair, into the mudroom to find her backpack and head to the bus stop.

By the time Lauren had traveled to school, done her locker, and sat down for homeroom, she had been asked so many times about her injury that she had a speech down by heart, so well practiced that she could riff and improvise on it, edit or remix it on the spot.

"I can see you are admiring my black eye," she said to Renée, who approached her with mouth agape. "But you should ask Danielle Sheridan how I got it."

Lauren's whole body buzzed. The thrill of a good lie. Her head filled with fizzy soda. It wasn't even a lie—it was a *suggestion*. Lauren could do the lie without telling it. Maybe this was the same thrill that Jeff Leidecki enjoyed every time he shouted *muthafucka* or the n-word on ski bus. And anyway, it was better that Danielle Sheridan got in trouble instead of her doofus little brother. Danielle had been way more obnoxious on ski bus than Sean ever was at home, and Sean hadn't insulted anybody's butt.

"Ask Danielle Sheridan," Lauren kept saying. The full name felt formal, correct, like an official grade-wide investigation was under way. She wasn't exactly accusing Danielle Sheridan of anything. She was just granting Danielle Sheridan the right to tell her own story.

Danielle happened to walk into homeroom at the worst time: as everyone else was settling into their seats, right before Mrs. Velasco called the room to order. Danielle walked in, and every head swiveled. Giggling, whispering. Somebody booed. An "EVERYBODY HIT THE GROUND!" from Gordie Garland's corner of the classroom. Muffled laughter.

"Did *boxing class* run late?" Jamie asked Danielle as she passed Jamie's desk. Danielle smiled helplessly at no one in particular, trying to be in on the joke.

Two periods later, earth science, Lauren sat at a back table with Shannon, Jeff, and Evan as Danielle approached. "Lauren, what is going on—" Danielle began, going to place one hand on Lauren's arm.

"Don't *touch* her," Shannon said, possessive, protective.

"I don't—how did you get hurt?" Danielle asked. Her doll's face wasn't crafted to show distress. Her cornflower eyes and upturned rosebud lips only knew a language of soft-spoken delight.

"Do you remember thrashing around on ski bus like a crazy person?" Lauren asked. An even tone. Again, it wasn't an accusation— it was a question, regarding an observable event with witnesses. Did Danielle remember? The question didn't assume one answer over another. Lauren wasn't lying. She was *acting*, she supposed, but she wasn't lying.

"But I didn't—" Danielle said. "I never touched you."

Jeff squealed. "You *just touched her*," he said. "Like five seconds ago, I *saw* you."

"You weren't jumping up and down and messing around?" Lauren said. "Didn't people see you? Weren't you dancing to the N.W.A song?"

"'One Hundred Miles and Runnin','" Evan said. Backing up the story. These were bland statements of fact. Lauren didn't single out Jeff or Evan as witnesses. They had to come forward on their own. No one likes to be put on the spot.

"But I didn't give you a black eye!" Danielle said. Her voice cracked. Her lashes blinked mechanically.

A Baby Born doll, with nine lifelike functions and eleven accessories.

"If *you* didn't give her a black eye on ski bus," Shannon asked, "then who did?"

"I have no idea!" Danielle said, one tear spilling down her cheek.

"So are you calling Lauren a *liar*?" Shannon asked.

Shannon was enjoying this too much. She and Lauren weren't even all that good friends.

"No, I am *not* calling her a liar!" Danielle spluttered.

Shannon was one of the first kids in school to get three-way calling at home. She liked using it with girls who were in a fight, but one girl wouldn't know that the girl she was fighting with was listening in on the conversation. Shannon would probably call Danielle tomorrow but not tell Danielle that Lauren was there, too, on the other line, cross-legged on her bed, hunched over her phone, one hand clamped over the receiver to hide her breathing.

"And when she was done beating up Lauren, she called you fat and ugly, Shannon," Jeff said as Evan bayed beside him.

Sometimes Shannon would telephone a boy and girl who were rumored to like each other and conference them in without saying anything, not even hello. If you lucked out on the timing—if both of them answered on the first or second ring—each would think the other had made the call; they wouldn't know a third person was involved at all, or not at first. Shannon called these "crush calls."

"No!" Danielle wailed. "I didn't say that about Shannon! I did not!"

"What is going on?" Mr. Philbin asked. "Evan, stop acting like a hyena. Danielle, what is wrong? Do you need the nurse?"

That's what all the male teachers always said when a girl at Mayer Middle School was crying. *Do you need the nurse?*

"No," Danielle said, looking back and forth between Lauren and Shannon.

"Then *sit down*, Danielle," Mr. Philbin said.

Shannon wore an ominous smile. "She will be *destroyed*," she whispered to Lauren, leaning across the table. "We will *crucify* her." She'd gotten that line from a movie about high school. If Mom heard Lauren saying that, she would want to wash her mouth out with soap—Mom wouldn't do it, but she would threaten it.

Lauren watched Danielle's back, two rows over and one seat up. She could tell Danielle was crying. Just then Lauren remembered Sean's bag of frozen peas, left underneath her bed. They would be a thawed lump right now, puddling into the baseboard. Hopefully the ceiling wouldn't leak. Danielle's head was bowed and her shoulders were shaking. It was all so easy it was boring. It was embarrassing.

NOW JAMIE AND Jeff were off to Kent, a bookish place with a strong Model United Nations team and a famous novelist among its alumni; Shannon and Evan to Knox, which was nick-named Jox. Kelly to Catholic school; Renée to Nichols, the private school near the Albright-Knox art gallery—Mom spoke of Nichols like it was a kingdom visible from a misty distance, a castle behind a fortified moat. Bethune was only a mile away from their house by road, and closer if you cut through the yards, out of the subdivision where the Brennans lived and through two more: first the rich one, where O. J. Simpson and Ahmad Rashad used to rent a mansion with a pool and tennis court and now where first-generation Indian and Korean and Jewish doctors lived, and then the "more modest" one, as Mom would say, where second-generation Irish and Italian and Polish factory foremen and secretaries and schoolteachers lived in one-story houses with one-car garages, extra bedrooms in the basements.

Although Lauren didn't know other kids at Bethune, with the exception of Danielle, some of the teachers knew her: the old-timers who had been there since the school opened, back when Mom and Dad had been part of the first graduating class. Both the chemistry teachers, all three of the gym teachers, almost the entire English department. Once in a while they'd call Lauren by Mom's name, or stare at Lauren like they didn't know what year it was.

"Brennan—any relation to Pat Brennan?"

"I taught your mother, didn't I? Jane?"

"You're Jane Thirjong's . . . little sister? Oh, right, pardon me."

Mom and Dad loved to go on and on about their days at Bethune, like they were on a talk show, because they liked to remember when they were young.

"Open-plan learning, they called it," Dad said.

"Very few interior walls," Mom said. "You didn't really have classrooms."

"You had basically one huge room."

"No desks, just sofas and big tables."

"The idea was to mix up the grade levels and subject areas and just have a whole *Free to Be . . . You and Me* situation."

"Sort of a hippie hangover from the sixties. We can have the Summer of Love all school year long."

"Oh, and no carpets, do you remember that? No noise insulation whatsoever."

"But the teachers rebelled. They stacked up filing cabinets as makeshift walls."

"And milk crates."

"They stole them from the cafeteria loading dock."

"Mrs. Norris brought in all those hand-painted floor screens, what do you call them?"

"Chinoiserie."

"Yeah. I read the Federalist Papers under those things."

"Treadwell stole thirty desks out of the basement that they'd already sold to a parochial school in Lackawanna."

"Oh yeah, of all the teachers Treadwell was the ringleader."

"Treadwell," Mom said, shaking her head. "Easiest A in the English department."

"Treadwell was at Woodstock. Speaking of hippie hangovers. You can see his hairy butt in a *Life* magazine spread, Lauren," Dad said.

"It sounds like a big, loud mess," Lauren said.

"Sure, but it didn't feel like it, because we didn't know anything else," Dad said.

"You're lucky to be going there, Lauren," Mom said, "because after that big, loud mess you'll be able to concentrate anywhere, under any circumstances. It will serve you well when you go to college."

"Why?" Lauren asked.

"Well . . . your dorm room might be noisy when you're trying to study."

"But then I could just go to the library," Lauren said.

Mom hesitated.

"Couldn't I?" Lauren asked, and stopped because she felt herself going mean. It could just hang there in the air that Mom didn't actually know what she was talking about, because Mom never went to college. Lauren was in high school now—the time was over for doing easy, embarrassing things.

Bethune felt pasted-together, low-stakes. Nobody could even agree on how to pronounce it. "Rhymes with buffoon," Dad said. "BETH-yoon," Mom said, or sometimes "BETH-un." Mr. Treadwell insisted on "Beaton," which he said was the Scottish pronunciation, although the school was named for a lady from Buffalo, an architect. Bethune had a sense of "make do," as Mom would say.

Lauren liked this. Important things happened at Kent and Jox, and the most important things of all happened at Nichols, because parents paid a lot of money for their children to go there.

"Well, usually it's their grandparents paying it," Dad said.

Lauren was tired of danger, tired of the tightrope feeling of middle school. Nothing dangerous or thrilling could possibly happen at a school attended by, for example, Paula Brunt. On their first day at Bethune, Lauren nodded hello at Paula as they walked into first-period biology class. They had attended the same schools since kindergarten but not interacted much. Paula was sour and ungainly, wide-hipped and flat-footed, dark hair in a blunt bob. She tended to have one close friend at a time. Lauren and Paula smiled at each other walking into second-period Speech & Communication class, tried to ignore each other walking into third-period Global Studies class, and burst out laughing when they discovered they'd been assigned the same fourth-period English class. By lunchtime, they shuffled wordlessly toward the same empty table in the sunken pit of the cafeteria.

Lauren didn't have to account for herself with Paula. None of their interactions had any danger to them—there was the sourness, yes, but nine years of proximity to Paula had made the sourness familiar, almost comfortable. She was steady and pleasingly boring. Her house, in one of the "more modest" subdivisions slightly farther north, looked like the house on *Roseanne*. You opened the front door, and inches away was the couch and the TV, and you sat down and watched the TV. There was even a crocheted throw over the back of the couch, like on the sitcom. Paula's mother was a nurse. She went to bed extremely early or extremely late, depending on the shift she'd been assigned at the hospital. Paula's father worked nights as a foreman at the brass factory, and he, too, was often at home sleeping or eating at odd hours, or he was in his pajamas when the rest of the world was dressed and out. They were quite lovely, as Mom would say, Mrs. Brunt especially so, usually offering Lauren something to eat, but they were too absorbed in trying to cycle their bodies into waking or sleeping rhythms to do a lot of chitchat. Their house was always tidy, but gray and cramped in a way that couldn't be fixed with a deep housecleaning or a paint job or a new piece of furniture.

Lauren liked it there because the Brunts' house had an intelligence of its own, orderly and near-silent, requiring no evident enforcement of rules and no meaningful adult supervision. The intelligence of the house might have had something to do with why Paula was the only person of Lauren's age, to Lauren's knowledge, who said she had had sex, more than once, with different boys. The boys didn't talk about it, or else they did and Lauren just didn't know—and Paula didn't have a "reputation" like some girls did, maybe because she was not someone the boys would brag about. It was mean to think that, but Lauren knew it was true. Somehow, something about Paula told the boys that she was available. Pheromones had nothing to do with looks. Maybe Paula was *practice*, like Kelly had seen her friends as practice. There was a power in that, and Lauren wondered if Paula resented that her power had to be concealed. There were boys as old as seventeen, boys one year away from college, who wouldn't acknowledge Paula if they passed her in the hallways but who, she said, had been inside of and on top of and beneath her. She had watched them lose their senses, and they had lost their senses because of her. When Lauren thought about it she forgot to breathe.

Paula was familiar and unknowable at the same time. She had taught herself a wordless language of looks and gestures, the secret history of how bodies fit together, an animal knowledge of scent. She knew what other people wanted and they didn't even have to tell her. There was a thrill and a danger in what she knew that Lauren didn't.

It is not so different over here, Paula seemed to say. *It may be strange now, but soon you will know what I know.*

BETHUNE'S TEACHERS APPEARED ready to accept Paula as a fellow member of their adult world, as they already did with some of the senior girls, like Abby Yoon and Claire Finnerty. Abby was probably going to be valedictorian and probably going to get into Harvard, and now she wanted to direct the fall play and she would probably get to do that, too. She worked hard and happily at things that apparently came very easily to her—debate team, first-chair violin—and her teachers regarded her as a minor celebrity, their gazes blushing and parental. Everyone thought that Claire—class treasurer, writer of award-winning poems, Seven Sisters–bound—was a shoo-in for homecoming queen, but then she wasn't even voted onto the court, and it was a minor scandal. It showed that a lot of people at Bethune didn't like her, maybe because she used words like *ersatz* and *perspicacious* in regular conversation and looked exactly like Jessica Lange, but the snub also made her seem less perfect and therefore more vulnerable, and that made her even more likable among people who liked her already. Mrs. Bristol, the hardest A in the English department, brought up Claire's exclusion from homecoming court in a class discussion on the theme of jealousy in Henry James's *The Spoils of Poynton*—Mrs. Bristol didn't mention anyone by name, but everyone knew what she was talking about.

It was the English teachers who loved Abby and Claire best of all. The English department was its own little fiefdom: no core requirements, no quizzes, no non-negotiable due dates, freshmen and seniors mingling in the same classes. All the teachers had tortoiseshell glasses and season tickets to the Buffalo Philharmonic, half of them with subscriptions to *The New Yorker* and half to *The New York Review of Books* so they could share around the table in the English department office, which was really just a bunch of carrels arranged in a semicircle. The men in tweeds, the women in floral blouses and peasant skirts. The English teachers didn't call on Abby or Claire or Paula so much as they chatted with them in the midst of class while the other students watched. This was especially true of Mr. Smith, the new guy. Midtwenties, youngest teacher in the department by a decade or more. Round hazel eyes, silky dark hair that curled just over the back of his collar. Sometimes he wore a sport coat, like his department elders, but mostly tucked flannel shirts, jeans, Converse sneakers. It was like he had grown out of being a student but not quite grown into being a teacher. Mr. Smith felt low-stakes, too. Just out of teachers' college—there was no way he knew what he was doing. He could spend half a class period dissecting a half-dozen lines of one poem, just going back and forth among Abby and Claire and Paula, not even trying to open the discussion out to the whole class. One day the four of them had some in-joke going about "Lines Written a Few Miles above Tintern Abbey," on the part about the cliffs "that on a wild secluded scene impress / Thoughts of more deep seclusion." Without raising her hand, Lauren asked if Mr. Smith ever used to live in Tintern Abbey. The four of them laughed, but Lauren didn't understand why the question was funny.

"How come you almost never call on Lauren in class?" Paula asked Mr. Smith. The top of her voice sounded like sympathy for Lauren, but the bottom of it was making an inside joke.

Mr. Smith winked at Paula. He said, "Eh, she knows I know how clever she is."

It was Paula who told her that Mr. Smith lived alone in a one-story brick house in the "more modest" subdivision next to the Bethune campus. Behind his back, Paula called him "the emancipated minor" and, occasionally, "the man-child," even if she did laugh at all his jokes.

Mr. Treadwell, still the easiest A in the English department, was coming close to retirement, and he was handing Drama Club over to Mr. Smith. Mr. Treadwell liked Noël Coward and Oscar Wilde—he did productions full of arched eyebrows and curlicue sentences. Characters holding unlit cigarettes in long silver holders from the Mélange thrift shop on Elmwood Avenue. Mr. Smith wanted to do the midcentury American tragedies: Arthur Miller, Eugene O'Neill, Tennessee Williams. Plays with yelling and boozing and monologues. And cigarettes, still, presumably. For the 1991 fall play, he chose Miller's *All My Sons*.

"Now there's a play that ends with a bang," Dad said.

"That's a heavy one!" Mom said. "It's got suicide—no, *two* suicides—World War II, negligent homicide. Smothering mothering. Usually when high schools do Arthur Miller, it's *The Crucible*."

"Is Chester the Molester still running the drama club?" Dad asked.

"I don't know who you mean," said Lauren, although she did.

"Patron saint of handsy drama teachers," Mom said.

"Mom knew Treadwell *very* well," Dad said.

"I did *one* play," Mom said, "and he's harmless, anyway. Big hugger. But that's all."

"It's a new guy," Lauren said.

Lauren tagged along to the *All My Sons* tryouts with Paula to "keep her company," by which she meant that her audition would give her a legitimate excuse for being late to swim practice. Lauren had been swimming competitively for so long that when she imagined quitting it was like imagining dropping out of school or eloping with Evan Lewis. She got her best times in relays, where three other swimmers were depending on her and judging her performance, but she honestly didn't care where she placed when she swam on her own.

"You were so smart about your audition," Paula said afterward. "Play it big and silly."

Lauren couldn't remember the audition very well. It was a blur of loud talking and arm-flapping and trying not to laugh or look down at her script.

"Like they say about kittens and puppies at the ASPCA—the ones that go crazy and throw themselves against the cages are the ones who get homes," Paula said.

"Blah, blah, blah," Lauren said.

"How you kept moving around, pacing around the stage even when it wasn't your line—like *Look at me, look at me*," Paula said.

"Well, I mean—wasn't that the point?" Lauren asked, raising

her chin with the effort of keeping her voice buoyant, unserious. "The whole point of the audition? To say, *Look at me*?"

Paula didn't answer. She wore a smile like she had won the game, upper lip pulled down, nostrils flaring. Her satisfied-piggy smile. She did that a lot. The smile was like Paula wanted you to know she had a secret that she'd never whisper in your ear.

THE CAST LIST for *All My Sons* was posted outside the band practice room first thing Monday morning. There was an exit door just down the hall, so Lauren could just happen past on her way out and take a peep at the list, out of idle curiosity. Abby and Claire were peering at the paper tacked to the wall as she approached. Claire smiled at Lauren. "So you're the designated freshman," she said, batting her eyelashes like Lauren had done something deliciously naughty.

"Who, me?" Lauren asked.

"There's one in every play—it's a tradition," Claire replied.

"It's a good thing," Abby said. "Mr. Treadwell always reserved one big role for a freshman, and Mr. Smith seems to be doing it, too. Take a look. And congratulations."

Lauren looked at the list. Claire was Ann, obviously, and Abby was the director, obviously, and Lauren was Kate, the matriarch.

"There must be some mistake," Lauren said.

"The designated freshman always thinks that," Abby and Claire said in unison.

After English class was over, Lauren hugged her books to her chest and stared at the corner of the desk Mr. Smith sat behind.

"I don't want to play this part," Lauren told him. "I'm grateful and everything. But I think another person would do a better job."

"You don't want to play the mother?" Mr. Smith asked. He was talking like Claire had told him the deliciously naughty thing that Lauren did. He leaned back in his chair. "That surprises me. Kate is *arguably* the most complex and fascinating character in *All My Sons.*"

"Mm." Lauren nodded. Mr. Smith talked so fast that it was like she had to start responding before she figured out what he said.

"So you agree?" Mr. Smith asked. A friendly challenge.

"Um." Lauren offered a pained smile that showed all her bottom teeth, like Mr. Smith was in a pickle and she was so terribly sorry that she couldn't help him get out of it.

"What are your objections?" Mr. Smith asked. "About Kate. Be specific."

"She's just—she's deluded," Lauren said. She was mumbling. "She's dumb. And old, although that's not her fault."

"Okay. What's so dumb and deluded about her?" Mr. Smith asked, straightening up and adjusting his glasses.

Lauren frowned. "She just lies to herself and her family about everything. She pretends her child isn't dead, and she pretends her husband is a good person. She's in total denial. She thinks she's protecting her family, but she's wrecking it."

"That's perceptive—I can see why you'd say all that," Mr. Smith said, "but I'm not hearing you say why you don't want to play her."

"Well, I also have swim team after school every day," Lauren said. "I can't go to swim practice and rehearse the play at the same time."

"Swim team will wrap up in, what, two or three weeks?" Mr. Smith asked. "We can nail down other parts of the play in the meantime and concentrate on your scenes later. Also, you were aware of that conflict with swim team when you auditioned. It didn't bother you then, did it?" Mr. Smith's grin was like he had caught Lauren in a fib but he wouldn't tell on her.

"I just . . ." Lauren shrugged, first one shoulder and then the other, her body corkscrewing on itself. She wanted to take up less space in the room. "I don't feel comfortable with this. I just don't. I'm sorry."

"Don't be sorry—this is great!" Mr. Smith said, leaning forward and clapping his hands together in glee. "Feeling comfortable is the last thing an actress should want. This *should* push you out of your comfort zone. You know you're doing something right," he said, tapping one finger in the air, "when it *hurts*. When you think, *Wait—should I even be doing this?*"

"Yeah," Lauren said. Dad would say that Mr. Smith was as oblivious as a bulldozer.

She stared over his shoulder at a collage of old political cartoons. Woodrow Wilson blowing a soap bubble out of a pipe inscribed LEAGUE OF NATIONS. She pushed her books into her chest. Her breasts had come later than the other girls', and sometimes she was still taken aback to discover them there. "Also, I'm—I'm only a freshman? It feels weird to play the mom."

"Weird how?"

"Not believable. I won't look like her."

Mr. Smith frowned and shook his head. "That's up to you. The audience wants to be told what to see. They give you their consent when they buy a ticket."

Lauren nodded and stared at the carpet. "So . . . um . . ."

"Were you hoping to play Ann, perhaps?" he asked. Ann, the would-be bride of the dead son. After he dies, Ann falls in love with his surviving brother, much to the distress of Kate the matriarch. "What's the first thing anyone in the play says about Ann?" Mr. Smith asked. "Do you remember?"

"No . . . that Ann's boyfriend died in the war . . ." Lauren murmured.

"That she's beautiful," Mr. Smith said. "Before we know her name, she's *the beautiful girl*. Well, who wouldn't want to play the beautiful girl? Beloved by all, widowed before she could become a bride, thwarted by tragedy, bearing up despite everything . . ."

Mr. Smith nodded expectantly, waiting for Lauren to pick up the thread, raising his eyebrows above his glasses. Lauren sensed that he was saying something else without saying it, or that he wanted her to say it, whatever it was, and she would only be able to figure it out later. President Woodrow Wilson was sneering at her from behind his pipe, and AP American History students were filing into class.

"Listen, any pretty girl can play Ann," Mr. Smith said, gathering up his things and standing up. "There are very few actresses, *young* actresses, who can play Kate. You are one of them."

"I don't have to do the play if I don't want to," Lauren said to the corner of the desk.

"How does your friend Paula feel about the whole thing?" Mr. Smith asked.

People already thought of Lauren and Paula as a pair. Paula was assigned to be property mistress. "She told me she's not even jealous," Lauren said, looking up. They both smiled like they were finally sharing something.

"And are there people in your family who object?" Mr. Smith asked.

Mr. Koslowski, the AP American History teacher with the comb-over, was standing beside Mr. Smith. He looked at his watch, looked up at the clock on the wall, sighed.

"My mom is super religious," Lauren said, frowning on one side, glancing back at the AP American History students to see who might be listening, "but no, I doubt she cares one way or the other."

"She's Catholic?" he asked. Lauren nodded. "Ah, my people," he said. "So full of remorse, so excited to do things to feel remorseful about."

"She's only Catholic for herself," Lauren said. "She doesn't make me go to church or anything."

Mr. Koslowski half placed, half tossed his things onto the front desk and started writing on the blackboard, hitting the chalk against the slate with extra dismissive force. Mr. Smith, still standing beside the desk, feigned that he didn't notice.

"Well, I'm glad we talked," he said. "An actress *should* get down and dirty and fight with her character and argue with her playwright. I admire that in you, Lauren."

Lauren tucked her chin against her chest, her hair falling in her face.

"Okay, you are now in *physical pain* due to this conversation, so score a hundred points for me," Mr. Smith said. Lauren laughed weakly and stood up straighter. "But just do me this favor," he said. "Before you decide—"

"I already decided—"

"Before you do that, ponder what Arthur Miller says about Kate in the stage directions. He calls her 'a woman of uncontrolled impulses, and an overwhelming capacity for love.'"

"Not impulses—uncontrolled *inspirations*," Lauren corrected him. She felt both pride and irritation with herself for pointing out his error.

"See, you know her better than I do," Mr. Smith replied, bowing in a joking way to Mr. Koslowski, who was now scowling at the two of them. A few students behind Lauren tittered.

"I need to start my class now," Mr. Koslowski said.

"Just trying to embrace some of that old open-plan spirit, Koslowski," Mr. Smith said. He danced his hands in semicircles, like a pitchman on a late-night infomercial. "Overlapping conversations, cross-disciplinary collaboration, hybrid vigor."

Lauren was inching away as Mr. Smith turned back to her, gathering up his things from the desk. "'A woman of uncontrolled inspirations,' right," he said, starting to walk alongside her. "Think about what an uncontrolled inspiration might look like. And think about the people in your life whom you could describe in the same way. We can't condemn anyone with that much inspiration and that much love to give. Even if they drive us crazy."

RIGHT BEFORE EVERYTHING changed, during those first weeks of high school, there were signs at home of what was to come. Stacks of paperwork left on the kitchen counter in the morning, then silently whisked away. A pamphlet titled *Adoption: The*

Ultimate Journey of Faith, on top of the refrigerator: Lauren accidentally swept it to the floor when pawing for a banana. Mom's general state of distraction, her spaciness, was nothing new, but now it was a single, distant object that seemed to hold her.

Mom was driving her home from swim practice in their wood-sided station wagon. The Chappaquiddick, Dad called it, because he said it was the same model some drugged-out blond newscaster had drowned in, "just like a Kennedy girl." The dragon wagon, Sean and PJ called it, for reasons lost to time. Past sunset, mottled lights fell on the hood and dashboard, painting geometric patterns on the backs of Lauren's hands. Whenever Sean and PJ weren't in the car, Mom padded out these commutes with some nonessential errand, or a drive through a neighborhood they hadn't seen in a while. Lauren liked the serene pointlessness of these detours. She could have walked or biked home or picked up a ride from a teammate, but here with Mom there was a privacy in the dark, a privacy-with-another she otherwise could find only with Paula. A key to feeling alone-yet-together was that they couldn't look directly at each other: Mom's voice trailing off in concentration as she made a left-hand turn against four lanes of Transit Road traffic; Lauren watching Mom's hands on the steering wheel and the stick shift, her long piano-player fingers, the veins flat and faint. She had a young person's hands, smooth and soft and musical. The other moms didn't have hands like hers.

They used to get this kind of intimacy on nighttime strolls around their neighborhood, but Lauren had grown sheepish about them. "We're not walking anywhere," Lauren said. "We start at home and then we just walk home." They could pretend the car trips had a point. Lauren did not want Mom to know how much contentment she took in these evening errand runs. She wanted Mom to see them as an act of daughterly generosity, almost condescending. She could keep her desire for her mother a secret from her mother.

Lauren curled up in the front passenger seat, knees drawn to her chest, her hair smelling of chlorine and burrowing a warm damp patch in the headrest. On the radio, AIDS activists chanted on the White House lawn.

"That's the same group that locked themselves to the pews in Saint Patrick's Cathedral," Mom said. "The famous church in the Big Apple."

"Why did they do that?"

"To get attention for their cause. Anything they would do in a church will cause a hullabaloo."

"So you must hate them," Lauren said, rolling her eyes.

"I don't hate anybody. Certainly not them. Jesus would have sat down there in the pews and heard them out. And here we are out in the boonies, talking about them, right? That's a good result for them."

Honeycombs of shadow and light moved across the dashboard and Mom's hands. "Mr. Smith is so weird," Lauren said into the half darkness.

"Who?" Mom asked.

"Mr. Smith. Remember when I told you about the Drama Club adviser?"

"Oh, yes, I'm sorry, I remember."

"He says that during rehearsals we should feel free to call him Ted."

"Hm."

"Not in class. Just when we're working on the play."

"Still. Do you think that's appropriate?"

Lauren shrugged. "I mean, I guess it's up to him what he wants to be called. Right?"

Mom didn't say anything.

"Some of the kids call his office the Tedquarters and hang out in there all the time," Lauren said.

Lauren considered whether or not she should tell Mom that Mr. Smith let kids drink in Tedquarters. Or didn't *let* them, exactly, but he "looked the other way"—that's what Dad would say whenever the Town of Amherst let him slide on a certificate or a piece of insurance or something. Lauren turned it over in her head. It seemed childish to tattletale, but it also seemed childish *not* to tell Mom—or not childish so much as sneaky, somehow ungenerous.

"I think it's weird," Lauren said, "because—"

Mom was turning up the volume on the radio. "Sorry, honey, just a minute, I want to hear this—"

The radio announcer called it a hospital siege, in a suburb of Salt Lake City. The perpetrator's wife had given birth to ten children. Two of them died shortly after birth; delivering one of the surviving babies, the youngest of them all, had nearly killed the wife. After recovering, she had "gotten her tubes tied," Mom was explaining.

"Is that the same as a test-tube baby?" Lauren asked.

"It means she couldn't get pregnant again," Mom said. "The egg wants to travel down a tube to the uterus, but the tube is tied off and there's nowhere for that poor little egg to go. That's why her husband was mad—not that he—I mean, there's no excuse for what he did. But he wanted more children. He thought God wanted them to have more children."

One night, the husband went to the hospital where his children were born. He had two guns and a bomb. He was looking for the surgeon who he thought had hurt the mother of his children. He took hostages: nurses, babies, new mothers, a woman in labor. In the end, a nurse—also a mother—was dead, shot in the back, and a baby was born while the man held a gun to her mother's stomach. Mom talked about the man and his wife like she knew them. She called them by their names, Rick and Karen. Before Rick went to the hospital with the guns and the bomb, he brought home ice cream bars for all his children.

"What kind?" Lauren asked.

"Rick said he and Karen had one more baby in heaven waiting to be born," Mom said. "It drove him crazy that he couldn't reach that baby. What kind of what?"

"How did he know that?" Lauren asked. "That there was another baby?"

"He just felt it, I guess. He probably couldn't explain it. He knew there was someone out there just waiting for him."

"They could have adopted, if they wanted more kids," Lauren said.

Mom took in a sharp breath. Startled, happy.

Lauren looked up at Mom. Her light brown hair in a ponytail, the *J* of its tip resting on one shoulder. The other moms wore bobs and pageboys, not ponytails. The night patterns moved across Mom's face like the veil on a film-noir heroine.

The next night, her mother was gone.

IT WOULD BE two weeks, Dad told them. Or maybe more. No return date set in stone. If Mom was gone two weeks, she would miss Lauren's Erie County Interscholastic Conference swim meet—Lauren probably wouldn't make sectionals, not even for the relay, so that would be it for the season. She would miss five of PJ and Sean's soccer games, and if she was gone two days longer than two weeks, she would miss Sean's science fair.

Mom was "doing church work in Eastern Europe," Dad said, slumped on the couch watching the Bills game, like nothing had happened. He was unsure about the details. *What work?* "Traveling around to different countries with her church group." *Which country?* "Ah, Eastern Europe." *That's not a country. What church group?* "Or it could be more accurate to say 'missionary work.'" *Since when is Mom a missionary?* Dad made a scoffing noise. "I don't keep very close track of this stuff," he said. *But didn't you talk about it first?* "It's a free country; she can do what she wants. Lauren, I'm trying to watch the game." *It sounds expensive, all that travel—did the church pay for it?* "Pretty sure I'm paying for it." *But you didn't even get to go.* "Hey, this is how it works. I earn the money and she spends it. What's hers is hers and what's mine is hers."

Sometimes Dad talked like this about Mom. Lauren felt that old thrill in hearing it, but it left a sick aftertaste, like she'd binged on candy just because Mom said she couldn't. Dad talked about Mom like she was his disobedient oldest child who would steal his credit card and run around unsupervised.

"Don't worry about any of this, Lauren," Dad said. "Your mom is going to come back home, and the Bills are going to win the Super Bowl."

LAUREN SAT CROSS-LEGGED at the lip of the Bethune auditorium stage at an evening rehearsal of *All My Sons*, Claire and Stitch Rosen on either side of her, as Mr. Smith paced around them. Abby in the audience seats. Stitch, a sophomore, played Joe, Kate the matriarch's husband, affable manufacturer of defective aircraft parts. The scene: Kate begs Joe to preserve the fantasy that their older son is still alive, somewhere in the Pacific theater, destined for a happily-ever-after with Ann, the beautiful girl.

Stitch had been one of the last boys to change. Over the summer, his voice dropped, his nose widened, his legs grew so fast that they bowed with the effort. He had bad skin and a glassy, distant affect, as if he were always five minutes away from falling asleep. It was often difficult to tell if he was bored by the task at hand, or in fact extremely engaged to the point of a trancelike state. Onstage, he projected his dialogue in a baritone singsong that didn't sound much like the mild tenor drone of his regular speaking voice. Maybe his delivery was a prank, but because he was so committed to the joke, and because he never broke character or revealed the punch line, when he was onstage there was a vibrating tension—a suspense of uncertainty, an essential mystery to his every word and gesture. Mr. Smith said Stitch had charisma.

" 'Nobody in this house dast take her faith away'—c'mon, that's a great line!" Mr. Smith was saying to Lauren. "It lands like a series of blows. It's pretty close to iambic"—he paused, whisper-counting the beats—"hexameter. Poetry in prose."

"It can still be a good line if I say *dare* instead of *dast*," Lauren said.

"And what an act of projection!" Mr. Smith continued.

"Or *should*," Lauren said. "No one in this house *should* take her faith away."

"Kate says they shouldn't rob Ann of her faith that her beloved is still alive," Mr. Smith said, "when really Kate is talking about herself. 'No one dast take *my* faith away' is what she's truly saying. She's saying, 'Nobody mess with the reality I've created for myself—'"

"You get that, right?" Stitch asked Lauren. Lauren didn't know if Stitch was making fun of her or making fun of Mr. Smith, or neither, or both.

"'—because—because I'm the one holding this family together,'" Mr. Smith–as-Kate finished.

"Are we sure it's not a misprint?" Lauren asked. "*Dast?*"

"Think about it: Kate had a son old enough to be a pilot in World War II, so even if she'd had him just out of her teens . . ." Mr. Smith's eyes widened, and he held his hands open toward Lauren, as if giving her some kind of cue, like this scrap of information was especially relevant to her. "So even if she'd had him very *young*, she would have been born at the turn of the century. You don't think people talked a bit different back then?" Mr. Smith said.

"Try the line again?" Abby said. She had to call out to be heard from the seats, yet she still sounded calm and patient.

"Nobody in this house—dast—take her faith away," Lauren said.

"You say that word like it's in quarantine," Stitch said.

"Words will never hurt you, Lauren," Claire beside her said.

"Think of people you know of—of great *faith*," Mr. Smith said. "Your mom, for instance."

Lauren glanced over at the auditorium exits as if Mr. Smith had spotted Mom there.

"My mom?" Lauren asked.

"Or, Ted, do you think it would be helpful for Lauren to imagine that she's doing Shakespeare?" Claire asked, and turned to Lauren. "You wouldn't change all the *thee*s and *thou*s in Shakespeare, would you, Lauren?"

"You're not even in this scene!" Lauren said.

Claire smiled languidly at Lauren from where she sat, her legs slung to one side under a long corduroy skirt. She shaded her eyes and looked out at the seats where Abby was sitting.

Paula said that there were two Claires, the cat and the dog. The cat was slinky and sneaky. She watched you and avoided you at the same time. The dog gazed at you dreamily and wanted your approval and you wanted to take the dog home, but then you found the cat sneaking around your house instead. Lauren missed Paula, just then.

"Okay," Mr. Smith said, clapping his hands together. "Lauren, you have homework. Tomorrow morning, when you're in the shower, say the line ten times fast. It will be just you in there, no one to make you feel self-conscious, and you can really—really wrap your mouth around it. Uh, wrap your tongue around it. Whatever!"

"Stop Harris-ing her, Mr. Smith," Claire said, teasing, and Mr. Smith shut his eyes and shook his head, putting his hands up. Everyone in the upper grades thought it was hilarious how the senators in the Clarence Thomas confirmation hearings said *Harris* instead of *ha-RASS*. Jason Harris, a junior, had to deal with a lot of jokes. The lower grades, as well as PJ and Sean, had more to say about the pubic hair on the can of Coke.

"Do you want somebody to walk you home?" Stitch asked Lauren.

"No, thanks, I can walk," Lauren said, shouldering her backpack.

"Is your mom still away, Lauren?" Mr. Smith asked. Claire cocked her head in sympathy. Lauren tugged at one strap of her backpack, pretending to adjust it. How did they know about Mom?

What did they know? Lauren paused in the space between the question and her response. She felt the space she took up in their imaginations.

"She is coming back soon," Lauren said to the strap of her backpack. "See you guys tomorrow." She kept her head down as she walked toward the stage exits. She heard Stitch yell "BYE, TED!" as he leapt into the orchestra pit.

AFTER REHEARSAL, STITCH practiced skateboard tricks in the Bethune parking lot, which bordered the football, soccer, and baseball fields that spread out behind the school. The hollow hiccupping roar of the wheels on the asphalt followed Lauren as she approached the chain-link fence that divided the school grounds from the ranch houses on half acres lining Fox Hollow Lane, narrow and winding. A chunk of the fence peeled back to leave a child-sized opening that Lauren could stoop and maneuver through, into an undeveloped lot, dense with trees and undergrowth. She kept forgetting to ask Dad about that lot. To reach home, Lauren would walk through the lot, cross Fox Hollow, and cut through the Reillys' yard, next door to Mr. Smith's house.

Centuries of tree growth shaded and blanketed the houses along this stretch. The Reillys' wooden ranch nestled under maples and pines. The unvarnished back deck was almost as big as the house. Mr. Reilly hunted deer. He aged the meat in coolers, placing them at the top of an old kiddie slide and opening the drain plug to let the bloodied ice trickle down the dingy yellow plastic.

Past the hedgerow behind the Reillys' house was the outermost street of the wealthy subdivision, half of it still woods. Stitch Rosen's house was one of those, on Sycamore Run. These backyards were where the auto mechanics and cosmetologists, the Reillys and Spizzotos, shared property lines with the physicians and attorneys, the Kumars and Epsteins and Kims.

"You never cut through the Rosens' yard, do you?" Mom asked at breakfast, the last morning she was home.

"No, I don't go that way," Lauren said, although she usually did. The Rosens lived in a five-bedroom colonial on a double lot, with a huge weeping willow out back. Half of their backyard was still woods, sprawling enough that Lauren liked to pretend she was lost in them, like Gretel or Red Riding Hood, although becoming lost was never a real risk. When she reached the weeping willow, Lauren could see them through their kitchen window: Mrs. Rosen washing dishes, one of Stitch's brothers putting something in the microwave.

"Good, I'd rather you took another route home," Mom said.

"Why?" Lauren asked, assuming the answer would be stupid before she heard it.

"Because Dr. Rosen is a *baby killer*!" PJ said.

"No, he's not," Lauren said, looking at Mom for an explanation.

"No, no," Mom said, as Dad rapped his fist once on the table and pointed at PJ. "No, he's a family man with children, religious, a good man. Or I can only assume he is a good man."

"*Religious* but not *Catholic*," Dad said.

"But he is misguided, yes—not because of his faith, it has *nothing* to do with that, don't be so *ridiculous*—and I do pray for him," Mom said.

"Good-lookin' guy," Dad said. "Fit. Served in the IDF."

"What does any of this have to do with me cutting through his yard?" Lauren asked. All Stitch had ever said about his dad was that he worked long hours.

"That is enough, Lauren," Dad said.

"And how do you know he wants you to pray for him?" Lauren asked, and then Dad was yelling. Yelling on Mom's last day.

Going home tonight, Lauren stopped under the weeping willow and saw Dr. Rosen through his kitchen window. Washing dishes, maybe. He was looking up and adjusting his glasses, focusing his attention on something Lauren couldn't see. Then he lifted his hand. He was waving at her. She stumbled over the Rosens' cat, slinky in the moonlit grass, and waved back.

The grass inhaled and exhaled, breathing her feet off the ground. The darkness was milky and changeable, like you could move your finger through the air and write a story. Silent armies of squirrels rappelling from the pines to assemble in tactical formations. Other people's parents having sex with each other in the Patels' swimming pool. A baby crawling alone through the damp thick grass, gurgling with determination. The rules change at night, and so the baby stands, delivers a stern speech in baby language, pulls up the Rosens' petunia beds, then creeps back into her house—Stitch's house?—up the stairs, into her crib. She wakes before dawn and cries out in shivering distress. Her mother rushes in, moving in a high-speed sleepwalk. The sodden, freezing clothes could be blamed on a faulty diaper; some hazy failure of housekeeping could account for the black bands of earth under her tiny fingernails. Whatever she had done was undisclosed to her now.

Lauren had reached home. She turned the knob of the back door and found it locked. She walked around the house, past her mother's impatiens, pachysandra, the little pussy willow tree she'd planted when Lauren was born, but the front door, too, was locked. No one in her house ever bothered locking the doors when they were at home. She fished around in the bottom of her backpack for her key.

The house was different as Lauren unlocked and opened the door. The light was yellower, more diffuse, bouncing off new surfaces. In the den, Sean was sobbing.

"But I don't *want* to sleep in PJ's room!" he wailed. "I want my own room!"

"Don't cry, honey." Nana Dee's voice. Lauren hadn't known she was coming over.

"It will be fun, like a sleepover," Mom called to Sean from the kitchen. Mom! Mom was home. How long had it been since she heard Mom's voice? Lauren had forgotten this strange, singsong delivery, like Mom was projecting from the Bethune auditorium stage.

Then, a nervous jolt of laughter from Dad. Had Lauren ever heard Dad laugh at all? The most he ever managed was a dry cough and a *That's funny*.

"I can't believe you kept this a secret all this time." Aunt Marie's voice.

"Well, we didn't want to get anybody worked up until we knew it was a done deal," Mom said. Who was "we"?

"Hello?" Lauren called as she closed the door behind her.

She heard the pounding of small feet against the parquet floor of the kitchen, then the thump of a small body hitting a wall.

"Oh!" she heard Mom say. "Ah—*este bee-nuh?*"

What was she saying? What was wrong with her? It occurred to Lauren that Mom was making a halting attempt at a foreign language. Another voice she'd never heard.

The pounding resumed, and a tiny figure appeared in the entryway to the kitchen. A scream rose up from the figure, who came barreling down the hallway into the foyer where Lauren stood. A glad running girl. There was a confusion in the girl. She wasn't a toddler, but she was a toddler's size, with a toddler's unsteady gait. She walked as if walking were new to her. Her legs were long spindles, her hips rotating atop them with a mechanical grind. Her brown eyes shiny as marbles. She cocked her head and windmilled her skinny arms and stamped her feet and screamed again. Nothing could make her happier than seeing Lauren there.

"Lauren," Mom said over the little girl's screams and Sean's diminishing sobs, "I want you to meet someone very special." Aunt Marie behind her, waggling her fingers at Lauren.

"Mom, you're home," Lauren said.

"Boo-nuh, cheh meh fatch!" the little girl was exclaiming.

"Mom?" Lauren was asking, trying to catch her mother's eye. Mom hovered over the girl, her expression warm and worried. "Mommy, what's going on?" The *Mommy* curled Lauren's tongue, forced and fake.

"Hiya, hew-you! Hiya, hew-you!" The girl nodded in Lauren's direction, staring over Lauren's shoulder with an expectant, open-mouthed smile. Her eyes reflected all the light in the room. "Bee-nuh! Bee-nuh!" She grabbed at Lauren's hand and shook it as she jumped up and down. She knew what she meant. She was delirious as she welcomed her sister to her new home.

"YOU HAVE A new sister?" Paula was chewing into the phone receiver, potato chips or something.

"An adopted sister," Lauren said. It was late, past ten. She was sitting up in bed under the covers, the phone receiver in her lap. Mom's and Mirela's voices muffled through the adjoining wall of Sean's bedroom, a bleating baby talk, *ooh*s and *whoo*s, little kids playing ghosts.

"That's so cool," Paula said, crunching. "It's cool, right?"

"I mean, yeah," Lauren said. "It's a nice surprise."

"A surprise?" Paula asked. "So you didn't know this was happening?"

"Oh, I mean, I had an idea, sure—we talked about it," Lauren lied. "It was a surprise just because we didn't know exactly when it would happen. My mom didn't want any false alarms."

Crunch, crunch. "Huh. Wow. That's awesome."

"Yeah, it's pretty awesome."

"Where's she from? What's her name?"

"Mirela, from Romania."

"Wow, you never mentioned it at all," Paula said, yawning.

Lauren sank into her bed, flat on her back, the phone at her ear half-propped against her pillow, the receiver and cord rising and falling slightly on her chest. A creak and a few soft clicks on Paula's end of the line, too: fidgeting, nesting. Putting each other to bed. Moments before, Lauren had felt a heavy certitude that she would confide in Paula how blindsided she felt, how confused. Now she felt that heaviness changing form, descending into imminent sleep. Sleep would whisk away the unconfessed hurt before it traveled down the phone line, before Paula could hear that Lauren was an outsider to her own life, home, and family, that her own mother was a stranger to her.

"How old is she?" Paula asked.

"She's, um—I think she's three?"

"You think?"

Lauren laughed softly. "It's been such a big day. I'm blanking out. I'll tell you more tomorrow, okay?"

"Yeah, of course. Hey, Lauren, I'm really happy for you and your family. This is so exciting." The sudden absence of Paula's usual sourness and skepticism made her simple congratulations feel startling, naked, almost painfully earnest.

"Thank you, Paula, so much."

"Hey, before we get off the phone—come see my tree sometime," Paula said. "Maybe tomorrow before rehearsal?"

"Your tree?"

"Yeah, the beech I'm making out of papier-mâché for the play. It's so big I've had to construct it in three parts that I can sort of stack together. It's taken over the prop room. I'm trying to figure out if I should make three different trees for each night of the performance—because they have to fall down every night, you know? Or maybe I can make one tree that's hardy enough to fall and get back up again. Oh, and maybe we need another one for dress rehearsal . . ."

Lauren laughed. "That sounds like a lot of work," she said. "I can help you. I promise. I'll come see your tree."

THE WORD MOM used a lot in those first weeks was *exuberant*. Also *vivacious* and *lively* and *full of life*.

"Our Mirela is so full of life—she just doesn't know where to put all that energy!" she would say. "Everything is so new and exciting for her."

Mirela was *exuberant*, and that was why she would grab the pen out of Lauren's hand as she sat at the kitchen table marking up her *All My Sons* script, why she grabbed and tore at the pages, why she grabbed anything in anyone's hand at any moment—Sean's Game Boy, PJ's Sony Discman, the crossword or the can of Budweiser in Dad's hand—in order to throw it or smash it or pound it into the floor.

"She's learning how to share," Mom said.

She was *vivacious*, and that was why she stumble-skipped up to every shopper in the supermarket, pawing at their coats and shoelaces, expressing her *vivacity* in loud, staccato vowels. She was *lively*, and that explained the constant motion, running, jumping, tripping over her own feet, spinning around and around until she collapsed into a kicking heap. And *everything was so new and exciting for her*, and that was why there was so much screaming. Nana Dee presenting her with a Peaches 'n Cream Barbie made her scream. The taste and feel of the ordinary parts of dinner—the crumby scruff of a chicken nugget, a runny slice of tomato—made her scream. Anything soft and fluffy—a stuffed monkey, the fur on Midnight, the cat—made her scream. Walking down a flight of stairs made her scream.

Bathtime was only screaming. Bathtime was the worst of all, by far. Mom would sit in the tub for hours in a bathing suit, draining and refilling the water when it went cold, pouring more bubble bath from the bottle, trying to coax Mirela into the suds with her. Mirela's screams recoiled off the tiles. She kicked the locked bathroom door. The scene would repeat itself later in the evening in Sean's—now Mirela's—room. Lauren sat in bed listening to Mom soothing Mirela, pleading with her to go to sleep, at least lie down, at least come close to her bed. Mom had replaced Sean's Buffalo Bills sheets with pink princess linens. Finally a silence.

"She's probably never had a doll of her own before, a bed of her own," Mom said. "She's never had American food. God knows what kinds of baths she's had. Everything is scary to her."

"But why does she have to *scream* all the time?" Sean asked. "It just makes everything scarier." Sean still refused to share a room with PJ. At night he took a sleeping bag to the basement.

"Maybe screaming was the only way she could be heard before," Mom said. "It's how she expresses herself. It's not like she only screams when she is upset."

"That's even worse, though!" Sean said.

"But it's our job to show her a better way to say what's on her mind. We just have to be patient. God will show us how. What she needs most is love."

"Her eyes are far apart," PJ said.

"Lauren's eyes are wide-set, too," Mom said, looking at Lauren. "Like Jackie Kennedy."

"Lolo!" Mirela said, pointing at Lauren. Her smile was electrocuted.

"Lauren and Mirela could be sisters," Dad said.

"They *are* sisters," Mom said.

I have a sister, Lauren thought, and felt a feral nothing, a gust of wind, present and unseen.

ABBY SAID THEY could find Claire's and Lauren's *All My Sons* costumes at the Salvation Army on Transit Road. Abby drove them there in her Volvo one afternoon. It was in the low sixties, unseasonably warm, and the sky and the air had a blush to them. Deepa Singh, who edited the literary magazine with Claire, came along for something to do. She sat in the back with Claire, and Lauren sat up front with Abby. This was new, driving places where no one wrestled or cried over who got the front passenger seat. Deepa wore her long hair differently every day: in two twisty buns, in four slim braids that started at the nape of her neck. She could twist it behind her head and stick a pencil in it while carrying on a conversation and it would just stay that way.

Abby smoked a Marlboro Light out the window. She had a tape in the deck of the Pixies' *Surfer Rosa* and turned up the volume almost as high as it would go. The music was ruined, screeching, but it also sounded right—there was no way to fix it. The songs sounded like they were recorded in a black and white world, everyone's bodies flattened into lines and circles, illuminated skeletons, and it was the music that pulled the lines of limbs around, yanking an arm out of its socket and reattaching it hand-to-shoulder, and the bodies howled in pain but they were happy, too, because what the bodies felt was new and interesting, and when it was all over the bodies would be different and better than they were before.

Abby singing along with every word granted Lauren permission to love the music the way Abby did; Claire and Deepa in the back seat, shouting over the music about submissions to the literary magazine, granted Lauren permission to just tolerate the music the way they did, for their friend whom they loved. Whatever happened in Abby's car, whatever Abby and Claire and Deepa talked about, was more complex and more real than anything else Lauren had known before, because they were capable of finding this music and understanding it well enough to enjoy it, and that understanding could vouch for anything else they were interested in and any other opinions they might hold.

Stitch, too. Lauren imagined him here in the car with them and chewed on her thumbnail.

This was Lauren's first trip to a Salvation Army. She wanted to ask the other girls if they got all their clothes there, but didn't in case it was a dumb question. Abby wore Converse and a hoodie and jeans, every single day. Deepa wore Converse and complicated layers of plaid flannels and jeans with colorful patches on them. Claire wore clogs and long, fuzzy cardigans over dresses and skirts that never rose above the knee, and Abby called it "frump chic" and Deepa called it "librarian chic," and both of these phrases were compliments.

At the Salvation Army, Claire came into Lauren's dressing room without asking, a brownish bundle over her arm, just as Lauren was stepping out of her jeans. "You have a lovely figure," Claire said, "and your costume sort of has to hide that, because Kate is lovely in her way but not like you are lovely." Lauren pulled the dress over her head and pushed the curtain open on the dressing room, stepping in front of the cloudy three-way mirror. Beneath her bare feet, the linoleum floor seemed covered with a layer of almost-dry nail polish. The dress smelled decayed, like a piece of clothing could die and rot. It was cotton, with a cinched waist, flared skirt, and a big brown-and-white floral print, spotted with mildew at the hips.

Abby and Claire nodded their approval of the dress. Abby ripped off the $5.99 tag before she bought it with petty cash from the Drama Club fund. The rule at Salvation Army, Abby explained, was if an item of clothing for sale was missing a tag, it was automatically priced at $2.99.

"What about Claire's costume?" Lauren asked.

"Oh," Claire said, tapping a finger on her chin. Like something small and amusing had slipped her mind. "I have mine already." She smiled and rubbed Lauren's arm. "I'll show it to you when we get back to Tedquarters. I hope you like it."

Tedquarters had wall-to-wall carpeting the color of creamed corn, a couple of halogen standing lamps, two sagging maroon couches pushed against perpendicular walls, a long cafeteria table, and a small battered desk that only Mr. Smith sat at. Natural light came through a single window, high and narrow. A film covered everything: dead skin, soda residue, a hoagie-ish debris. If Lauren spent too long in there, she started to feel itchy. The week of the performances of *All My Sons*, the senior girls decided that Tedquarters needed what they called "a woman's touch." They said this in a high singsong, like it was a joke and yet it wasn't. Deepa brought in a chevron tablecloth and a colorful crocheted throw for one of the sad couches. Abby brought in succulents and a snake tree. Claire brought a bamboo bowl filled with satsumas. Lauren had never heard of succulents or satsumas. She wondered how they'd found out about them like she wondered how they'd found out about the Pixies. She had decided to bring a satsuma to Paula next door in the prop room when Claire appeared in front of her in her costume, pretty and airy, a lilac confection with a sweetheart neckline and frilly cap sleeves.

"So pretty," Lauren said.

Claire shrugged. "My mom insisted on sewing it herself. According to the script, it has to twirl," she added, and twirled. "I am so *ready*," she said. "I think it's because of *you*, Lauren. You are so *on point*." She flopped girlishly onto one of the sagging sofas, her dress fanning around her. She looked up at Lauren and patted the sunken spot beside her. Lauren sat down and dipped her head toward Claire romantically. They laced their fingers together. At this moment, they were friends. Lauren would just sit here a moment, and then go help Paula with her tree.

"So your mother stole a gypsy baby and brought it home." Andy Figueroa was standing over them, hands in the pockets of his one-size-too-big suit. A sophomore like Stitch. In his role as the surviving son, Andy had to kiss Claire toward the end of Act I, and he was always going on and on about how revolted he was about the kiss. He felt embarrassed to be in love with Claire, and resentful of it, just like a lot of their classmates.

"My family is none of your business," Lauren told Andy. With her index finger, Claire was drawing tiny circles in the palm of Lauren's hand and humming lightly. A song of solidarity, no questions asked—Lauren hadn't talked to anyone about Mirela, except for Paula.

"It *is* my business," Andy said, "because that little freak attacked my mom when she was picking up my brother from football practice."

Lauren could picture it easily: her mother waiting for PJ or Sean in the parking lot behind Mayer Middle, Mirela running up to Mrs. Figueroa, Mrs. Figueroa trying to wrap the girl in a hug, Mirela rejecting the touch, thrashing, kicking. Maybe Mrs. Figueroa had come away with a fat lip or a scratched cheek. She had been Lauren's and PJ's and Sean's third-grade teacher.

"Your mom is scared of a three-year-old?" Lauren was saying to Andy. "Sounds like your mom is the one who's got problems."

On Lauren's second day of kindergarten, she took a wrong turn down the long corridor to her classroom, froze, and saw Glinda the Good Witch in a doorway. It turned out to be Mrs. Figueroa. She must have been wearing her regular school clothes, but in Lauren's memory she sparkled and twinkled and stood seven feet tall. A voice like a flute from the land in a lullaby. A wand on the desk just behind the door, just out of Lauren's sight. Kindergartner Lauren ran into her arms. Mrs. Figueroa scooped her up and buried her face in Lauren's neck, as if she'd been waiting for her all that time. They'd never seen each other before.

"That kid should be locked up in a loony bin," Andy said.

"Andy, enough," Claire murmured, shifting languidly, hanging on to Lauren's hand.

Or maybe it had been the second day of first grade, not kindergarten. Because there was a teacher's aide who helped the kindergartners to their classrooms, Lauren remembered, but by the time you were in the first grade, you were on your own. More likely she would have lost her way in first grade. You could tell the story however you wanted it.

"You should probably stay home from opening night tomorrow, Andy," Lauren said, "because that little freak will be in the audience, scaring your mom."

Claire took her hand away. Mrs. Figueroa's *r*s purred and a *shhh* threaded and rounded through her speech. It twirled in Lauren's ears like a figure skater, like Claire's dress.

"Shut up, Lauren," Andy said.

"I just want you and your mom to feel *safe*," Lauren said.

"Lauren! See me outside." How long had Mr. Smith been standing in the doorway? Claire got up from the couch, not looking behind her, humming as she joined Deepa and Abby at the long table.

Lauren lowered her head as she followed Mr. Smith down the hall.

"Come in here. I want privacy," he said.

"You can't go in the girls' bathroom," she said.

"Lauren," he said. A bark. The sound of an impact, like his voice was striking something in the way and what was in the way was her. He sounded like Dad.

He shut the door behind them. Three stalls, the harsh cleanser smell and then another smell beneath it, loamy and animal.

"Lauren, what's gotten into you?"

"Andy was—"

"Andy is Andy is Andy," Mr. Smith said. "I don't think it's any surprise to anyone who Andy is. This is not who *you* are."

Mr. Smith was standing too close. Lauren wanted to move away, but she was already against the wall. He wasn't that tall, had only a few inches on her. Maybe that was part of why he came across as so young, why people might underestimate him.

"I'm sorry. I shouldn't have said those things," Lauren said.

"At the beginning of the school year, you seemed like such a sweet girl. You *were* such a sweet girl. What happened?"

"I don't know."

"You will have to do better than that."

"I don't know what to say. I'm really, really sorry."

Lauren had done something very bad. What she did had cornered her in this small, dank room with an angry man in charge of her. He was everywhere, it was like he was on top of her, but the menace was also coming from inside her—she was the one who was doing it, she was the one who could stop it, but she didn't know how. She needed to say whatever could get her out of the room.

"Things are just—a lot has happened at home. My mom."

"What's going on with your mom?"

"I don't—it's just—please, I'm sorry. I wish I could go back and rewind. I'm sorry, Mr. Smith."

He was relenting. "Mr. Smith is what my mother calls me," he said. "Call me Ted. Outside of class, I mean. You can call me Ted."

"Ted."

"So you're having trouble at home." She nodded. He smiled. "Well, we can talk about that."

"Do we—do we have to talk about it in the bathroom? Because someone might—"

"You can have trouble at home, but you don't need to have trouble at school. Nobody is going to cause you trouble at school. Andy Figueroa, he's noise, he's static—just ignore him. Be smart. Switch the dial on the radio and get a better station." He pantomimed turning a knob with his thumb and forefinger. "You can tell me anything, you know," he said, "even the things that make you angriest or saddest—*especially* those."

"Okay. I'm sorry."

"You said that. I got that part. You are that sweet, smart girl that I remember. Don't forget that."

She nodded. "Yes."

"Even if you're not feeling sweet, we can pretend. Like a role. My class, my play, is a place where you can be sweet. And smart. The two can go together, you know? You don't have to play the role anywhere else, unless you want to. Just here. Maybe it will become a habit. Okay?"

"Okay."

"You play the sweet girl and it's just what you become."

With a chivalric little bow, he held the door to the girls' bathroom open for her. At the door to Tedquarters, he made the mock-simpering bow again, adding a rotating flourish of one hand. She felt sick and then a jubilant petulance, an irresistible full-body rejection of the premise that this ridiculous small man could set the terms by which she could talk to a peer or enter a room.

She walked straight past him, past Tedquarters, her eyes cast impassively ahead.

"Lauren, what the hell?" he called after her.

She found Paula in the prop room, cheeks smudged with wet flour, sucking on the index finger she'd just nicked with an X-Acto knife, but humming along in an undaunted way to Steve Miller

Band on the tape deck. Music that Lauren's parents liked. The linoleum eddied with climbing cardboard branches and cascades of butcher paper. Paula swiftly set up a workstation on the floor for Lauren, assigning her to the dress rehearsal tree: presumably the least consequential of the four beeches. Lauren tore the strips of newspaper, dipped them in the thin gruel congealing in chipped cereal bowls, and laid them down, moving from root to trunk. She bent into the lulling monotony of the task and Paula's voice *wooing* to "The Joker." She observed with appreciation how the work became incrementally more difficult as the dribbling glue hardened around her fingers and clinched her wrists, as if Paula had chosen this work especially to still her shaking hands.

MOM WOULDN'T TALK about what she had actually done to find Mirela and bring her home. "The way you forget childbirth, you forget Romania," she said. Mom liked this joke so much she kept making it, whenever she wished to avoid a question. The joke meant adopting Mirela was both private and gross, and so it was inappropriate to ask about it.

Here and there, things trickled out by accident. The cigarette breath of the "baby broker"—he was the guy who seemed to be in charge, who talked too close and wore a beat-up leather jacket over a patterned acrylic sweater. That was very Mom, to notice if someone wasn't wearing natural fibers. The big day, day three, was when Mom began to suspect that all the babies she met were a bait-and-switch.

"In Romania, the kids age in dog years—you'd meet a newborn girl, and the next day she'd be a five-year-old boy!" she said.

Then she caught herself. "But forget all that. Mirela's here with us now, and that's all that matters."

Lauren pleaded with Mom to leave Mirela at home for opening night of *All My Sons*. "Even if we had already found a sitter whom we could trust to handle such a lively little girl," Mom said,

"Mirela is part of our family now. We don't shut one another out. We're all in this together. She will be so proud of her big sister, in her stage debut!"

Lauren considered. "If you can't get a sitter, maybe *you* could stay home with her?" she asked.

Mom laughed. "Lauren, if you are trying to hurt my feelings, you might succeed, but you're not going to change my mind. I wouldn't miss your play for the world. We will be there. For you. As ever."

"Mom," Lauren said, "did Mirela get into a fight, or something, with Mrs. Figueroa?"

Another laugh. "No," she said. "She crawled into her car and asked, in her own special Mirela style, for Mrs. Figueroa to take her home. It was a struggle for us to get her out of the car, but it was all fine." She was nodding, still laughing. "Oh, just fine."

When it got bad with Mirela, Mom did what she called the squeeze. She showed Lauren how to do it with a Raggedy Ann doll. Sit down on the floor, pull Mirela into your lap, wrap both of your arms around her from behind, pinning her arms to the sides. She's hitting and kicking all the while. The two of them rocking back and forth, Mirela arching and butting against the hold, grunting, thrashing. After long minutes the tantrum would die, like it had been suffocated with a pillow. Mirela and Mom on the floor, panting, emptied out.

"So she didn't hurt Andy's mom at all?" Lauren asked. "He was lying?"

Her mother rubbed one wrist absently. "She didn't hurt anyone. The only one Mirela ever hurts is me."

"LOLO!"

It happened—and Lauren had known it would happen on opening night, she just hadn't known how or when—during her big early monologue. Kate the matriarch, in her floral-pattern housedress and matronly bun—Abby had swept and sprayed and bobby-pinned it herself—has a headache. Through a haze of pain, she recounts a dream about her probably-dead son. She talks to her living son about her dead son. She sees her dead son's face in the cockpit of his plane as he flies past their house, the house her boys grew up in. She reaches out to touch him, try to stop him, but stop him from what? Dream logic can't account for it. She hears his voice. She looks into his eyes. The tree she planted in his honor, Paula's papier-mâché beech, snaps and falls in his wake.

"Lolo! Lolo!"

The *slap-slap-slap* of tiny patent-leather shoes on the auditorium floor. Murmurs and giggles from the audience. Mom in a stage whisper: *"Mirela! Come back here!"*

"It's a—I have a headache—" That wasn't Lauren's line, not exactly. The audience laughed at the symmetry of screaming child and aching head.

"I couldn't sleep," Lauren said over Mirela's noise. The audience laughed again. What were her lines? She couldn't remember them, only the gist.

"Just give me the gist," Dad always said whenever Mom was boring him.

The *slap-slap-slap* pounded down the dialogue until it was flat and illegible.

Mirela ran into the stage, the *thump* of her little body against the wood. Lauren felt it through her feet, in the low beige heels she'd borrowed from Nana Glenis. Mirela leaping against the lip of the stage again and again, trying to hoist herself up onto the boards.

"Lolo! Lolo!" Mirela's screams were strangling her. Mom was trying to pull her away. Mom wore lipstick and pearl earrings, Lauren saw, her hair upswept. Mirela wore a blue gingham dress and a soft pink cardigan. Her hair in two braids. They had tried.

"I—I was tossing and turning—" Lauren said.

"What was it, Mom?" Andy asked, staring at Mirela. "The dream?"

Lauren was looking down at Mirela, too. The top of her head had thin patches—Lauren hadn't noticed before. This little girl who all of a sudden lived in their house. "A dream . . . but I didn't know it was a dream . . ."

Mom was whispering into Mirela's ear, but her hands on Mirela and the puffs of her breath against Mirela's face only spurred the girl on. Again she tried to jump onto the stage. The audience's laughter quieted, replaced by a rustling: people turning in seats, or standing up, searching for someone who could do something, wanting to help but not knowing how.

Lauren walked to the front of the stage.

"I was fast asleep, and . . ." Lauren bent down and reached for Mirela. One of her hands could span Mirela's upper arm. How tiny and thin she was—Lauren had seen it but not felt it. Mirela, who usually pulled away from touch even as she begged for it, went strangely limp as Lauren hoisted her by both arms onto the stage. She weighed nothing. She was a doll out of the prop room, slumped and boneless, staring out from a shelf in the dark.

Below them, Mom jabbed both index fingers toward the exits, and Lauren nodded in agreement. The anonymous audience heads turning toward Mom as she ran to the exits, and then turning back to the stage. Lauren knelt down in front of Mirela, holding her hands loosely. Mirela's face was slack, her eyes trained somewhere over Lauren's shoulder. Silence.

". . . I was fast asleep and I saw my child," Lauren said. "Right in front of me. I saw my child's face."

"Mom—then what happened?" Andy asked. Andy was still there. Lauren had forgotten him. His voice trembled.

"She was calling to me," Lauren said, looking back and forth between Andy and Mirela. "I could hear her like she was in the room with us." Her tone was confidential, a message intended only for Mirela, yet her voice carried to the back rows.

Mirela swayed back and forth, her face still blank.

"She was so real I could reach out and touch her." Mom was

at the edge of the stage wings, just out of sight of the audience. "I took her hand, and . . ." Lauren stood up and began guiding the girl toward her mother.

"I knew I could save her, if only she would stay with me . . ." Lauren was saying.

The two girls had reached the edge of the stage. Lauren pressed her free hand onto Mirela's jutting shoulder blade, urging her toward Mom, whose arms were outstretched.

". . . if only she held on to my hand," Lauren said as Mirela took a few mechanical steps toward Mom, then ran past her into darkness.

"But then she was gone," Lauren said. She clasped her empty hands and cast her face upward. One periwinkle stage light shining square on her face, one eye glinting like a dying star. "She was gone. And then—I woke up."

The applause, an ocean wave, infinite sound and infinite weight, tossed Lauren upward and caught her again. She floated on it, stunned and still. She broke apart in it, dissolved into the stage lights.

"We—we never should have planted that tree," Lauren said as the applause retreated into foam, and the play went on as intended.

LAUREN—KATE—WAS SUPPOSED TO break down in tears at the end of *All My Sons*, weeping for her husband and her child. Stage-sobbing was easy to do in rehearsals: hide face in hands, shake those shoulders, work up a little extra saliva and suck at it to mimic the sound of sniffles. But when the gunshot rang out on opening night, a starter's pistol on loan from the phys ed department, Lauren jumped and wailed, her fight-or-flight systems activated. She moaned her husband's name and took her surviving son in her arms, and her body believed her, issued signals and responses according to what she had seen: Stitch's silhouette through the window of the plywood stage façade, the shot, the fall. The stage directions said to push her weeping son away—with love, with firmness—and to move toward the porch, toward the silence upstairs in the house where her husband's body lay. But instead Lauren hung on to her stage-child Andy Figueroa and sobbed real tears as the curtain fell. She cried through curtain call and then she ducked into the dank bathroom down the hall behind the stage, the one where Mr. Smith had told her to be sweet, and she sobbed to the edge of retching, forehead pressed against the stall door.

She felt herself altered. Bewitched. As if the only way to trick Mirela had been to trick herself. She made-believe and it was just what she became.

She fixed her makeup as best she could with wet paper towels and reported to Tedquarters. The cast and crew spilled out the door as Mr. Smith was wrapping up some speech. Lauren pushed against the flow to get inside the room. Everyone looking at her, the swiveling heads, some smiling and proud, some confused. Paula moved with the crowd toward Lauren, wearing her satisfied-piggy smile. She clapped Lauren's shoulder in either congratulations or sympathy. Stitch was right behind Paula. "Lauren, you were good! Ted was asking for you in his speech—I don't think you were here," he said, one hand on Paula's shoulder and the other holding aloft a beer in a brown lunch bag.

Lauren couldn't look at Mr. Smith when she reached him at the back of Tedquarters. "I am so sorry," she said into the breast pocket of his corduroy blazer, the color of honeyed tea. She pressed her face into his chest, his sternum, and felt a strange surprise—she didn't know what she had expected to find there, a shirt stuffed with wood chips or goose feathers, not something hard and curved, smooth and implacable. She turned her face to see the *Blue Velvet* poster hanging over his desk, across from a rectangular grid of old *Playbill* covers, swimming in front of her. "Mr. Smith, I asked her not to bring her!"

"Lauren, no," Mr. Smith said. He was holding her so tightly, both of his hands rubbing up and down her back. She stiffened against his hold on her, startled and pleased, and she wondered who was watching.

"That was astounding, truly," Mr. Smith was saying.

Lauren's breath was shallow between Mr. Smith's arms and chest. "Mr. Smith?"

"My personal rule is never to be the one to break a hug," he said.

"Okay," Lauren said, slowly pushing out of the hug. She hoped he wasn't offended.

"Those were your sisters?" he asked.

"My mom and my sister."

"That was your *mom*?"

Now it was Mr. Smith who was acting. He knew Mom was young, young in a way people noticed.

Claire was at her side. "Lauren, you were incredible," she said. "Celebrate with us, come on." She handed her an elegant silver flask. Lauren took a swig.

"Oh my word," Claire said, "we have to get Lauren's vodka face into our next stage production."

"I don't know anything about that, by the way," Mr. Smith said, waving his hands around.

"I couldn't do the lines—I couldn't even remember them—I just had to deal with what was in front of me," Lauren said, smacking her lips to deflect the taste of the vodka.

"Exactly," Mr. Smith said. "You know, a great acting teacher once said, 'The art of the actor is living truthfully in imaginary circumstances,'" Mr. Smith said. "But you, Lauren—you were living *imaginatively* in very *real* circumstances!"

"You people are ridiculous," said Andy from the floor, his head and arms draped over his knees. "This was a disaster, and we're acting like it was some great thing."

"Andy, please," Mr. Smith said.

"That's not constructive," Abby told Andy.

"I'm sorry, Andy," Lauren said. "I didn't mean for this to happen."

"You're not supposed to hug me at the end!" Andy said. "You're supposed to let go of me! You're supposed to do what the script says!"

Lauren lifted her chin and stared down her nose at him. "Andy, you lied," she said. "You lied about Mirela. She didn't hurt your mom. She didn't hurt anyone."

"Just do what you're supposed to, the next time!" Andy said.

"I did," Lauren said. "I did what I had to."

"I think our boy needs another hug," Claire said.

"Do you want to come out with us tonight, Lauren?" Abby asked, and Claire was drawing little circles on Lauren's shoulder again.

IT WAS GOING to be Claire and Abby, and Deepa and Julie, who was Deepa's best friend and wore the same layers of flannels and patches, like they chose from the same closet every morning. And Stitch, a kind of mascot. Abby's car.

"Hey, I'll come," Paula said.

"Oh, I don't know if there's room in the car," Abby said. "I don't think there is. Maybe you can find another ride?"

Paula nodded and said good night, ducking her head and speed-walking out of Tedquarters, down the hallway, past the band practice room, and out the door. She got it, nothing personal. It was best that it came from Abby, practical and clear-eyed Abby, who could squint at the situation like it was a tricky math problem, solved by subtracting one.

Claire in the passenger seat, everyone else in the back: Lauren in the middle, Julie to her right with Deepa on Julie's lap, her legs slung over Lauren's, and Stitch on the left. Lauren had changed back into her jeans and sweater after the performance, but she worried that she had absorbed some mildewy essence from her costume, and the others might discern it in the closeness of the back seat. She could smell Stitch. He smelled like outside even when he was inside, like trees and dried leaves or some sleek small mammal who lived in the woods but took his meals indoors. Like he lived in his own big backyard, up in the weeping willow. He breathed laboriously through his nose, except when he was onstage. Abby stopped at the 7-Eleven so Julie and Deepa could run in for jumbo Slurpees.

Claire twisted around in the passenger seat to look at Lauren. "How's your sister?" The wide-eyed solicitousness in her voice, the predatory purr, the cat and the dog.

"Like, tonight, or in general?" Lauren asked.

Claire shrugged, almost flirtatiously.

"I didn't get a chance to talk to my mom before they left," Lauren said. She tried to introduce a businesslike clip to her voice, as in the thirty-second addresses they had to prepare each week for Speech & Communication class. Thirty seconds to summarize the Gulf of Tonkin resolution. Thirty seconds to encapsulate the Bush administration's response to the AIDS crisis. Synthesis of facts, stripped of analysis or interpretation. "My mom says Mirela's behavior will calm down when she learns English—she won't be so disruptive if she can express herself in the same way everyone around her can."

Claire nodded. "That's probably true. Did you know that Abby didn't speak a word of English until she was *five*?"

"What? No way!" Lauren heard the edge of screeching shock in her voice. She looked at Abby in the rearview. Abby's mouth twisted down on one side, in concentration or annoyance.

"Yup," Abby said after a moment.

"How come?" Lauren asked, softly. "I mean, if you want to say."

Abby puffed through her nose and her frown deepened. "It's not some big secret. That's when my family came here from Korea. I went to kindergarten, there was no ESL where I went to elementary school, so I just figured it out." Claire had turned back around in her seat and started singing to herself, like the conversation had nothing to do with her.

"Hey, I made you this," Stitch said, handing Lauren a cassette.

He had written down the names of the songs on the sleeve of the cassette, in pencil. "That way," he said, "if you don't like the record and you want to tape over it, you can just erase the track listing and write in the new songs." The instructions were so straight-forward and obvious, and his delivery of them so wide-eyed and earnest—like he was slightly unsure whether she would under-stand or remember—that Lauren could not figure out if he was putting her on or not. In the front of the car, Claire was looking over at Abby with a hand over her lips, pretending to stifle a giggle.

Julie and Deepa came back, poured out part of each Slurpee onto the asphalt, filled each cup to the top again with vodka from the elegant flask, which, it turned out, belonged to Julie, and passed the cups around.

"I also have cough syrup if anyone needs it," Deepa said, and everyone but Lauren nodded in appreciation of her foresight.

The movie was called *The Man in the Moon*, about a family in the South in the 1950s. The scenes were humid and sleepy, and the movie and the spiked Slurpee made Lauren feel the same, and she faded in and out of sleep. The pretty teenage sisters in the movie lived with their golden-backlit mom and sweaty, attractive dad and adorable toddler sister in a nice old house on many acres of farmland. They didn't have much to do. Whenever Lauren woke up, one of the sisters was brushing her hair or swimming in a pond or lying around. Their mother was pregnant, although her oldest was about to go off to college. Lauren wondered why Mom hadn't just had her own baby if she wanted another one—she had to be younger than the mother in the movie.

Then a boy showed up and both sisters fell in love with him, and they thought of little else but him. Lauren thought about who her new friends might be in love with. Claire was dating a foot-ball player, Dan DeFilippo. He wasn't a particularly good football player, and he had the highest GPA on the team. Lauren was pretty sure they'd had sex. Abby was sort of seeing a guy who went to Buff State and worked at the Home of the Hits record store on Elmwood Avenue and had tattoos on his arms and maybe other places. They'd definitely had sex. Deepa was sort of seeing a guy at Canisius College who she'd met through Habitat for Humanity. They probably hadn't had sex. Julie, who was an aspiring opera singer and always played the lead in the spring musical, wasn't dating anyone. Neither was Stitch, obviously.

Lauren woke up again with her head slumped toward a man sitting beside her, her hair falling on his sleeve, and she put a pinky to the corner of her mouth to wipe some drying saliva as she started to tell Mr. Smith she was sorry for invading his personal space when she smelled Stitch's outdoor smell. It was Stitch's arm—it was Stitch sitting beside her. She heard someone giggle, and someone else passed her the Slurpee.

"I've never seen a movie where nothing really happens," Lauren said in the lobby after it was over. Everyone laughed, although she hadn't meant it as a joke. "Not like that was a bad thing. Just new to me."

"Nothing happens except for when the hottie farmer boy runs himself over with his own tractor," Deepa said.

"I think Lauren was asleep for that part," Claire said.

Abby dropped Stitch off at his house and pulled into her own driveway, on the opposite end of the block. It had been decided that all the girls would sleep over at Abby's. Lauren felt an intense contentment in the drift of the evening, how she swam along in the calm, unyielding current of these efficient and leaderless girls. They seemed to view their boyfriends as casual hobbies—they wouldn't obsess or compete over a boy like the girls in the movie. They came to decisions about food and entertainment and sleeping arrangements and the arc of their lives' destiny with little discussion and no apparent conflict.

"May I use your phone? I just have to call my mom," Lauren asked Abby, and she felt very young.

LAUREN WAS THE first one to wake up the next morning. Abby's house was bigger and nicer than hers. The living room where they all slept had an arched, double-height ceiling. Great wooden beams, windows down to the floor. She lay still under her down sleeping bag, Claire and Abby in sleeping bags on either side of her on the piled rug, Julie and Deepa under blankets on the sectional sofa above them. Lauren's throat was scratchy-dry, and her eyes were clumped and sticky with the stage makeup she'd slept in. Last night's hairpins were piercing her scalp and she was holding back a cough and she badly had to pee. Still she lay there, listening to the *tick-tick* of the mantelpiece clock, comfy mounds of living blankets rising and falling slightly all around her. She wanted always to feel this cozy, this embracing joy of belonging.

She crossed her arms in front of her, each hand on the opposite bicep, and felt Mr. Smith's hand gripping her upper arm, squeezing, sliding up and down, in the doorway to Tedquarters last night, just before they'd left for the movie.

"Congratulations again, and listen—don't worry about Andy, all right?"

His thumb nicked the side of her breast, and again. He hadn't meant to do it. She put her hands on her hips, to move the arm he was rubbing away from her chest.

"I won't, I promise," Lauren said.

"I think what it is, is he *likes* you, and he doesn't know how to handle it."

"Um, okay," Lauren said, looking over his shoulder at her classmates milling around. Anyone could overhear. Gary Wisniak, the affable head of the set construction team, came past them, offering Lauren a high five. She returned it, taking the chance to step back a foot from Mr. Smith, his hand slipping off her arm. "Well, thanks for everything," she said to Mr. Smith.

"Don't you think so?" he persisted, stepping forward. She was cornered again.

"I don't think he thinks about me much, unless I'm getting on his nerves for some reason."

"To be honest, I'm surprised that boys your age pay attention to you at all."

"What?!"

He stepped back and grinned. "Because they're all *terrified* of you."

"Huh. I doubt it."

"You're too mature for them. Way out ahead of them. That's why they don't appreciate you. When you get closer to college, all of that will change."

"Okay, well, I guess I'll look forward to that. Good night, Mr. Smith."

She turned over onto her other side in her sleeping bag and thought about the movie. At the beginning, the two sisters are lazing in the screened-in porch of their house at twilight, in their old-timey underclothes, listening to a love ballad on the phonograph, telling their small troubles to the man in the moon. The sisters are bored and bickersome, but this is when they are happiest in the whole movie. Not when the boy shows up and the excitement starts, but right then, when they are just rolling around in themselves and taking each other for granted and waiting for something to happen.

Lauren wondered if either of the sisters had figured out how to masturbate. It was the ugliest word she had ever heard. Mrs. Graziano, the health teacher at Mayer Middle, had taught the word to them. Lauren had figured out how to do it by accident two summers ago, lying on her stomach on the living room couch reading *Flowers for Algernon* while everyone else was out of the house, and she was pressing her hips against the cushions because it felt so nice, and then it all overcame her and she knew from then on she'd have to do this at least once every single day.

Lauren crept out of her sleeping bag inch by inch, working to preserve her new friends' sleep, a game she could play and win by herself. She found her backpack in a little pile on the hearth, found a bathroom in the hallway off the kitchen, peed, splashed some water on her face, dabbed at her clotted eyelashes with a tissue, wiped at smeared eyeliner, plucked out the hairpins. Crimped locks of her hair stuck straight out from her head. She rummaged around in her backpack for a comb and found the tape that Stitch had given her. Claire and Abby had noticed how Stitch had underlined each word in the title of each song.

"Song titles should be in quotation marks, but still, that is *so* cute," Claire had said.

Lauren tried to tamp her hair down with wet fingers, then bent over and held her head under the running faucet. The water ran cold then tepid. She was relieved that none of the other girls had seen her like this. She rubbed her hair with a hand towel, and her face went hot as she remembered: Mirela onstage, Mom running into the wings, the tears, the speeches. As cozy as she had felt just a few minutes before, she now felt urgently that she needed to leave this house, that she could not be seen, that the older girls had only been doing a kindness by asking her out with them, that they would not want to see her now, having caused such a commotion with her weirdo family.

Abby's mom was in the kitchen, slicing strawberries and watermelon, frying eggs. "Good morning, Mrs. Yoon," Lauren said, putting up a goodbye hand. "I'm Lauren. Thank you very much for having me over." A promise not to bother her further, to get out of her way.

"Hello, good morning!" Mrs. Yoon waved at Lauren with a charming urgency, as if from some distance. "Stay, please stay." She put one hand on Lauren's shoulder, the gentle pressure of her touch substituting for the language Lauren didn't speak.

"I couldn't bother you, ma'am, but thank you so much."

She cut through the dewy yards in the thin morning light. The front door was locked—Mom always locked up the house at night now—and Lauren let herself in with her key. Everyone was still asleep. After weeks of getting home late or sleeping over at Paula's, she hadn't seen her house in a while, not in daylight, not alone without somewhere else she already had to be.

Dark scuff marks all over the hallway walls. Puncture wounds here and there. In the living room, the carved-wood mallard ducks on the mantelpiece and the clusters of framed photographs on the piano had disappeared. The chunk of rock from the trip to Italy when Mom and Dad fell in love, gone. The line of Lauren and PJ and Sean's school pictures that climbed the wall opposite the staircase—all gone, too, each frame leaving behind a faint rectangular footprint. A lingering vinegary odor, the result of Mom's iffy attempts to cook *sarmale*, thick glutinous rolls stuffed with beef and bacon and salty cabbage. A Romanian dish to remind Mirela of home—not the true home she was taken from, but a pretend home she might have had under different circumstances, one filled with the smell of hot, wet garbage.

It occurred to Lauren that Abby and Mirela had something that she did not: a first country, a first language, the other life that provided the first strand of the double helix of a real person. Lauren's was a half life. She imagined that if she tried to describe this insight to Abby, she would twist her mouth to one side and look away.

Midnight slinked down the hallway and rubbed herself against Lauren's ankles. She was thinner, her tail bigger in proportion to her body. Lauren had chosen her from the shelter, but Mom had given naming privileges to Sean, then aged five; he chose Midnight for her black fur. Lauren had been mean to Sean about the name, called it "tacky," and she felt bad about it now—it was a good showing for a five-year-old, she had come to realize, and Midnight always loved Sean best. These days, Midnight and Sean spent a lot of time together in the basement, because Mirela could only reach the basement with great hollering effort. Creeping down, down, with slow noise.

Lauren sat cross-legged in the hallway and rubbed between Midnight's ears. The cat's eyes rolled back in her head as she leaned into the rub, overwhelmed by Lauren's touch, baring her teeth. Lauren let her nibble roughly at her knuckles and bite down into her palm.

"We've been through a lot," Lauren whispered to Midnight, wincing as she tried to ease her hand out from between Midnight's jaws. "Let's just let off some steam."

"SEAN IS REGRESSING," Mom said, the following weekend. She was driving Lauren to sleep over at Paula's house, Mirela strapped into the car seat in the back.

Sean had moved more of his things into the basement that week after Mirela destroyed the planetarium he constructed with paint in primary colors, foam and string and Christmas lights. Sean cried so hard he fell into a fit of dry heaves and refused to go to school.

"It's annoying you went to all that trouble of baby-proofing the house when it didn't even work," Lauren told Mom. There were zip ties on the pantry door and cutlery drawers. Chunks of adhesive rubber stuck to table corners. A padlock on Mirela's door, which was still decorated with construction-paper cutout letters, with shoelace stitching in pigskin brown, spelling S-E-A-N.

"Annoying to who?" Mom asked.

"To you, I guess," Lauren said.

"Dad helped, too," Mom said.

"*Sure* he did," Lauren said. Dad was always at work lately, even at night. He said he had paperwork, but he could just as easily do the paperwork at home.

"Parents always have to take precautions," Mom said. "It honestly wasn't much different when you and your brothers were babies."

"But Mirela isn't a baby," Lauren said.

"But if you count from the day she joined our family," Mom replied, "it's like she's still a newborn."

"Babby," Mirela said, pensive. She could sit happily for hours strapped into her car seat, looking out the window and babbling to herself, kicking the back of the front passenger seat.

They were learning Mirela. One thing they had learned was that she was best in the car and worst at home. "That's because home is where she feels safest, " Mom said. "She can test boundaries. You and your brothers were the same. So often perfect angels out in the world until we got back to the house and all heck broke loose."

"Mirela is never a perfect angel out in the world," Lauren said.

"Anyhow, Sean feels displaced," Mom said. "It's probably just a phase. You had a minor regression phase, too, right after PJ was born, when you weren't the baby any longer."

"I did?" Lauren asked. "I don't remember that."

"Of course you don't. You were only about the age Mirela is now."

Do you even know how old Mirela is? Lauren thought.

"That's one of the funny parts of all this," Mom said. "Mirela probably won't even remember it."

"Everybody else will," Lauren said glumly.

"You know what Sean asked me the other day?" Mom asked. "He said, 'Mom, when will Mirela be normal?'" She laughed.

"And what did you say?" Lauren asked, trying to sound uninterested in the answer.

"Well, I told him that Mirela has a very unique way of experiencing the world—"

"There's no such thing as *very unique*," Lauren said. "You're either unique or you're not."

"—and her *unique* way of experiencing the world is one of the many gifts she has to share with us," Mom said, looking up into the rearview mirror. "Isn't that true, Mirela?" Mirela kept humming out the window.

"So Mirela destroying Sean's solar system was a *gift*?" Lauren asked.

"That's pretty much what Sean asked, too. No, it wasn't a gift. But it was her own way of showing enthusiasm—I know that's hard to understand, but it's true. Or—think about the play."

"I never want to think about the play ever again," said Lauren, who thought about the play frequently.

"Okay, well, however you feel about it now, there's something wonderful about being able to create a moment like that. The moment that you and Mirela had together. That's a gift. No one who was there will ever forget that night."

"And I'm sure Sean will never forget Mirela destroying his solar system."

Mom sighed. "The gift that we can give her is patience. Love and patience is all she needs." Mom was turning onto the circular drive that bisected the lawn in front of Saint Benedict's.

"All she needs to become normal?" Lauren asked.

"All she needs to become herself." Mom glided into a spot across from the rectory in the near-empty parking lot.

"What are we doing?" Lauren asked. "You go to mass tomorrow morning. Aren't you doing the dead baby mass?"

"*Lauren.* I expect that sort of talk from your brothers, not from you." Mom took her keys from the ignition. "I've got some boards and plywood from a couple of your dad's construction sites in the trunk. Flimsy stuff. We're going to break them down and—"

"We?"

"Not you. Unless you want to."

"'We' who?"

"We, you know, uh, the Respect Life committee. We're going to try to use them for signs at our next day of action." Mom was already opening her door and sliding out of the front seat.

"Mom . . ." Lauren whined. She slumped in her seat.

Mom was opening the door on Lauren's side. "C'mon, you don't have to carry anything—I mean, not if you don't want to. It won't take long. Just be another pair of eyes on Mirela for me," she said, and walked around to the trunk to start removing the boards.

Lauren got out of the station wagon and opened the door to Mirela in the back seat as Mom lugged a stack of plywood to the rectory. As Lauren unclipped the car seat straps, her diaphragm collapsed and the air in her belly coughed out of her throat; she crumpled over in surprise, a shrunken balloon. Mirela had punched her in the stomach, and now she was scooting under Lauren's hunched frame to escape the car, and Lauren wheezed as she caught Mirela around one thin wrist, the girl pulling and scratching to get away. Lauren steadied herself on the door frame, then sat down on the pavement, her hand clenched around Mirela's arm, to keep the screaming, fighting girl safe at her side. She watched as Mom hurried out of the rectory and back to the car. Mirela was tugging at her with mounting fury.

"Lauren," her mother said, exasperated, "why are you sitting on the ground when you could be helping?"

"Lolo!" Mirela screamed.

Ridiculous tears filled Lauren's eyes as she tried to remember what Mom had demonstrated with the Raggedy Ann doll. The squeeze. It had looked like it would be so easy, Mirela had roughly the proportions of Raggedy Ann, but her head was a swinging club, her arching back was a rubber band she could use to catapult herself out of the hold, she had ten hitting limbs, she had teeth. A fat tear fell from Lauren's eye into the crook of Mirela's neck, and Mirela wailed like she'd been scalded.

Lauren again felt herself altered. Bewitched. Her internal organs had grown or shifted around, or the casement of her body had shrunk. She'd been tricked. Her anger was childish, and she was embarrassed by it, and the embarrassment magnified her anger. It was Mom who had staged this, but why? This was not where she was supposed to be. This was not supposed to be her sister. Mom was not supposed to be this strange child's mother. This strange child was not calling her name.

"You offered me a ride to Paula's!" Lauren shouted, as Mirela bicycled her legs in an attempt to escape her grip. "If you didn't want to just give me a ride to Paula's, you should have said so!"

"Lauren—"

"Lolo!"

"I didn't ask for this!" Lauren said. "I don't want to be here! I'm not supposed to be here!"

"Be here!" Mirela said.

"Ladies, can I be of some assistance?" a man's voice called out. An average man of average build, striding out of the rectory toward their car. Salt-and-pepper hair and beard, pressed jeans and a blue crewneck, eyes crinkling with benevolence. It took Lauren a couple of seconds to register his priest's collar, long enough for Mirela to break free and run to the man, her stick arms outstretched. Mirela flung her head away from him as he scooped her up into the hug she begged for and refused, screaming in delight as he tossed her around and dangled her upside down.

He was new here, Lauren remembered—he was the one who had replaced Father Paul, who had been put on "medical leave." Mom and Dad would always laugh with each other in a secret way when Father Paul's "medical leave" came up, usually when Nana Glenis went out of her way to mention it so she could go on and on about how Father Paul had gotten "railroaded," and then Dad would make some horrible dirty joke about "railroading" that PJ and Sean would repeat for days, and Dad would find that funny at first and then he would get mad at them, even though they learned it from him, so really it was like Dad was mad at himself.

This new priest, Father Steve, was the one Mom would get giggly about, and he appeared to know Mirela already, well enough to understand that she seemed happiest when she was spinning and flying and losing her breath.

"Father Steve," Mom sighed, sheepish, relieved, as Lauren got to her feet. "Could you just keep an eye on Mirela while we finish unloading these? Oh, and this is my older daughter, Lauren—I'm sorry you haven't met before now."

"How do you do," Father Steve called. Lauren ignored him and took the last pile of boards out of the trunk.

"*Manners*, Lauren," Mom said.

"Nice to meet you, sir," Lauren mumbled, pushing her palm against an edge of plywood, hoping for a splinter.

"Maybe next time you can be thoughtful toward your sister and me, even when you think no one is looking," Mom murmured to Lauren as they dragged their parcels over the sidewalk and into the rectory.

By the time Mom and Lauren reached the classroom where the Respect Life committee convened, Mirela had moved on from Father Steve to the Huebler sisters. She danced ring-around-the-rosie with Summer and she climbed Charity like a ladder.

A door-sized poster was laid out on the table closest to the entryway, all reds and purples, the imagery dripping, steaming hot.

"Jesus, Mom, what is this?"

"Lauren, watch your language," her mother said.

"What are you going to do with this?" Lauren asked.

"We are trying to be truth tellers, Lauren," Father Steve said. "We just wish we had a different truth to tell."

"But that's disgusting," Lauren said. Her mother began silently rolling up the poster, her face unreadable.

"You are absolutely right, Lauren," Father Steve said. "It *is* disgusting. I'm afraid that's why we're here."

It wasn't Mom who'd staged this after all. It was this man with the creamy voice, stroking his beard like he could extract a sermon through his fingertips. Pick some scripture out from under his fingernails. This was the man, or the kind of man, who would have talked Mom into bringing Mirela home. He was why they were here, why Mirela had punched her.

"Lauren, wipe that look off your face *now*," Mom said.

There were more posters splattered with the same reds and purples and black block-capital letters stacked up against the classroom windows. An impression of bawling offal, a rotting mess in the back of a truck, no one discrete component that could be recognized and named. The horror was so far inside that it couldn't be dug out.

"Mom," Lauren asked, "tell me, please—what are you doing with these signs? Where are you—why do you have these?"

Mom looked down silently at the poster in her hands, a monk with her scroll. Her ponytail had come loose and strands of hair hung in her eyes.

Father Steve cleared his throat. "So, Lauren. Your mother tells me that you and Mirela made quite the big impression in your stage debuts," he said.

A chair toppled over behind him, a Mirela scream.

"Mom?" Lauren said again. "Mom, please."

"Perhaps—uh, perhaps you should do an all-ladies production of *All My Sons* called *All My Daughters*." Father Steve had an easy confidence, like he could convince other people he was clever just by believing it himself, puffing up his chest like he was converting the oxygen he extracted from the air into something pure, edifying, forest-sustaining.

"That's interesting," Mom said. "What would the corrupt matriarch produce instead of defective plane parts?"

"Hmm. Pretty dresses, I would think," Father Steve said.

Lauren wiped the look back on her face. "Tampons," she said. A drop of spit on the *p*.

Mom smiled hard. "Lauren says things just for effect," she said. "My apologies, Father."

"No apologies necessary."

"And, Father, you're missing a plot point—pretty dresses never killed anyone," Mom said, a jingle-jangle in her voice.

"Tampons kill," Lauren said. "You ever hear of toxic shock syndrome?"

"Lauren, that is *enough*," Mom said, closing her eyes.

"I suppose I haven't thought this through," Father Steve said. "But it seems to me that mothers like yours, Lauren, think of everyone's children as all their daughters, all their sons."

"Yup, that sure is the title of the play," Lauren said. She was acting like her brothers.

"Mothers like yours feel called upon by God to love and serve every human life," Father Steve said. "Your mother has set a great and Christly example in welcoming Mirela into our community of life."

"Mirela!" Mom gasped. "Where is Mirela?" She darted out of the room. They could hear her calling the girl's name up and down the hallway.

"You were supposed to be watching her," Lauren said to Summer and Charity.

Charity snorted. "That's news to us," she said.

"She's always running away," Summer said.

"I'm so afraid we'll see her picture on a milk carton someday," Charity said.

"Mind your own business," Lauren said.

"In that case, I guess we *weren't* supposed to be watching her," Summer said, snapping her gum in victory. Charity giggled.

"We are all one another's business," Father Steve said, as Lauren moved past the sisters to follow Mom out the door. He opened his hands, a gesture of philanthropy. "We are all responsible for one another. And, Lauren . . ."

Lauren stopped in the doorway and looked back at him.

Father Steve folded his hands and smiled. "Lauren, this is God's house. No one could ever go missing here."

PAULA DIDN'T SEEM to mind that Lauren started coming home with her almost every day after school without really asking. Maybe she thought Lauren felt bad about going to the movie without her on opening night. Or maybe she didn't care and never thought twice about it—that was probably the answer, because she never brought it up.

For two weeks straight, as soon as she got home every afternoon, Paula wanted to catch the last couple of hours of the Kennedy nephew's rape trial. Lauren pretended to do homework, but she was watching, too. She could gather that it was vulgar to follow the trial, or at least it was vulgar to talk about it; she wouldn't have wanted Claire or Abby or any of the other senior girls to know she was following it. Now that the play was over, Lauren suspected that she was a toy that the senior girls had grown out of, a doll, like the old G.I. Joes that Sean would bring down from the attic and then, in a flourish of maturity regained, banish upstairs again. Lauren feared she wasn't useful to the senior girls. She couldn't drive; she could only be driven around. She didn't know the right music; she could only be appreciative of the music they listened to. She couldn't ask the senior girls over to her house; she didn't ask Paula over, either, even though she didn't care what Paula thought of the Mirela situation.

"He's like Blane, how he nods and bugs out his eyes when he wants to fake being sincere," Paula said of the Kennedy nephew. Blane was the cute, rich boy who dumps Molly Ringwald in *Pretty in Pink*. They get back together in time for the prom, but you know he'll just dump her again after the movie is over and no one is looking anymore.

The Kennedy nephew was a good witness for himself. A studious young doctor in training, calm, measured. A polite and upstanding fellow who trusted the process and who could feel his innocence, just like he could feel the family blood in his veins, its density and temperature. All reasonable people could share his innocence with him, feel it pumping through them, too, once they had heard his side of the story. He could keep his story straight. The woman who accused him cried a lot and couldn't describe exactly what happened and forgot so much and wanted everyone to take her word for everything and insulted the defense attorney just for doing his job. "Please help me get this over with!" she said, crying, but that wasn't what anyone was there to do, and Lauren had to look away although she couldn't see her face. The television plopped a big, blue-gray dot over her head.

"Saves her the embarrassment," Nana Glenis had said, over for dinner on the opening day of the trial. She kept a corner of her attic devoted to Kennedy memorabilia: clippings, buttons, *Life* magazines, the negatives of the roll of film she shot the day President Kennedy gave a speech in Niagara Square. She could name all eleven of Robert and Ethel Kennedy's children in order of age, middle names included. Nana Glenis left before dessert, after Mirela threw a fistful of mashed potatoes at her and poured a cup of water over PJ's head.

"No, it's not about embarrassment—it's more about privacy," replied Mom, who was upset that the alleged rape had occurred on Good Friday. "For any of them to be out carousing on Good Friday, of all days!"

"Jesus needed a couple of beers up there on that cross," Dad said. "You gotta beat the heat."

Paula was sure that the Kennedy nephew did it, and Lauren was, too. It wasn't a conclusion that Lauren reached after weighing the evidence—that the sobbing woman who said she was raped had been raped by the man she said raped her seemed a self-evident truth, available without benefit of a jury trial or news coverage. Yet there was another, equally self-evident truth in the trial, which was that the Kennedy nephew knew how to behave correctly, how to control and parcel out his presentation of himself, and his shrieking accuser did not. Carrying on like that. She was messy. She had ginned up this whole mess. She was messed up in the head.

"Making a scene," Nana Glenis said. "Hasn't that poor family been through enough?"

There was what happened, and then there was the story of what happened. The story was what was more important, because the story would keep itself alive in the retelling of it, long after what happened was dead.

MOM HAD BEEN nervous about Thanksgiving, and it's true that Mirela ripped both legs off the turkey and then locked the turkey and herself in Aunt Marie's downstairs bathroom. Mom had been nervous about Christmas Day, and it's true that the youngest cousins were distraught when Mirela tore the wrapping paper off every present under Nana Dee's tree before anyone else woke up. Now Mom was nervous about Lauren's birthday, but it was Mom who wanted a big party at their house, not Lauren. Lauren's birthday fell right after the holidays, when most people felt gorged on parties and presents. But Mom said this birthday was extra important because it was the first one in the immediate family since Mirela came home.

Both sets of grandparents came over, Uncles Brian and Mike and Joe and their wives and all the cousins. The uncles and Granddad, Mom's dad, sat in the den watching the Bills, who were two games away from making it to the Super Bowl for a second year in a row.

"Norwood's really been redeeming himself this season, don't you think, Lauren?" Uncle Mike asked with his crinkly smile. Lauren's baby pictures looked like Uncle Mike's when they were both smiling. Scott Norwood was the kicker who had missed a long, difficult, but not strictly implausible field goal at the end of last year's Super Bowl, which the Bills then lost by a single point. Lauren didn't follow sports, but she sensed that one's attitude toward Norwood could be a litmus test for a person's entire worldview. A small minority of Bills fans wanted Norwood banished to another team for spite; others had nothing against him personally but found it nearly unbearable to see his number on the field, like the other Bills and all their fans were being haunted by the ghost of his defeat; still others wrote impossible movie scripts in their head about a Super Bowl sequel on the order of *Rocky II*, whereby the Bills not only win the match but by one point, courtesy of a long Norwood kick, one that would avenge the man, the team, the blighted city, and of course, the tragic squandered genius of O.J. in one perfect arcing firework of a field goal. Dad, like most Bills fans, was soft and forgiving toward Norwood in a way that felt out of keeping with his personality generally, calling him "a good guy who had a bad day at work." Lauren was surprised and moved that Dad could acknowledge an uncomfortable, unfamiliar feeling and put it into words, and it helped her understand why so many of the men in her life spent so much time sitting still watching sports.

The great-aunts came to her birthday party, Eunice and Faye, with their crumpled-paper voices and ashtray kisses. They mixed big polyester prints with dark brocade scarves, and all their clothes smelled like the Salvation Army, and they wore bulbous brooches in iridescents and jewel tones, clip-on earrings that rattled and dangled, clacking fake pearls. Sometimes they gave their jewelry to Lauren on the spot: a cameo locket with a sapphire-green eye; a yellow-gold signet ring of adjustable size. Lauren wore the baubles to school, feeling like an heiress, until Claire told her, with apologetic discomfort, that her great-aunts' things were cheap. Lauren appreciated knowing this. But how did Claire know? How could she tell? Her mom must have explained it to her.

Lauren didn't ask Julie or any of the other senior girls to the party. Paula came, a couple of PJ and Sean's friends. Danielle Sheridan, of all people, owing to a chance encounter between Danielle's and Lauren's mothers at Bells market. A buffet spread, a Bells sheet cake from Nana Glenis, and a homemade malted chocolate drip cake from Nana Dee. Balloons that PJ and Sean had blown up and tied themselves, streamers that Mirela tore down, a construction-paper banner that Mom had cut, mounted, and strung herself, using supplies from the Jo-Ann fabric store on Transit Road, reading HAPPY FIFTEENTH BIRTHDAY LAUREN. Mirela ripped it in half. Mom taped it back together, and Mirela ripped it in half again.

"She's just so excited about Lauren's birthday," Mom explained. "She means well. We have to celebrate who Mirela is, not who we might think we want Mirela to be."

The house filled with people, smiling faces bobbing in Lauren's direction, but before they reached her there was Mirela, Mirela in every room, corner, doorway, Mirela in front of you and behind you and under your feet, Mirela laughing, jumping, hitting plates of potato salad and soft-cooked baby carrots out of surprised hands, pulling at sleeves, kicking at ankles, *being herself.* A car backfired in the crowded kitchen, raising a whoop from Nana Glenis; it was Mirela, who'd stolen a smoldering cigarette from between Aunt Faye's fingers and attacked the balloons with it, *pop-pop-pop.* Lauren leaned against the sink, watching, wondering who might volunteer to try taking the cigarette away from Mirela.

"Happy buh day!" Mirela hollered at everyone, every conversation, every face scanning past. "Happy buh day!"

"I wanted to thank you for inviting me to your birthday party." It was Danielle by Lauren's side, holding a small white box with a large blue bow. The words sounded practiced. Danielle looked ill at ease in a starched white blouse. Lauren imagined her taking it off as soon as she got back home, pulling on a loose T-shirt, flinging her legs over the side of the couch to watch *Yo! MTV Raps.*

The box flew out of Danielle's hands onto the floor tiles, landing with a clinking crunch. "Ohhh," said Danielle, crestfallen, as Mirela ran past her to kick the box into the next room. A group shout rose up from the den, signaling a happy development in the Bills game.

"It's okay," Lauren said, picking up the cigarette Mirela had dropped on the floor and flicking it into the sink behind her. "Thanks for whatever was inside that box."

"So, uh—yeah, I just, I wanted to thank you for inviting me to your—"

"Happy buh day!" Mirela was back, she was there, she was always there, yelling, looking back and forth from Danielle to Lauren. "Happy buh day!" Danielle smiled down at Mirela as if through great ennobling pain.

A familiar feeling burbled back, coating Lauren's synapses. It was the feeling of sitting back in class and watching Danielle disintegrate. *Pull on her string.*

"Hey, Mirela," Lauren said, leaning over her like they were in a conspiracy. Lauren wasn't sure if she wanted Danielle to hear what she was about to do. "Has Mom ever told you," she asked the girl, "the story of what I did the day before I turned three?" She held out her palms to Mirela for pat-a-cake. "Before the sun went down, I went from room to room turning out all the lights in the house, yelling, 'Go to bed, go to bed!' because I thought that way my birthday would come sooner." Danielle laughed, and Mirela pummeled Lauren's palms with her little fists.

"My mom has told that story a million times," Lauren said, looking up at Danielle. "You'll probably hear it from her before you leave today, Danielle."

She turned again to Mirela. "What did *you* do," Lauren asked brightly, "the night before *you* turned three?"

Lauren had conjured something on the night of *All My Sons*. A new scene, another girl. She could do it again, whenever she wanted to.

Mirela hit Lauren's palms harder, harder.

"Go ahead, tell us, Mirela, we're listening—what did you do on *your* birthday?"

Harder, harder.

"Mirela, listen—do you know what a birthday is?"

"Mah buh day!" Mirela said.

"Nooo, Mirela," Lauren murmured, catching both of the girl's fists in her hands as she got down on her knees. "It's not *Mirela's* birthday. It's *Lauren's* birthday. I don't know when Mirela's birthday is. Do you?"

"Mah buh day! Mah buh day!"

Danielle was fading out. It was just the two sisters in the room now. They were onstage together again, alone, holding hands.

"Nope, sorry, Mirela," Lauren said. She controlled the edge in her voice. She heard Andy in her head. *Little freak.* "Your birthday is the day your mommy gave birth to you. But we don't know your birthday. And we don't know your mommy."

"Mama," Mirela said, pointing across the room where Mom

was stringing the HAPPY FIFTEENTH BIRTHDAY LAUREN banner for the third time.

"That's not your mommy, Mirela," Lauren said, shaking her head ruefully.

"Mama," Mirela said. She was blinking rapidly. She was trying to think. "Mama. Mama."

"But where's your real mama, Mirela?" Lauren asked, her throat constricting and pinching the words, choking them off.

It was torn. It was over. There was no use stopping now. Lauren had dragged them all the way under. Their lungs were filling with water.

"Where is *Mirela's* mommy?" Lauren asked. Altered, bewitched. "Not *Lauren's* mommy. Mirela's mommy, who gave birth to Mirela, on Mirela's *birthday.*"

"Mama," Mirela said, her finger stabbing the air, her eyes darting everywhere. "Mama. Mama." She jabbed both arms, she stomped her feet, she spun around and around, screaming "Mama," then screaming no words at all, strangled vowels and pure pain, sirening up from the child on all fours.

"*My* mommy doesn't know your birthday, Mirela," Lauren whispered, although no one could hear her. Her brow was dotted with sweat and her eyes were dry. "I'm so sorry."

"Lauren, honey, what happened?" Mom was by her side.

Danielle was back. Danielle had never been gone. She was backing away. Lauren rose to her feet again, her knees knocking together. "I think . . ." She leaned back against the sink, reaching behind with both hands to grip the edge of the counter, unsteady with what she'd done. "I think Mirela is sad that it's not her birthday."

"No my mama!" Mirela was wailing like she'd been burned. "No my mama!"

Even that day, after Dad asked everyone to leave and Mom had taken Lauren's place at the sink, holding a washcloth to her bloody nose—even then, Lauren knew it wasn't Mirela's fault. Mirela didn't have any say. Lauren didn't, either. No one asks to be born. No one chooses their family. No one gets to say, *You. You're the one. You're the one I want to be my mother.*

That night, Lauren said to Mom, "Mirela is special because she is chosen." She was trying to be kind. Lauren didn't feel guilty, not yet. "You chose her, Mom, you just didn't know how hard it would be."

"But I chose you, too, Lauren," Mom said. "I *conjured* you. I'd seen you before. They put you in my arms and I knew it was you."

JANE

It had to be bigger than Wichita. Wichita, they could quantify. Last summer. Forty-six days of siege. Two thousand six hundred arrests. Thirty thousand protesters in all. Flattening heat, clothes soaked and throats dry. They sang and clapped and refused to budge. Their action was slowness and stillness. They locked arms in front of the entrances to the clinics, laid prostrate before the doors. They propped themselves up on their elbows, joints and pelvic bones grinding into the scorching pavement. They lay beneath the wheels of cars, filling their lungs with miasma, coughing out prayers for the dying. They felt the hooves of police horses in their ribs and went limp in the arms of arresting officers. One hundred at a time, they crawled toward the police, cornering the cops against fences and clinic walls, a military-precision pincer move. In came the federal marshals, and still they crawled and clapped and sat. "God's law before man's law," they chanted, cross-legged on the concrete. They knit baby caps and booties where they sat, crocheted colorful blankets. A college-aged protester with tangled mermaid hair was knitting a white woolen baby sweater, tiny fabric roses embroidered along the collar. She was swept off to jail, flat on her back, hair swimming behind her, dozens hauled off along with her, only for busloads of new protesters to take their place. Sometimes a protester would take her own place: arrested and jailed and released and then arrested and jailed again, all in the same day.

The protesters aspired to be Paul fallen from his saddle, Peter crucified under his own terms. "A woman's body, a woman's choice"—that was the other side's refrain. But they could make choices with their bodies, too. Their bodies were not their own. They could give up their bodies on behalf of others. And they won, for a time. For seven days last summer, then ten days, then a month, in July, straight into August, they said that there were no abortions in Wichita. Jane didn't know how they knew for sure.

There was nothing unattainable about the victory in Wichita. These were ordinary people. They did things anyone could do, things a baby could do. Sitting in place, crawling, singing, clapping, unwilling to budge, refusing to cooperate—these were a baby's pastimes. They made choices fit for babies. Along with the bloody placards and bundles of baby blankets and newborn-sized clothes, they also brought folding patio chairs and Styrofoam coolers. One man, stout in his navy polo shirt, sat cross-legged in a patch of grass, red rubbery carnage propped against his knees, eating a sandwich. Working men and women, moms and dads, putting in an honest day's work.

"Thirty million," the reverend was saying in the video. The Respect Life members were watching a television set on elevated wheels that Father Steve had pushed into the classroom. The reverend had beige hair and beige skin and beige trousers; he was smooth and bland as batter. "Can you imagine?" the reverend asked. "Thirty million innocents. Once you think about it, once you truly wrap your head around it, you start to see them everywhere. That extra, empty desk in your son's classroom—"

Their eyes moved to various empty desks in the classroom, then back to the video.

"Whom did God intend to be sitting at that desk? Learning the alphabet, his multiplication tables? Would he have grown up to be your own son's best friend? Grown up to be the doctor who delivered your babies? Grown up to be president?"

The reverend was walking through a lakeside scene, green and rolling, denuded of people. Could have been Lake Chautauqua.

"You see them everywhere, even though you can't see them. Is that mother, beside you at church, missing a baby? Is that little girl, running on the playground, wondering where her brother went? We can't answer all these questions. But God can. God has the answers. God knows us before we are born. God is with us even then. God is with the babies when they are murdered in the womb. We cannot know why God allows the sin of abortion. Why God allows a baby to be slaughtered inside her—"

Father Steve turned off the video. "The language gets a little heated at times," he said, flipping the lights on. "The reverend comes from a different rhetorical tradition than we do. But we can find inspiration in his passion, even as we forge our own path."

Drizzle chattered on the classroom windows. It was the end of March, sky slushy gray with lake effects, last crumbling patches of snow melting into newborn grass. They were aiming for Good Friday or Easter. "As it happens," Father Steve said, "a baby conceived during Wichita's Summer of Mercy will be born during Buffalo's Spring of Life."

"The message is very powerful," said Betty among nodding heads. "It's a bit *much*, but—yes."

"Where are the Catholics in this?" Jane asked. "Is there a Catholic video?"

"We are the Catholics," Father Steve replied. "This is a multidenominational effort."

"You know," Betty said, "just the other day, this Presbyterian gal said to me, 'Oh, but you're not Christian—you're *Catholic*'—"

"Will this nonsense ever stop?!" Phil exclaimed.

"—so, I mean, there are many boundaries to be broken here," Betty finished.

"Our work will not be without its difficulties," Father Steve said. "At times it will be painful. It's a battle, and it won't begin or end with us. But a soldier in battle knows to find interludes of respite and sustenance. We will remember to rest, to eat, and to drink. Our labors should not preclude folding chairs, coolers full of drinks. For the Lord is my shepherd—"

"I shall not want," the group replied. "He maketh me to lie down in green pastures: he leadeth me beside quiet waters."

"We know how to tailgate, after all—we are from Buffalo," said Father Steve, who was from Schenectady.

In Wichita, the cops had to drag and carry so many protesters that the police department purchased wide leather lifting belts, like the ones Pat and Colin and Brad Bender used to wear for weight training during football season.

"To every thing, there is a season, and a time to every purpose under heaven," Father Steve said to murmuring assent.

"Will we—will people who participate in the Spring of Life risk getting arrested?" Mr. Glover asked.

"We may be arrested," Father Steve replied. "It's nothing to fear. I can't imagine a jail in the suburbs looking like Attica. Arrests are one thing, but in terms of *convictions*, if we are speaking of an actual prison *sentence*, it's very unlikely."

"How can you be sure?" Mr. Glover asked.

"The necessity defense," Summer and Charity said in unison.

"The activists in Wichita shouldn't have been arrested in the first place," Summer explained, "because of the necessity defense. The courts recognize that sometimes breaking the law can be justified for a greater good."

"It's straight out of Thomas Aquinas," Mr. Glover said.

"Any fair-minded judge will understand that we *have* to do this," Charity said.

The ultrasound images that Mr. Glover procured from his doctor friend at Children's Hospital made Jane think of seafood. A shrimp submerged in brine. A jaunty seahorse. Sean was the only one of her babies who Jane saw on ultrasound. They rubbed a gel on her belly that conducted sound waves through a plastic wand as big as a mixing spoon, and a computer assembled the pictures that bounced back, much like a bat assembles a mental floor plan of his environment through echolocation. Or a dolphin. Sean, her little dolphin! Bouncing his clicks and squeaks around the pool until they etched his self-portrait. The wand was smooth and beige as the reverend. The technician pushed and dug in and worked it over Jane's belly, like she was moving cold butter through batter with her dumb wooden spoon, like Jane was in the way, or like Jane wasn't there at all. Trying to reach the baby, to see the baby's clicks and squeaks. The messages Sean wanted everyone to hear.

Sean. That was Sean. Never anything but Sean. She could have ended Sean, by law.

The gleaming instruments could have ended Sean. She closed her eyes against the glare. She shuddered as the nurse brushed past.

"We obey God's law before we obey man's law," Charity said. "It's the first commandment."

"You might argue it's also in Romans, which is incidentally the most law-abiding of the Gospels," Father Steve said. "Romans says, 'Love doeth no harm to a neighbor, therefore Love doth fulfill the Law.'"

"I understand that the doctor in Wichita was doing abortions very late, when the baby is, well, *really* a baby," Betty Andrower said.

"It's always a baby!" Summer and Charity said.

"Okay, but there's a continuum—" Betty said. She was fussing with the gold cross around her neck, drumming her plum-colored nails against the brief line of décolletage that disappeared into the V-neck of her sweater.

"You sound like Tiller the killer," Phil said, not a condemnation so much as a correction, like of course Betty didn't mean what she had said. Tiller was the worst one, his name a curse.

"Well, yes, I know, it's always a—you know what I mean," Betty said. "My question is—do we know if any of the clinics in Buffalo—just to play devil's advocate—"

"And why would we advocate the devil?" Phil asked.

"—are there any, shall we say, *special cir-cum-stances*," Betty enunciated, an actorly warble entering her voice to protest all the interruptions, "under which they perform—"

"What type of special circumstance could possibly justify murder?" Phil asked. "This is science. This is a genetically unique, growing, living being. That living being has never existed before and will never exist again. What justification can there be? Why would we look for one?"

"Well, I don't like even to say the word, but"—Betty's voice dropped to a scandalized whisper—"*rape*." She tugged at her cross.

"There's no death penalty for rape," Summer and Charity said in unison.

"Okay, but—it's hard," Betty said. "To put someone through all that." Phil opened his mouth to reply—and Jane knew what he would say: *If it's so hard on the mother, then how hard is it for the baby?*—but he stopped himself.

Jane didn't think Betty's conundrum was hard.

"Don't get me wrong," Betty said, her head stooped prayerfully. "It's a terrible thing. No words. I mean, that's why I'm *here*. Because I think it's all just *terrible*."

Jane had one that was hard. "What about a case where the mother's life is in danger?" she asked. "Women used to die in childbirth all the time."

"*Used to*," Mr. Glover said.

"It's rare that a baby would put his own mother's life in danger," Father Steve said.

"It's a myth created by the pro-abortion forces," Mr. Glover said.

"But even if it's rare," Jane said, "even if it only happens to one woman—"

"That woman is a child of God and a whole world unto herself, and that is a tragedy. You are right, Jane," Father Steve said, nodding.

"Pardon?" Mr. Glover asked.

"Jane," Father Steve said, "you have heard of the term *fetomaternal chimerism*."

It was neither a question nor a statement, and the ambiguity was intended to flatter the listener. "*Chimera* in the Greek myths is a fire-breathing monster," she said. "Part lion, part goat, part dragon. Always a woman."

Surprise or pique crossed Father Steve's face, but then he was beaming indulgence at her again. "I used to read a lot of fables and myths to the kids," Jane said. "Sorry," she added.

"*Chimera* is also an illusion," he said, nodding. "A mirage born out of magical thinking. Like in your myths, Jane. The irony, in this case, is that it's in fact entirely appropriate to think in terms of magic and miracles when it comes to the bond between a mother and her unborn child. Science"—he popped a tiny exclamation point on the word, like in the goofy English pop song the boys used to like so much—"has discovered that a baby's cells can remain inside his or her mother's body for years, even decades after he or she is born. They might stay there forever. And those young, new cells can help repair the mother's body when she is sick or worn down."

Mr. Glover, reassured, patted the top of his little desk. "It's good when science and faith are shown to be harmonious," he said. "Though it's no surprise to me."

"But we must pause to think of the mother whose child has died inside her," Father Steve said. "That poor woman. What toll does it take, to carry around that child's spirit, in the form of her cells?"

Charity hugged herself. "I can't imagine," she said. "A ghost, clinging to your insides."

"That's why it drives me crazy when people say, 'It's just a clump of cells,'" Summer said.

"I know it's not," Jane said. "Four times over, I know it."

"Do you mean three?" Summer asked.

"I guess it's clearest and best for us if we think in terms of no exceptions," Betty said.

"Romans again, my friends," Father Steve said. "'And thinkest thou thus, o man, that judgest them which do such things, and doest the same, that thou shalt escape the judgment of God?'"

"No exceptions," Jane said.

We believe in what we can't see, she thought, as she heard a sound coming closer, a rhythmic slapping, a rapid pounding, the screams of a child in peril.

A circle of adults crammed under children's desks, exchanging ideas in shared faith, all of Scripture in their hands—for an hour or so, Jane had mistaken her world for being at least as big as a kindergarten classroom. But really it was the size of one spinning, wailing, inconceivable little girl.

IT'S NOT THAT she hadn't talked to Pat about it. She showed him the brochures. She talked about flights, training sessions, paperwork. He indulged her with the same bright solicitous voice he used to put on when Sean became convinced that Midnight could be taught sign language. Soon, though, he became aggravated.

"I don't want to get all worked up about something that is not going to happen," Pat said. "Not in a million years."

He didn't forbid her from doing it. All he said was that she wouldn't do it.

You would never.

The bet she made was that he would want to save face. That's why she made sure, the first night back, that his mother was there, his sister was there. He could not admit to them, or to his coworkers and friends, his daughter and sons, that his wife had blown up his life without his consent. Blown it up *again*, in fact, and worse this time. Gone nuts, run away, brought home another man's child. Commanded him to call her his. And he didn't admit it. He didn't say much at all. He just started leaving for work earlier and earlier each day, and coming home later and later.

Jane and Mirela lived on an eroding isthmus, then an archipelago. Sinking dots they tried to string together driving along in the dragon wagon. Possible playdates ebbed away, one by one, after Mirela peed all over Bitsy Spizzoto's bedspread, after Henry Bingham went face-first into a glass table—three stitches to the chin, talk from Henry's blustery lawyer father of pressing charges. Sean's basketball games sank away after Mirela flung herself backward off a bleacher into two rows of sitting fans, the brunt of the impact again falling on the Figueroa family. Mirela emerged bruised along one arm and leg, laugh-screaming, her hair sticky with crying little Susie Figueroa's grape soda.

They could do Wegmans grocery store, but only just after the store opened in the morning, when it was still almost empty of shoppers. They could do Sunday mass for about ten minutes, fifteen, before the stares got too much. Worse than the glowering stares were the friendly, sympathetic ones, for conveying that Jane and Mirela were there to put on a show for an audience that would laugh and smile and clap along. Mirela was the instrument by which the parishioners could express their virtue and tolerance.

They could do playgrounds at dusk, after most other children had gone home for supper and bathtime. If other children were there, and especially if those children were talking to one another, Mirela would put her face in theirs and yell until they stopped. If any other children happened to be holding a stone or a stuffed bear or a Ziploc bag of animal crackers, Mirela would slap the object to the ground. If a child hung from the monkey bars, Mirela would try to pull her down; if a child was sitting at the top of the slide, Mirela would try to push her not down the slide but off the side of it, in a dead drop.

It wasn't so much that Mirela wanted things. It was that she wanted others not to have them. Most of all, she didn't want Jane to have her. She ran through any open door, climbed into any unlocked car. Trying to go off with strangers not because they were so enticing, but because they were not Jane.

Jane's own mother could barely look at her anymore. Jane suspected that her mother felt a grim triumph in what she perceived to be the catastrophe of Mirela—how it proved, once and for all, that Jane was a performer of catastrophe, setting off explosions for attention and expecting others to clean up the wreckage. But her mother needed to relish that triumph privately, away from the gaze of her daughter, and it was inconvenient for her mother's case that Jane was peering out from inside the wreckage. Their telephone conversations now were all cold logistics: her mother wanted to take the older kids to the mall, or out for pizza.

"Just trying my best to give them a bit of their childhood back," she said.

Mirela could do almost anything once. Anything that was strange, anything for the first time. She did best when there was no history, no memory, when the question of what *is* she had not been answered, not even posed yet. She excelled at first impressions. She would home in, her eyes all over yours, her hands on you, your fingers intertwined, her spaghetti arms wrapped around your waist, such a happy, friendly girl—what would you do, push her away? Would you refuse to answer her questions—and you couldn't be sure what the questions were, the consonants and vowels familiar but strung together out of order, curving upward questioningly at the end? Would you refuse to reciprocate her smiles, her unprompted and delighted laughter? A typical girl her age— and, sorry, how old is she again?—was so shy, thumb in mouth, turning away, one shoulder rising up to shadow her face, hands clutching at her mother's legs. This one wasn't clingy, no sirree, no stranger danger here. What a charmer. Gotta keep your eye on that one, Mom.

They did the garden center once, when the ground was still frozen. "She'd be at home most anywhere," the owner said, tousling Mirela's hair as Mirela headbutted her midsection repeatedly, with mounting force. The woman had a silky worn face, grays at her temples. Surely she had raised children; by now her children had children. She should know better. She should know that shyness in small children was a sign of security. Shyness was discernment: of who was safe and who was unverified. She should know, as a mother, not to be flattered by Mirela's attentions.

Stop polishing the apple was what Jane's mother always said about flattery. Jane could never take a compliment with grace. Maybe that was the problem—she couldn't take a compliment paid to Mirela, either.

"So much spirit!" the woman at the garden center said. Jane made herself grin and nod. The woman meant well—most of them did. Jane heard this a lot, about Mirela's spirit. A spirit was a ghost; Jane heard a deadness in this word. She used to see a glint in Mirela's eyes; now she suspected she had misapprehended it. It wasn't Mirela's own light. It was just a reflection of light, bouncing off a cold, hard surface.

"Is she yours?" the kindly gray woman asked.

Something else Jane heard a lot. The color of Mirela's skin, her syllables, how she walked and danced on invisible stilts—it all placed her elsewhere. Outside of a family that Jane would belong to. Mirela was here yet somehow not. *Whose do you think she is?*

"She's adopted," Jane said.

"How lucky she is to have you," the woman said. Always that. *How fortunate.* They wanted to weigh in on Jane's goodness. *How God has blessed you both. You are doing the Lord's work. What a sacrifice.*

The worst was *God bless you for rescuing her,* like she was a dog at the pound. Or *saving her,* like she was money, or leftovers; like she was a recyclable that got mixed up with the regular trash. Jane imagined herself responding, *No, she saved herself, by surviving long enough for me to find her.* But that would trigger more praise and more questions.

Where is she from?

What is she?

Mostly, Jane tried to foreclose further discussion with what she intended as an enigmatic smile, but what resulted, she suspected, was a tight little smirk. If Jane was smug in her goodness, that meant she wasn't good.

The language of the dog pound came at times to Jane's mind unbidden, too. *I rescued her.* She knew she shouldn't judge others for saying it. She should first and only judge herself, and God would judge her last.

Once in a while, she prayed penance for her thoughts. There were so many of them. One was *I never got to go to college, but this poor Romanian orphan will!*

Maybe Mirela was insane like a saint. She ate next to nothing. She had a startling capacity for pain. She spoke and behaved in ways that were impossible to explain. She arrived in a vision. She was impervious to reason. Like Catherine of Siena, she eschewed friendship. Like Catherine, she would take her family's belongings without asking—she was a prodigious stealer and hoarder of the food she didn't eat, squirreling it in closets, drawers, dollhouses, pants pockets, air vents.

The thief is not looking for the object that he takes. He is looking for a person. He is looking for his own mother, only he does not know this. That was Winnicott.

They could have a babysitter once or twice. Unsuspecting teens, at first all from Bethune, but then Jane had to cast a wider net. An hour or two, sometimes only long enough for Jane to donkey up Muegel Road and back for groceries, or attempt a nap upstairs, although she would just lie there awake, spent and manic, listening out for trouble. The first time, the sitter would leave the house flustered but intact. Perhaps she went home feeling a small sense of accomplishment. The assumption was that the next time would be better, calmer, because by then Mirela and the sitter would have learned each other. This was the narrative Jane presented, almost certain that it was false. If Mirela learned you, she could beat you. After the second job, the sitters didn't come back. A bruised lip, a torn shirt. A sobbing heap on the kitchen floor when Jane came home, the sliding glass door to the back patio cracked diagonally across and Mirela spinning in the yard, her hands smeared with blood or raspberries. Angry calls from the sitters' mothers. Strange looks at Wegmans. Word got around.

A rapid pounding. The screams of a child in peril. Holly Haverford was standing in the door to the classroom. Holly, the babysitter of the day, was a senior at Knox and a friend of a girl whose brother used to be on a basketball team with Sean.

"No exceptions," Jane was saying as she looked up to see Holly. Mirela was grabbing at Holly's hand. An older, aghast version of Holly stood just behind them.

"You don't have to pay me, and don't call me again," Holly said, yanking her hand away from Mirela and turning to go. The older Holly, shaking her head in pity and horror, followed Holly out.

"We are glad to have you join us, Mirela," Father Steve said as Mirela ran to the center of the room and overturned a desk piled with flyers and laughed at him. He was the funniest joke she'd ever heard. As Jane started to wedge herself out from under her desk to go to Mirela, the words Summer Huebler said scattered, locking into partial formation as Jane's attention cohered on them after the sounds had left the air.

"What did you just say?" Jane asked, turning in her seat to face Summer.

She wasn't sure.

"What did you just say," Jane repeated, her hands gripping the desk.

She was seventy percent sure. Eighty percent.

"*Summer?*" Jane asked, because now she was one hundred percent sure, because Charity was talking at a fast clip about transportation arrangements for the protests and because Summer was sitting silently, hands folded, wearing the enigmatic smile that Jane aspired to in moments of foreclosed discussion.

"Did you just say that you *can think of one exception?*" Jane asked, and then Mirela was crawling into her lap and pushing away from her at the same time, pulling at Jane's hair, her screams inside her and outside her and surrounding her.

JANE TRIED TO think of Mirela as she would a newborn. What helped Jane through the early, sleepless days and nights with her infants was the thought that they were working past exhaustion and despair just to stay alive outside of her, to adapt to the cold, blinding world they'd been exiled to. This was their *kenosis*. Jane remembered taking Lauren out into the demented whiteness of the post-blizzard landscape, swaddled in too many blankets, just her little snout visible, the steam of her warm breath meeting the freezing air. She looked like a breathing mummy, neither alive nor dead. For a couple of wrenching days when she was about ten weeks old, Lauren shrieked with gas, her cries piercing and rhythmic as contractions, and then she whimpered for a while as she fell into an exhausted sleep, only to be struck awake with new pain. Photographs of Lauren in her first few months—you could see it with PJ and Sean, too—depicted passages of blissful sleep but also something closer to sweaty collapse, her eyes screwed up against the marauding light. Getting air into her lungs, finding the milk in her mother's breast, gaining control over the reflexing limbs that kept jerking her awake—it required a strenuous trial and error.

Lauren's systems weren't prepared for this. Nearly forty weeks' gestation, yet she felt she had come too soon. Her stated position was that she was not supposed to be here.

Was Mirela supposed to be here? In this body, in this place? She had the height and the canter of a child still new to walking, but her limbs were thin, older, worn out, as if they'd already been stretched and whittled by this task they had not yet completely learned, and her face was drawn, literally—there were lines etched from either side of her nose to the corners of her mouth, years too deep. If they arrived at Saint Mary's playground before other kids had cleared out, Jane could watch other parents watching Mirela, trying to figure out her age, her origin. Just what *is* she.

The foundation of the health of the human being is laid by you in the baby's first weeks and months. . . . You are founding the health of a person who will be a member of our society. This is worth doing. That was Winnicott.

But Jane hadn't done the thing worth doing. Not with Mirela.

She wasn't present at the laying of the foundation. She didn't know who Mirela was.

THERE WAS THE pediatrician who recommended a sedative, which calmed Mirela down for a while until it didn't, and when it stopped working, it caused her to sleepwalk. Mirela couldn't walk up or down stairs, but she could sleepwalk them. Late one night, before they had locks on all the doors, Jane found Mirela in the kitchen, kneeling by the light of the open refrigerator. She had taken out all the produce and arranged it in a grid on the tiles, and fortified it with a snaking perimeter of jars: jams, ketchup, relishes, Jif peanut butter. She stacked the emptied areas of the refrigerator with cans of cat food. The child worked grimly, silently, mapping her inventory for some harrowing siege that lay ahead.

There was the pediatrician who recommended an anti-anxiety medication, which calmed Mirela down for a while until it didn't, and when it stopped working, the tensions it uncoiled produced a new and frightening energy that contracted her muscles with supernatural force as she raised her tricycle over her head and bashed it over and over into the ribs and flanks of the poor dragon wagon. She went about her violence mute and dispassionate, a tiny lumberjack splitting logs on an ordinary morning.

There was the pediatrician who recommended a cognitive stimulant, which calmed Mirela down for a while until it didn't, and when it stopped working, her sleep grew threadbare and tenuous. That was the worst. Because she did sleep. "She's a good sleeper," Jane told everyone. Sometimes, not always, Mirela didn't want to wear clothes (the rubbing of the cloth against her skin taunted her, smothered her), and sometimes, not always, she didn't want to use the potty (though the messes seemed at times less like accidents than decisions, statements). But at night, she wanted to sleep, invariably, and there was a miracle in this. Jane remembered to pray thanks to God for it. The endless chaos, the screaming, the smashing, and then silence. Like flinging a sheet over a noisy bird's cage. Mirela fought in her sleep, kicked and punched against sleep like someone was holding her down. But she slept.

There was the pediatrician who spoke of "cut points" for Mirela. Emotions, behaviors, cognitions that were placed out of her reach after twelve months at the institution. After eighteen months. After twenty-four months. There had been a year, almost to the week, between Barbara Walters and bringing Mirela home. A year of cut points. Neural pathways choked off and wasted away. Her brain pruning itself, weeding the dead patches, sealing off the dead ends. Maybe these deaths were reversible, or maybe Mirela was out of time, or close to it.

"The child who is loved learns to be lovable," this pediatrician said. "The child who is not loved learns the opposite. Being lovable is not necessarily in itself a sign of character. It's a sign of how you were raised."

There was the specialist in "theraplay," Miss Amber, who wore a tiered flowing skirt and Birkenstocks. She had a degree from Buff State and looked like an editorial cartoon of a disarmament activist.

"All the gals at Buff State have flowers in their hair and hair under their arms," Jane's mother said. She must have overheard this somewhere, and every time she said it, it was with a smug surprise, like she had just thought it up on the spot.

In the patchouli-and-jasmine-scented parlor room of Miss Amber's Queen Anne house on Elmwood Avenue, Mirela sat cross-legged on a mat amid a pile of toys: play-kitchen utensils, dolls, trucks, blocks.

"Does is?" Mirela asked, slapping at a truck. She didn't yet pick things up: she slapped at them, scrabbled and pawed at them, before trying to grab hold. In her unrehearsed and tactile way, she was sizing them up. "Does is?"

"That means *What is this?*" said Jane, sitting off to one side of the mat.

Miss Amber, in the lotus position, held up a hand. "Here, words can mean whatever Mirela wants them to mean," she said.

Mirela picked up the truck and smiled expectantly at Miss Amber.

"Now you've decided to pick that up," Miss Amber said. "What is that?"

"Does is?" Mirela asked.

"It's a truck, Mirela," Jane said, to a disapproving look from Miss Amber.

"What do *you* think it is, Mirela?" Miss Amber asked. "It can be anything that Mirela wants it to be."

"Tuck," Mirela said, smiling harder. She scrabbled at a baby doll. "Doe-ie," she said.

"A doll," Miss Amber said. "You wanted a doll, and now you found a doll."

Forty-five minutes and $150 later, Jane said to Miss Amber, "I'm sorry, but with all due respect, what is this meant to accomplish?"

"We're putting the child in the driver's seat," Miss Amber said, flipping her wavy auburn hair over both shoulders. "The child is empowered to make her own decisions. We are simply there to facilitate those decision-making processes. The goal is for the child to develop self-efficacy at the somatic level."

"I'm not sure that Mirela wants to be empowered to make decisions," Jane said. "I think Mirela just wants control."

"What is the difference?" Miss Amber asked. Mirela smiled over Miss Amber's shoulder.

"I mean that she wants control, but—control of what?" Jane shook her head, frustrated that she couldn't articulate herself. If she was presented with a pad of oversized white construction paper, Mirela would grab a crayon and scrawl upon every single page. Scribble-scribble-scribble *rip* scribble-scribble-scribble *rip*, through ten pages, twenty pages. She did this with seething focus, aimed not so much at claiming what was hers but rather at ensuring no one else could claim it. It was spite, Jane thought—a chip on Mirela's skinny shoulder. Yet Lauren used to do similar things as a toddler, and Jane had interpreted those acts as the opposite of destructive: a proof of self-assurance, manual dexterity, an announcement of the self.

"Once she had control, what would she do with it?" Jane asked. "She's practically still a toddler."

"Well, so many of these words are labels," Miss Amber was saying. "*Toddler, controlling*—when we over-rely on labels, rather than experiencing and observing a uniquely beautiful set of gifts and challenges, we're communicating to the child, and to ourselves, that there is something wrong with the child."

"There *is* something wrong," Jane said.

"*Wrong* is a word," Miss Amber said.

". . . Yes," Jane said.

"Think of a cup." Miss Amber held up her mug of tea. "What if instead of saying, 'This is a cup,' we said, 'This holds liquid'? Try the same substitution with Mirela. What if instead of asking, 'What is this child?' we ask instead, 'What does this child do? What does this child hold inside her?'"

"Does is?" Mirela asked, reaching for the mug.

"We can absolutely ask those questions," Jane said, "while also trying to find a diagnosis."

"Well, if we must use labels, then choose different ones," replied Miss Amber, holding the mug over her head. "What if we decided to label Mirela as an empowered child?"

"What do you think of that, Mirela?" Jane asked as she helped the girl with her coat. Mirela punched her in the stomach, and Jane did not react, except to ponder, for a split second, her lack of reaction. A breath-sucking impact to the gut was no longer, in the present scheme of things, a sufficiently novel impetus to merit recognition from Jane's psychological or physiological pathways.

"Sometimes a mismatch of temperaments simply calls for a change in communication styles," Miss Amber said, saluting Jane and Mirela with her mug of tea. "Until next week!"

The following week at Miss Amber's, Mirela stood up, and Miss

Amber said, "Now you've decided to stand up!" She sat down and Miss Amber said, "Now you've decided to sit down!" Mirela stood up and sat down, stood up and sat down, for the remainder of the allotted time, with Miss Amber narrating, their smiling faces locked in a feedback loop. Miss Amber wore a tiara of wildflowers.

"The same and the same and the same," Mirela admonished Miss Amber at the beginning of their third session. Then she smashed a green dump truck into the rug over and over until it splintered and flew into pieces, shards of plastic whirligigging in the air. As Miss Amber tried to intervene, Mirela screamed, "*I DE-SY-ID! I DE-SY-ID!*" She was about to crash a Fisher-Price barn through an oriel window when Jane caught her from behind and pulled her close, wrapping both arms around her as they both sat down on the parquet. Jane waited for the girl to wear herself out against her grip.

"Oddly enough," Jane gasped from the floor, pressing her chin against Mirela's collarbone to keep the girl from smacking her head against Jane's nose, "this eventually calms her down. Keeps her from hurting herself, too." Mirela arched her back and tipped them both backward.

Mirela was the child who touched the top of the hot stove once, and then again, and then turned up the heat on all the burners and climbed into the oven, and there was no pain or shock that could override the necessity of chaotic control, of being in control and having wrested that control away from her captor, the exaltation of *I DE-SY-ID!*

"I don't think you will find what you are looking for here," Miss Amber said to the writhing pile on the floor.

A WALKING CATATONIA sometimes took possession of Mirela in the late afternoon. Her no-Mirela face, her eyes cloudy and unseeing. Usually Jane tried to break the no-Mirela spell, despite the respite it could provide for everyone around Mirela, and

perhaps for Mirela herself. Jane spoke soft commands and entreat-
ies, cupped Mirela's chin lightly between her thumb and forefinger, tried to beam her eyes into Mirela's eyes. If Jane aimed that
beam correctly, it risked alighting the girl's fury. Or Mirela's eyes
would dart and dance away from the beam, the effort agitating
her, activating her motors of constant talk and constant movement.
Still, any Mirela was better than no-Mirela. There were many Mi-
relas, but no-Mirela was the only version of her in whom Jane saw
no hope. She was quiet without peace, cauls forming over her eyes.

Still, in the corner lot down the street from Miss Amber's house,
strapping the girl into her car seat, Jane was tempted to take icy
refuge inside no-Mirela. She could consent to the thought. *She is
tired. Let her be. She'll snap out of it. You don't have to do everything
all the time.* Jane stepped back from Mirela, forgetting the door
frame behind her, and as she stood up she knocked the top of her
head against it. She felt the stunned freedom in the pain—not an
ennobling ache you could pray thanks for, but real pain, the erasure
of any intellectual or emotional or physical sensation but the blow
itself and the response of her nerve fibers, the white flashes of light
popping just above her field of vision that a saint would take for a
sign, and then a notion Jane could somersault into: what if she hit
her head against the door frame again and again, what if she did
it enough times to knock herself unconscious, what if she split her
head open against the door and her brain was impaled on her skull
and she never woke up again and she just *made it all stop*, and she
turned the thought inside out and thought what if she could hit
Mirela, what if she allowed herself to do it once, just once, which
would of course allow her to do it again and again and what if she
never stopped until it all stopped, all of it, done, gone, over, and she
understood why Pat had never hit her, not even once.

THAT NIGHT, AFTER Mirela was in bed and the boys were
watching TV in the basement, Pat still at work, Lauren at a friend's

house—Paula, probably—Jane was shelving books in the den when a giant set of cartoon teeth swiped past her vision, a glancing blow, and her whole body surged with chemical overwhelm. She held still on the floor as panic coursed over her.

The Book of Teeth. One of a stack of little-kid books Pat had brought down from the attic for Mirela. A sweet gesture, for him to remember the books, to cull thoughtfully from a larger pile and bring them downstairs. *The Book of Teeth* had been one of Lauren's favorites when she was two, two and a half. One weekend afternoon, Pat had erupted over—the laundry? The bedsheets? Linens and detergent were somehow implicated. Jane locked herself and Lauren into Lauren's room, Pat shouting and throwing things elsewhere in the house, Jane quietly weeping, Lauren oddly calm. She toddled up to Jane with a smile and handed her a book like a tissue. It was a compendium of snouts, fangs, tusks, chompers, with pullout tabs that made the animals' jaws work up and down. Lauren sat in Jane's lap as they moved the tabs back and forth. The *snap-snap* of the shark's teeth. The *crunch-crunch* of the bear's jaw. Lauren turned around in Jane's lap and hugged her, patting Jane's shoulder.

"Book for Mommy make it better."

There was much that Jane could forgive Pat, but she could not forgive him this.

Now *The Book of Teeth* between her fingers beat an electric current through her. On all fours on the carpet, Jane pressed her head against the book's cover and waited until her heart slowed and her skin stopped prickling. When Pat's anger was over, there was always the memory of it to confront. The memory could contaminate anything, at any time: *The Book of Teeth*, photographs, songs, the children's toys. Her friendships, dead or saved. It grabbed hold of the things they and she loved best. It ripped up and desiccated those things, and turned them into sentimental lies.

A dinner party at the Samersons', early summer. Pat tripped over a step to their back deck, and as he recovered himself he looked back at Jane behind him, his features spasming. She turned away as if she hadn't seen—sympathy or humor made everything worse. If she identified herself as a witness to the crime the step had committed against Pat, then she was admitting her guilt—her complicity in the crime. She read the story in his head. She knew about the step and didn't warn him. He wouldn't say it out loud, but he thought it, and he *knew* it, and he would behave according to what he knew. What he knew *she* knew. She foresaw him tripping on the step. She'd built the step. She'd built and designed the whole deck for the Samersons and planned this party and finagled an invitation all to orchestrate this one humiliating stumble. Because that was the sort of person she was. Spiteful. Devious. And what kind of people were the Samersons, to cooperate in such a ruse?

"Your *friends*," he said. Spat it out, disgusted. *Friends* was an accusation. He accused her of *friends* a lot, even after she'd mostly stopped trying to make them. Respect Life was a bunch of *friends*. The venom of it was cryptically sexual—she was spreading herself around. She'd been around the block and the kindergarten classroom and the Samersons' deck.

Jane never had the Samersons over for dinner. She wrote them a thank-you note, brought them blueberry muffins she baked from scratch, but she didn't properly reciprocate their invitation. When PJ and Sean went to play with the Samersons' twin boys, Pat would say, just audibly, "Those goddamn people with the *deck*."

The dinner at the Samersons' happened back when Jane worried about appearances and niceties, about seeming rude or avoidant, about reciprocating dinners. She regarded this old self with benign condescension. It was a time before Mirela, when her husband didn't yet have anything to be angry with her about. It was before Jane herself had experienced cut points as Mirela's mother. One of her cut points came when she stopped hoping that people wouldn't think they were strange, and instead she started hoping that people thought they were very strange indeed, strange enough that they should be left alone.

Jane put *The Book of Teeth* back on the shelf, leaving a pile of other books on the den floor, and got to her feet. She walked past the downstairs bathroom and heard the *thump-thump-thump* of Mirela self-soothing. The panic coursed again—Mirela was in her bed, Mirela was asleep, the door was locked, had Mirela sleep-walked downstairs again? Then Jane realized the sound she heard was her husband, a man she once thought she knew, hitting his head against the wall tiles. He was home—Jane hadn't realized. And where was Lauren, exactly? Pat would know, and he would know if Lauren needed a ride back from somewhere. He knew more of these things, nowadays, even though he never seemed to be here. Or had Pat driven Lauren home, while Jane was wallowing in *The Book of Teeth*? She raised a loose fist to knock at the bathroom door, hesitated, and instead continued toward the stairs, the *thump-thump* trailing off behind her.

Their marriage was the ficus in the dining room that Jane was occasionally startled to discover was still alive. She would dump water on it, its leaves would go swollen with abject thanks, she'd resolve to pick up the right plant food from the nursery and add watering to the daily morning routine, and then weeks later she'd happen upon its almost-corpse once again. It would not die passively. For the ficus to die would demand a decision.

Jane climbed upstairs to check on Mirela, and lingered in the open doorway to Lauren's room instead. Not home. Jane didn't know the bands on the posters anymore. Lauren no longer kept her stuffed animals and dolls on her bed. Jane slid open the door of Lauren's closet and saw them in a jumble on a high shelf, her favorite purple bear's hind leg dangling.

Lauren would have slipped away anyway, she told herself. The boys, too. You lose them no matter what, everyone said it. Marie had been telling her since Lauren was born that if you lose them it means you've done everything right, you've prepared them to become independent in the world, and after all, she wasn't losing them solely for the usual prosaic adolescent reasons but also for the good cause of Mirela, the cause of saving a child. Jane slid the door shut and lay down on Lauren's unmade bed, fitting her own body to the imprint that Lauren's body had left. She buried her face in the quilt and the pillow.

She smelled smoke. She sat up and the image assembled itself: Lauren kneeling at the headboard of her bed, smoking cigarettes out the window, blowing through the screen. Jane opened the drawer of Lauren's bedside table and rummaged around toward the back. A pack of Marlboro Lights and a Bugs Bunny lighter. She laughed to herself. Next would be cloves, and after that, marijuana. Beer would sidle up soon enough, maybe after the cloves but before the pot.

She checked that the child safety latch was in place on the Bugs Bunny lighter and put it in her pocket. She paused over the cigarettes, then returned them to the back of the drawer and pushed it shut.

She should confront Lauren about the smoke smell, Jane thought as she made her way back downstairs, dropping the lighter into her purse hanging on the bannister. Or not *confront*—just talk. Make helpful observations. Before Mirela, Jane had found these sorts of semidisciplinary situations both easy and false. Jane's children regarded her less as a moral-philosophical authority and more as a faucet to be turned on, a car that went go, a refrigerator holding a bottle of orange juice. In her role as a utility that went largely unnoticed unless it was broke-down or temperamental, it was difficult for Jane to make her children happy, exactly, but if it was ever the case that the faucet didn't turn on or the car wouldn't go or the refrigerator was out of orange juice, then it was absolutely, definitionally Jane who had made her children unhappy. This state of affairs didn't particularly trouble her; the nice thing about being a light switch is that your day-to-day life is plain cause and effect. The connection between terminals is either open or it is closed. The children are upset, and here is why.

Cause and effect did not apply to Mirela. You could not extract remorse from her. She took a transactional satisfaction from her misbehavior, with all its rewards accruing to herself. Punishment could provoke her anger, but just as often, punishment seemed to be a source of repletion. Jane gave Mirela time-out after time-out before she realized that Mirela was misbehaving to get the time-outs—that she was hunting down her punishment because she wanted to be alone, but it wasn't safe for Jane to leave her alone, but refusing to leave her alone intensified Mirela's fury and thus the danger that she would cause herself or others harm, but it was increasingly the case that no one but Jane was willing to be alone with Mirela, or be with her at all.

Maybe what Mirela thought she wanted was an empty room. Blank and scrubbed. That room was where she went when she was no-Mirela. She met the warm smile of a familiar face as a mask, a trick played on her. She played the trick right back at first, to keep things balanced. She couldn't be fooled. She played the part of the bright, happy girl as long as she could, but in truth she lived in the dark, and she was perpetually outraged to be dragged from it, to be known, to be made not a stranger, to be *found out*.

Inside the blank scrubbed room, Jane could see the tall nurse in white. The counterfactual was always present with Mirela. The terror of the counterfactual used to lie in the image of Mirela in her crib, in that place, waiting for a year, and another and another, crying until she accepted that her cries would not be answered, while her family, an ocean away, puttered around ignoring her, Lauren on a stage or in a swimming pool, the hollering octopus that was the boys, Pat in the garage, Jane donkeying the groceries up Muegel Road. But now the nurse was beckoning Jane out of her own living room. Barbara Walters was blowing a kiss and saying, "Good night, dearest Jane." The nurse was switching off the TV, guiding Jane up the stairs, into the bath, into her bed. She'd been so tired, the night of *20/20*. She couldn't remember if she'd even taken a shower after cleaning up that poor man's shit.

Jane didn't always turn away from the nurse. Sometimes she closed her eyes and sank into the almost-scalding bath, the warm towel just out of the dryer—had the nurse taken care of the laundry?—the sheets susurrating against her body as she pressed her face to her pillow, the curtains drawn in the warm dark, the nurse sitting on the edge of the bed, smoothing Jane's hair, rubbing her back, singing a soft, wordless tune until she fell asleep. The uniform crackling and rustling like white noise, like the wind on the window, so starched it could snap. A branch scraping along the glass, the old leaves crumbling against it. Jane wakes up in a house where Sean still has a bedroom of his own upstairs, where Midnight doesn't live with the Schecks down the street, where pictures hang on the walls, where there aren't bars over the windows, where nobody locks the doors.

THERE WAS THE early childhood development center at UB, a one-way mirror reflecting and penetrating the playroom. Every playroom that Jane and Mirela visited had its standard chorus of toys: the stacking rings, the shopping cart, the rotary phone in primary colors, the cheerful croaking puppy-on-a-string. Each toy a standardized test, a multiple-choice bubble that a child filled in by the order in which she stacked the rings or by how lovingly she offered the clacking puppy a strip of plastic steak.

In this playroom, they met Delia, a graduate student whose research focused on emotional regulation. Jane liked Delia immediately. She spoke at low volume and high rapidity, she preferred observations over opinions, and she didn't interrupt. Her kind and sleepy demeanor, her hooded eyes, reminded Jane of Dr. Vine, how a gauze of exhaustion wrapped his evident quickness and sharpness in a cottony bundle.

"Have you ever heard of the strange situation?" Delia asked Jane.

"There are so many jokes I could make right now," Jane said. Mirela babbled like a schoolmarm at her own reflection.

"Ha, I believe it," Delia said. "It's an experiment. Dates back to the 1960s and '70s. What happens is—"

"No, wait, I remember," Jane said. The small wings of a memory opened and retreated along the top of her head; she squinted slightly as if to glimpse it flapping away toward the Clearfield Library. "I've read about this before."

"So in the strange situation, you put a mother and her child, who's around one year old, in a room with some toys. The kid crawls or toddles around, plays with stuff, looks back from time to time to see that Mom is still around, gets onto Mom's lap, gets down, wanders around some more, does his whole baby thing."

"Yes, yes, I remember this! Then Mom leaves for a while."

"Exactly. Maybe the baby cries while Mom is gone, maybe he's okay, maybe he's anxious. Doesn't matter all that much, because Mom comes back. The kid who was anxious or crying is happy to see her again."

"He finds comfort in her return," Jane said, nodding.

"Yup, and the kid who was fine when she was gone is also happy she's back. I'm oversimplifying, but those are basically the two outcomes you'd want to see: sad-then-happy, or fine-then-happier. Pretty neat. That's where you're seeing what we'd call secure attachment."

Mirela laughed and spun herself around in circles until she fell down. She got up again, spun, fell down laughing.

"But in the strange situation, sometimes you don't see secure attachment," Delia said.

"Sometimes you get a baby who's clinging to Mom from the get-go, whining, crying, not wanting to explore the playroom," Jane said .

"Yup, something like that. Then Mom leaves and the kid explodes. Just totally freaks out. When Mom returns to the room, everything should be okay again, right? But sometimes it's like Mom coming back makes the kid more resentful. She's darned if she does and darned if she doesn't. So that's another type. We call that anxious-avoidant."

Mirela spun and fell down and stayed where she was, on her back in a snow angel. She watched the ceiling, engrossed by a shadow-puppet show that only she could see. She softly sang along to the song she could hear them playing up there.

"There's a third type," Delia said. "This third type of kid doesn't explore the room and doesn't seem to care what Mom is up to. Mom is there, she leaves, she comes back—whatever. This type is what we call anxious-ambivalent, and in some ways, that's the worst-case scenario. When a baby just doesn't care."

"Is it possible to overanalyze it? It could be just that the baby is relaxed. Or having an off day."

Some children are never allowed even in earliest infancy just to lie back and float. They lose a great deal and may altogether miss the feeling that they themselves want to live. That was Winnicott.

"Sure, it's possible," Delia said with her sleepy smile. Jane liked her so much. "What it also might be telling us is that already, at just one year old, the baby has been conditioned *not* to care, not to place any bets on Mom coming back or his environment having something to offer him. He's not a dumb kid—he knows he's going to lose that bet because he's learned it through experiences of neglect or trauma, because he's been paying attention."

"He cries, nobody answers, so he takes that feedback and she— she uses it . . ." Jane trailed off.

Delia waited and nodded. "Yes. And that's the most challenging scenario, because the kid has been given information and he's acting on it in an intelligent and rational way, in what he thinks is a self-preserving way, and it's challenging to talk him out of what he's learned from his own experience."

"I wish we could go back in time and put Mirela in the strange situation," Jane said. "Although I think Mirela would be the one to leave the room."

"Could be," Delia said.

"If I'd found Mirela back when she was young enough for the strange situation," Jane said, "we probably wouldn't be here."

"All the same, I'm glad you're here now," Delia said.

"It's hard to think about—before—what could have been."

"No, of course."

"I try to avoid thinking about it. Because there's no——"

"I understand——"

"——no possibility of going back."

"It's a room that is shut. The past."

"It's over. The door is closed and locked. Why knock at that door when you know it won't open?"

"And so you concentrate on the now. That's healthy."

"I wish she could have a do-over," Jane said. "I wish I could give her that. I wish she could just start all over again."

"In all of your research, have you come across the Arden Attachment Center?" Delia asked. Jane shook her head. "I have some literature for you. It's a clinic that focuses on kids with attachment issues. They're in Colorado."

"Oh, I don't know about that—it's only been five months," Jane said. "Going on six. I started taking her to doctors almost as soon as she got home. I knew she'd need help adjusting. It just takes time."

"Right. The thing is, you don't have a lot of time," Delia said.

It wasn't a judgment or a warning; it was an empirical observation, a recitation of numbers, a result, a sum. How much time Mirela had lost plus how much time she was losing. Or multiplied by. Six months was one-sixth of her life. Eighty-three percent of Mirela's life was lost time and cut points.

They watched Mirela. Now she was lying tummy-down on the floor, legs kicking the air, tapping Mr. Potato Head's nose against his cheek, singing the tuneless little song to herself.

You would never know. There were moments when you would never know, and you could string enough of those moments together to add up to an hour, a day, a whole child's life.

WELCOME TO ARDEN: WE BUILD BONDS
THAT LAST FOREVER

Amid the peaceful splendor of the Colorado mountains, the Arden Attachment Center is a world-renowned sanctuary for families facing the challenge of attachment disorders. At Arden, your child will learn the language of love, trust, and human connection. And you, the caregiver, will be your child's most important teacher.

What Is Attachment?

Just as a child is taught to read and write, to swim or ride a bike, an infant is taught to love and communicate by receiving the attentions of his mother. Picking him up when he cries, feeding him when he is hungry, changing his diaper when it is wet, gazing into his eyes in loving attention: in these elemental interactions, the mother is helping her baby learn, through example, how to love and be loved. The cells of the baby's brain and body store those learning memories, which are activated when the child is touched or spoken to.

Who Is the Unattached Child?

Due to earlier experiences with severe neglect and abuse, the unattached child is alienated from all sense of safety and security. She is a stranger to a loving touch. In fact, she associates love with pain. Instability and trauma are the normal state of affairs for the unattached child, who seeks a grim solace in control.

At Arden, we know that love *can* conquer all. First, though, love must be taught. Love is a language the child will learn to speak fluently. For the child who was loved badly or not at all, there has to be a process of unlearning as well. At Arden, your child will find firm and gentle shepherds to lead her through this challenging but rewarding journey.

What Is the Unattached Child Thinking?

It's the universal question for the caregiver at her wits' end: *What is going through this kid's head?* But it's important to understand that the unattached child does have a rational belief system, taught to her through abuse and neglect. Her belief system has two main tenets: that she is not loved, and that she cannot trust others to provide for her needs. A loving, authoritative caregiver is a mortal threat to both of these beliefs. That is why she attempts to defy and disrupt the caregiver's efforts wherever possible. At Arden, we break down this defensive belief system, brick by brick, through evidence-based therapeutic interventions.

What Are the Responsibilities of the Unattached Child?

The child must unlearn her abuse by performing it.
The child must unlearn her rage by giving voice to it.
The child must unlearn her imprisonment by reentering it.

The unattached child was denied the opportunity to grow, explore, and become who she was meant to be. She feels a rational rage at this injustice, and that rage is complicated by the grief she feels for the lost birth mother. In short, she has been imprisoned by neglect, abuse, and unprocessed grief. The teams of caregivers at Arden can help her reclaim that freedom for herself through our special two-week therapeutic intensive. During this rigorous program, the unattached child is reborn into a world where once again she has no power, no autonomy, no control—but this time she is completely safe, in the arms of a caregiver who is teaching her unconditional love. At Arden, your child gets a second chance at her childhood—and so do you.

KEY CONCEPTS OF THE THERAPEUTIC INTENSIVE

1. Building trust.

2. Teaching love.

3. Valuing rage. Think of the unattached child's rage as a fever. A fever must be treated, but it also must be understood as a cleansing reaction to a bigger threat—a fire that the body sets to smoke out danger. Rage is a rational response to the grief and pain caused by neglect and abuse, and under the right circumstances, it, too, can be cleansing. In the safe, controlled environment provided at Arden, the

cathartic release of rage can break down the barriers the child has built against love and trust.

4. Reeducating the body. The body is a mosaic of cells. Those cells hold learning memories, and in each of those memories is a lesson, good or bad, about love, trust, and safety. The unattached child must, in a sense, unattach from her dream—or her nightmare—of the biological mother, and transfer her attachments to new caregivers. This is a physical process as much as it is a mental one.

Elements of the Therapeutic Intensive

BREAKING DOWN DEFENSES. The unattached child can be a citadel of deflection and controlling behavior. His defiance and disruptions may seem *out of* control, but in taking over his family's lives, his oppositional behavior is also a means for him to stay *in* control. The therapist's first task is to deconstruct those defenses through games, guided play, verbal correction, and other techniques that are therapeutically designed to throw the child off balance.

"BABY"-ING. Another step in dismantling the child's defenses is to guide her back to a state of infancy, where she feels both helpless and safe with a caregiver who is both all-powerful and nonthreatening. These techniques include swaddling, cuddling, cooing, and singing lullabies.

ROLE-PLAYING. The child is guided toward reimagining traumatic incidents in his early life, unearthing memories that lead to the cathartic release of rage and other emotions.

HOLDING THERAPY. Just as the infant must be protected from her own kick and startle reflexes through holding and swaddling, the unattached child can be shored up against her fear of touch and trust through holding therapy, where she again finds herself at once powerless and completely safe. During the two-week therapeutic intensive, holding therapy is the punctuation mark that ends a hard, fulfilling day of learning, unlearning, and relearning.

REBIRTHING. This profound event grows organically out of holding therapy. It re-creates the child's first and greatest embrace in the womb: where her mother's body holds her, safe and warm.

LAUREN

Paula liked to talk about how different boys kiss. The senior, captain of the lacrosse team, who did it like he was slurping soup. The sophomore on the Model UN team, who thrust his stiff long tongue in and out, like a dowsing rod, "like he could fuck with his mouth," she said. When Paula described kissing, it was like she wasn't one-half of the kiss. It was like the guys were sucking at the air or a mirror, and Paula was off to the side taking notes.

When she was having sex with a guy, Paula said, she would imagine him doing normal things—writing a term paper, standing in line at Mighty Taco. And sometimes when she saw a guy doing normal things, she would imagine him having sex. "But, like, it's *all* normal," Paula said to Lauren.

They were sitting across from each other at the big table in Tedquarters, sharing a bag of Doritos. "Why is it weird to have sex in front of people but it's not weird to eat in front of people?" Paula asked. "They're both totally regular, boring, gross sticky things that everybody does."

"Not everybody," Lauren said sheepishly.

"I mean, *eventually*," Paula said.

Kurt Cobain was in one of Paula's magazines with his girlfriend. He had cherry-red hair and an itchy blue cardigan; his girlfriend was kissing him in profile, her lemony hair waxy and curling like a doll's. "She's *ugly*," Paula said, and she was so happy about it. Paula loved Kurt Cobain, lately seemed to think about Kurt Cobain all the time, and could work Kurt Cobain into any conversation, much like Mom could with Father Steve. "I think Kurt goes out with her just to piss people off," Paula said.

"Or maybe he goes out with her because they like each other," Lauren said.

"I bet she weighs more than Kurt does," Paula said. "Did you know he's so skinny he wears long underwear under his clothes? To stay warm and pad himself out."

Lauren had started to wonder whether Paula made up all her stories of sex with boys, or at least some of them; if she placed herself in their arms the same way she placed herself inside Kurt Cobain's head as he picked out his clothes in the morning.

"Is Kurt Cobain an Asshole, a Creep, or an Unspeakable?" Lauren asked. Paula and Lauren had categories for all boys and men, famous or not. Assholes were usually extroverts, Creeps were introverts, and Unspeakables were unable to be fully comprehended in their assholishness, their creepiness, and/or their dreamy perfection. Stitch Rosen was a Creep. Andy Figueroa was an Asshole, and so was Rajiv Datt, who was Stitch's best friend. Assholes and Creeps tended to pair off with one another. Brendan Dougherty, a quiet junior, with his pale-blue eyes and choirboy singing voice, was an Unspeakable.

"Kurt Cobain is Unspeakable with Asshole tendencies," Paula replied, swallowing the word *asshole* as Mr. Smith entered the room. Instead of heading toward his desk, Mr. Smith sat down at the big table, next to Lauren and across from Paula. Their elbows touched for a moment.

"I would have guessed Unspeakable leaning toward Creep," Lauren said.

"He's an A-hole who wants you to think he's a Creep," Paula said.

"Wouldn't you have to be a little bit of an A-hole to be the lead singer of a band?" Lauren said. She rustled the bag of Doritos. "You need a lot of confidence."

"He has a stomach condition," Paula said. "Maybe it's because all the attention stresses him out. Maybe he's a Creep after all."

"I think when you're a rock star, *I have a stomach condition* really means *I do a lot of drugs*," Lauren said.

"You can cut out the middleman and just say *I am a rock star* really means *I do a lot of drugs*," said Mr. Smith, pulling a sheaf of papers from his satchel. "It's a good illustration of the transitive property."

Paula thought that Mr. Smith was an Asshole, and Lauren thought he was a Creep. He was the only teacher they disagreed about.

"Maybe Kurt Cobain does a lot of drugs *because* he has a stomach condition," Paula said. "But I hope they're not doing drugs, because they want to have a baby. They say so in this interview."

"If they can get heroin, they can get birth control," Lauren said.

"That's why they call it a drugstore!" said Mr. Smith, making a flourish with his red pen.

"My mom put me on birth control as soon as I got my period," Paula said, darting a glance at Mr. Smith, who sighed loudly and started to murmur aloud as he read his papers.

"Me too," Lauren said, without knowing why.

"But isn't your mother super Catholic?" Paula asked. Paula knew the answer. She was saying this just for Mr. Smith's benefit.

"Your mom goes to church, too," Lauren said.

"But she doesn't make *me* go."

"My mom doesn't make me go to church, either," Lauren said. "Not anymore."

Paula stared at Lauren so long that Lauren looked away. "People are complicated," Lauren said, rustling the Doritos bag again.

"I have to go to studio art now," Paula said, standing up. "What a very interesting conversation this has turned out to be, Lauren."

Lauren pretended to highlight some important passages about the Treaty of Versailles in her Global Studies textbook as Paula walked out.

"Will we see you at tryouts for the spring musical soon?" Mr. Smith asked, not looking up from the papers he was grading. Their elbows touched again.

"Maybe, I don't know," Lauren said. She thought about moving to where Paula had been sitting, across the table from Mr. Smith, but she wondered if he would be offended by this, or if the doubtful sensation of inappropriateness hanging over them would only become concrete if she acknowledged it by moving, or if he was waiting for her to move and would become frustrated that she didn't, and as these thoughts talked past one another and canceled one another out, she remained still and glazed in her chair, as if she weren't thinking at all.

"What could be *Uhh, maybe, I dunno* about it?" he said.

"What's the play again?" asked Lauren, who knew that Bethune's 1992 spring musical would be *Grease*, according to the posters advertising the upcoming auditions that hung all over school. Paula had designed the posters herself in the studio art printmaking shop while Lauren sat beside her studying for an algebra test.

"It's Gilbert and Sullivan's comic opera *The Mikado*," Mr. Smith said, turning a page.

"What?" Lauren asked. Mr. Smith always had these references ready to go, like he had a filing cabinet full of them and he chose five at random each morning to spread like bread crumbs through the halls and classrooms of Bethune.

"Lauren," he said as he made a note in the margin of the essay he was grading, "you know that I know that you know what the play is, and your too-cool-for-school act is ironically quite befitting of Jim Jacobs and Warren Casey's classic musical in its portrayal of teenage rebellion as manifested largely in a wholesale rejection of the state academic apparatus."

"Uh-huh."

He was so smart, and she would be as smart as him one day, but she wasn't yet. He'd had more time to learn the words, the names. All she caught was *too cool* and *act* and *rejection*. Or *rebellion*? But she wasn't acting cool, and she hadn't rejected anything. She was just sitting here. What was she doing that she didn't know about?

"The pose you strike, of the disaffected, eye-rolling adolescent alienated from the opportunities extended to her, and to a great extent alienated from speech and language itself, is spot-on," he said.

Mom hated it when Lauren rolled her eyes. She said that nobody wanted to be around that kind of negative energy. That was the threat—that everybody was looking at Lauren and nobody liked what they saw.

"Too good to talk to me now, huh?" Mr. Smith asked.

Lauren breathed faster. His joking tone was a warning. She needed to explain herself, to say something he couldn't criticize or argue with.

"I need to be home more, these days," she said. "Might not have time for the musical. I'm sorry. I—I've told you about it—my situation at home."

Mr. Smith frowned at his papers. "Don't I remember you trying to get out of the fall play, too? You don't mean it."

"No, I mean it. I need to be around more to help my mom with my adopted sister."

"And how is that going?" Mr. Smith asked, putting down his pen and turning to look at her. "You've said that it's been challenging."

"It's good. She's good. It's just a lot of work for my mom."

"Your adopted sister has tantrums?" He was turned ninety degrees in his seat to face her fully, Lauren staring straight ahead.

She shrugged. "Probably like any kid. I don't know. It's not such a big deal, I guess."

"I thought you were in the middle of explaining to me why it *is* such a big deal."

"I don't know."

"What does your mom do when your adopted sister has a tantrum?"

"Different stuff. She just deals with it."

"You are incredibly difficult to talk to."

A pumping in her throat, in her ears, rings of sound, gold rings, rattling, visible.

"Just deals with it? How?" he demanded.

"Sometimes she holds her tight." A metallic ringing at the front of her head, behind her eyes. Gold spotting her vision, like she'd won a prize.

"How do you mean?"

"She just tries to hold her close. My mom puts her on her lap, turned away, so they're both facing the same direction, and she wraps her arms around her from the back, like this"—Lauren wrapped her arms around an invisible child on her lap—"to stop her moving around so much, to calm her down. She wraps her, like swaddling a baby, and she rocks her like a baby, too. Sometimes Mirela hums, like she is singing to herself. And they just hold and rock like that until she calms down."

"Your mother learned that from a licensed professional?"

Lauren suspected she had said too much, or said the wrong thing, but she didn't know what. It was hard to hear her thoughts over the ringing, to see her thoughts through the gold spots. "I think it's just instinct. She calls it the squeeze."

"Why is your voice shaking?"

"I'm nervous."

"You're nervous? Because you're concerned about your adopted sister?"

"I don't know."

"It's okay." Mr. Smith was rubbing her back. Mom used to do that. Blood pounding in her ears. The gold spots turning black at the center, the black blooming, the gold a dying outline. But she also had a warm pooling feeling in her chest, a pleasurable sadness.

"My mom said when I was two I had an ear infection," Lauren said, "and the medicine I had to take gave me crazy tantrums, and she would hold me like that and I would calm down." There was a creak in her voice, like after sobbing or like when PJ and Sean would do frog-monster voice, like Lauren was fake-crying in an

All My Sons rehearsal. "It was bright pink medicine. I liked how it tasted. I don't remember that, though—it's what my mom told me. I think she just goes on what feels right."

"What feels right." He was holding her hand with one hand and rubbing her back with the other. He played variations: rubbing circles and then up and down, tracing ticklish patterns and pushing with the heel of his hand.

"Yeah, it's just—sometimes my adopted sister is out of control and she needs to calm down and be in a safe place." She tried to talk in a higher voice, like she could put her voice out of reach of the creak, but she couldn't. She couldn't stop faking.

"That sounds hard," he said, his hand low on her back.

"It's okay."

"Okay. So you can't try out for the spring musical because your mother is taking care of your sister? And you can help her, somehow? Is that right?"

His rubbing hand traced an oval near the base of her spine, just under the waist of her jeans.

"Well, there's also . . . to be honest, I can't sing," Lauren said, shrugging again.

"That's just another put-on," he said, squeezing her hand.

"No, I can't."

"Ah, come on," he said, leaning in so their heads were pressed together, "try me." He had coffee breath.

"No, it's true," she said. "That's why I used to play the flute, to get out of singing."

"And how was your *embouchure*?"

Lauren blushed. The *bouch* puffed against her ear. A cloud of coffee grains in her eyes, in her nose. She was dizzy. She squeezed his hand back and pulled away.

"Maybe I can help Paula out with the props, if she does that again," she said, standing up.

"Mm-hm. Just be aware," Mr. Smith said, taking his pen and looking down at his papers again, "that I'm onto you."

Her stomach flipped. "What do you mean?"

"That business from before about the birth control," he said, licking a finger and turning another page. "You and I and Paula all know very well that's yet another put-on. You're just full of put-ons today."

"I don't know what you mean," Lauren said.

"Lauren, give me a break."

"I wasn't putting anybody on."

"There is no way," Mr. Smith said, head down, voice dropping although they were alone in the room, tapping his pen on the desk, "that your very proper, very Catholic mother would do that."

"She's only Catholic for herself," Lauren said. "She doesn't force anything on me. I'm not even getting confirmed."

It was odd to be standing over him like this, talking down at him. He was the one who'd started it.

"These are *my* people you're talking about, too, you know," he said.

"It's none of your business," Lauren said.

"You *made* it my business by bringing it up," Mr. Smith said, looking up but not in her eyes, "and as your teacher, it is certainly my business if a student is *lying* to me."

Her body buzzed with the old thrill, a tingle that traveled up her neck and spidered across the top of her scalp. She stood at the gate between telling a lie and making it true.

"I'm not lying," Lauren said. "How much do you want to bet?"

"Wagers of any kind are prohibited on school property," Mr. Smith said. "Did we learn nothing from the strip poker controversy of last fall?"

"I can prove to you that I'm not lying."

Mr. Smith put his hands up. "This conversation needs to end here."

"Why?" Lauren asked.

"Because it's not *appropriate*," he said with an air of finality, twirling his pen. "You are being *inappropriate*."

"You mean it's inappropriate for me to lie to you, which I am not doing? Or it's inappropriate for us to be talking about birth control pills?"

"Stitch, Rajiv, how nice to see you both," Mr. Smith said as the boys cartwheeled into the room.

THESE DAYS STITCH and Rajiv moved around Bethune by means of cartwheels and pogo jumps and froggy hops and single axels, thanks to their shared interest in the Red Hot Chili Peppers and the women's figure skating program in the Albertville Winter Olympics. Sometimes, in mid-conversation, Stitch set his mouth in a perfect line and began whipping his head around in the manner of the band's jumping-bean bass player, then he would pick up the thread of the conversation he was in as if nothing had happened, and no one commented or criticized him, just as no teachers told him off for *boing-boing*ing in a zigzag down the passageway between the yearbook office and the math department, slashing at his air guitar, screwing up his eyes and working his lips in a rubbery ecstasy.

"What a little punk-ass bitch," Rajiv was saying.

"Rajiv has a case of the Mondays," Mr. Smith said in an exaggerated pouting voice, and everyone cringed.

Rajiv was upset about the Red Hot Chili Peppers' appearance on *Saturday Night Live* that weekend. Lauren had watched it at Paula's, flopped next to Paula on her bed. Lauren hated that band but didn't say so, because Stitch and Rajiv loved them. Stitch and Rajiv talked a lot about the band's "musicianship" and their "influences," which Lauren knew nothing about. She did know that all their songs were about fucking—they wore barely any clothes onstage or in their videos, probably because they wanted to be ready at any time to do all the fucking they sang about—and even the songs that weren't about fucking seemed to be them trying to prove they could write a song that wasn't about fucking, like the cheesy ballad that Stitch and Rajiv would yell-sing down the hallways. They were big dumb naked red-faced fuck machines, except for the guitar player. John. John was the one. Sad brown eyes, ridiculous cheekbones. Paula had a picture of John smoking an emotional cigarette taped to the headboard of her bed. In the video for the cheesy ballad, John wore a Kurt Cobain outfit, cardigan and baggy grandpa trousers and a knit hat with a pom-pom on top, and maybe the outfit was like an upside-down distress flag to show everyone that John was in the wrong band and he needed out, and the outfit would look stupid on anyone else, but on John it looked cool, the same way whatever Stitch did was cool because it was Stitch who was doing it. On *Saturday Night Live*, John didn't wear a shirt on the first song, but it was more like he had forgotten to wear a shirt, or he was too sad to put on a shirt, or like the lead singer had ripped off John's shirt to force him to fake being the rebel fuck machine he so clearly was not. John hunched over his guitar on the far side of the stage, looking cold and hungry, doing the bare minimum. Falling asleep on his feet like a horse.

"John is so depressed," Paula said. "He can't handle the fame." Paula talked about all her rock stars like this, like they were her friends who confided in her, but in cryptographs through the pages of *Kerrang!* and *Spin*, and now she was gossiping about her famous pals behind their backs. She talked about Kurt Cobain's mysterious stomach condition like she was his personal physician.

John did look depressed up there on the *Saturday Night Live* stage, but pointedly so, focused and industrious in his depression, like he was studying for the depression SATs, and the lead singer was so infuriated with him by the end of the first song that he kicked John right in the ass—flung himself to the ground and spun around on his back and brought his knee to his chest and punched his foot forward and *awp!* It was like something PJ would do to Sean, except then Sean would have sat on PJ's face and farted in vengeance. John just took it. Lauren and Paula looked at each other to confirm that the kick had really happened. Paula was taping the show, and when it went to commercial she stopped and rewound the tape so they could examine the kick, frame by wobbly frame. When the band came out for their second song, the cheesy ballad, John had put on his Kurt Cobain outfit and he was playing the familiar notes of the song's introduction but in the wrong order, backward, slowed down, bent, in a different scale, or de-tuned, his arpeggios a vortex, a drain that his bandmates were circling, and as the song reached what should have been its apex and John, poor dear scrawny gorgeous kicked-in-the-ass John, stepped up to the mic to sing the climactic chorus that was also the title of the big hit cheesy ballad, he screwed up his face and instead of singing the words, he went, "*WOOOOOOO!*"

Paula burst out laughing.

Again, higher-pitched this time. "*WOOOOOOOOOOOOOO!*"

John sounded like a girl, like a fan. Paula flung herself back on her bed and bicycled her legs in the air for joy and laughed some more.

"Why did he do that?" Lauren asked Paula, but she knew why. No one knew how much power John had until he decided to use it to say no, to reject what was happening and create something anarchic and better. He said no without saying it. It was startling and childish, and that's why it was beautiful. At the end of the song, the lead singer glared at John like he was a swiveling head in middle school, but it didn't matter. It was done. They'd been in a war and the war was over and the big dumb fuck machine had lost and John had won.

"John is so lovely," Lauren said, and Paula *WOOOOO*ed in agreement.

"It's so unfair to the rest of the band," Rajiv was saying in Tedquarters now. "What an asshole."

"And what a choice of insult, Rajiv!" Mr. Smith said.

"But we'll always remember that he did that," Lauren said. "Would we be talking about them right now if John had just shown up and played like normal?"

"Like you know anything about music," Rajiv said. "Name *one* song of theirs that isn't on the new record." Stitch stopped-dropped-and-rolled to a spot just behind Rajiv, drew his knee to his chest, and extended his leg until his foot pressed on Rajiv's backside.

"I just think it's cool that he took a risk and did something crazy that we would all remember," Lauren said. "I bet he was scared."

"Answer me—name *one* song," Rajiv said, shimmying his ass against Stitch's heel. Lauren was always in the witness box when Rajiv got started on music.

She looked at Stitch on the carpet, his foot grinding into Rajiv's backside. Stitch screwed up his face and hit the note exactly as Lauren could hear it in her head: "*WOOOOOOOOOOOOO!*"

The tape that Stitch had given her the night of *The Man in the Moon* was a copy of *Gish*, by the Smashing Pumpkins. She liked how the music on *Gish* sounded literally like metal, as if someone had translated into music the sound of metallurgic processes that she was vaguely aware of through factory field trips and reading *Johnny Tremaine* in eighth grade. Casting, forging, extrusions. A gleaming sound that hinted at a gruesome suffering beneath it, like Johnny Tremaine's mangled hand were at the mixing board. But the singer was trying too hard to be hard, nasal and sneering, like he was mocking the listener for her poor judgment in listening to him, or for thinking she was good enough to listen to him. She could imagine Stitch singing the songs instead.

After *Gish*, Stitch gave her a cassette with *Nevermind* by Nirvana on one side and their other record, *Bleach*, on the other. All the songs written in pencil, each word individually underlined. Lauren had listened to *Gish* and *Bleach* enough to be able to speak with Stitch about them in a knowledgeable way, but *Nevermind* was the one she listened to over and over. Everyone was listening to *Nevermind*. Danielle Sheridan had a Nirvana T-shirt, and Rajiv gave her endless shit about it. For Lauren, *Nevermind* offered freedom in an enclosed space. The space could be Abby's car on the

way to Delaware Park or to the record stores and cafés on Elmwood
Avenue, or the space could be the width of two headphones on the
days when Lauren took the bus to school. Or at night, to drown out
Mirela screaming.

"I don't really pay attention to lyrics," Stitch said, which struck
Lauren as a radical idea. "I pay attention to production." Stitch was
interested in how a sound was constructed, compressed, how it
scrambled the air around it. He wasn't interested in words because
they didn't mean anything without the sound—an isolated lyric
couldn't bear to stand all on its own. There was a song on *Nevermind*, "On a Plain," about not having words and not making sense.
It made fun of itself for trying to have a message. Stitch had read
that Kurt Cobain just dashed off the lyrics right before he recorded
himself singing them. It was strange to be so careless about words
that millions of people would hear and think about. But the emotions in the song were clear: restlessness, irritation, but also humor and not taking yourself seriously. The song was about caring
about not caring. It had the feeling of marking time just before
something big was going to happen. In class, Mr. Smith called this
"liminal space," and told the students to watch out in their reading for characters having important conversations on thresholds or
staircases or through the windows of trains departing the station,
one person on the train and the other left behind on the platform.

Kurt Cobain liked R.E.M., who had a big embarrassing hit record out when Lauren was in eighth grade, but Stitch said they had
a lot of older records that were okay to listen to. He said *Reckoning*
was the best R.E.M. record because the band wrote it very fast and
didn't have much time to think about it. A lot of second records
were like that, he said—*Nevermind* was a second record.

That night, Lauren lay in bed listening to the tape of *Reckoning* that Stitch had made for her. Mirela was asleep, so Lauren
could listen to the music chiming out of the small speakers on the
tape deck, nothing to drown out. The most unfinished song on
Reckoning was "Second Guessing," because the entire chorus was

"Uh-oh-oh, here we are," over and over again. The song was stupid in a Smashing Pumpkins way, like it was daring you to become bored and frustrated with it, but it also made Lauren think of Kurt Cobain saying "Here we are now," like he was in liminal space, like party guests standing in the doorway announcing themselves, bringing big expectations that they were expecting to be disappointed. Lauren imagined everyone she liked standing in this doorway, singing along with Nirvana or R.E.M. or the Pixies: Abby, Deepa, Stitch, even Claire. The only friend she couldn't see there was Paula.

The phone rang, and Lauren knew it was Paula, like she was calling to ask why she wasn't included in the doorway, and Lauren yelled, "I got it!"—remembering Mirela too late, hoping she wouldn't wake up—and grabbed the receiver. "Hello?"

A click, and someone lightly breathing. "Hello?" a voice asked, and it took Lauren a moment to place it.

"Hello? Who is this?" Lauren asked.

"This is—wait, you called me," the voice said.

"No, I didn't."

"I'm confused. Hello."

"Stitch? Is that you?" Lauren asked.

"Yeah. This is weird. Uh, who is this?"

"This is Lauren."

A crush call. They were back in middle school.

"I don't get it—what happened?" Stitch asked. He sounded lost but so close, inside her head. Like there were doors opening inside her and he was walking through them, not knowing where he was. For the second time that day, Lauren felt the old thrill. She wanted to play—she hadn't realized how much she missed this.

"What happened is that you called me," she said lightly, like she was the one in charge of the joke.

"I didn't—this is crazy," Stitch said.

"It's okay," Lauren said. "If you've changed your mind about talking, that's fine."

"What?"

"Thanks for calling, Stitch," she said.

"Wait—"

Lauren hung up the phone and sputtered a laugh like someone was watching her. She started to pick up the phone again to call around, try to figure out who had done it—but no, on second thought, better not to seem interested in a kiddie prank.

She switched off the lamp on her bedside table, and then she was alone in the dark with *Reckoning*. There were songs on *Reckoning* that felt ancient and bottomlessly sad, a sadness as old as a riverbed. Listening to some of the songs made her imagine sitting on the banks of a creek where a classmate had drowned—not a best friend, maybe someone you knew was nice and said "Hi" to and had always meant to get to know better, and now you never could.

She wouldn't tell Stitch that sometimes she put on Crowded House at night as she fell asleep, because Crowded House wasn't the type of band he would think was okay to listen to. They were too old and sweet, too nerdy. But the harmonies and the organ, the chimes of the guitars, created the same warm pooling feeling in her chest that she felt listening to *Reckoning* or in Tedquarters or at the sleepover at Abby's: the pleasurable sadness, like the lush sadness of autumn leaves, the sense in autumn that everything was full with loss and longing, with memories so beautiful that they couldn't be spoken before they were washed away with winter's thaw, and the spring would begin unaware of all that had been lost. These sentiments were too embarrassing to be put into words, too melty and mushy to be pounded into shape. She probably couldn't tell anyone about them. They could only travel through chord progressions, vibrations through hollow chambers, compressed air through pipes. They were secrets and needed to be enjoyed in secret, like the nighttime car trips she used to take with Mom. The best and realest parts of life were unspoken, or unable to be spoken, the things that no one would tell you about—you had to teach yourself the language alone, and it had no words. You had to be in the right place at the right time, and paying attention. You had to be with the right people in the right doorway.

Crowded House had a new song called "Fall at Your Feet," and to Lauren it naturally paired with Billy Bragg's song "Trust," because both songs had lines about a man being inside a woman. Weirdly, in the Billy Bragg song, the singer—a man—was singing from the perspective of the woman, and on top of that, she was pregnant. "He's already been inside me," Billy Bragg sang. So much of the character of his voice was located in the damp thrusting of his lips. The voice, the words, and Billy Bragg's adenoids pressed against her wet and close, a squeaking-squishing that Lauren found almost unbearable and that she kept rewinding and listening to, squirming, because it was so strange and obscene and she wanted to understand it.

"I feel like I'm moving inside her," the wimpy nice guy from Crowded House sang in "Fall at Your Feet." She squirmed at this, too. He *feels* like it? Or was he *doing* it? *That* nerdy little noodle of a guy? What would it feel like? How would he know?

She thought about Mr. Smith. She felt his hand on her back from the afternoon. She'd been trying not to think about it. She put her hand between her legs so it could all overcome her and she could go to sleep. She thought about what he was like when he was alone, or alone with his girlfriend, if he had one—Paula had asked him if he did, and he'd shaken his head vehemently and said "No, *no*," in a manner that left ambiguous whether he was denying having a girlfriend or denying Paula's right to ask the question, and certainly left no space for clarification. During the school day, he could use up all his jokes and puns and sarcasm, alternate them as offense and defense as he dealt with all those dumb kids like Rajiv and Andy Figueroa, and by the time he came home he would be drained of anything that wasn't serious and compassionate and *ardent*. That was a word Lauren had learned from him, *ardent*: overcome with admiration, loyalty, and passion for the one you love. Stunned by her. When he was alone and only one other person in the world was looking—a person that hadn't been foisted on him but the one he wanted—that's when you could see who he really was.

"WHERE'S JAMIE LEE?" PJ asked as he and Sean piled into the back of the dragon wagon. Mirela's car seat was empty and Lauren was in the front passenger seat. Sean and PJ's latest nickname for Mirela was Jamie Lee, after the actress who screamed through the old horror movies they taped off HBO.

"Where's who?" Mom asked.

"Jamie Lee is PJ's special name for his binky," Sean said. "Where's your binky, PJ?"

"Oh, I remember, I left it *up your butt*," PJ replied as they punched each other in the arms, laughing at how much it hurt. Throwing their heads back, thrilled with the pain.

Mom turned up the car radio over PJ and Sean chanting, "Kill! Kill! Kill!", which was a key line from a Jamie Lee movie called *Prom Night*. A woman on a call-in show was talking through her nose, her voice echoing behind her on her own radio that she'd forgotten to turn down. "I'm not pro-abortion, I'm pro-life," the woman was saying. "I think abortion is wrong. I want to be clear about that. But what is also wrong is these out-of-towners coming in here telling us what to—"

Mom turned off the radio.

Lauren flipped it on again.

"—when this is about overwhelming our local police, overrunning our local court system, spending taxpayers' money to—"

"Even the people on your side aren't on your side," Lauren said.

"Don't be smart," Mom said. "It's not just out-of-towners who will be participating in the protests. Is Father Steve an out-of-towner?"

"Yes, he is!" Lauren said. "He just came to our church a couple months ago, and you act like you've been best friends forever."

"Well, wherever they're from—good people can disagree. I want to listen to all sides."

"That's why Mom turned off the radio!" PJ said from the back seat. "So she could listen to all sides!"

"The *mayor* invited them, after all," Mom said. "It's not a crazy fringe thing."

"A federal judge has ruled we have to keep a minimum of one hundred and fifty feet from the clinic doors," a voice on the radio said. "But it is our constitutional right under the First Amendment to provide sidewalk counseling to—"

"This is not primarily a free-speech issue," another voice interrupted.

"Is that what you do? Sidewalk counseling?" Lauren asked.

"Okay, well, *that*—that *is* an out-of-towner thing," Mom said. "They try to talk the patients out of what they're doing. I—we don't do that, in our group."

"Whatever it is you're doing," Lauren said, "please, seriously, Mom, don't do anything to embarrass me."

"We're not doing anything to embarrass you," Jane said. "We are doing it to save children. None of this is about *you*, Lauren."

"I'm doing this to embarrass you, Lauren," PJ said, and blew an enormous fart between the heels of his hands.

"No, it needs to sound wetter than that to really embarrass me," Lauren said. "Try it in the crook of your arm." Lauren, PJ, and Sean blew farts into the crooks of their arms for the remainder of the radio segment.

"You still haven't told us where Mirela is," Lauren said to Mom as the station switched to the weather report.

"Dad took her long enough for me to pick you guys up and drive you around to all your stuff, which is my absolute favorite thing to do when I'm not driving Mirela around to all her stuff," Mom said.

"Mom, Mirela thinks there's a ghost who lives in the trunk of the car," PJ said.

"She yells and points her finger at the washing machine when it's turned on," Sean said.

"And she tries to go to sleep in it when it's turned off," PJ said.

"She puts my shoes in the refrigerator," Sean said.

"When it rains she says it's her birthday," PJ said, and goose bumps came up on Lauren's arms.

"When she goes up the stairs she holds on to the bannister like somebody's trying to push her off, and she gets angry at them, but there's nobody there," Sean said.

"When she goes down the stairs she just *lies down*," PJ said.

"She gets upset if she has to wash her hands, but she also gets upset if her hands are dirty," Sean said.

"She pooped in the bathtub and washed her hands in the toilet," PJ said.

"She thinks my bike is alive," Sean said.

Mom turned the dragon wagon onto the driveway of Paula's house, and Lauren got out without saying goodbye. She heard Sean and PJ pummeling each other trying to claim the front seat as she approached the front door, tapped on the screen, opened the door halfway to pop her head through. "Hello?" she called. "Mrs. Brunt?"

Paula's mom was inches away, sitting on the couch in her nurse's scrubs, watching *Oprah*. "Hey, honey," she said dreamily. "It's nice to see you. Paula isn't home yet—she's at a meeting, I think? A club?"

"Yearbook," Lauren said, smiling.

"Do you want to wait for her here?"

"If that's okay?" Lauren asked.

"Sure, honey. Are you hungry? Do you want a sandwich or something?"

"No, thank you, Mrs. Brunt."

Lauren shut the front door behind her with elaborate care and walked up the wooden steps to the second floor of Paula's house. Lauren closed the door of the upstairs bathroom, turned on the taps, knelt down, and opened the bottom drawer beneath the sink. There, inside a shoebox-sized plastic tub, were rows and rows of small rectangular boxes. Lauren peeled open the seal on one box. In it were six trays, each as thin as a pack of matches and sealed with gold foil. She took out a tray, which held twenty-eight tiny pills, each packed beneath its own clear dome. Iridescent opals retrieved one by one from the bottom of the ocean. Lauren peeled the foil back. A pill popped into the palm of her hand. She slipped the single pill under her tongue, then took it out and put it into her jeans pocket instead.

Lauren slipped the tray back inside the box and the box inside her backpack. She arranged the boxes remaining in the plastic tub so that there were no conspicuous gaps between them. She slowly closed the drawer, biting down on her lip and shutting her eyes as the wheels on the rail squeaked into place. She hoped that the running tap masked the noise. She flushed the toilet, counted to three, switched off the tap, and opened the door. She was alone.

She shouldered her backpack and went into Paula's bedroom. The ceilings on the top floor of Paula's house were too low; more than once Lauren had bumped her head on their sloping sides. The skirting boards had been torn from Paula's bedroom walls. A crack in the ceiling snaked down the wall and behind a 10,000 Maniacs poster. Lauren sat down on the edge of Paula's bed. It was big enough for both of them. Flannel sheets, periwinkles on white, the same as on a nightgown Mom used to wear. The sheets were musty, dank like the air in the room. "Like you own the place" was something her father said to Lauren and her brothers when they were messy or rude or loud or taking up too much space for his liking, but Lauren did, in fact, act like she owned Paula's place, coming and going when she pleased, eating the Brunts' food, using their shampoo and electricity, leaving stray hairs and motes of skin and oil on their bedsheets for Paula's mother to launder. Drool on her pillowcases, probably. She kept a toothbrush in the bathroom that Paula shared with her brother, a change of clothes on one shelf in Paula's closet.

Paula and Lauren moved about freely with each other, as if they were alone and unseen, unacquainted with shame or inhibition. They got changed in front of each other, peed in front of each other, reported to each other in forensic detail about their periods and shits. They admitted to each other that they made themselves come although they didn't tell each other what they thought about when they did it—that was a boundary. And Lauren didn't do it in Paula's room, only in the bathroom with the door locked. Another boundary. The other night they'd taken off their underpants, squatted over compact mirrors, and described to each other what they saw, mixing floral anatomy with the raw ruddy language of the butcher's shop. The reflection was objectively frightening: marsupial pouch, hungry eyeless mouth—if you pulled back the lips you could see if its teeth were coming in. The dark hair thin and flat as Mr. Koslowski's comb-over. She tranquilly observed the thought that even Mr. Koslowski, who was married and had kids, had had his head between somebody's legs at some point, perhaps even recently. You reached a certain age and that became part of your life, somehow.

When Paula came home from yearbook, Lauren was going to practice her number for tomorrow's spring musical auditions. A silly old show tune that stuck in her head from the days when she took piano lessons. Lauren had sung it to the tiles of the shower that morning as PJ and Sean barked and banged outside the bathroom door. She sang the song to herself as she sat on Paula's bed, tracing her sock along the floorboards. Downstairs, the television droned. Lauren would know that she sang her song badly if Paula grunted and nodded and avoided meeting her eye, and that she sang it passably well if Paula flared her nostrils and smiled and said something acerbic.

Sometimes Lauren thought she trusted Paula more than anyone else, and sometimes she thought it wasn't a matter of trust, but rather that she didn't care what Paula thought of her. Maybe she had found a perfect, safe intimacy with Paula, or maybe Paula was just a receptacle—that is, mostly a dump, which is once in a while a place where useful things can be fished out and taken without consequence or remorse. Maybe Lauren served that same function for Paula.

Lauren turned on Paula's television, like she owned the place, and stared at MTV. There was a new U2 video that was boring-on-purpose: black-and-white footage of buffalo galloping in slow motion, alternating with pictures of flowers and various translations of the word *one*. It was sort of transfixing in how boring it was, or just in how different it was from any other video. Mom or Dad would say the video was "arty," which was maybe the same as boring, although Lauren suspected that you developed a taste and preference for arty things the same way you developed a taste for vodka. Until today she hadn't watched the video through to the end, when it froze on an image of buffalo hurling themselves off a cliff, their bodies seconds away from breaking against the rocks below. One of the buffalo was upside down, its hooves poised daintily in the air, comical and ghastly. Lauren felt the purposefulness of how boring the rest of the video was in a new way. It added another layer of horror to know that galloping toward your own certain death could be tedious.

Lauren pressed play on whatever tape was in the deck. It was still the Red Hot Chili Peppers on *Saturday Night Live*. She rewound to the beginning of the cheesy ballad and waited for John to do the *WOOOOOOO*, and when he did it she forgot herself and laughed out loud. At the end of the song she rewound to the beginning and watched again. It was a stupid waste of time to just lie here watching something she'd already seen, laughing at the same joke like she was hearing it for the first time, but if Paula walked in right now Lauren wouldn't be embarrassed. Paula would just sit down and watch with her. They wouldn't even have to talk about it.

Lauren wondered what Mirela was doing now. Mirela was why Lauren was sitting here, alone, in another family's house, which was funny since Lauren was always telling Mom to try leaving

Mirela alone. "Just let her be," Lauren said. "Give her some room to breathe."

"She doesn't truly want to be left alone," Mom said. "Not deep down. It's just that being left alone is what she's used to. She is comfortable with neglect and isolation. And that's unfair to her. No child should have to get used to that. We have to break her of the habit. We have to teach her how to love us and how to be loved, how to accept love."

Lauren understood why Mom took it personally. Mom told Mirela she would never leave her. She said it over and over, like one of her prayers. Mom thought Mirela was afraid she'd be left alone. But maybe Mom had that all wrong. Maybe Mirela was afraid that Mom would stay.

"—I'M A LITTLE lamb who's lost in the wood—"

"Okay, Lauren, we get it," Mr. Smith called out.

Lauren squinted out into the seats from where she stood on the auditorium stage, beside the piano and Deepa, who was playing for spring musical auditions.

"What?" Lauren asked.

"What?" Deepa asked.

"We're good here," Mr. Smith said.

"I just started—I didn't even get to the bridge—" Lauren said.

"You told me you couldn't sing," Mr. Smith said. "Remember? I'm taking you at your word."

"I don't get it," Lauren and Deepa said in unison.

Mr. Smith showed his teeth in a rectangle, like he'd just smelled something rotten.

"Should I run lines with Stitch now?" Lauren asked, glancing over at Stitch, who was waiting in the wings. "Isn't there a—dance component? To the audition?"

Mr. Smith clapped once and jabbed his thumbs toward the exits. "Lauren! You're done! Goodbye!"

Lauren threw up her hands and walked offstage, Deepa calling after her to take her sheet music.

"What an asshole," Stitch whispered as Lauren passed him, and she laughed loud, hoping Mr. Smith could hear her. She hoped he could see that it was Stitch who had made her laugh.

She arranged a tight smile to screen off the surprised faces of the students waiting outside for their own auditions: Andy's smirk, Claire's pitying pout, Paula's piggy smile. Lauren couldn't have been onstage more than five minutes before Mr. Smith ordered her away. She grinned and shrugged as she walked past them— strolling with stringent casualness toward the front entrance of Bethune and, just beyond it, the sunken cafeteria—and the performance didn't feel fake. It felt great—she would not have to be in the stupid musical! She would not have to spend weeks slouching around in Tedquarters, slimy Domino's pizza boxes strewn around, listening to Andy bitch about his costume or his fellow castmates' poor vocal modulation! She would not have to pursue Mr. Smith's erratic approval except for English class, and in a few short weeks she would have the option of switching out of his class for Mrs. Bonnano's poetry module, where students got to go to Delaware Park to write sonnets. She could be composing lines on the landscape architecture of Frederick Law Olmsted instead of trying to figure out why Mr. Smith was paying her so much attention today, or why he was ignoring her today, or why he'd forced her to rewrite her quite fine essay on the first half of *The Things They Carried* ("This is so bad I can't bring myself to grade it") or why he'd given her an A+ on the bad essay she'd written on the second half of *The Things They Carried* the morning it was due ("Loose yet incisive—love to watch you think!"), or what she had done *this time* to make him mad, and whether or not she would escape consequences for making him mad, and if he thought that not casting her in the musical, after pressuring her so intensely to audition, was some kind of *consequence*, a punishment—well, she had escaped granting him that satisfaction, too. She could try out for spring track instead, or swim laps in the afternoon so she wouldn't be out of shape for summer swim club, or she could do both, if she was feeling ambitious—and maybe she was! Or she could spend afternoons with Dad at his new development, like he was always asking her to, learn about the family business. Or she could do some of the volunteer work that Mom used to do but couldn't anymore because of Mirela.

Or she could help Mom with Mirela. She could take the lie she'd told Mr. Smith and make it true. Mom was having such a tough time, and whatever mistakes Mom had made, Mirela was with them now, she was part of the family, she was Lauren's sister—she'd never thought she'd have a sister!—and Mirela deserved better than a sister who was always hiding from her playing make-believe in a school auditorium or watching MTV in Paula's poky house. They all made fun of Mirela for running away, but really Lauren was the one running away from Mirela, from all of them. And that was about to change.

"Lauren!" Paula was following her. They stopped at the edge of the cafeteria pit. "What happened back there?"

"Eh, wasn't my day," Lauren said, throwing her hand like she was shooing a fly. A brave smile, the smile of someone who rose above. "You should go back—you'll lose your place in line."

"Okay—do you want me to meet you at my house after?"

"You know, I should probably spend some time at home. Good luck!" Lauren grinned wider and walked out of school.

THE CAST LIST for *Grease* was posted just outside Ted-quarters on Friday afternoon, just as classes let out for the weekend. Lauren breezed by to take a look, just out of curiosity, and she saw that Andy was chosen for hotfooting greaser Danny, and Julie was goody-two-shoes Sandy, and Stitch was auxiliary greaser Kenickie, and Deepa was sweet, stupid Frenchie, and Abby and Claire were in the chorus as secondary Pink Ladies—as they explicitly wished to be, as a low-time-commitment senior-year lark—and Lauren, incredibly, was wisecracking Rizzo, de facto head of the Pink Ladies.

"You? Again?" Andy blurted behind her. Lauren knew who he meant. Without turning to acknowledge him, or the several voices murmuring congratulations to her, she walked down the hallway, past the band practice room, and out the door, like she couldn't care less about any of it, like she hadn't noticed all the attention she was getting.

"Another lead!" Mom exclaimed when Lauren got home. "And only a freshman. Lauren, you're an absolute star. I'm so proud of you!"

To celebrate, Mom sent Mirela to Nana Dee's for the night and rented *Grease* from Blockbuster for the rest of the family to watch together. They ordered pizza and wings from Bocce's, with extra celery and blue cheese for Mom. Dad came home from work on time like he used to. Mom went to kiss him hello and he put his hands on her shoulders—a feint at an embrace, but really a defensive block—as he thrust one cheek at her, saying something about needing to brush his teeth after having Ted's Hot Dogs for lunch.

"I haven't seen this in so long," Mom said as the movie began with Danny and Sandy kissing on a beach, which PJ and Sean found very upsetting.

"Suck my kiss!" PJ said through a mouthful of Sean's ear. The Red Hot Chili Peppers had infiltrated the area middle schools.

"This movie was huge when Lauren was a baby," Mom said.

"All I remember are the songs and the leather pants Olivia whatshername wears at the end," Dad said. He was sitting up quite straight on the couch, not picking at the bottoms of his bare feet like he usually did after a long day. Like he was a guest. He hadn't gone upstairs to brush his teeth like he'd said he would.

"Is Lauren Olivia whatshername?" Sean asked, wiping his ear on PJ's pant leg.

"No, Lauren is Ritzy," Mom said.

"No, Rizzo—like Ratso Rizzo," Dad said.

"Like *Fatso* Rizzo," Sean corrected him.

"Yes, I have to sew my own fat suit to be in the musical," Lauren said.

"You won't need one!" PJ yelled, pinching the skin above her knee, and Lauren smacked him on the arm and PJ ululated and turned a somersault on the carpet and their father pounded his fist three times on the arm of the couch.

"I don't think of Dustin Hoffman as fat," Mom said.

"Rizzo is the one that gets pregnant," PJ said from the floor. He was eating a wing and bicycling his legs.

"No wings on the carpet," Mom told PJ.

"Wait, how have you seen this?" Lauren asked PJ.

"No, Rizzo is the gay hooker," Dad said.

"Who?" PJ asked. An orange globule of wing sauce arcing through the air.

"PJ, the carpet," Mom said.

"Fatso Rizzo," Dad said.

"A pregnant hooker," Sean said.

"No, *Lauren* is the pregnant hooker," PJ said.

"Only in the movie, I bet," Mom said. "They probably clean it up for high school."

In the movie of *Grease*, all the high school students looked twenty-five except for Rizzo, who looked thirty-five. Sean thought Movie Rizzo was a teacher's aide who just liked to hang out with kids. "Like Steff in *Pretty in Pink*," he said.

"Like Mr. Smith," Lauren said.

"You're always talking about that guy, but nobody knows him and nobody cares," Sean said through a mouthful of chicken, in a tone more observational than critical, and Lauren smiled and pretended to yawn, stretching her arms above her head for enhanced effect. She felt her muscles opening, her fingers laced and limbering against one another, and remembered daybreak at Abby's house, that same embracing joy of belonging. The fake yawn became a real one, and she sat back on the couch, closer to Mom.

"She looks too pure to be pink," Movie Rizzo said of Sandy. Dad whistled low through his teeth, and Mom laughed.

The phone rang and rang. "Are you going to get that?" Dad asked Mom.

"Let it go. Let's just have a night," Mom said.

"What is going to be left of this script once they cut out all the sex stuff for the school play?" Dad asked as a high schooler lay prone on the bleachers, leering up a classmate's skirt, while PJ and Sean, repeating the patter of one of the secondary greasers, yelled, "She puts out? She *puts out?!*" They continued reciting this for weeks, at any provocation and no provocation at all.

"'Model of virginity'?" Mom asked. "They're not going to let anybody say that in a high school production."

"Are you allowed to come up with your own substitute lines?" Dad asked Lauren, who shrugged.

"Wholesome times infinity," Mom said. "Master's in divinity."

"Cops in the vicinity," Dad said.

The phone rang and rang.

"Rizzo is a bitter old hag," Lauren said, to her brothers' screeching approval. "Even her big musical number is just about dissing some poor girl she barely knows."

Lauren did admire how Movie Rizzo could manipulate the people around her into doing what she wanted them to do, like when she contrived a scene between Sandy and Danny at a pep rally that left both of them feeling confused and down. Movie Rizzo's biggest problem was that she was always bored, like her boredom was a low-grade illness brought on by being a thirty-five-year-old still in high school, and the boredom made her do things that were impulsive and self-defeating, like climbing down a trellis to meet up with five guys—five!—or throwing a milkshake at Kenickie, or engaging in unprotected intercourse with Kenickie, a character whom Dad thought had some kind of endocrinological disorder. When Movie Rizzo said that she felt like a broken typewriter because she had missed a period, Mom objected, not because Rizzo was possibly pregnant and that would say something about her moral compass and the inappropriately adult themes and situations of *Grease*, but because "defective typewriter" wasn't a strong metaphor.

"How many things could 'I'm a defective typewriter' mean?" Mom asked. "Aren't there better typewriter jokes they could come up with?"

"I got my ribbon in a twist," Lauren said.

"I couldn't find any space at the bar," Dad said. "The space bar."

"A fight broke out at the Star Wars Cantina and a starship pilot broke a typewriter," PJ said, as Sean did the splits in a handstand and PJ knocked him over.

"'I skipped a period' is not really a joke, it's more like a bad crossword clue, where you have to have most of the letters already before you can figure it out," Dad said.

"Yeah, it's like the feeling when the clue to eighty-five across is 'See eighty-five down' and so you look at eighty-five down and it says 'See eighty-five across,'" Mom said.

"Locking in on a punny crossword clue should feel like the teeth of a zipper coming together," Dad said, steepling his fingers, as lights in their driveway flooded the den windows and reflected off the television set. Nana Dee's Saab. Dad hit pause on the VCR as Mom went out the front door to investigate.

"Fuck," Dad blew through his teeth, peering out the window.

"*Mother* fuck?" PJ whispered.

When Mom came back, she looked harried and resigned. "We'll have to finish up movie night another time, everybody," she said. "Mirela's having a rough one."

"I DON'T WANT to keep playing the old lady," Lauren complained to Mr. Smith after English class.

"Maybe you're just an old soul," he said.

"I watched the movie," she said.

"Don't go by anything you saw in the movie. Everything gets edited for the school version."

"Rizzo is a hag, and I'm not."

"Didn't we have the same conversation about *All My Sons*? I've told you before: the audience wants to be told what to see."

"Mr. Smith——" Lauren began. Her hands were trembling.

"Speaking of old ladies, Mr. Smith is what my mother calls me," he said with a grin. "When class is not in session, you can call me Ted."

"But class *is* in session," she said.

"Are we not in fact *between* classes?" he asked. "Does Bethune not lack walls and doors? To be a teacher or a student here now is to stand poised in a threshold space, where convictions blur and identities mingle. Like the balcony in *Romeo and Juliet*—we are both inside and outside, lending our every encounter a jolt of the uncanny."

"Real fast—I have something to show you," Lauren said. Her hands shook so badly that she had trouble unzipping her backpack. The zipper caught on the fabric, and she felt the shuddering in her ears as she worked the cloth out of its teeth. She reached into the bag, looked quickly around her, flashed a single tray of birth control pills in front of Mr. Smith just long enough for his face to change, and dropped them back inside.

Then she said the line she'd rehearsed in her head a million times. "Unlike a broken typewriter, I'll never miss a period," she recited, zipping up her bag and striding away without looking behind her, a small secret smile on her face. She was in a movie walking into her close-up, hitting her mark. She could turn on her heel and cue a popular song. Other students would leap onto their desks, tap heels clicking, jazz hands in formation.

"That line is not in the school version of the play, by the way!" Mr. Smith called after her. The punch line in the movie.

THE FIRST REHEARSAL was short: permission slips, announcements about costumes and fund-raising, an abbreviated run-through of the big ensemble song, "We Go Together," with Mindy, the choreographer, who ran the ballet school in the Bells strip mall. Mr. Smith didn't even hang around to watch. Paula was home sick, officially, although Lauren suspected she was home sulking about having been made property mistress again. Walking home, Lauren cut through Stitch's yard, reached the weeping willow, looked through the kitchen window. Nobody home yet. She passed PJ and Sean shooting hoops in the Schecks' driveway three houses up from home. Lauren walked through the front door and into the living room, pausing a moment when she saw Mirela asleep on the sofa. Mirela was taking Ritalin, which was something she had in common with Andy Figueroa. Her morning dose wore off in the late afternoon, making her ravenously hungry. She could eat a sleeve of Chips Ahoy! in a sitting, half a box of Hostess Powdered Donettes, great heaping BLTs, a tall glass of orange juice and half of another. Sedated by food, she would then fall asleep anywhere, almost like she was unconscious. Lauren tiptoed past her into the kitchen and saw Mom sitting at the table alone, hands folded in front of her, staring intelligently at nothing.

"Lauren," she said, her voice just above a whisper. "Come sit with me."

Lauren maneuvered carefully into the round-backed chair opposite her mother. It was pulled too close to the table, but she didn't dare push it back, in case the scraping sound stirred Mirela. It felt as if a hushed and jumpy team of surgeons huddled over the girl in the next room.

"So," Mom murmured, letting out a half sigh, half laugh, "what's new with you?"

Lauren shrugged and looked out the window that faced the backyard. "How is Mirela?"

"The same," Mom said.

"I was thinking of how I might be able to help you more with Mirela," Lauren said. There was a cardinal in the beech tree. Mom and Dad would get so excited when they saw a cardinal in the backyard—they always wanted everyone else to come see. "I wasn't expecting to be in the musical, and I'll have a lot of rehearsals, but—maybe after it's over—this summer."

"That's sweet of you, Lauren. Don't worry about Mirela. That's my job. How are you?"

"I'm good."

"How's school?"

"Good."

"How's the play? The musical?"

"Good."

They sat in silence for a while. Watching the cardinal preen and tic and nod and go about its business, Lauren felt the warm pooling feeling in her chest.

"How's your friend Paula?"

"She's home sick today. But she's good."

"Good," Mom said, and they both laughed almost noiselessly under their hands.

"She's a little negative," Lauren admitted. "Negative energy." Mom didn't like negative energy.

"Does she have stuff going on at home?"

"I don't know. I don't think so."

"It must be hard for her."

"What do you mean?"

"Well, she . . . she didn't win the lottery in the looks department. And you're so pretty. It could be that she wants what you have."

"No. I don't think she cares," Lauren said.

"Your friend Skip Rosen is in the musical with you again?"

"Stitch. Yeah, yeah, I know, you hate his dad."

"I don't hate anybody."

"He's a doctor, Mom. He helps people. He doesn't hurt people."

Mom sighed through her nose and rubbed her eyelids. "Andy Figueroa, too? He's in the musical?" she asked. This was something Mom did when she was straining for conversation—she would pose factual statements as questions, as if she didn't know the answers.

"Yeah, he's playing Travolta," Lauren said. "He has laryngitis, although Mr. Smith thinks he's faking."

"Oh?"

"Or not faking, but he says it's—it's psycho—psychodramatic?"

"Psychosomatic."

"Yeah. It's anxiety. Or that's what Mr. Smith says."

"His vocal cords work, but he thinks they don't work, so they don't work, because he's nervous."

"Something like that. But he didn't have it during auditions, when it would make more sense to be nervous. He only has it now that he needs to practice."

"They used to call that hysterical blindness. Happened more with girls, supposedly. So Andy has hysterical laryngitis."

"I wish I had that excuse," Lauren said.

"What do you mean?"

"I don't think I'm a very good singer. Or dancer."

"Malarkey—you wouldn't have been picked for the musical if that were true."

"I stepped on my own foot when we were running through a song today. And Andy kept glaring over at me whenever I sang with the group, so I lip-synched."

"Ignore him. He sounds like a fruitcake. Much as I like his mother."

"I think I'm going to be the worst one in the whole play."

"Mamie Figueroa. She always has been such a nice woman. She asks after Mirela. She wants to know how to help."

"Mr. Smith asks, too," Lauren said.

"You like him a lot, don't you?" Mom asked with a big smile, her chin in her hand.

"I guess so."

"It's nice to have some younger teachers in there. Someone closer to all of you in age. That youthful vim."

"I don't know," Lauren said. "He's weird. Moody. He, um—he just wants to be everyone's friend all the time."

"Oh. What's wrong with that?"

"I don't know. It's creepy. It's kind of pathetic."

"Lauren, that isn't very tolerant. Maybe you have been spending too much time with Paula."

"You're the one who said—" Lauren stopped. The warm pooling in her chest was turning cold. The cardinal flew out of the tree, and Lauren felt a new quick strange pressure on her sternum, a little phantom shove, like the cardinal had pushed and lifted off her chest to take flight, and then a ridiculous sadness, one she could not articulate or admit to anyone, and it occurred to her with a dull thud to the head that it would always be possible to feel this way, for the rest of her life she would be stalked by this panicky sorrow, even a stupid bird could bring it on, that it wasn't the bird but it was *her*, it came from inside her, she was the one who was doing it.

"I'm sorry," Lauren said. The *o* on *sorry* quavered like a soap bubble.

"What's wrong, honey?"

Lauren stared into the wood grain of the table. Something was spilling over, and she didn't know what it was. She didn't have words for it. It was a tearful harmony over an organ line. *Use your words* was something Mom used to say to Sean when he was little. Or Mom said it to all three of them, but Lauren could only remember her saying it to Sean. There must be so much that she'll never remember.

"You can tell me anything, honey."

"Mom?" Lauren asked. "Do you remember my birthday party?"

Mom laughed. "How could I forget it?"

"I wasn't—I wasn't nice to Mirela at my birthday party."

Mom put up a hand. "Lauren. You are so sweet. Don't worry about it. It's so long ago now. And it was perfectly understandable."

"No, I—"

"Anyone in your place would have been frustrated with how she behaved. That should have been *your* day. It's okay, honey. Don't be so hard on yourself."

"But the thing is—"

"The important thing is—"

The phone was ringing, and Mom leapt up to get it. Often Mom let calls go to the answering machine, so she could screen the caller. The other night she didn't answer it at all. Maybe Mom was worried now that the ringing would wake Mirela. But she jumped up so fast to answer that her chair scraped the floor.

"Mom, could you—"

Mom held up a hand with a confidential, apologetic smile, as if she was going to get rid of the caller as soon as possible. She *beep*ed the new cordless phone awake and put it to her ear. "Oh, hello, Dr. Zeller." One of Mirela's therapists, Lauren guessed. She couldn't keep track of them all, and they all eventually disappeared anyway, so it wasn't worth learning their names. Lauren could learn them all this summer, when she had more time to help out.

She held eye contact with Mom for a beat. Mom looked up at the ceiling and twirled her finger in the air, pantomiming her impatience. She held the phone to her cheek with one hand and, with the other, raised the antenna.

"Could you tell them you'll call back?" Lauren asked, but before she could finish, Mom turned her back to face out of the kitchen, toward the foyer.

Lauren panted. Like a dog, she thought.

"Yes, I see," Mom was saying. "Well, what about—right, right." She was walking slowly into the foyer, her head bowed in consultation with the voice on the phone.

Lauren, still sitting at the kitchen table, heard the weak groan of the carpeted stairs beneath Mom's feet. She walked into the foyer to the bottom of the stairs and watched her mother climbing to the top, the tip of the phone's antenna scraping against the ceiling.

"Mom?" Lauren asked.

"In a minute, honey," Mom's silhouette said as she closed the bedroom door behind her.

"Mama," Mirela said from the living room.

"Mom," Lauren said, more insistently, to no one.

"Mama mama mama," Mirela called. The syllables were sticky, like she was dreaming and trying to talk herself into waking up.

NOW THAT PAULA had quit the show and was refusing to spend study hall in Tedquarters, it meant that twice a week, from 2:10 p.m., when Mr. Smith usually walked in after his post-lunch staff meeting, until about 2:30 p.m., when Stitch and Rajiv came somersaulting or skateboarding in after Phys Ed, Mr. Smith was usually alone in Tedquarters. Lauren wondered why he was always in there, why he never spent any downtime with his colleagues in the English department office, picking up some gardening tips from Mrs. Bristol or catching up on back issues of the *New York Review of Books* that Mr. Treadwell stacked in his carrel.

"It's so cute how you can get all that alone time with Ted," Paula said. "I bet he always sits down right next to you."

"Whatever," Lauren said.

"You two are so *close*," Paula said. "It's crazy that you could get a lead role without really even trying out. I guess it's just that he knows you so *well*."

Depending on the day, if Mr. Smith had seemed moody in English class, if he'd waved Lauren off when she raised her hand, she then had twenty minutes in Tedquarters to try to fix it, to convince him with a perfect offhand comment that she really had done the assigned reading, no matter what he thought or assumed. And if English class had gone well, in Tedquarters she could, as Dad would say, "capitalize on the win."

"I had an idea," Lauren told him. It was a bit awkward to have conversations at the big table, facing their books and paperwork and not each other. "I was thinking that Paula and I could switch places, and she could play Rizzo and I could be the property mistress."

"Paula quit," Mr. Smith said.

"No, I know, but she could come back, couldn't she?"

Mr. Smith continued marking papers like he hadn't heard her, like their elbows weren't touching.

"I think that would make her happy," Lauren said. "And I wouldn't mind at all."

"No, I'm sure that's an issue of utmost prominence in your life right now, Lauren—just how ecstatically happy you can make your good friend Paula," Mr. Smith said. "You'd give it all up for her, wouldn't you?"

"Paula is a good singer. I've heard her," Lauren said.

Lauren hated Rizzo like she was a person. She had a dream that she was suspended from school after arguing with Rizzo in the cafeteria—Lauren shoved her across a table, sending Stitch's brown-bag lunch spinning onto the linoleum, and Mr. Smith had to intervene. In another dream Lauren surrendered Midnight to an animal shelter because Mirela wouldn't stop pulling her tail, and when the door shut on the cage, Lauren realized that Midnight had Rizzo's face.

Mr. Smith flicked his pen onto the table and rubbed his eyes. "You wear me out, Lauren," he said. "You keep trying out for my plays and you keep trying to weasel out of them and it's just a lot of drama for one Drama Club."

Lauren hated Rizzo for her curdled crudeness, her spiteful pride in being the unpretty slut. These traits came through even in the sanitized school version of *Grease*, although it got rid of the sex jokes and jeering puns and Rizzo's pregnancy scare. "I can't sing," Lauren said quietly. "And I can't dance. And I definitely can't do them at the same time."

"I doubt that."

"You didn't come to the first rehearsal," Lauren said. There would be weeks and weeks of rehearsals. "And you barely let me try out. That's why you don't know that I suck."

Mr. Smith sighed, and put his hand on Lauren's back. In the usual places, rubbing up and down in the usual rhythms, covering the usual distances. His hand on her back was apologizing for being so tough on her, but also it was underlining, with feathering fingers and knuckle-presses, that he was so tough on her in class and in rehearsals because she was *different*, she was special, he had higher standards for her, and anyway they had an understanding. His head was low and leaning into hers.

"Sing for me," he said. He took her hand with his free one.

She looked at his hand on hers and did not say anything.

"Come on, try me, sing." A cooing whisper. His coffee breath. "What's the song? I know you know it. Everybody knows it. It was a big hit when you were a baby."

Lauren laughed and shook her head, and her hair brushed against his cheek.

"You're the one that I want, doo, doo, doo, honey," he whisper-sang.

Lauren laughed again. Her whole body laughed like a seizure, like his tuneless croon was tickling her sides.

"You're the one that I want, doo, doo, doo, honey."

A knot in her side tightened as if it were about to pop open. She forced herself to stop laughing and pulled her hand away. "I'm gonna go now."

As she stood up, his hand on her back held its position in space, caressing down her spine and landing on her ass. "Excuse *you*," he said as she maneuvered past her chair and then his.

"Oops, sorry," Lauren said, her hair falling in her eyes as she shambled to the door. Stitch and Rajiv were in the hallway trying to do the splits, and she was relieved that they hadn't seen her in there and she was hopeful that they wondered why she was in such a hurry, why she was so flushed and happy.

THE BETHUNE AUDITORIUM. Another rehearsal. Lauren sang a line of her solo, "Look at Me, I'm Sandra Dee," raised a hand, then she was supposed to go to the next line and the next hand motion, but she saw her hand still suspended in air, a beat too late, and tried to move it to where it was supposed to be, and as she did that she forgot the next line of the song. "Ugh!" she exclaimed, stamping her feet in frustration. The girls looked away. The boys licked their lips and stared. Her shame and embarrassment were a confession to Rizzo's shame and embarrassment. Rizzo was messy, and Lauren made a mess of playing her. She was stumbling through the worst version of her real life while a smooth fictional production swirled around her, elegant and vigorous as a ballet. She was an isolated lyric. Rizzo's song was about pretending to hate a perfect girl, but the whole thing was a front for hating herself. Eye-rolling and jealous and *so ugly*. Negative energy. Sour and stinking.

Mindy said, "You know what, Lauren, let's not worry about the dance steps for now. Okay? You can just stand still and concentrate on this important song—let the others worry about the dancing." Lauren hated Mindy, too, for trying to be kind, for letting the effort show.

"Lauren is a Method actress," Andy Figueroa said. "You run lines with her and you catch an STD."

"I hear herpes gives you two left feet," said Brendan Dougherty, in a strangulated *duh* voice, like Lauren wasn't worth the effort of a proper joke. Scattered laughter.

"Jesus, Brendan," said Claire, shielding her eyes with one hand. She wasn't defending Lauren so much as protesting her own discomfort. Before *Grease*, Lauren had seen Brendan as a pretty void, flat as a poster of a boy-band heartthrob on Danielle Sheridan's bedroom wall. It turned out that he was a person, too.

"Guys," Mindy said in an admonishing tone, but she wasn't a teacher at Bethune, so she had little authority, especially when Mr. Smith wasn't around. Or what authority she did have derived from how likable she was. The boys would think Mindy was likable so long as they also thought she was fuckable, but that could go wrong if the boys started to get an inkling that Mindy herself also thought that she was fuckable.

Lauren was too incompetent to be fuckable. Mingling with the

sour and the stink was a scent of pity, the close air of a funeral.
Something had died. Lauren stared at her sneakers, which were
bolted to the stage. She watched herself wielding a chain saw, slicing at the section of stage her feet were bolted to, carving out two
snowshoe-sized wooden blocks, clomping out of the auditorium
atop her great big stage clogs, and throwing herself into Lake Erie.
Except wood floats, she thought. Even her fantasies of erasing herself were incompetent.

"Lauren dances like she just shat her pants," Brendan said.

"Yeah, yeah," Andy said, revving up, "and she's moving around
real careful so—"

"—so it doesn't run down her leg!" Andy and Brendan yelled
together, and they fell all over themselves laughing.

"You guys are fucking *assholes*," Julie fumed at the two boys,
and this was what brought tears to Lauren's eyes. Of all of them,
she was maddest at Julie, with her rich pirouetting voice. Julie's
pity gave the taunts their meaning. Inside herself, Lauren ripped a
chunk of the stage off her feet and dashed her head against it.

AFTER REHEARSAL SHE locked herself in a stall in the bathroom farthest from the auditorium, behind the studio art work-
shop. She sat on the edge of the toilet hugging herself, eyes closed,
humming to cross out Brendan's voice, Andy's voice.

Nevermind was about the length of a class period, if you didn't
count the long silence and then the secret thrashing song that
came after it. The song woke Lauren up if she didn't remember to
switch off the CD player at night. If she ran each song through her
head before she allowed herself to unlock the stall, that would buy
her forty minutes. She would sing every word, hum every guitar
line, tap out every beat, but quietly, quietly, she'd have to listen out
in case someone came in and heard her, and by the time she got to
the end everyone would have gone home. Rehearsal had run late as
it was, she wouldn't have to face them again until tomorrow. She

pressed her fingers against her eyelids and watched the bluish-reddish shapes pump and drift, an amoebic wash of strange living things buoyed and eddied by the submerged guitar lines.

"*Memoria*," she whispered to herself. "*Memoria*." The chorus of the second single, the one that sounded like it was recorded underwater. She didn't know what it meant. Memory-ah. She made up what it meant, to help pass the time: the memory of Maria, the phantom of an Italian mob widow who lived long ago, who only wore black mourning garb, black lace and veil, after her husband was killed with a pistol—by her own hand, people whispered, but she always denied it, blaming the local Black Hand, as anyone would. *Memoria* was the word you used, three times fast, to ward against her vengeful ghost. Maria dropped the gun in the ocean, off the coast of Sicily. Lauren would recite this story to Paula, tell her it was the origin of the song, that she'd read about it in one of the music magazines.

Lauren had gotten to the second-to-last song—*I'm on a plain, I can't complain*—when Carl, the school custodian, called out from the doorway to the bathroom and said whoever was in there had to leave. He sounded apologetic; he probably thought she was having woman problems.

Lauren could hear Stitch's skateboard before she pushed open the side doors to the Bethune parking lot. She saw he was alone and exhaled. It was cold and wet and the light was thinning out, down to a bruisish purple.

"Hey," he said, looking down as he flipped his skateboard. It spun twice, spiked the ground on one corner. He watched it roll out of his reach, not moving after it. "I was wondering where you went. I was waiting."

"I didn't ask you to wait for me," she said.

"I wanted to ask if you liked the last tape I made you," he said, his hands in the pockets of the red buffalo-plaid jacket he wore every day.

Lauren stared at him. "Are you kidding me?" she asked.

"No. The Replacements. Did you like it?"

He watched her patiently. His eyes always seemed faintly rheumy, as if he used special drops that unlocked a blurry fourth dimension, visible just over her shoulder.

"You waited an hour in the parking lot to ask me if I like the Replacements?"

"It hasn't been an hour," he said. He shrugged and skip-hopped toward his skateboard. "I'm just practicing," he said, rolling back toward her.

"You aren't—you're making fun of me, right? I don't get it."

"What?" asked Stitch. He stopped pushing the wheels forward and back with one foot and squinted at her. Mouth open like no one was watching, like he was alone with himself. "I'm not making fun of you. If you get a chance to listen to it, let me know what you think."

"Okay. I'm sorry," Lauren said. Her tongue and lips were numb and slow, like she'd been out in the cold for too long. "I did listen to it."

"What did you think?"

"I liked it. It feels very—close. Like they're playing live."

"Like you mean the production?"

"They leave in the mistakes, the missed notes. But in a good way, like they're excited to be playing for a crowd. Like they practiced, but they're nervous."

Stitch nodded. Both of them were looking at the ground. "The drums speed up and slow down sometimes."

"I like the singer's voice."

"Paul Westerberg," Stitch said.

"Yes—and I liked—I liked how I feel like I'm in the room with them. And the singer is talking to someone he knows very well. Like, sometimes the other person is there, and sometimes he's pretending they're there, like he's getting up his nerve to talk to them later. And sometimes he's mad at them, and sometimes he's mad at himself and taking it out on the other person."

"Why are you crying?" Stitch asked.

Lauren wiped her eyes with the sleeve of her coat. "Why are you asking me that?! You were there! At rehearsal! You know—you saw what happened."

Stitch shrugged and said nothing.

"God, it was so embarrassing," she said.

"Don't pay attention to them," Stitch said.

"How can I not pay attention to them?"

"I don't. It's a waste of time."

"They're your friends."

"Just because I'm around them doesn't mean they're my friends."

"What do they say about me when I'm not around?"

"Probably nothing, because they can't hurt you when you can't hear what they're saying."

Lauren laughed and wiped her nose with her other sleeve. "That's clever."

"I didn't say it to be clever."

"Please don't feel sorry for me."

"I do a little bit. I'll try not to. Are you sure you don't want me to walk you home?"

Lauren nodded at the ground.

"Suit yourself. I hope you feel better. See you, Lauren." He began to turn away.

"Hey—why did you—that one time, why did you call me and act like you didn't?" Lauren asked. Her sadness had given her permission to be a brat, a middle schooler.

Stitch stopped and looked back. "I didn't call you," he said. "Do you want me to call you?"

Lauren shrugged. "Yeah. I mean, do what you want."

"Okay. I'll call you later."

The skateboard faded out, and Lauren was alone, still staring at the ground. Her body rotating like a drill, pounding like a jackhammer through the top line of tar into the roadbed, into the stones, down to the earth, until she hit water, until she could hear the submerged guitar from the *memoria* song again and she could know she was alone. Not alone in this parking lot, in this place that she knew, where the people who knew her would return tomorrow, but alone in a place where she could not be found or known or remembered, the songs looping in her head for company.

Stitch just felt sorry for her. He wasn't going to call her later. She didn't want him to. He would call her and whatever they said he would just go and tell his friends.

She went through the gap in the chain-link fence, over the shallow line of trees, crossed Fox Hollow Lane, cut through the Reillys' yard and then the Rosens', waved at Dr. Rosen through his kitchen window. Across Sycamore, then the overground pool, across Northridge, then the O'Tooles' yard—careful to keep an eye out for their anxious shepherd, Ireland—and into her own. The late afternoon light had almost completely leaked away, like the light had liquefied and was puddling into the part-crunchy, part-soggy ground. Lauren stopped short at what was more or less her family's property line, placing one hand on the trunk of the old beech. She could hear Mom yelling, "No, no," then a clattering explosion. Lauren could picture it: Mirela had figured out how to climb up on the kitchen counters, and now she was emptying the high cabinets of their bowls, casserole dishes, tumblers. Crash after crash. Dad was home, bellowing. Knives in his voice, ricocheting off the walls with Mirela's screams. A pause, the crashing stopped, and now Mirela was laughing. Someone was crying. Lauren didn't wait to listen out for whether it was Mom or one of the boys. She turned back, cut through the O'Tooles' yard again, ignoring Mrs. O'Toole's wave and taut disapproving smile from her back porch. Northridge, overground pool, Sycamore, the Rosens', the Reillys', Mr. Smith's.

She was in Mr. Smith's backyard, under the canopy of maples and pines. It was odd that she had never done this before. She turned around in the center of the yard, a full 360 degrees. Juddering in her throat, in her ears. Yet she felt hyper-calm, her surroundings supersaturated despite the darkness and tree shadow, intensely clear, outside of time. She took a pedantic interest in how marooned his little red house looked from behind, no patio or deck, just two steps to a back door and a rusty wheelbarrow slumped beside it. The little red house a crouched and thinking thing beneath the sighing trees, untethered to its neighborhood, poised to stand up on its legs and collapse again atop her. Her reflection scattering yellow on a back window.

The grass inhaled and exhaled, breathing her feet off the ground. The darkness was milky and changeable, like you could move your finger through the air and write a story.

She walked around to the front of his house. A curving path, pachysandra and stunted hedges in front of his windows. She knocked softly on his door. Her breath came shivering. The door opened.

"Lauren, what are you doing here?" He seemed almost angry at her, or angry at the unseen conspiracy that had dropped her on his porch.

"Um," she said. She ducked her head and scratched the sole of her shoe on his front step. "I just—I need—I'm sorry."

"Don't be sorry, just—come in—but wait—are you okay? Shouldn't you be at home?"

"I don't want to go home," Lauren said, her eyes filling with tears. "I want to be here. I want to be with you." She pushed through the doorway and into Mr. Smith's chest, hands on his shoulders. The door tapped shut behind her, and he wrapped his arms around her.

"It's all right," he said.

"Can I stay here for a while?" she asked.

"Lauren—you aren't—are you all alone?"

She nodded and sniffed into his shirt. His arms tightened around her.

SHE HAD KNOWN that what happened next was a possibility. She didn't expect it, exactly. It wasn't what she said she wanted. But she couldn't pretend she hadn't pictured it. Of course she had. She thought about it all the time. She made herself come with it. And she wasn't stupid. She had friends who were seniors. She still decided. Her decision belonged to her.

It was like he was trying to get something over with. Her dad used to watch boxing on *ABC's Wide World of Sports*, and she remembered a fight where one of the boxers obviously had the upper hand, but he was holding back, round after round, maybe waiting to tire out his outmatched opponent. Maybe he was trying to be benevolent. But then in the eighth or ninth round, the guy who was winning just went nuts—combination after combination, blow after blow to the kidneys, on the ropes. A controlled frenzy. Like he'd gotten bored, like he wanted to finish the other guy off, get it over with. But he couldn't and he couldn't. The other guy just stood there and took it.

She just took it. She decided to. She came here on her own. It was on his couch in his living room, ten feet from his front door. Every image sharp and discrete: the last light almost violet through the half-drawn shade, the *Stranger Than Paradise* movie poster tacked to the particleboard paneling, the nubby seams of couch cushions bearing into her lower back, the twelve-inch television set on the egg crate topped with worn, softened paperbacks. The pictures cycle through relentlessly, like an automated slideshow, shuffle and click, shuffle and click, a crunching *snap* as each image turned, like the same photograph taking itself over and over for the rest of her life, and the clearest picture was not something she could see or feel but rather the presumption, the unspoken assertion that *this would be the thing that they would be doing now.* That a person could jam himself inside another person, without consulting her first, should not have seemed so remarkable to her. She should have taken it for granted. He had a lot of trouble getting inside, which made him more frustrated and more excited. There was no more room and no more room and then he found it and he was all the way in. The stretching and straining and pulling became all at once a burning pain, like a pop of sizzling grease, and it was funny and it hurt and she cried out and he clamped his hand over her mouth, only for a second, like he was afraid someone could hear them but there was nobody there.

He's already been inside me

Was her body her own, just then? That's the thing she would always wonder. Who did she belong to? To herself? To her parents? To him? Did he take her, or did she give herself away?

She decided to.

"Lauren says things just for effect," Mom would say. "She does things for effect."

Here, then, was the effect.

She remembered afterward wanting to comport herself with a dignity bordering on primness. She cantilevered herself upright. She willed herself to look fluid, casual, offhand, like she was strolling out of *Grease* auditions. She walked around his couch into his bathroom and closed the door. She sat to pee, and observed the pink jellyfish-like consistency of what was on the toilet paper before she dropped it into the bowl. She wasn't sure if this was her period or something else. Her period wasn't regular enough to keep track yet. She observed the pinkness of the water in the toilet before she flushed it. On the tile she saw the end point of a trail of blood dotting the fifteen-foot path she'd taken. She stepped outside the bathroom door to see him slumped in a reclining chair, his body evacuated. Yet it was her body all over the floor, clotted and textured in spots. She put on her underwear and jeans, went into the kitchen to find paper towels and liquid soap, returned to the living room to wipe up the mess. There was blood on the couch, and she went to work on the stain.

"You don't have to—it's all right—" He didn't move.

"I'm almost done," she said.

When she was finished, she sat down on the floor by the front door and put on her shoes. "Lauren," he said from the reclining chair, "this is our secret. There would be trouble if anyone found out about this. No one—they wouldn't understand."

"I know," Lauren said as she tied her laces.

"Lauren, I'm serious."

Lauren looked up at him. He wouldn't meet her gaze. "I know," she repeated. "It's okay. You don't have to worry about anything."

She decided to. She was still deciding.

She left his house through the back door, took the usual route back to her house. Her legs, dumb as lumber, moved her through the yards and her head, a balloon, floated slightly above her. She didn't know what she expected. An announcement. A card or certificate, some kind of witness, her mom ordering pizza and wings. When she got home, she remembered dully the chaos in the kitchen. She went straight upstairs without saying hello to anyone.

"Lauren?" Dad calling from their living room. "Your friend Stitch-'em-up called."

She closed and locked the bathroom door. She had to pee again. It stung, and there were rusty stains in her underwear. She stared at the stains. This was the witness. More soap and water was all.

She reached into the pocket of her jeans, in a lump on the floor. She'd been wearing this same pair of jeans every day for weeks. She used to think that was gross, but Abby and Deepa and Stitch all did it with their jeans, too. The single, tiny pill was still in the pocket.

She took a shower, turning the handle hotter and hotter until she could barely stand it, got used to it, then hotter. Whenever she ran the water now, she thought she could hear Mirela screaming beneath it. She could turn it off, stand dripping in the silence, turn it on again and then she'd be sure this time, she'd be absolutely sure she could hear the screaming. Off, nothing, on, off, nothing. She watched herself melting down the drain. She dried herself. Avoiding the mirror. Wrapped in only the towel, she climbed under her bedcovers. She remembered stupidly that she had unfinished homework. Knees drawn to her chest, her hair burrowing a warm damp patch in her pillow, she saw her mother in the spotted darkness of the dragon wagon, her profile backlit by the streetlamps, before the other pictures began cycling through again, shuffle click *crunch*, and she lay in the dark with her eyes wide open for a long time, enough time for the slideshow to go around once, twice, again, each thick *click* like the smacking of lips, but when her eyes did close she slept within seconds.

JANE

Jane's children had accustomed her to the arbitrariness of time. The hourless blur of cluster-feeding a newborn, the dilating minutes and hours of a rainy afternoon confined indoors with toddlers, when the stutter-stop ticking of the clock became the clenching of a diseased and faltering heart. She remembered the shattering seasick disorientation of looking at the clock and knowing that whatever time it really was, it could not possibly be the time shown on the clock, that surely someone in charge would be here soon to work this all out, and quite frankly it was unacceptable that it hadn't been worked out already, before all this time had passed.

On this third day of the Spring of Life, three days after Easter, Mr. Glover pulled up to the redbrick WellWomen clinic on Main Street—Jane in the passenger seat and the Huebler twins in the back, Betty and Phil in Phil's car just behind them, the vans of out-of-towners, the Operation Rescue types, descending all around as planned—the clock in Mr. Glover's Datsun said 5:58 a.m., and Jane's wristwatch said 5:58 a.m., but it was not 5:58 a.m., it could not be, because they were supposed to be first, and they were last.

"These aren't our people," Mr. Glover said, peering out the window.

The other side was already there, waiting for them. The other side had sneaked into their homes, turned back their clocks, unplugged their phones, they had papered over their windows and blocked out the rising sun, they had stolen time itself and used that time to conspire with local authorities to install yellow tape and wooden barricades all around WellWomen.

"Crime-scene tape around an abortion clinic—how appropriate," Mr. Glover said. "Well, here we are. You people get out here and I'll find someplace to park."

The other side milling around behind the barricades nodded at one another as Jane and her friends approached. The cops in their matching ponchos and squirrel-brown mustaches milled in their own small groups.

"Good morning, ladies and gentlemen." A thirtysomething woman with a squinty, ironical smile, her skin like tallow, waved at them from behind the barricades. She opened her arms in welcome, rather grandly, as if WellWomen were her estate and the cops her uniformed waitstaff. She wore galoshes and baggy jeans and a big puffy drawstring coat like the one Jane wore through her pregnancies, like she was ready for a long hike through inclement weather. No one could be this persuasively upbeat at six in the morning.

"My name is Bridie. I'm with the Choice Action Network." Her hands, in Gore-Tex gloves, gripped and patted the barricade like it was her trusty steed. "I would be doing you folks a disservice if I didn't tell you that you're going to want to keep across the other side of Main Street today."

"Tell it to the First Amendment," Charity Huebler said.

Another woman, slightly older, scarecrow-thin, came scowling up behind Bridie's shoulder. She wore a blue vest that read ESCORT. "We know you folks made it onto *Good Morning America* just for praying and singing your little songs—" she started.

"All three of the morning shows, actually," Summer interrupted. "National news."

"But you won't be happy with that, will you?" the scarecrow-woman asked. "You need more attention?"

"What my friend Jill here means to say by that," Bridie continued, "is that we know that you folks are escalating today. Attempting a full-on clinic blockade."

Jane looked around at the other Respect Life members, who looked as surprised as she felt. "Hello, my name is Jane," she said. "I'm pleased to meet you. I'm being honest with you when I say that we haven't heard anything about any kind of blockade. We're here peacefully. Just as we were on Monday and Tuesday."

"We're not all that creative," Phil said with a chuckle, and the Hueblers glared at him.

"Is there any coffee?" a pale skinny girl in all black called out behind the barricades.

"Coffee is a diuretic," Bridie said mildly over her shoulder. "You don't want to find yourself in a scuffle with an anti and have to take a piss." Bridie folded her hands and rested them on the battered wooden beam. "Pleased to meet you, Jane. Thank you for your honesty. I don't want any of you folks to take this personally. But you will need, eventually, to move to the other side of Main Street, if you don't want the police to be involved."

Fragments from twenty minutes earlier, and from days gone past, began to assemble themselves. At the meetup at Saint Benedict's that morning, Jane looked across the front lawn laid with thirty gravestones, to mark the thirty million dead babies. Past the graves, she could see a maroon Oldsmobile parked at the outer edge of the lot—a car she hadn't seen there before. Yesterday, driving past the Rosens' house, she saw cars filling the driveway and the street in front, and people—all women, she thought—assembled on the stoop. Jane assumed it was a "house call," the kind of aggressive, in-your-face action that Respect Life avoided but that might appeal to plenty of Oh-Rs who'd shown up over the weekend; now she wasn't so sure. Nor was she sure she had really seen a maroon Oldsmobile in Mr. Glover's rearview. Maybe her memory had maneuvered the car into view after the fact, in order to explain the irrational scene laid in front of them now at WellWomen, this mocking party at which they were the guests of honor.

. . .

THE FIRST PATIENTS started arriving around eight thirty. The Oh-Rs called the other side the "pro-aborts," pronouncing it *probort*. Probort sounded like the name of a humanoid blob from the arcade games the boys used to play at Darien Lake: a colleague of Q*Bert, Dig Dug, Evil Otto. The proborts worked in formation, looping themselves around a patient's car as it arrived, as many as five or six of them at a time, and then encircling the patient herself, guiding her and whoever was with her—a mother, a friend, once in a while a father of the doomed child, or so one presumed—through the crowds. Summer and Charity yelled, "Deathscorts!" at the escorts in their blue vests. Jane was sure that they'd picked that up from the Oh-Rs. Father Steve, when he finally arrived, wouldn't approve of it, surely.

Looking back and forth on Main Street, Jane saw Choice Action Network sentinels in position for patients who arrived on foot. They wore neon-yellow vests that said PEACEKEEPER. They had headsets and talked into their hands and crackled when they walked, like cops. They could radio ahead and form protective circles blocks ahead of WellWomen. They closed into a phalanx as they came closer to the redbrick building.

A few Oh-Rs were unfurling a hand-lettered banner that said DR. ROSEN KILLS CHILDREN. Jane came closer to them. She held her own ABORTION KILLS CHILDREN sign across her chest to show she was one of them. The Oh-Rs wanted to hang their banner between two stakes plunged into the front lawn of WellWomen, like laundry on a line. They argued with some cops about it for a while, yelled about freedom of assembly and their First Amendment rights, but not one of them was getting through the barriers and yellow tape.

"Excuse me," Jane was saying. "May I ask you about your sign?"

They weren't listening. Now they had a notion that they could climb onto the roof of the Pancake Palace down the street and drape the sign over the restaurant's awning. Dr. Rosen ate his lunch at the Pancake Palace most days. The cloth banner, strung on dowels, drooped and accordioned between them as they debated, soaking up dew from the grass.

Jane came a few steps closer, tried again. "How do you know about Dr. Rosen?" she asked.

She heard shouting, not just an argument but something violent. A half block west, some Oh-Rs were scuffling with proborts. Jane turned toward the commotion, and in front of her stood an out-of-towner, maybe an Oh-R, a large, tuberous man in a dark fleece and a fisherman's hat, holding a sign twice as wide as he was. It was pasted with side-by-side photographs of Dr. Rosen and a bloody fetus. Under Dr. Rosen's photo, it listed his name, home address, and telephone number in block letters, easy to read from a distance. The words printed over the top of both pictures were WHICH ONE OF THESE IS HUMAN GARBAGE?

Jane rehearsed a quick speech in her head, like the first time she stood outside the Respect Life classroom. She opened her mouth and balked, lifted her foot and put it down again. She would tell him that she is Dr. Rosen's neighbor. That her daughter is friends with Dr. Rosen's son. That we hate the sin and love the sinner. That this is a community, and yes, we have our differences, and we all want what's best for women and babies, but even if Dr. Rosen has lost his way, there's a better path to—

"Just so's you know, Rosen has a practice of his own, three blocks east of here," Mr. Glover was saying to the man in the dark fleece.

"Three blocks from *this* place?" the man replied, incredulous. "Y'all got more abortion mills than gas stations around here. You walk out your house any direction and somebody's killin' a baby. Buffalo has gotta get its house in order."

Jane opened her mouth and closed it again. Mr. Glover's mustache twitched. "We love our city," he said. "We hope you do, too. Anyway, a house is what you're looking for—big brick entryway tacked on the front—can't miss it. He should be able to see your sign. It would do him good to see it."

JANE LOOKED AT her watch. It was time to meet Pat in the 7-Eleven parking lot, just past the Pancake Palace, where he would hand off Mirela so she could attend the protest with Jane for a couple of hours.

"It's not too late!" the Oh-Rs were yelling at a cordon of escorts concealing a patient as they approached the barricades around the WellWomen building. "You don't have to go through this! Who's making you do this? Who's gotten into your head? Come talk to us! You're going to be okay, just don't go through that door!"

Jane walked west on Main Street toward the 7-Eleven, past the proborts chanting, "Pray! You'll need it! Your cause has been defeated!" There were so many of them, skies and rivers and glaciers of them, beneath the low dirty clouds. Or they moved as one body, one endocrine system, heeding orders from the same glands, activated by the same secretions. Receptors and plasma membranes. Instincts but no intentions. Some of them didn't live anywhere near western New York. Others were students from UB or Buff State— they didn't grow up here, or they wanted to pretend like they hadn't. Sometimes, though, Jane could hear the flat hoof of the accent stomping in the chant. *Yer kaaz. Gunna stap.*

An Oh-R leapt toward a barricade and clapped a sign over the head of a probort who had unlocked arms with his comrade for a thoughtless instant. Culling the herd. The moan of a fallen beast. The sign buckled in half and a cop tackled the Oh-R. The sign read ABORTION KILLS A BABY BUT NOT HER MEMORY.

The protesters thinned out as Jane approached the intersection with Harlem Road. Bridal shop, knitting supply store, bakery. When she reached the Pancake Palace, she turned around to watch the scene of the protest from a distance, scanning it for the heroic detail, the single black-and-white freeze-frame that could run on all the front pages—the moment of the water cannon's impact, the protester confronting a bayonet with a chrysanthemum. But this was just people yelling at each other while other people stood around and watched. Father Steve was right—it had the busy idleness of a tailgate, one where too many people had started drinking too early in the day.

Hubris was the thing Jane hated most in herself, and hubris had brought them all here. They thought they could do Wichita all over again, in a different town and a different season, with a different cast, like a traveling show, like the proborts couldn't rewrite and restage it with just a little heads-up. Jane turned back and could see the dragon wagon idling in the 7-Eleven parking lot. She sprint-walked toward the car. She turned her ABORTION KILLS CHILDREN sign facedown against her chest and stomach with one hand, and with the other, she waved at Pat as he walked around the car to open Mirela's door. Forget all this hullabaloo, Jane would say to the two of them—let's all head home together instead, or grab a bite at the Pancake Palace first. It was so rarely the three of them together, they could make something nice out of it, play hooky—

"Are you *sure* about this, Jane?" Pat was asking. His face was gnarled, like he'd just tripped over the Samersons' deck. "Is this an appropriate place for a child?"

He was already angry with her, and she hadn't spoken a word. Of course he was angry; of course he would ask this question. He was right to ask it. And he did seem genuinely aggrieved. And yet he had agreed to this drop-off plan. And yet he had driven Mirela here, to the protest at the abortion clinic that he so avidly disapproved of. And yet he was already lifting Mirela out of her car seat and handing her over to Jane like she was a sack of groceries. And yet he was getting back inside the car. And yet he was staring at Jane through the open window, appalled at the things she made him do.

A memory: Jane in their driveway, trying to get PJ, not yet three, into his car seat as he arched his back and flung his body around, howling and pulling at her hair as Pat hovered over them, so close and so useless, telling her to *get control over the situation, Jane, for Christ's sake*, when Sean, not yet two, toddled off down the driveway toward the street, and Pat yelled, "Excuse me, Jane, your child is running into the road!" and she bolted to catch Sean, leaving PJ crying and tangled in his straps, and as she lugged her youngest back up to the car, Pat's face contorted in disbelief at this preposterous woman and her preposterous children. From beginning to end, he hadn't moved one inch from where he was standing.

The "Excuse me, Jane" was what really made the memory special, the preening fake gentility of it. Jane laughed. Mirela, her hand in Jane's, laughed, too, and pointed accusingly at Pat.

"I don't see what's so funny," Pat said. Age and anger were pulling downward at his face, draining it.

She couldn't remember where Lauren was in the memory. Jane spaced out, staring at the asphalt, trying to find Lauren.

"What is *wrong* with you?" she heard Pat asking.

Jane smiled, because she knew the answer.

Pat knew the answer, too. He wanted so badly for her to be wrong, and now, for once, she was. Bringing Mirela here was a bad idea. But there were so many times when Pat had wanted Jane to be wrong when she wasn't. It was a crushing debt he'd racked up. She couldn't forgive it, not yet. First he had to pay some of it down.

"Wish us luck today, honey. See you later—we can grab a ride home with a friend," Jane said, and she let Mirela spin her round and round.

They swung arms and skipped as they headed back toward the protest. Things might go well for Mirela today, Jane thought, because Mirela would be surrounded by nothing but new people, engaged in nothing but new situations. The first two days of the Spring of Life, the mostly peaceful tedium of it, had convinced Jane of this. Maybe even Jane would seem like a new person to Mirela when she was out of the house and playing another role.

They walked past the Pancake Palace. Bakery, knitting supply store, bridal shop. "Baby killers!" was the first refrain that reached them from the crowd as they approached WellWomen.

"Babby koowa!" Mirela cooed. Pat had chosen appropriate dress for her—a lined windbreaker, thermal socks—but had put her jeans on backward.

"Don't say that, Mirela, it's not nice," Jane said. "Wait, what happened here?"

The crowds around the barricades were suddenly much thinner. On the opposite side of Main Street, the pro-life protesters stood behind the curb, facing a line of police. They sang a forlorn hymn that she didn't recognize.

"What happen!" Mirela cried with excitement, jumping up and down, still holding Jane's hand. "What happen!"

"Jane, over here!" Betty Andrower among the crowd, hoisting her ABORTION KILLS CHILDREN sign over her head. Jane realized that she must have left hers behind on the roof of the dragon wagon.

"Mirela, let's cross the street," Jane said, squeezing her hand.

"It was that Oh-R moron who sucker punched the pro-choicer," Betty said, maneuvering past a protester and stepping off the curb as Jane reached her side. Jane let go of Mirela's hand long enough to clasp arms with Betty. "It was his fault—they pushed us all back after that." Betty's hands on Jane felt mysteriously nice, sending out slinky little lines of euphoria that shimmied through her shoulders and met in a puff of surprise at the base of her throat. To investigate the feeling further, she threw her arms around Betty, so small and so full, for a long hug, and she could have cried for how nice it felt, but she had to break the hug to grab on to Mirela's hand again.

"Back behind the curb, people, on the sidewalk, nobody in the street," the cops said. They sounded as forlorn as the hymn.

"Do you think we can sneak back up?" Jane asked Betty. "That Bridie woman told us this would happen."

"Oh, let's just keep as close to the curb as we can," Betty said. "What do they think we are, criminals?"

"It is absolutely absurd to suggest that our action has brought violence to Buffalo," tiny red-haired Kitty Stenton from Witness for the Innocents was yelling at a cop who stared past her. "I was born and raised here in Buffalo. Witness for the Innocents is a local, grassroots organization. This is our home—"

"This clinic is open! This clinic is open!" the proborts were shouting.

"Where is Father Steve?" Jane asked Betty. Mirela tugged at Jane's hand.

Betty shrugged. "God knows," she said. "No one's seen him. I bet he knew this would be a bust."

"We don't know it's a bust just yet," Jane said. She was watching the curb. The protesters were inching forward. A few more of them were off the curb. The cops creeping backward, arms crossed, exchanging glances, nodding in acknowledgment.

Mirela tugged harder and started to whine.

A sign that read ABORTION STOPS A BEATING HEART migrated forward, the length of itself. A cop took a step backward, then another. Mirela tugged and Jane almost came off her feet.

"Mirela—wait—"

Three more pairs of pro-life feet shuffled off the curb and onto Main Street. One woman was chest to chest with a female cop, a hand patting her uniformed shoulder, her face pleading, appealing to her sense of reason. The female cop looked at her colleague beside her, and Jane tried to read their expressions. A glint of indulgence, mischief—an opening. The cops had the air of the midday parent: already tired, sure, but plenty of patience left, wanting above all just to keep things on an even keel, there's a long way to go yet, no reason to risk a meltdown by being too rule-bound about snacks or television time or precisely where a pro-life protester could stand on Main Street without being arrested and charged with criminal trespass.

Three more pairs of feet came off the curb. The female cop took two more steps back as Kitty Stenton's voice rose in volume and pitch.

Mirela's hand twisted inside Jane's and she was gone. Running in her crooked *slap-slap* to the barricades across Main Street, ducking under the tape, Jane just behind her but then a cop body-checked her, a big mitt grabbing her shoulder.

"Is this a joke?" Jane asked, one hand on the asphalt, the other pointing over the barricades. "That's my kid who just ran past you!"

The cop let go, unbothered, concealed behind his sunglasses. He folded his arms and reassumed his wide-legged stance in front of the barricades, elbow to elbow with his colleagues, like Jane held no interest for him, and never had. They were a tighter operation over here on the north side of Main Street, wearing more equipment, not inclined to chitchat.

"Whose side are you on?" one probort shouted at Jane.

"Just let her get her kid," another probort said.

Two cops down the line nodded at Jane. She slipped between them and under the yellow tape and began pushing into the crowd. "Mirela, where are you? Mirela, come to Mommy!"

"You're desperate, you lost! You're desperate, you lost!" the proborts were chanting. Their side was younger. Not all of them were sensibly dressed for the gray weather. Band T-shirts over flannel. One read FUDGE-PACKIN' CRACK-SMOKIN' SATAN-WORSHIPPIN' MOTHERFUCKER. Their side had more women, but not mothers, Jane thought—just college students and lesbians, not women like her. There were women kissing each other on the mouth—in greeting, nothing more, but still. She shouldered and elbowed past and through their bodies in a *shush-shush* rhythm of polyester coat sleeves and calling out her child's name. They would know who she was and that she didn't belong among them. Jane came against a tall tomato-red coat, her nose pressed against a *shush-shush*ing armpit and a Columbia brand insignia, and she felt the obscure pleasure again, the longing to squeeze her eyes shut and wrap her arms around this body in this coat, push her head inside it, un-button the buttons on the shirt underneath it, and breathe in the skin inside.

"Mirela!" she called.

"Someone help this gal find her child!"

"She's here—we've got her," a woman's voice called out. Jane moved toward the sound.

A pocket had opened in the crowd, a protective circle around Mirela. She turned and turned, smiling and waving at each face watching her, the rosie in the ring.

"Mirela, thank God . . ." Jane said, reaching for the girl's arm, but Mirela eluded her and ran over to Bridie, pulling at Bridie's hand, laughing, jumping up and down.

"Aren't you a charmer!" Bridie said to Mirela.

"Our bodies, our lives, our right to decide!" they were chanting.

"What's your name, sweetheart?" Bridie asked.

"Babby koowa!" Mirela replied readily.

Bridie's colleagues tittered. Even here, Jane and Mirela found themselves putting on a show.

Bridie's eyes fell on Jane. "Ah, Jane, you've made it back to us. Hope you had a safe journey. This cutie pie is yours, I presume?"

Jane nodded and swallowed. She had her speech prepared. "My name is Jane, and this is my daughter Mirela," she said over the clamor. "She got a hard start. The first few years of her life were hell. But she had a right to be born, and I'm so blessed and humbled by God to—"

It had felt so right in her head lying in bed last night, and in the shower long before dawn this morning. When she was still in the shower and the proborts were already here.

"Hey, lady," a white woman in dreadlocks on Jane's right called out, "I spoke with God today, and you know what? She's pro-choice! And she told me that my body is mine alone!"

"—I'm so blessed to be given the chance to show her a good life—"

"Ho-ho, hey-hey," three college-aged protesters on Jane's left sang in unison, "Operation Failure, go away."

"I'm not from out of town—"

Someone had given Mirela a glazed doughnut, and she was trying to stuff it into her pocket, backward on her hip.

"I'm not with Operation Rescue," Jane said. "I live here. I'm from Buffalo."

They could hear a cop on the other side of the tape, somewhere in the no-man's-land between the opposing sides, maybe smack in the middle of Main Street. He was trying to give orders over the feedback of a bullhorn. Everyone gasped and covered their ears and Mirela laughed and spun. The cop started yelling. "Everyone has to back up!" he bayed. "Everyone who is not an officer of the law or an identified escort, back up, back up, back up!" She hoped Mirela's disappearance had caused some kind of diversion, and now the street belonged to their friends.

Jill came up behind Bridie, sidled around in front of her. "Out!" She was pointing at Jane. "Get her out of here!"

"Jane, unless you've had some radical change of heart, I think it may be time—" Bridie's voice was caustic.

"Your kid was trying to tell you something, coming over to our side," said a young bearded man in a poncho.

"Maybe she was," Jane said, fixing him with her best earnest gaze. "Scripture tells us always to listen and consider what our children have to say. Scripture says—"

"Yeah, time's up, lady. You got what you came here for," said White Dreadlocks.

"Scripture says, 'But Mary treasured up all these things, and pondered them in her heart.' I try to do the same," Jane said.

Poncho Guy nodded. "Uh-huh. She's adopted? That girl?"

"Where is she from?" asked White Dreadlocks.

The bullhorn was screeching again, and Mirela laughed at the beauty of the painful sound. Poncho Guy and White Dreadlocks grimaced and crumpled inside the feedback, and Jane saw her chance to lead Mirela back to their group. They pushed and pulled through the crush back to Main Street.

"Racist, sexist, anti-gay, born-again bigots, go away!"

"We don't want any of your sidewalk counseling! You need your own counseling!"

The pro-life protesters had covered Main Street on their hands and knees. Their bodies were not their own. These were the bodies of vulnerable children, barely able to crawl. Jane watched Phil as he knelt straight down in a puddle—he could have easily avoided it. He was acting out a child's clumsiness, or indulging his own thirst for martyrdom. "Hold the line!" Phil was shouting from the puddle. "Hold the line! Link your arms and link your feet! Crawl toward the yellow tape! Keep your eye! On! The tape! If they're not touching you, move!" A dozen of the Oh-Rs had linked themselves together, arm in arm, with horseshoe-shaped bicycle locks. A larger swell of cops now stood between the pro-life side and the clinic. A few cops were leaning over the kneeling protesters, their fingertips resting primly on their bowed heads.

"Come down here on the ground with me, Mirela," Jane said, and Mirela obeyed, getting on her hands and knees in imitation of Jane, as Jane had been almost certain she would, because she had never asked Mirela to do such a thing before.

"It's not your body, honey," Summer Huebler was calling out on her knees, "it's a child."

A chant began. "There will never be another you! There will never be another you!"

An officer took up Summer's hand as if to place a ring upon her finger, and instead he fitted plastic handcuffs around her wrist. Summer went limp, as they had all been instructed to, and the cop dragged her toward a line of police cars. The pressure of her dead weight against the pavement prodded a loafer off her foot. Mirela pointed and laughed at the abandoned shoe. "Babby koowa!" she screamed at Summer.

Charity Huebler cried after her sister from her hands and knees. "Summer, I'll come find you!"

"Charity, I'm okay!" Summer called back.

Mr. Glover was sitting up on his knees with his hands cuffed behind him. His arresting officer had left him there to consult with two colleagues on various clamps and implements that might

succeed in separating the bike-locked Oh-Rs. "Jane," Mr. Glover
called out to her, "what you and Mirela did before was *galvanizing*.
We never would have made it back into Main Street without Mirela's bravery."

"That's nice of you to say, Mr. Glover," she called back, "but if
you've ever been to Wegmans with Mirela, you know that bolting
away is just how she does things."

Mr. Glover offered a magnanimous shrug and fell backward.
"God works in mysterious ways, Jane!" he shouted, prone.

Mirela climbed onto Jane's curved back. "Ho-sey wide!" she announced.

"Mirela, you're going to break my back," Jane gasped, spreading her hands apart and bending her elbows to distribute Mirela's
weight. Mirela tumbled onto the pavement, on purpose, and let out
the laugh that meant she was hurt. Charity stared at Mirela and
murmured the Hail Mary as a cop cuffed her.

"That kid is Teflon," Mr. Glover was calling over to Jane. "Just
watch. She's your Kryptonite. Your human shield!"

"Lady." A different cop was admonishing Jane, looming over
her bent shoulder. Jane waited for the pinch and click of the cuffs
around her wrists. "Just get outta here already, and take the kid with
you," he said. "I won't tell ya again."

"She gets to leave?" Charity was asking. "Just like that? Because
she brought a kid with her?"

"I'm not moving," Jane called back to Charity.

"Jane, Jane, go to Rosen's—" Mr. Glover was calling.

"That's a good idea, actually," Charity yelled as a cop began lug-
ging her away. "Go to Rosen's, Jane!"

"Go to Wozen!" Mirela said, rolling around on the pavement.

"I'm not leaving all of you," Jane said.

"Ma'am, I need you to get up," Jane's cop was saying.

"Get up!" Mirela said, rising to her feet.

"Go to Rosen's, Jane," Mr. Glover repeated. "See what you can
make happen there. Mirela is our Joan of Arc!"

"Go to Wozen!" Mirela agreed. She started running east, the

right direction. Jane followed her, darting and weaving through the mazes and chains of kneeling protesters in various states of prayer and arrest, feeling the vertigo of impunity. Mirela was running away and for once no one was telling her not to, no one was grabbing her by the arm or saying *no, don't, bad, stop.*

Three blocks. That was nothing to Mirela. Mirela could outlast and outrun them all.

DR. ROSEN OPERATED his practice out of a timber-frame clapboard house with a rolled-tile roof. Similar houses nearby had wraparound porches, but Dr. Rosen's entrance was through a brick enclosure, one that looked like it was added to the original house later, as a fortification. Two young women sat cross-legged atop the roof of the brick addition, like snipers, one peering through a camcorder with a blinking red light. Cheap roofing sheet curled upward around them, like a rotting carpet. There were no police barricades erected around the house, but police in riot helmets and neon-orange smocks were everywhere. The proborts had wrapped themselves around the house five deep, arms locked. The swaddling mass of bodies was claustrophobic, sickening, annihilatingly sexual, a python consuming its prey. The obscure pleasure placed its hand again on the small of Jane's back. To push, to press, to bear another body, to be wrapped in another body. No faces, just rising and falling musculature under *shush-shush*ing fabric and clammy, clinging fingers. To submit to the python, to struggle against its impersonal, motiveless crush.

A line of cops on the sidewalk in front of the house, separating the two sides. In the street, another crawling procession toward yellow tape, like the scene in front of WellWomen. "Hold the line!" a man was calling from his hands and knees.

"Go to Wozen," Mirela was imploring Jane, tugging on her coat sleeve.

Mary treasured up all these things, and pondered them in her heart.

Jane took Mirela's hand as they came close to the rear of the crawling procession. A riot cop materialized in their path, arms crossed.

"You brought your kid to this?" the cop asked.

"Babby koowa!" Mirela said.

Jane smiled apologetically at the cop. "I can't believe the language she's picked up already this morning," she said. "We just, uh—we need to get through?"

"You live on this block?" the cop asked. "You got ID?"

"Uh, Dr. Rosen is my neighbor," Jane said, careful not to lie.

"Dee-ya! Dee-ya!" Mirela was pointing at the python. Jane glimpsed Delia in the outer ring of the python, arm in arm with protesters on either side. "Right-to-life, your name's a lie, you don't care if women die!" she was chanting.

"Yes, that's Delia!" Jane called out.

"Hey, Mrs. Brennan!" Delia called back, pulling one arm free of her companion and waving.

"Nice to see you!" Jane said, waving back, hoping the cop would take note of this neighborly exchange. Mirela smiled sweetly at the cop, mimicking Jane.

The cop shrugged and looked away. "Do what you gotta do," he told Jane. "But this is no place for a kid."

"I'll get her home safe, Officer, thank you," Jane said. Jane and Mirela walked silently past Dr. Rosen's practice, the python on their left, the line of riot cops on their right. Jane recognized the reverend's voice, calling from the front of the kneeling procession.

"What do we do when they scream in our faces?" the reverend was asking. His batter-beigeness in person put Jane in mind of the gingerbread man. "We stay calm. We sit. We sing. We pray. We think about the babies. We need to stay with them. Stay right there with the babies. Feel them in your hearts. They need to know they're not alone."

This all sounded like a speech Father Steve would give. Jane wondered if he had arrived at WellWomen yet. She hoped the cops hadn't snagged him before she'd had a chance to talk to him about how the protest was going.

"Let's pray for the women who have been scheduled here. There are appointments that will be happening right now." The members of the procession folded their hands on the pavement and rested their heads there. Butts in the air. Each of Jane's kids had slept like that at some point in their babyhood.

Jane could see, as she and Mirela came closer, that the reverend was standing atop a wooden crate. The sun had come out just for him. Three local camera crews were set up in front of where he stood, as if he had summoned them, directed them.

"You, there," the reverend called. "The woman in the blue coat, with the child. Welcome!"

"Hello, howyoo!" Mirela replied.

"Keep moving, lady," said a cop on her right.

"Ladies and gentlemen, a mother with her child—we haven't seen enough of that today, have we? Because that is what this is all about, isn't it? Join us, please."

The cop moved to place himself between Jane and the kneeling procession, and Mirela darted around him and into the street. "I have to . . ." Jane began, and the cop put up his hands, allowing Jane, too, to run into the street and catch Mirela by the arm just as the girl tripped over a praying leg.

"What did Jesus say?" the reverend was asking. "Jesus said, 'Suffer the children and forbid them not to come unto Me, for such is the kingdom of heaven.' Who is this child, ma'am? Come closer, both of you."

Jane and Mirela edged closer to the reverend, praying bodies shuffling aside to let them past. Jane got to her knees on the asphalt and pulled Mirela down beside her.

"Tell us of yourself and of your child, ma'am," the reverend said.

"My name is Jane, and this is my daughter Mirela," she began, and faltered. She could not find the rest of it. "She is—I am—blessed and humbled by God."

"Your soul is a masterpiece, Mariella!" someone called out behind them.

"Every child deserves a birthday!" another yelled, and others began chanting the refrain.

"Mah buh day?" Mirela asked.

Behind her Jane sensed the cops moving in on the procession. She could hear the *clink* of handcuffs, the grating of the bodies on the pavement. Jane craned around to watch the last testaments of the witnesses before they were swept into police vans.

"We are not the ones disturbing the peace and killing babies! Over there—arrest them, arrest *them*! We are here for peace!"

"I pray to God for a peaceful resolution of the child-killing issue before other people get hurt!"

Jane turned back. The reverend was rummaging around beneath his crate. There was Tupperware under there.

"There is a doctor who performs late-term abortions at Children's Hospital! At a *children's hospital*! Can you imagine the *depravity*?!"

The reverend stood up and held aloft—

He held—

He had—

Held in his hands—

What was it? What did Jane think—at first, at the time—it was? A doll? A package? A parcel of victuals for the tailgate they had all been promised? A rubbery cross-section of internal organs used as a teaching tool in middle-grade science classrooms? She blinked and cocked her head and still it refused to come into focus. She could not see what she was seeing. She heard a gasp, a shout, a collective groan. Other people were seeing it. What was it?

You are far enough along that we have two choices here.

(The first choice, of course, was they could break down the baby inside her and take it out with instruments.)

She'd seen her before.

(The second choice, of course, was she could give birth to the baby, who was already dead.)

They put you in my arms, and I knew it was you.

"This! This is what abortion on demand and without apology looks like—that says it all, doesn't it? Nips it in the bud."

"Buddy, what is—is that what I think it is?" A man's voice, a Buffalo accent, from over near the camera crews.

She glanced over at Mirela, who had acquired an ABORTION KILLS CHILDREN sign and held it over her head as she spun in circles.

"What do you think it is?" the reverend asked.

"Buddy, that is—you are disgusting. That is the most disgusting thing I've ever seen in my life."

"It is, isn't it?"

"That's horrible."

"Isn't it horrible?"

"*You* are horrible. That is sick, what you're doing. You are sick."

"This is sick? Well, I would agree. We agree with each other."

"How did you get that?" a woman's voice called.

"I agree with you that—"

"How did you get that? Where the hell did you get that?" More and more voices. Bystanders, Jane could see. Not necessarily proborts.

The python couldn't see the reverend.

"See, we have found a place where we agree. We agree that this is sick."

"Is that real?"

"This is not a political issue. This is not a partisan issue."

"Is it real?"

"This is not politics."

"Guys, it's real—he says it's real!"

"It's not real."

"That is sick!"

"If it's real—"

"Would you like to touch her?"

"You are sick—"

"Say what you want about me—but would you like to touch her? Her name is Thea."

"You are fucking sick, man."

"Would you like to touch her, and decide for yourself if she is real?"

"This is sick, man."

"I understand why you might feel sick."

"We are going to have to take that thing away from you." Two cops were pulling the reverend off his crate.

"Reverend—" Jane said from the ground.

"She's a she, Officer. She's not a thing," the reverend said calmly, cradling what he held in his hands.

"Reverend—you don't know—" Jane said.

"She's a human being, murdered, Officer."

"Reverend," Jane said, "that's not a—you don't know she's a—"

"We're going to have to take you into custody, sir."

"A real aborted baby, Officer, sir, dead at nineteen weeks."

"Why are you arresting him?"

"Sir, why in the world did you bring that here?"

"Nineteen weeks?" Jane asked.

"More or less," the reverend replied. He was looking at her again. "What difference does it make?"

"Nineteen weeks?" she asked again.

"Ma'am, please stand up."

"Reverend," Jane said, "that's a stillborn baby."

This is the body of Christ.

"Jane? Jane, is that you?"

This is the blood of Christ.

"Reverend, that's a stillborn baby."

He gave his only begotten son.

"Where is the baby's mother?" Jane said. "Does she know you've done this?"

"Ma'am, I already told ya—"

We have two choices here.

"Jane—"

"Did you ask her—did you tell her—that baby had a mother—"

Where is the mother's body? Jane thought, and one arm twisted behind her back.

"That baby had a mother——"

Are you my mother? asked the baby bird.

Hands all over her body. "Please don't touch me——I have every right to be here——you do not have the right to touch me——"

The officer pulled her other arm behind her back.

"I didn't say that you could touch me——"

Her arm twisted back and her chest cavity opened and her heart fell into her stomach and something, a brittle thought, the recognition, flapped out of her sternum, fell on the ground dead.

"Mirela?" she asked, almost to herself, as she wrenched her head around to one side and the other as far as she could. "Mirela?"

ANOTHER YEAR, ANOTHER wedding. Their table had started talking about a movie. What was it called? Karen Allen was in it, or Brooke Adams—one of those. All those toothsome, tough-pretty brunettes from around the time when the boys were born. Debra Winger. Margot Kidder? Pat corrected Jane on a minor plot point, and Jane countered that Pat's correction was incorrect, and Pat ended up throwing his dessert fork down and stalking off who knows where, and in the car home the dispute became a fight about Pat's incessant need to prove Jane wrong on everything and Jane's incessant need to show herself to be perfect and both of their incessant needs to embarrass each other in front of good, respectable people who would never see them the same way again or invite them to their homes or their families' weddings, and what was different about this fight was that when Pat and Jane returned home, Pat paid the teenager who had watched the children and drove her home and drove back, and Jane did some tidying up, and then they both went to bed. They did not speak to each other, though they slept side by side. The next morning, they still said nothing, locked in a businesslike stalemate. And then Pat asked Jane if she had time to go to the dry cleaner that day and Jane asked Pat if he'd remembered to fill the tank of the dragon wagon, and regular communications more or less resumed.

All at once, silently and together, they had reconsidered their options. They could argue and fume for days, which was what they usually did. They could whisper-fight in their bedroom for hours in hopes of coming to some resolution, the failure of which would still result in more days of arguing and fuming. Or they could forget about it. Let it wither for lack of sunlight. Finally put the ficus out of its misery. A wound should not be allowed to fester, but perhaps their marriage would heal over adequately enough if they could both just resist the urge to pick at it, because neither of them was going to change, because nothing could ever happen to prevent these fights in the future, because their marriage had mutated into a third person, a fourth (now fifth) child, a toddler, whose tantrums were debilitating but also a normal, unavoidable aspect of development—except this was worse, so much more debilitating because they did not love this toddler, could not bring themselves to pay more than grudging attention to this toddler, who would never develop out of the tantrums, in fact would never grow up at all, but wouldn't die or go away, either, would just continue to whine and weep and Magic Marker the walls and shit the diaper and rip the shitty diaper off for laughs for the rest of their godforsaken lives.

Their conflicts and their resentments were weather. Nothing could be so trite as to talk about the weather.

So Jane felt something like surprise, lying in bed with the lights out at day's end—the day Mirela ran away and went missing, not that she'd gone missing very long, not that she was ever really missing at all, as the whole affair was totally blown out of proportion—when Pat sat down on the other side of the bed and said, "We need to talk about what happened today and what's next."

"Not now," Jane said into the dark.

"Yes, now."

"I've been up since four a.m. and I'm very tired."

Pat snickered. "And why are you so tired, Jane?"

"I know that how things are now is not tenable."

"Tired from your *pro*-test? Because you're a *pro*-tester now? Saving babies? Washed in the blood of the lamb? Who are you, Jane Fonda on a tank?"

"And I know we need to do something to make things better."

"And what are you going to do about it?"

"Well, seeing as it's all on me to figure it out and I can't hope for any help from you—"

"You made this happen! You want my help to clean up your mess?"

"I know what I'm going to do. There is a clinic in Colorado that specializes in treating children like Mirela."

"*Hmmm*, another *clinic*. Not sure we've had the best of luck with *clinics* lately."

"They are very highly regarded, cutting-edge. I heard about them from a brilliant graduate student at UB—her name is Delia Reizer. I've had the clinic's materials for a while and I've thought it over carefully."

"Sure, just make a few phone calls, right?" Pat sneered. "Easy as calling in the electrician. Just do a little rewiring, presto."

"You would know who Delia was, and what she had to say, if you paid any attention to the challenges Mirela faces," Jane said.

"If *you* knew anything about the challenges Mirela faces, you wouldn't have brought her to that *shit show*—"

"Who brought her there, Pat? Who brought her there?"

"You told me to! It was your decision! All of this is your doing!"

Pat flopped back on the bed and stared at the ceiling.

"I made you do it," Jane said. The *nyah-nyah* tone in her voice was ugly and stupid and intoxicating.

"Fuck you, Jane!" he hissed, bolting up from bed again and pacing the carpet, his hands balled into fists. If she pushed a little further, *nyah-nyah*ed one more time, she could make him punch the dresser, rip the curtains from the rods, try to strangle a bedpost. She could make him do it.

"In any case," Jane said. "I called this afternoon, the second I got home——"

"Home *from jail*," he said.

"Pat, they took us to the Clearfield rec center. In a Metro bus. It was like a field trip the kids would go on. I mean, we could have dropped by the library afterward if we wanted to. Clearly nobody took any of it all that seriously."

"You were *arrested*."

"The clinic is in Colorado—I called them when I had a chance to breathe after Dee and Marie came over, and by the way, I'm grateful that they could help out today, Pat, and I'm grateful that they are in our lives——"

"Oh, shut up, Jane." He was grinding his fists into his eyeballs, groaning.

"All righty, then. Just to finish my thought——"

"And you're always accusing *me* of being passive-aggressive. What a joke."

"——the clinic can take us on short notice. I can buy the plane tickets tomorrow. And yes, Pat, this has all been a joke. All I ever think about is how can I do a funny ha-ha joke on you and make you feel bad, bad, bad."

He sat down on the bed, back turned to her. She was still on her back, hadn't even bothered to raise herself on one elbow, but she'd moved him all around the room, with just her words.

"And that'll fix it, is that right?" Pat said. "Some clinic, God knows where?"

"I didn't say it would fix it. Colorado is not God knows where. It's one of the fifty states of America, the country of our birth and citizenship. It's spelled *C-O-L-O-R-A*——"

"You just pick up the phone, buy the tickets—oh, and I have to wonder who's paying for *that*—and that's it, all better? If that's the case, then why didn't you take her to the clinic in the first place?"

"Mirela. Her name is Mirela."

"Why did you do this to us, Jane?"

"You never say *Mirela*. It's always *she, her. It,* why don't you call her *it?*"

"You are an id-ee-*it.*"

"And it's only been six months."

"And it feels like six goddamn years." The mattress nudged and eddied Jane as he got up again and flipped on the bedside lamp. Jane shaded her eyes as her pupils shrank.

"I had no say in this." Pat was standing over her, pointing his finger in her face. "You turned my life upside down, you turned the kids' lives upside down, and you didn't even ask me."

"I did ask you."

"You didn't ask *them.*"

"I did ask you. We talked about it. You just didn't take it seriously."

"Bullshit."

"And I didn't need your permission."

"I never adopted her, Jane. There was no legal process—"

"No. Enough. I didn't need you."

"Did *you* adopt her? Legally? Where is the paperwork? Whose is she, Jane?"

"Stop."

"Where is her mother?"

"I am her mother."

"Her *real* mother!"

"I am her real mother."

Now Jane understood why it rankled her when people asked about Mirela's real mother. The implication was not only that Jane was unreal, but that Mirela was, too—that she was false, fake, unverifiable until her real mother could be located and interrogated.

Jane got out of bed. "Whose is she?" Pat demanded as she slipped past him out the door.

She moved down the hallway, pausing to steady herself against the wall, hand flat against the spot where PJ's first-grade portrait used to hang, the one where he was missing all four front teeth.

"Lauren?" she whispered, opening the door to Lauren's room.

"Yeah, Mom," Lauren said. She sounded wide awake, like she'd been listening to her parents fight. Her room was closest to theirs.

"Honey, Dad is snoring, so I'm going to sleep with you tonight, okay?"

"Okay, Mom," Lauren said, moving over in the bed.

Jane tickled Lauren's hair with her fingers, rubbed her arm. Lauren lay so eerily still in the spoon that Jane knew she wasn't asleep but rather wanted to be thought asleep. Jane worried the bottom hem of Lauren's T-shirt between her thumb and forefinger. It had been a long time since she had prayed before bed. She begged Jesus Christ, the only Son of the Father, for forgiveness for her sins, and when she had run out of her own sins she said the Hail Mary and the Act of Contrition, alternating between them over and over, lips silently forming the words, starving herself of sleep like a saint would, although a true saint would never share a bed with a man, or with a child of her own making.

Jane's mind whirred. She was ground beneath its wheels. She stopped her prayers and instead took an inventory of the child or the girl or the almost-woman whose body was in hers. Lauren's knees pulled chestward, almost seated in her mother's lap, her mother's outline curving around her. As they had begun.

Once upon a time, it was just Jane and Lauren. Or it could have been. *Duck* and *bight* and honey-almond folds. The grimy rental on Evans Road. If only they had gotten that far. What difference did it make what other people thought of them, if they knew who they were and knew their love for each other? Surely it would have been the first stop on a big adventure. Jane consented to the thought that erased PJ and Sean and Mirela. Or worse than erased Mirela—just left her where she was, in a dank cot across an ocean. Jane lay down in the thought. The best time of all had been just Lauren, because that was the time when they could get away.

Lauren had gotten away. Or almost, she was almost there. She had what she needed: she was pretty and slim and she got straight As. She was an athlete, she was smart, creative, her teachers paid her lots of attention, they wanted to see her up on a stage—she belonged there, all eyes on her. Two lead roles in a row as a freshman, and no training, no voice or dance lessons, nothing. A natural talent. She was special. Jane had been distracted from her lately, yes, but others were captivated. Lauren was fine. So much more than fine. She wouldn't be like Jane. She would go to college. She would create a life that was her own, intentional. She would date different boys before deciding on one forever. Her children would be—if she chose to have—her children would be—

The whirring again. She felt herself driven to dust. She pressed her face against her baby's hair, her ribs under her light hand rose and fell. The baby, the baby, the baby is okay, she is still in her arms, the baby is okay, the baby, the baby is okay.

LAUREN

They were pretty sure Mom would get onto the news on all three local stations, but they could only watch one while recording another, over a soundtrack of Mirela's screams from the backyard, where Nana Dee was trying to play with her.

"I still don't understand how you could have lost her," Dad was saying, "when at any moment you can hear her in six counties."

"Shh, it's starting," PJ and Sean said.

"Jane Brennan of Williamsville never thought of herself as an activist," the reporter began.

"You know, I've got four kids; they keep me pretty busy."

Lauren still startled by *four*.

"It's Mom!" PJ and Sean announced. "Mom's on TV!"

"You look pretty, Mom," Lauren said. On the screen, Mom's cheeks were flushed with the wet spring cold, and her hair swept across her brow in a curtain.

"But when Operation Rescue came to town to protest abortions in the area, gaining nationwide attention for what they are calling the Spring of Life, Jane just knew she had to be part of it," the reporter continued. "You see, her youngest child, Mirela, is adopted." Slo-mo shot of Mirela spinning on the sidewalk beside Mom, doing the electrocuted smile. "For Mirela to join the family, Jane had to launch her own kind of rescue operation, saving the girl from an overcrowded orphanage in Communist Romania. To see Mirela now, you'd never guess the horrors she escaped, thanks to this Williamsville family."

"She is adopted," Mom was saying as the camera cut back to her, then to a scene of chanting crowds, then back to Mirela. "And so, you know, you just want to show people there's another way, you— you can choose life."

"Wait, I just saw—was that Dr. Rosen's picture?" Lauren said.

"But what began as a protest on behalf of lost little lives . . . almost ended with a little girl lost."

"*Ooooohh*," Sean and PJ said in unison, Sean clutching his stomach in mock-pain and PJ slapping his forehead with his palm. "*That's a little straaaiiinnned*," Sean ululated in his opera voice, clutching at PJ's arm. PJ elbowed him in the gut, and Sean keened with gladness.

"The irony is not lost on me," Mom was saying on TV. "I'm just glad she's okay."

"Mom, you were protesting Dr. Rosen?" Lauren asked. "What was that sign with Dr. Rosen's picture on it?"

"The protesters had a big reveal in store—one we can't show you on TV."

"It was pretty dramatic, yes," Mom was saying into the microphone.

The news cut to a slow-mo of Mom, her jaw dropping open.

"Mom?" Lauren asked again. "That's Stitch's dad. Stitch is my friend." Mom, on the couch, shook her head and closed her eyes.

"Didn't that Rosen kid call here the other night?" Dad asked.

"Mom, you promised that you wouldn't do anything to embarrass me," Lauren said as the phone started ringing.

"Hi, Glenis," Dad said. "You've got Channel 4? We're watching Channel 7, and we're taping Channel 2. Talk to you in a bit."

"In all the hubbub," the reporter said, "Mirela slipped away. And Jane Brennan the activist. Had to rediscover. Jane Brennan. The mom."

"I mean, she was fine," Mom was saying to the reporter, "but I had quite a fright for a moment there."

"Good Samaritans found Mirela at the nearby Pancake Palace

restaurant, where the little social butterfly had already made acquaintances with diners as well as hostess Joanie Schmertz."

"Joanie from bowling league?" Dad asked.

"She's a very happy, very, *very* friendly little girl," Joanie was telling the reporter.

Cut to Joanie on a ladder propped against the side of the Pancake Palace, inching the DR. ROSEN KILLS CHILDREN banner off the roof with a broom.

"Jesus H. Christ," Dad said.

"Today, Operation Rescue is back out on our streets, on day four of the Spring of Life protests that have already resulted in two hundred arrests. But Jane Brennan, activist *and* mom, is on the sidelines for now. She is back home with her kids, including little Mirela, who has now been the happy beneficiary of not *one*. But *two*. Rescue. Operations. Deena Sobel, WGRZ News, Buffalo."

"Who writes this shit?" Pat asked.

"Shit, shit, shit, shit, shit!" PJ and Sean chanted.

"Mom, why were you even talking to a reporter?" Lauren asked.

"We're supposed to take any opportunity to put a face to our cause," Mom said. "I had Father Steve's blessing."

"He wasn't even there!" Dad said. "Your hero stood you up!"

"Why did you have that awful sign about Stitch's dad?" Lauren asked.

"I had *nothing* to do with that!" Mom said.

"Oh, *sure* you didn't," Dad spluttered.

Lauren felt a crystalline desire, a longing she could feel calcifying under her brow and the nape of her neck, for Dad to stop talking, stop being there. She did not want to have to share her anger with Dad's anger.

"And why were you talking to them about Mirela?" Lauren asked. "She has nothing to do with any of this."

"She shouldn't have been there!" Dad's voice had climbed to a yell.

If Lauren had to halve her anger to make room for Dad's, then her pity would see its chance to sidle in and smother her resolution. She did not want to pity her mother, so small and helpless on the couch, so reasonable and remorseful.

"Mirela is nobody's business but ours," Lauren said.

"I didn't volunteer that Mirela was adopted," Mom said. "The reporter asked me, and I said yes. And then the reporter said, 'Could you answer in a complete sentence, so it's easier for us to edit together later?' so I said, 'She is adopted.' Or whatever I said. Then there was an awkward silence, like they wanted me to say more, and I didn't know if it was just going to be dead air on TV. I guess I forgot it wasn't live. I was trying to be polite. Notice how they keep cutting away to Mirela or to the other protesters? You can see there that they edit it together to twist the meaning. They manipulate the conversation like that. They manufacture it."

Dad was talking over her. "They wouldn't have had any footage to manipulate if you had just shut up! Just shut the hell up! What the hell were you thinking, Jane?"

"Don't tell Mom to shut up!" Lauren yelled, and Dad stamped out of the room.

Jane slumped deeper into the sofa. "Dad is right. Father Steve stood us up," she told Lauren. "And as far as I know, the reverend is still in jail."

"What for?" Lauren asked.

"Or not in jail, in the rec center."

Mom had gone to all that trouble, and she hadn't even made it to real jail.

"Why's he in the rec center?"

"For disorderly conduct and for creating a physically offensive condition," Jane said.

Dad by the door again. Shifting from foot to foot, snorting, shuffling. Nobody ever accused Dad of wanting attention.

"What does 'creating a physically offensive condition' mean?" Dad asked, gripping either side of the door frame like he could tear down the walls if he received the wrong answer.

"It's when Sean lays a log and forgets to flush," PJ said from his spot inches away from the TV. PJ said this tentatively, like a peace offering.

"The reverend pulled a bit of a stunt," Mom said.

"He threw a dead baby into the crowd!" Sean said.

"No—wait, how did you hear that?" Mom asked.

"Everyone heard that," Sean said.

"Who is *everyone*?" Dad asked.

"I heard a bunch of lesbians started playing Hacky Sack with the dead baby," PJ said. He paused and looked around, still concerned that he was interpreting the mood of the room correctly. "That was a joke."

Sean laughed, trying to reassure PJ. "Right, I get it, because Mom thinks all the baby killers are lesbians!"

"No, I do not—it's not—it was a *doll*," Mom said. Her throat audibly constricted on the word *doll*. Lauren wondered if her dad or brothers had heard it—that was the tell.

"You don't know it was a doll," Lauren said.

"A very realistic doll," Mom said. "People assumed it was real, and he was shoving it in everyone's face."

"I shove my *balls* in your face," yelped Sean, and PJ clamped his hand over Sean's mouth, and Sean slurped at his brother's palm.

"How do you know for sure it was a doll?" Lauren asked.

"A cop threw up," Mom blurted out.

"So, right—why would a cop throw up *if it was just a doll*?" Lauren asked.

PJ made retching noises, opening his mouth wide enough for Sean to hock a loogie into it.

"When you were born, Lauren, Dad said you looked like a doll," Mom said.

"I did?" Dad asked.

"I don't remember that," Lauren said.

"Of course you don't—you were just born," Mom said.

Mom only told stories about the three of them that they were too young to remember, stories they couldn't tell themselves; they couldn't quibble over details. Maybe that was when Mom loved them best, before they could make memories that she couldn't have all to herself.

"Did it have a smell?" Lauren asked. "The baby?"

"Lauren, that's kind of an awful question," Mom said.

"Lauren, that's kind of an awful smelly ass you have," Sean said.

"It doesn't even matter whether or not it was real," Mom said. "They made their point."

"Did you make your point, Jane?" Dad asked. "Did you *get your point across?*"

"Leave her alone!" Lauren screamed at Dad, standing up as Mom caught her arm, and he punched the door frame with his fist and walked out of the house.

"HEY, LAUREN," ANDY said. The tone of a swiveling head. Andy, Stitch, and Rajiv were walking out of Tedquarters. She was late for rehearsal. "Seems like your mom is so busy saving babies that she can't keep track of her own kid."

"The irony is not lost on her," Lauren said.

"Sucks for you to have to kiss her," Andy said to Stitch, "seeing as she thinks your dad's a baby killer."

"I do not think that," Lauren said. Andy knocked into her opposite hip as he and Rajiv walked past. "Whoops, sorry!" he sang over Rajiv's screeching cackle.

Stitch hung behind. "I'm sorry he said that," Lauren told him.

"We're expected to go to the auditorium now to practice 'We Go Together,'" Stitch said, looking past her down the hall.

The big closing number, entire ensemble, the fastest choreography, lyrics full of junk and nonsense, mortifying *wompa lompa lompa*s and *dippety doo bee dah*s. Lauren had skipped the previous run-through of the song, and she hadn't practiced on her own at all.

Lauren followed Stitch to the auditorium. "Stitch, honestly, I'm sorry about everything that happened with the protest and all that junk."

"Thanks," Stitch said, stopping outside the entrance to the wings. "I think they're set to go. Everyone's up there but us."

"Are you okay?" she asked him.

He peered nervously into the wings. Lauren had never seen him nervous before. They could hear Mr. Smith's voice, sounding tired and frustrated. "The city gave us a round-the-clock guard," Stitch said. Hands in pockets, head down, pushing the toes of his Converse into the carpet. "Two cops all the time, all night. If you cut through our yard going home tonight, you'll probably see them." He shrugged. "Or you could cut through somebody else's yard, for a change. You know, it's up to you."

"I'm sorry you have to have guards," Lauren said. "That's terrible."

"No, it's not—they're nice guys." He was almost stabbing the carpet with his Converse now, like he was trying to crush a cockroach.

"Oh, I'm sure, but—it sucks that you need that."

"It's not the first time this stuff has happened. They used to picket us every year on Hanukkah. Right on our front lawn. Screaming 'baby killer' through the dining room window while we played dreidel and lit the menorah. My dad used to get so mad."

"Stitch, I am so sorry."

"My little brother on my mom's lap, watching them bang on the window. I remember that." He tapped his foot three times on the carpet and looked up at her, mouth a thin line, eyes not rheumy but gleaming, appraising. It astonished Lauren to realize that Stitch could cry. He wasn't going to cry in front of her right now, but he had cried before, and he would again; he was capable of it.

"I'm sorry," she said.

"Yeah, you keep saying that."

"I also want you to know that I don't agree with my mom about this stuff."

"I get it." He was looking down again, grinding his toe. "You are not your mom."

"I think what she's doing is messed up."

"It's messed up to bad-mouth your mom, though."

"I'm not bad-mouthing her. I'm just saying we disagree."

"Okay. Congratulations."

Stitch turned his face and took a deep breath. Lauren stared at his profile as he exhaled. "You know," he said, "my grandmother died a couple of weeks ago, and—"

"Oh, I'm so sorry—"

"I don't need all that—"

"—on top of everything else your family has been through—"

"No, I don't need all that. But it reminded me. There's this old rule about sitting shiva. You probably don't know it. You're Catholic, right? So you wouldn't know about this. People don't follow this rule all that often anymore. But the old rule was if you came to the house of the bereaved, you weren't supposed to speak unless they spoke to you. You were supposed to bear witness to their pain in silence. If the suffering person wanted to talk, then they could make that decision themselves. It wasn't up to you." He looked up at her again. "Do you get it? It's not up to you."

"Lauren, Stitch—what the hell?" Christo, the accompanist, was beckoning them from the door to the backstage. "We're all waiting for you."

Stitch slipped past Christo in the doorway and into the wings. Because it appeared to Lauren to be the least impossible option—because it seemed just barely plausible that she could follow familiar instructions as an interchangeable component of a large coordinated group, as opposed to being left alone and unassimilated in the silence of an empty hallway, where she would be immediately swarmed by the full volume and velocity of her current predicament—Lauren followed Stitch and Christo through the wings and onto the stage, where she took her place in the back row, pulling in her shoulders in hopes of bringing down her height by an inch or two, keeping her eyes on Deepa directly in front of her, following as closely as she could, the two-step, the turn, the pat-a-cake clapping choreography. If she could move as Deepa's shadow, maybe Mr. Smith wouldn't call her out for falling just behind the pace. She moved her lips. Deepa had told her that, if you forgot the words, you could lip-synch "watermelon cantaloupe" on repeat and probably get away with it.

Halfway through the second rendition of "We Go Together," Mr. Smith out in the seats called out for Christo to stop.

"Lauren," he said. "Come up here."

"*Bus*-ted," whispered Brendan Dougherty beside her. He was only in the back because he was so tall.

Lauren walked to the front of the stage.

"Now sing it," Mr. Smith said. "All on your own."

Christo played a few prompting notes. "No," Mr. Smith called to Christo. "A cappella."

Lauren cleared her throat. "We go together, like rama-lama-lama, ka-ding-ety-dinga-dong."

The laughter behind her like fingers flicking her ears.

"Keep going," Mr. Smith said.

She pressed two fingers just below the waistband of her jeans, as if to check that her diaphragm was in flattened singing position, but actually to make sure her zipper was up. She was in the dream where you're onstage in your underwear—everyone had the same stupid dreams. Now everyone standing behind her would have a new dream, that they were her.

"Um—uh—" Lauren started.

"Remembered forever . . ." sang Claire, just behind Lauren, trying to find a volume at which Lauren could hear but Mr. Smith could not.

"Claire, I did not ask you to sing, I asked Lauren to sing."

His glasses caught the light, hiding his eyes in opaque whiteness.

"Remembered forever," Lauren sang, "like doo-wop-sha-diddy-diddy-bing-ety-bingy-bong."

The howling behind her, a dying moan, lions tearing open an antelope's belly, the organs piling out, steaming, fogging Mr. Smith's glasses.

Mr. Smith started applauding. All the boys except Stitch and a few of the girls behind Lauren applauded, too. Claire stepped closer to her, not clapping, close enough to take her hand, although she didn't. Abby wasn't clapping; Lauren could almost feel Abby's breath on her neck. The applause died down, and then it was just Mr. Smith applauding, hard, like he was trying to hurt himself.

"Lauren, I'll cut a deal with you," he said, hitting his palms together three last times. "You learn the words to this song, you show up to rehearsal on time, and you can have your 'busted typewriter' line, okay?"

"What?" she said.

"What?" whispered Claire and Abby.

"That was a *joke*," he said, his white mask glinting. "The terms of that deal will not be upheld. Let's take a break."

ALL THE WORST things Lauren had done had always been held with herself alone. Mirela was too young and Danielle too estranged to understand what happened at Lauren's birthday party. And when Lauren told everyone at school that Danielle gave her a black eye, she was the only person who knew it wasn't true— not even Danielle knew. Right this second, Danielle could be alone in her bedroom on Wellington Lane, sitting on the edge of her canopy bed with its Laura Ashley floral bedspread and eyelet dust ruffle tabbing out the chords to "Lithium" on her acoustic guitar and trying to remember if and when and how her head had made bruising contact with Lauren Brennan's eye socket on ski bus two winters ago.

But this new secret was different, because someone else had seen the whole thing. Was seeing it. Had known from the start.

She had to keep the story straight. She had to remember what it was she told Mom about where she'd be late that evening. Had she said Paula's house or Abby's? Or rehearsal? Would Mom remember, had she been listening? What if she'd said Paula's house, and then Paula called and Lauren wasn't home? She could dissolve into these questions in the middle of any class, leaving the husk of her body behind. Words slid into page gutters, x and y axes switching places. Her outward attention idling on a patch of dried gum on the carpet, catching his anger. "*Pay. Attention. Lauren.* Thank you," he said, almost like a hiss, like the sound Dad made when he wanted to yell and couldn't.

"But she *was* paying attention," Stitch murmured, from his desk directly behind her. She would have looked like a model student from behind—sitting up straight, head facing forward, hand holding pencil poised over her notebook. But Stitch couldn't see all of her. She didn't want him to, and she hadn't asked him to. Even now, Stitch tried to be nice, but he was making assumptions.

She had to keep the characters straight, their motivations. The people at school and the people in the wood-paneled living room. There was a trench between the two spaces, an energy constantly traded between them, matter changing states: ardor then anger, anger then ardor. His anger a substitute for his ardor. His anger a waste product of concealing his ardor. She was ennobled, inert; she sympathized with his predicament, and her sympathy exalted her. She saw her body lying along the trench, or her body as a single match dragged along its seam, her hand engulfed in flame as she tried the knob on the front door of his house at night, as she tried to write on his classroom blackboard, neat, calm, everybody watching and no pain.

She *made him mad*, he said. She *drove him crazy*, he said.

The trench opened up and he pulled her down, her arms tight around his neck to break her fall.

How strange and funny that everyone else thought they could see her, that all eyes were on her from every side, that Stitch presumed to know where her attention lay—that he could see her face through the back of her head. There she was, fumbling questions in English class, flailing around onstage, off-key, off-step, pissing off Mr. Smith again. That guy was always up her ass. How did she get cast in the first place? Oh, she couldn't do anything right. There was her crazy mother and crazier sister all over the news. It's just one thing after another with that family.

But no one could see what was really happening. What she was making happen. She could decide when she wanted to slip through the gap in the chain-link fence through the yards into a parallel world, behind one-way glass. She could look back through the glass and smile, and know it was real where she was, elemental, irradiated, irrefutable. A living world of soil and salt and blood. She could smile through the glass at everyone icebound, eyes midblink, mouths open and dumb, and she could laugh at them, because they would never know, and they couldn't know, they weren't capable of knowing, because even if she told them, even if she were telling them right now, she could not prove it, and they would never believe her.

JANE

ARDEN ATTACHMENT CENTER —
INTAKE FORM FOR NEW STUDENTS

Mirela Brennan, F
D.O.B. 03/01/1988 (est.)

PRINCIPAL GOALS: Focus student's goals are to learn skills related to trust, cooperation, and family integration.

FACTS ABOUT THE STUDENT AND FAMILY: Focus student is a ca. 4-year-old girl who resides in a single-family home in western New York State with her adoptive family: mother, father, sister aged 15, brothers aged 12 and 11. She has lived in the home for 6 months and previously resided in a state institution for children in Ghiorac, Romania. She was admitted to Arden for the 2-week therapeutic intensive with her adoptive mother.

AREAS OF STRENGTH: Focus student is described by her adoptive mother as bright, friendly, and outgoing in public settings. She has rapidly learned many English words and phrases and is eager to practice her English with people she meets at shops, playgrounds, etc. She has high energy and enjoys running, climbing, and acrobatics. She approaches peers with confidence and enthusiasm. She takes great interest in her siblings and in her natural surroundings.

AREAS FOR GROWTH: Focus student exhibits both indiscriminate attachment and resistance to attachment. She attempts to show physical affection to strangers in public places, in the form of hugs, kisses, and hand-holding. She asks strangers if they can take her home. She rejects physical affection from family members, particularly the adoptive mother. Adoptive mother reports that focus student displays physical affection only if she wants something or if she suspects that she is in trouble for misbehavior. She hides or hoards food while also declining most meals and snacks and disrupting family mealtimes. Focus student has physically damaged or destroyed toys, dolls, books, and furniture provided for her enjoyment. Though focus student's violent intent is mainly focused on objects, it is sometimes directed at other family members, most frequently at the adoptive mother, resulting in occasional minor injuries to herself and her adoptive mother.

HOME SETUP: Focus student's home is a two-story house on a one-acre lot on a quiet residential street. Because focus student exhibits a fear of stairs coupled with a lack of appropriate fear of heights, the ground-floor dining room has been repurposed as the focus student's bedroom. Focus student's adoptive father, who works as a contractor, has installed fire-rated steel doors that lock from the outside as well as steel bars over both windows following multiple escape attempts and incidents involving broken doors and glass. Focus student currently sleeps in a bare room on a mattress on the floor.

PRECIPITATING EVENT OR EVENTS (IF APPLICABLE): Focus student ran away from adoptive mother during a large public gathering, attracting local media attention.

The room at the Holiday Inn in Evergreen, Colorado, had one big bed for both of them. It was good in the room, quiet and dim, and Mirela had Jane all to herself. Mirela zonked out under the covers in front of the TV, before her usual bedtime.

They woke up in the deep dark, cold and wet. Jane flipped on the bedside lamp, called the front desk for new sheets, stripped the bed, peeled Mirela's pajamas off. She soaked the pajamas in the bathroom sink and filled the tub with warm, sudsy water. Mirela didn't fight the bath, although she did fight the towel, the rubbing of it, as if her skin could peel off with the water.

"Air-dry, all right, Mirela, whatever works," Jane said. She felt a purposefulness that edged into happiness. She felt sated by what she'd accomplished. The two of them understood each other.

There was a knock on the door. Jane went to answer it, and a lethal wail went up behind her.

"Mirela, my love, it's the new sheets, that's all," Jane said. "This nice helper is bringing us clean sheets for the bed."

"Are you all right in there?" came the voice on the other side of the door.

"We're fine, hang on a sec—just a tantrum situation with my kiddo—" Jane said over Mirela's noise. Jane wanted to get the door open to get the new sheets. Mirela wanted it shut to keep out the light and sound and people. The door slammed into Jane's hand— the fingers, between the big and middle knuckles—and Jane cried out, and Mirela was all of a sudden calmer. Now they were both in pain. Fair enough. Mirela curled up in front of the shut door.

"Are you sure you're okay?" the voice asked, and Mirela pounded her fists against the door to drown out the talking with a more righteous noise.

"Yes—please, just—I don't mean to be rude, but it would be best if you would leave," Jane said. "Thank you, good night." She crawled past Mirela to the bathroom and stuck her hurt hand in the sink, with the soaking pajamas.

"Usually you love meeting new people," Jane said from where she was kneeling next to the sink. "I wonder what's different tonight."

"I want nobody," Mirela said from the carpet.

"Honey, do you want a blanket?"

"I want nobody!" Mirela yelled. She was naked and shivering. Jane wondered if shivering was even better than rocking, more precise and efficient in its calming effects, like a cat's purr, a velvety real thing burring in her throat, curled inside her rib cage buzzing. Jane's hand throbbed through her whole body, a rhythm in search of a discordant music. Her throbbing hand and Mirela's shivering limbs in syncopation.

"We have an early start tomorrow," Jane said, taking her dripping hand from the sink. "It's going to be a big day, Mirela. The people at Arden will help us get better."

She considered attempting to open the hotel room door and decided against it. With her hand that wasn't hurt, Jane took the top bedcover off the floor, gave it a quick whiff to make sure it wasn't soaked with pee. A shiny-satiny sheath of green. Jane laid it down a couple of feet away from Mirela. Mirela inched close enough to the blanket to kick it away.

"I want nobody," Mirela said.

"You won't always feel that way, sweetie," Jane said, sitting down next to the heap of blanket. "The people at Arden will help you feel a different way. Don't you want to get better?"

Mirela said something that Jane couldn't hear.

"You look cold—are you sure you don't want the blanket?" Jane asked.

Mirela said the same thing again that Jane couldn't hear.

"What did you say, honey?"

"I want you."

The cumulus cover of the pain had started to clear, and Jane could think a bit about this. This was, on the one hand, the type of "nice" thing Mirela would say when she thought she was in trouble. On the other hand, here they were, on the same side of the slamming door. Ordinarily, Mirela would be alone behind it. This was progress.

Mirela crawled over to the blanket and pulled it over herself. She hugged her knees to her chest and rested her forehead on the floor.

Jane got up, lay down on her side on the bare mattress, and watched the quivering little heap on the floor.

"Do you want to come back into bed with me, Mirela?" she asked. "We could share the blanket."

Mirela lifted the blanket to watch Jane with one eye. They watched each other to the beat of Jane's throbbing fingers and Mirela's waves of shivering.

"What are we doing here, Mirela?" Jane asked her.

Mirela lowered the blanket.

"Are we sure we want to do this, Mirela?" Jane asked.

Mirela didn't answer.

With her good hand, Jane switched off the bedside light with a theatrical crispness, a gesture to extinguish all doubt.

Session 1 — Rapport-Building

MODULE: Establish relationship with therapist through directed small talk, enforced eye contact, question completion, and holding therapy.

NOTES FROM SESSION: Focus student appeared happy and engaged with conversation about favorite foods and activities. Focus student maintained poor or no eye contact. When co-therapist redirected her to resume eye contact, focus student deflected through laughter, jumping, turning, and making "funny faces." Therapist interpreted this behavior as attempt to maintain control. Introduction of holding therapy led to similar deflective responses of smiling, laughter, fidgeting, and kicking.

Session 2—Body Work

MODULE: Rapport-building continues. Intensive verbal directives/ corrections, compliance exercise, biographical narration, and holding therapy.

NOTES FROM SESSION: Focus student engaged with Simon Says and hide-the-shoe game. Deflective response (laughter, spinning, falling on ground) as commands became faster and more complicated. Deflective response (laughter) when therapist used therapeutic hostile command tone. Difficulty during biographical questions and answers. Focus student repeated questions back to therapist but did not answer. (Prompt questions included "Were you a bad baby?"; "Did no one take care of you?"; "Why didn't anyone love you?") Second holding therapy session cycled rapidly through deflective response to frustration response. Focus student exhibited physical resistance requiring compression-therapeutic intervention from co-therapist.

Session 3—Role-Playing, First Module

MODULE: Compliance exercise continues with additional rules, increased speed, and intensified therapeutic hostile command tone. Regression role-play followed by holding therapy.

NOTES FROM SESSION: Role-play cast therapist as focus student's birth mother and co-therapist as orphanage nurse. A third co-therapist placed focus student in modified holding position. Focus student was asked how she felt to see her birth mother and nurse. This question only elicited laughter and other deflection. Third holding therapy session bypassed deflective and frustration responses to rage response, with extreme physical resistance to therapy requiring compression-therapeutic intervention from two co-therapists.

Session 4—Role-Playing, Second Module

NOTES FROM SESSION: Therapists attempted to direct the focus student's anger toward birth mother. (Prompt questions included "How does it make you feel that she left you?"; "Why did she leave you?") Adoptive mother expressed concern that drama practice was inappropriate for focus student's age and English-language skills. Fourth holding therapy session commenced during rage response, again requiring therapist and two co-therapists. Therapists introduced use of blanket during holding therapy as precursor to forthcoming rebirthing session. Adoptive mother expressed concern that focus student could be injured during holding therapy.

Session 5—Minding the "Baby"

MODULE: Therapeutic return to state of infancy using bottle-feeding, cradling, swaddling, rocking, lullabies.

NOTES FROM SESSION: Focus student's deflective response to first set of babying tactics converted immediately to rage response when swaddling was introduced. Responded well to bottle-feeding and sweets. Responded well when given a teddy bear she was "in charge" of. Repeatedly told therapists throughout the session that the teddy bear belonged to her. Adoptive mother again expressed concerns about potential injury to the focus student during holding therapy. Adoptive mother also expressed concerns about the next day's planned rebirthing session.

CAROLYN DEWEY, FOUNDER and clinical director of the Arden Attachment Center, shrugged her marathoner's arms out of her lavender blazer. She folded her hands on her desk, which contained two short stacks of papers, plaques and awards to her left, wood-framed photographs to her right. She took a lip gloss and a compact mirror out of the mauve leather handbag on her desk, flipped the compact open with her left hand while glossing her lips with the right, pulled her lips over her teeth and kissed them together twice, *pop-pop*, baring her teeth at the mirror to check for stains, and slipped the gloss and compact back into the bag—all in one flowing vapor trail of a gesture, without breaking the line of her monologue.

"When mothers bring their children to Arden, I want them to see something to aspire to. To see it inscribed in me. To be sure, it's not *about* me or what I have done, it's not about envying me— I'm not that vain—but rather envying the *time*, wanting the time back, seeing the *intent* and the effort expended, and thinking, *If I had all the time she had to work on myself, I would walk across all the deserts of the world, or I would rekindle three friendships I lost to the parenting years, or I would read all of Proust*, or whatever it would be.

"I see my upkeep, if you will, as a pact I keep with myself and with all of my fellow Arden parents. I see myself as one of you, and I want you to see yourself in me. In all this paint and coiffuring and visible workouts I want you to see a clock, and the hands of the clock are moving backward and giving you back your life. Not the life you had before you were the mother of an attachment-challenged child. You're not getting that life back, and you wouldn't want it back. But a life where you come first again, because if you're not taking care of yourself, then you can't take care of anyone else."

Carolyn started almost imperceptibly, as if sensing a mosquito somewhere behind her right ear. Her frosted blond hair was brushed and blown to curl under, tickling at the places where her slim shoulders met her neck; a front curtain swooped out of a deep side part and over a thinner translucent canopy of wispy bangs. In another compound gesture, Carolyn put her hand inside the mauve leather to retrieve a small aerosol spray can. If Lauren were here, she might scold Carolyn for ripping a slightly bigger hole in the ozone layer. Carolyn misted the area in question with a spiraling flourish, and patted the calmed zone with one hand while slipping the can back inside the bag with the other.

A few stray particles of the spray misted onto Jane's face, and with them a memory. The party at Rhonda's. Brad Bender swinging the cheerleaders around, Pat setting his hand on fire with the hairspray and the lighter, Colin screech-laughing at Pat in pain. And yet nobody whisked them off to Colorado for behavior modification therapy. Fifteen years later, a patch of Pat's left hand was still raw pink and mottled where it had gone up in flames.

"Sore paw?" Carolyn asked, and Jane felt a momentary calm surprise that Carolyn's clinical training equipped her to read minds. But it was Jane's own bandaged hand that Carolyn was pointing to.

"Oh, this—it's nothing. I caught it in the door . . ." Jane said.

Carolyn nodded, eyes wide, lips pressed together significantly.

"I judge no one who comes here, though I do invite them to judge me," she said. "Because no one failed like I did at putting myself first. When my boys were four and six, when we hit that first wall after I adopted them out of foster care, I lived on Hershey's bars and Wonder bread. Literally, when I was hungry I would take a piece of bread out of the wrapper and ball it up in my fist, like I was returning it to its primordial dough state, and take bites off it, or if one of my boys was about to light the other one on fire I would cram the whole lump into my mouth at once and start yelling at them with my mouth full. I mean, sell the movie rights, right? I wore the same grubby sweatpants for days. I didn't leave the house except for therapy appointments—not appointments for *me*, God forbid I do something for *me*, only for my sons. Sometimes I didn't bother brushing my teeth. I thought that I didn't have time for me to matter, which is the same as saying that *I* didn't matter. And if I didn't matter, then how could I possibly matter to my boys? How can someone who doesn't matter be a mother? You get to a point where you think, *I'm a wreck because my boys need help*, when it's really *My boys need help because I'm a wreck*."

Carolyn twirled a strand of iridescent beads around one finger. An artful tangle of gold and brass nestled against her chest under the open collar of her silk blouse. "I took women's studies in college. Bryn Mawr. I know, I know. The clothes, the jewelry, the dieting— it's all a trap. I read the books. I know the theory. But I was also learning how to live in it. You start to see living in the prison as a form of rebellion. I mean, if you're in jail, you must have done something transgressive to get there, right? I used to only wear clothes I didn't care about, dark machine-washable fabrics that didn't stain—now I wear creams and pastels. I wear *white*, for goodness' sake." She motioned to her blouse. "I wear stuff you only want the dry cleaner to mess with, because I now refuse to see myself as an object you can puke or piss or shit on, pardon my language. I wear a lot of jewelry because I now refuse to accept that someone is going to rip my earrings out of my ears or try to strangle me with my own necklace. I eat well and sparely because I refuse any longer to self-medicate with food, I refuse any longer to eat ice cream straight out of the pint over the sink for dinner because that's all I have time for and that's all I deserve, stuffing sugar and fat into my mouth like a pacifier, like a drug—shove it all in the garbage disposal that is me, grind it up, fill the empty hole inside."

Carolyn patted her collar and smiled. "I hope none of this is shocking to you. I can speak to you like this because I am no longer that person. She no longer exists, so I can't hurt her feelings. And, again, none of what I have to say is a judgment on others. Everyone should wear what they want and eat what they want. But whatever one does should be a conscious *choice*. What I'm saying is that every Arden mother needs to choose her own forms of resistance. Smart, tactical, self-affirming resistance. You have biological children, yes?"

"Three," Jane said.

Or four. *Had* or *have*. She was never sure which to say.

Two choices here

She had had four babies inside her.

It wasn't that she hadn't had four children.

Mirela is her fourth child.

Mirela was her fifth child.

With her good hand, Jane rummaged around in her own handbag for a mint or a stick of gum. Like the version of Carolyn that no longer existed, Jane had not brushed her teeth that morning. Her fingers curled around something unfamiliar: the Bugs Bunny lighter. She couldn't remember how it had gotten there. Had Mirela been playing with the lighter? Her eyes darted to one side as if the girl would appear beside her, laughing and on fire. But no. Mirela was down the hall, in another room, in front of another one-way mirror.

"You must have questions," Carolyn said at last. "What are they?"

Jane stuck a piece of Juicy Fruit in her mouth with the hand that held the lighter. Carolyn's eyebrows sat up. "Do you smoke?" she asked.

Jane smiled as she put Bugs Bunny away. "Maybe I should start," she said. "So—your literature has prepared me well so far, and I recognize a lot in it—a lot of Mirela, a lot of myself—but can you explain the idea behind the holding therapy?"

"I'm so glad you asked," Carolyn said. "We are in the process of trademarking holding therapy, in fact."

"Oh, congratulations," Jane said. "So is it like—like holding her *down*, like showing her who is boss, breaking down her ego?"

"That's a way of putting it," Carolyn said.

"Because that starts to feel like corporal punishment, and we don't do that in our house, we don't spank—"

"Oh my goodness—"

"—we wouldn't ever use any kind of physical coercion with our kids—"

"Jane, please, do let me interrupt. Holding therapy is not corporal punishment, it's not abuse or coercion; it couldn't be further from it. Holding therapy is also known as compression therapy, which, come to think of it, might be the preferable term."

"You could trademark that one, too."

"A good idea. Think of applying pressure to a wound when a patient is bleeding. Under normal circumstances, pressing an artery against bone is the last thing you'd want to do, because you're keeping the artery from working properly. But in an emergency, your only option is to suppress it, shut it down—temporarily, of course. Same goes for the unattached child. Under normal circumstances, holding down a child, inhibiting his movement, goes against everything we think and feel about caregiving. But the children who come to Arden express their trauma through their bodies, through movement: the hitting out, the rocking, the spinning. These are memories activating at the cellular level. The memories and trauma are kicking the kid around, jerking his arms and legs like a master puppeteer. It's an emergency, and so in holding therapy, we step in and apply pressure to the wound. We stop the trauma from working."

"But the holding is—what? What does it do?"

"There are several different techniques. One that you've seen is the basket hold: the child has his arms crossed in front of him, his back pressed against the therapist's chest, and the therapist is either holding his hands behind him or has her arms wrapped around him."

"I do this with Mirela," Jane said. "I didn't know it was a—a technique—"

"You used your intuition. Because you're a born mom."

"I get her turned away from me and hold her tight—not *tight* but *firm*, and I rock her and sing to her until she calms down. I showed my older daughter how to do this, too. Mirela rocks and hums and holds herself when she is upset, so I'm kind of mirroring what she does anyway, but in a way that gets her more under control."

"Yes, you're doing the basket hold."

"I call it the squeeze."

"Basket hold is an easy one—it's rather like the Heimlich maneuver. It gets results, simple as that."

"I don't know that it does. Maybe Mirela would calm down on her own without it. But it helps me feel as though I'm doing something."

"There are also the prone positions, which you've seen. The position where the child is laid out on a therapist's lap, looking upward at her, with perhaps a co-therapist helping to apply pressure. Or the child laid out on the floor, with a second or third co-therapist applying therapeutic pressure."

"Yes, this is what concerns me—Mirela flat on the floor, these people on top of her. It's just—I know I'm new to this, but—"

Carolyn nodded. "It *is* intense. But it's a perfectly safe, evidence-based therapy carried out by trained professionals."

"But why is it done?"

"Well, the child doesn't want to be held, right? And that refusal affords us an opportunity. As the child—"

"Mirela."

"—as Mirela strains against the hold, she feels on the cellular level that she herself is both powerless and profoundly safe. The universal condition of the loved infant. In this powerless and safe condition, she can release her rage against the absent mother, returning the rage and pain back where it belongs."

"She's giving the rage back to Mom."

"Well, she's giving it back to bio-Mom. Bio-Mom, or absent Mom, or abusive Mom will always be in the room with her, but she can no longer get a seat at the table. In the holding position, the rage of the child—I must speak in generalities, forgive me—the rage eventually succumbs to exhaustion, and the child surrenders to a feeling she hasn't experienced before, sinking into rest in her loving caregiver's arms."

"But she's being forced to do it. She's not coming to it on her own."

"Think of infancy. During the baby stage, the mother is the baby's prisoner, you might say, but the baby is the mother's prisoner, too. The baby didn't choose that, but she's mostly okay with it. In fact, being okay with that arrangement is the foundation of her whole life to come—because that's the beginning of attachment, and attachment is the name of the game."

"But these are—you're talking about it like it's surgery, but really it's metaphors. You know? How does such a small child grasp these metaphors? Somehow this narrative is taking shape through her own experience?"

"On an intuitive level, yes. You talked about intuition before, and she has it, too. On a cellular level, most definitely she can grasp it all. The body knows these things even if it cannot put them into words. Words aren't everything, you know. But the thing is happening even if you can't articulate it. You have to temporarily make something stop working in order to save it—break down cells in order to give birth to new ones."

"And rebirthing? That's what's on the schedule for tomorrow."

"I think, as with your questions about holding therapy, that what you're really asking is *Why does she need that?* and I can't tell you exactly until we're in the middle of it. Attachment therapy, for all its rules and protocols, doesn't necessarily follow a script. It's more of an improv class."

"But what are the basic, I don't know, principles of rebirthing? The brochure didn't say."

"Well, we can't fit everything we do into one brochure."

"How does rebirthing grow out of holding therapy?"

"So when we talk about attachment—what was the first attachment? It was the embrace of the mother's womb, yes? But for the child who comes to Arden, that embrace may have been poisoned by—well, let's back up. What do we know about bio-Mom?"

"Not much. Mirela had hep B, but we don't know where she got it from."

"But—was the mother dead? Unfit? Did she sign away her rights?"

"I adopted Mirela out of an institution. An orphanage."

"But that can mean so many things. A lot of kids in Eastern European orphanages aren't orphans—rather, their parents have signed away their rights. I mean, you know this."

"Yes, I do, and I didn't meet anyone claiming to be Mirela's mother. What I have are reams and reams of paperwork."

"And what did the paperwork say?"

"I don't—I'm sorry, but I don't see how this is any of your business."

"My goodness!"

"I'm sorry, I just—I don't know if anything in her medical records is accurate. I don't know what happened to her before I met her. I do not. I never will. I can only imagine, and I imagine the worst, and it's unbearable, so I don't. So—so we just have to deal with what's in front of us."

"I see. Well, then. We can keep to generalities. The embrace of the mother in utero may have been poisoned by drugs, alcohol, or nicotine; by poor nutritional choices; by abuse or trauma suffered by the mother during her pregnancy; by a difficult delivery. These environmental toxins were force-fed to the baby during her earliest stages of development. But it goes back further than that. It is no coincidence that we say a sperm 'attaches' to an egg: the journey of attachment begins at that moment of conception, in the nature of that mother-father relationship. So what was its nature? Was it abusive? Loving? Respectful? A one-night stand?"

"Like I said, I don't have any answers. I know nothing about Mirela's mother. The biological mother. I mean, I'm—I'm her mother now. I'm the mother she has known."

"And there is rage born there as well, because Mirela deserved better than that. By which I mean that she deserved to find her mother—to find *you*—sooner than she did. Deep down, she knows that, and she's angry about it, and that is only right and rational. And then to be torn from whatever family she did know, whatever its shortcomings. Being ripped away from the only body she ever knew. Familiarity is its own privilege."

There is one further point; his own mother was really his, because he invented her . . . From Johnny's point of view, however, when he was born this woman was something he created. That was Winnicott.

"Well, Mirela doesn't remember any of it, or she wasn't aware of it in the first place. There's no—there's no history."

"She is aware of all of this on the somatic level. The cellular level. That's where her history is inscribed, although we can't read it. She knows, at the very least, that something went very wrong. Otherwise, why would she be here at Arden?"

"So—so what you're proposing is a sort of do-over. She was born once into bad circumstances, and now, here, she can be reborn into something else?"

"And in that rebirth she needs to release the rage of that first and greatest loss, so that she can accept your love."

"But is that—the rebirth takes the form of more people holding her down? Like they're re-creating the birth canal or something, and she has to escape?"

Carolyn smiled. "You look scandalized."

"It's a little hard to take in, I guess."

"It seems fringe to you. Do you want to know how fringe CRT is? Elvis does it in a movie."

"CRT?"

"Coercive restraint therapy—what you do with Mirela, essentially. You and *Elvis*. Fifty million Elvis fans can't be wrong."

"Elvis?"

"*Change of Habit*, from 1969. Elvis plays a doctor. He does CRT with a young girl who has autism. Gets results, too. Mary Tyler Moore plays the nurse, or perhaps she's a nun—I can't recall now. But you can't get more all-American mainstream than those two, can you?"

"Mirela and I can inquire about screening the film tonight in our hotel room," Jane said. "But could we go over—"

Carolyn looked at her watch and tapped at it significantly. "We're going to have to end there, Jane, as I have another appointment."

"Okay, but maybe we could talk again? Before tomorrow and the rebirth?"

"My assistant can see if my schedule will allow for it. And I'll be there, Jane—I make a point of observing all the rebirths. Wouldn't miss it for the world." Carolyn stood up.

Jane remained seated. "I don't know," she said. "I'm not sure about this." She looked up at Carolyn in what she hoped was a pose of supplication.

"You are at the end of your rope, Jane, and you must trust us to catch you."

"I don't know that," Jane said. "I don't know where the rope ends."

"Usually mothers call us when they've found it."

"I haven't found it. But I wonder if she's already run out of time."

"She has not."

"If you took my kids away from me when they were born and then a few years later you just handed them back—"

Jane stared at the biggest plaque on Carolyn's desk until it went double.

"I meant my *other* kids," Jane said. "If you took my other kids away."

"I understand, Jane." Carolyn prayed her hands together in a chop-chop motion. Jane got up.

"Here at Arden, we're composing a new origin story for Mirela," Carolyn said. "We're going to write it down and keep it safe. It won't erase that first legacy of pain, but now she'll have another story to tell, and that story will belong only to her and those who love her."

"Well," Jane said, "I guess I'm proud to be Mirela's biographer."

THEY COULDN'T LEAVE Colorado with nothing to show for it.

This had to be Jane's thesis.

She fitted all of her available evidence to its mold. She disregarded any clues or data that couldn't be pounded into its shape. She poured her doubts into the chasm of all that she lacked: expertise, a college degree, fluency with diagnostic jargon and acronyms and Elvis movies. When her doubts overfilled that space, they flowed instead into the one left open by her shame—the shame of the expense, the flight and the hotel and the astronomical price tag on the clinic itself, the shame of what she'd brought on herself and her family and Mirela, the shame of her arrest, of her bad marriage and her teenage sluttiness and swinging her hips in front of Dr. Vine, the shame of staring at a naked, freezing child on the floor of a hotel room and thinking that this, on balance, all things considered, *this* had been a good day.

In the morning, she would get Mirela into the rental car and drive back to Arden with no qualms, the open road winding ahead of them, mountain majesty all around, or so she gathered. As in Romania, Jane hadn't gauged her surroundings beyond how they matched up to the map in her hands. Perhaps she could blame Buffalo for her tunnel vision. Living between two Great Lakes meant living under a watery gray dome—you forgot to look around you because there was so little to see. Tomorrow she would remember to look.

Maybe Jane watched a CRT session and saw violence where someone knowledgeable and credentialed saw closely observed protocol and measurable progress. This dichotomy could apply to so much of medicine, in fact. What would brain surgery or a cesarean section look like if you didn't know what you were looking at? What would you say, thirty years ago, if a doctor had given you polio to keep you from getting polio?

Arden prided itself on innovation, boldness, being first. Getting out in front required ruthlessness, ambition, a willingness to make mistakes. How many patients had been butchered in the first brain surgeries and cesarean sections?

Jane's mother had a great-aunt Katinka back in Hungary who died of cancer, not yet thirty-five. She left behind two small children and a handsome widower, who remarried within the year. They opened up Katinka's body, Jane's mother told her, and tried to burn out the cancer cells with gauze soaked in disinfectant. "It was before any of those so-called doctors knew what they were doing," Jane's mother said. "She suffered. She wasn't the only one."

Katinka's timing was bad: a few years earlier, she might have died peacefully in her bed, dreamy with morphine or ether as loved ones stroked her hair, held her hand; a few years later, there would have been others who had already suffered in her place, and the surgeons would have learned from their pain. Somebody had to be the first one. The first to be cut open, or poisoned, or held down while they screamed, for their own good. And somebody had to be the first one to commit these premeditated acts of violence, and accept that they would almost certainly end in disaster, because disaster was integral to success.

In the darkness, as Mirela's light snores wafted up from the carpet, Jane's mind was shrugging out of her grip—and this was another form of the obscure pleasure, to reject nighttime prayer in favor of submitting to the most irrational urges of her memory and imagination, walking half willingly right up to the monster, letting him put on the blindfold and turn you around, one, two, three. She floated in the shallows of sleep and corpses floated past in the stream, black tornadoes above in the shapes of gaping mouths and Saint Teresa's billowing dress. Bugs Bunny stood on the shore, detonating a blast on the outer bank. His whiskers were singed, fur blackened in patches, one of his eyes swollen almost shut. As the rapids pulled her under, it occurred to Jane that somebody had to be the first one to start a fire with a lighter and canned aerosol, long before Pat's hand had gone up in flames. Somebody was the first to think of it, and then attempt it, at great risk of harm. And that person, too, might have thought of it as a necessary violence.

JANE FREQUENTLY ASKED members of her family to try to see things from Mirela's perspective, but until the last day at Arden, she had never demanded it of herself.

Every day at Arden they held her down, at least for a little while. On the day of the rebirthing session, they used a blanket. A quilt, really, heavy, almost like a carpet. It looked like it smelled like stains. Two therapists, then three. She called out for Jane. She could see shapes through the blanket, arms and legs, but the blanket got tighter and the pressure got more and more until there was nothing to see, nowhere to move. She was laughing and then she was screaming and then she couldn't scream, or she tried to scream but only empty air came out, and the air had nowhere to go and so she was breathing in her screams, she was screaming backward, her whole body was a scream that made no sound under the blanket. No one could see or hear or feel her. The only way to get away from the blanket was to become the blanket, and the only way to become the blanket was to stop fighting the blanket. Her skull going soft, the knobs of her spine spinning into cotton. Her arms knitted to her sides, her legs stitching themselves together. Her whole self flattening and going stretchy like the webs between her fingers. She could be spread on the grass for a picnic, or laid out on the floor with toys for a baby. The toys in all the rooms were always the same: the stacking rings, the puppy on wheels that goes *tock-tock-tock*, the barn with the swinging clacking hinges, the popcorn-popping vacuum cleaner, the trucks, the blocks. All laid out on the blanket. She could keep Jane warm at night without Jane having to know she was there. The tiny gaps between the threads inhaling and exhaling, like a frog who breathes through her skin, like gills she could use when she went through the wash with the sheets and towels and pillowcases. Then she would be clipped to a clothesline outside, the breeze would nudge her up and back like on the old swing at Saint Benedict's, the air going past and through her, and as the sunlight drew the damp from her, she would grow lighter and lighter, so that one big push from the wind could send her up, up, like a lost balloon that caught briefly on the highest branches of the beech tree before continuing up, up, past the blue and into the clouds and the white, into the light that exploded her, only she was the light now, she was the air, she was herself, and she was everywhere.

Then the clouds burst with rainwater, and she was inside the clouds, and as she fell back to earth her arms and legs ripped away from their sutures, her head yelled as it hardened into bone, and she was thrashing to get away from herself, but her self was not the blanket anymore—the blanket was on the floor of the room and she was on her feet, and inside it was raining and out the window the sun was shining and the grass was brilliant green, and the people who had held her down were screaming "Fire!" and running out of the room, and they were gone and it was only Jane in the room now with her, the rain pouring down and Jane staring down at her hands, what looked like two small toys she was holding.

"Mirela, I set a fire!" she said, laughing, and holding up her toys. "Mirela, we set this place on fire!"

She was saying they had to get out of there, right now, Mirela, let's go, Mirela, listen, we have to go, and over the sibilant din of the fire sprinklers Mirela called out, "No Mama! No Mama!" and she was laughing, too, laughing along with Jane, and she spun around and around in the rain, tilting her head upward to drink the sky.

LAUREN

She had to pee all the time. There was a feverish itchy pressure on her bladder, revolting, more than a distraction; it was a chronic emergency signaling in a high whine behind her eyes. She would get up in class and take the laminated bathroom pass off the teacher's desk twice, three times. Even the teachers who liked her most started glaring, rolled their eyes. Sometimes instead of going to class at all she sat on the toilet in the lavatory outside the studio art classroom, straining, crying with the effort of getting out a few drops. She drank no water for one whole day, rinsing and spitting at the sink when she got desperate, then she changed tacks and drank glass after glass of water, trying to "flush out her system," which is something Mom always said to do whenever Lauren or her brothers got sick. She lowered herself into an ice-cold bath, cupping gasps of water from the tap. She got up three times when she and Paula went to see *Howards End* at the Eastern Hills Mall.

"You missed the best part—the poor bastard got murdered by a *bookshelf*," Paula said after the movie. They were sitting in the food court having Icees.

"I'll have to read the book," Lauren said.

"I know what's going on with you," Paula said, wearing her satisfied-piggy smile. "I've had what you have."

"That's great," Lauren said.

"I'll tell you what you should do," Paula said, "if you tell me how you got it."

"Got what?" Lauren asked. Everything about her felt red and swollen and hostile.

"You should see a doctor," Paula said.

"When you flare your nostrils like that you look like a pig," Lauren said.

LOS ANGELES WAS burning on the TV in the Brunts' kitchen when Lauren got up a second time from dinner, passing through the front room, where Los Angeles burned from another angle on another TV, upstairs to the bathroom. This time, Paula's mother followed her and asked to come in. Mrs. Brunt opened the door on her, sitting on the toilet, jeans around her ankles, and Lauren didn't even care. Mrs. Brunt rummaged in the bottom drawer, reached past the stash of birth control, and came up with a small bottle.

"Lauren, I want you to take one of these now and then one pill every morning until they're all gone," Mrs. Brunt said, filling a glass with water as Lauren buttoned her jeans. "They will turn your pee bright orange—don't worry about that, it means they're working. The pill will mask your symptoms, but it won't make the infection go away—for that you need to see a doctor for an antibiotic. You will need a full checkup before they can prescribe you anything. Is your mom away?"

Lauren nodded, swallowing the pill with the water. They were sitting cross-legged on the bathroom floor together. Mrs. Brunt's first name was Nicole. Her hair was a shining chestnut brown. She looked so young up close. Her skin was unlined, her cheeks downy like a cushion.

"Can I call your mom to talk to her about how you're not feeling well?"

Lauren shook her head.

"If she were here, would this be something you could talk to your mom about?"

Lauren shook her head.

"It's okay. It's normal—well, it's not normal, but it's common. And, you know, there's all sorts of reasons you can get one of these. It doesn't mean anything all on its own. But you need to see somebody. Can you try to reach your mom in—where is she?"

"She's in Colorado with my adopted sister."

"Honey, listen, I want you to try to get hold of her tonight. It's, what, a two-hour time difference? Tell her that Paula's mom is going to make you an appointment. I'll set it up through Rumson, where I work—"

"My mom takes us to Children's Hospital," Lauren mumbled.

"Okay, but you wouldn't go there for this, sweetheart," Mrs. Brunt said. "I'll take care of the appointment. I could get you one on very short notice, but you just have to clear it with your mom. You can't let this go—it won't get better on its own. It's nothing to worry about, so long as you get it checked out and treated. You have to do that."

"Okay."

"Lauren," Mrs. Brunt said, "I need to ask you something. Is it possible you could be pregnant?"

Lauren's vision smeared on the bathroom tiles. The husk. She couldn't have told anyone how long she stared like that, she couldn't have guessed.

"Oh," Lauren whispered. "I just remembered something. Mrs. Brunt?"

"Yes."

"I took some of Paula's birth control pills. I stole them. I'm sorry. The ones in there—I'm sorry."

Mrs. Brunt pulled Lauren into her lap and hugged her. She rubbed her back. "It's okay. Next time just ask."

They heard Paula calling up the stairs. "You're going to be okay," Mrs. Brunt whispered to Lauren, kissing her cheek. She left the bathroom. Lauren heard her talking outside in low tones to Paula. She didn't try to hear what they were saying.

"Lauren, is it okay if I come in for a second?" Paula asked from behind the door.

"Yes," Lauren murmured from where she was sitting on the tile. Paula entered, knelt down, and hugged her.

"I'm sorry you're not feeling well," Paula whispered in her ear. "I love you."

"I'm sorry, too, and I love you, too, Paula," Lauren whispered back, her tears wetting Paula's hair, and Paula turned to go.

Mrs. Brunt returned with a cordless phone. Everyone had them nowadays. She called information; she called the front desk of the hotel in Colorado; they were put through to Mom's room. She handed Lauren the phone, winked, and closed the bathroom door behind her.

"Lauren, my love." It was really Mom. "I miss you so much, but this call is going to cost a fortune."

"I need to talk to you."

"I know, baby, but can we talk when I'm back? Mirela and I are flying home in a couple of hours. We're gonna catch the red-eye. If they don't run us out of town before then."

"Mom, I need you to come home."

"Lauren, I just told you—"

"No, you don't—I need—"

She wanted Paula's mom. She wanted Paula. She wanted to make Mom understand, because she needed Mom to come home to her, but she couldn't, because she was someone else's mom now, and this wasn't her home, and she wasn't herself.

THE RUMSON PARKING lot was three-quarters empty after Lauren's appointment. The midafternoon sun was fat and congenial, lending a blood-orange glow to the interior of the dragon wagon. Lauren slumped in the back, behind the driver's seat, her arms crossed, staring at nothing. Mirela beside her, slumped and staring, too, as Mom was strapping her into her car seat.

"Where are you? Where is Mirela?" Mom was asking. She tapped two fingers on Mirela's cheek, tickled her ribs. Nothing. No-Mirela.

"Leave her alone," Lauren murmured. "She'll come out of it on her own."

Mom did as she was told. Back in the driver's seat, she put the key in the ignition without turning it. She folded her hands in her lap. "Lauren," she said. "My darling girl. Why don't you sit up here with me? I feel like a chauffeur. You're right behind me but I can't see you."

Lauren said nothing.

"So. We have a big decision here."

Lauren mumbled a response so that Mom couldn't hear it.

"What did you say?" Mom's eyes in the rearview, straining to see her.

"No 'we.' *We* don't have a decision."

"Okay. *You* have a big decision."

Lauren mumbled.

"Lauren, I can't—"

"There's no decision!" Lauren yelled.

"Lauren, keep your voice down—"

"It's not a yes-or-no, will-I-or-won't-I situation. It's happening."

"But you have a—you have a *choice*." It sounded like Mom was reading the words off a placard held aloft outside the clinic.

"That is hilarious coming from you," Lauren said. "The hock— the hiccup—" She shook her head and flushed.

"Are you trying to say *hypocrisy*?" Mom asked.

"You are a *joke*," Lauren said.

"I *am* a hypocrite, Lauren," Mom said. "I confess to it. But right now, we're not talking about all the craziness from before. We are talking about today. We are talking about you." Mom looked away from the rearview and into the mostly empty parking lot. "I'm not proud of what I got caught up in," she said. "With Father Steve and all of that. I made a mistake."

Lauren *pffff*ed a scoffing sound.

"You made a mistake, too—"

"You know *nothing*," Lauren said, and Mom shut her eyes against the impact.

"Lauren," Mom said, "who—who did this to you?"

"*I* did this to me," Lauren said.

"Honey—was it the Rosen boy? Skip?"

Lauren threw her head back and gagged. "Yeah, Skippy Rosenboy. That's the one. We're getting a shotgun marriage, just like you and Dad did."

"Honey—"

"The abortionist's son. That could be the title of a great romance novel, right?"

"Lauren, was it Skip?"

"His name is Stitch, and *no*. We're *friends*. Is it so beyond you that a girl and a guy could just be friends?"

"Who is it, my love?"

"It doesn't matter. It's my *choice*," Lauren said, in a mocking whine. "Just like you said. That's all you need to know. I decided."

"Lauren—it's so early. You understand me, yes? It's so early. We wouldn't have known for weeks, for months, maybe, if you hadn't needed to see the doctor anyway."

"So what?"

"It's barely even—"

"It's barely even what?"

"They could take care of it and it would be like it never happened. You've—it's barely started."

"It's barely a baby?"

"It might—end on its own. It happens a lot."

"It's barely a baby? Is that what you mean?"

"This doesn't have to define you for the rest of your life. You can decide something different for yourself."

Lauren said nothing.

"You don't have to go through—you can decide to end—"

She couldn't say it. She was talking to no one. No-Lauren.

"We also have to consider the practical side of things. If this happens. How will I be able to help you and also care for Mirela?" Mom asked.

"I don't need your help."

"What help don't you need, Lauren? Financial help? Help taking care of a baby?"

"Any of it. I can do it. I can decide for myself."

"Oh, it's that easy, is it, Lauren?"

"Maybe it's not. Maybe it's hard. But that's no reason for *murder*. Isn't that your whole thing? That it's *murder*?"

"I don't know what my whole thing is anymore, honestly, Lauren."

"Using Mirela as an excuse for *murder* is pretty gross, Mom."

"Shush," Mom said, eyeing Mirela in the rearview. No-Mirela was still staring, eyes filmy, lips parted.

"You want me to do it because you wish you'd done it," Lauren said. "When you had the chance."

"What? What are you talking about?"

"It's not true that you wish you'd done it? Admit it."

"First of all, this isn't about me. It's about you and your future. And second—"

"I have a future because you *had me*. Because you didn't do it. So I don't want to do it, either. There. Done. End of story."

"It's different. It's not the same thing. You are you, and I am me—"

"I am me because you didn't do it!"

"—and our lives are different. Your life belongs to you."

"What if this was me? What if it was me inside of me?"

"It's not you. It's not *you*! *You* are *here*."

"But I wasn't always! Not like this!"

"No—what—"

"You regret having me! Just admit it!"

"We're not—Lauren, keep your voice down, remember Mirela— we're not talking about me, we're—"

"Yes, we are. If we are talking about *you* and the decision *you* made, we are talking about *me*. It is literally the exact same thing. You are—"

"Lauren, honey, listen to me. Your life has value—"

"I totally agree! Thank you for proving my point!"

"—your life has value independent of any other person or any other thing. Independent of me. No one's mother can regret their— regret doesn't work—it doesn't work like that. A *person* is not some- one else's *decision*."

Mirela was softly humming.

"You can't regret a *person*," Mom said. "That's not a sentence that makes sense. I can't—"

"*You* are the one who is not making sense," Lauren said. "You are twisting things. I am here because of a decision you made. I would not be here if you had made a different decision."

"And now you are here and you can make your own decision. Your life is not my life."

"And clearly I ruined your life."

"No. No."

"Say it. Have the guts to say it. You regret that I was born."

"I cannot say that."

"You can't, but that doesn't mean—"

"I can't because it's a lie."

"You would have gone to college. You would have left Buffalo and had a whole other life. You wouldn't have gotten stuck with Dad."

"Wait, what? What's wrong with your dad?"

"He wouldn't have *been* my dad, and you would have a whole other life."

"I do not regret that you were born."

"You do, you do, you do!"

The humming grew louder, as loud as Lauren's voice, rhyming and dissonant.

"Lauren. You are my life's treasure. You are the core of my be- ing."

"What if you had *aborted* me? If you'd had an *abortion*, we wouldn't be here right now having this stupid conversation!"

"Lauren, stop it, right now—"

Hmm-MMM, hmm-MMM, hmm-MMM

"You wish I wasn't born, but you love me and you don't want me to make the same mistake you did. Is that right?"

"That's not what I think. How are you so sure of what I think?"

"I don't know exactly what you think. I just know you are lying."

"Mama lie," Mirela said and kept humming.

"That's a terrible thing to say."

Hmm-MMM, hmm-MMM, MMM-mm-MMM-mm-MMM-mm-MMM

"Then tell me something that's true."

"Mama lie," Mirela said and kept humming.

"You seem to think only terrible things can be true."

"Just be honest. Like that's so hard."

"Lauren. You are the love of my life and you have been from the moment you were born."

"You want to know who did this to me," Lauren said. The tears came all at once, fast and hot, spilling and sidling past one another. "You're dying to know."

"You can tell me if you want to. But I'm not going to ask again. It's up to you."

Mirela's shoe *thump-thump-thump*ed against the plastic bottom lip of the car seat, in rhythm with the *hm-MM-hm-MM*.

"You do want to know. Don't lie."

"Mama lie," Mirela said and kept humming.

"It doesn't matter to me. You can tell me or not tell me."

"You can't stand the idea of me having sex. Your daughter *had* sex. With a specific person. And not just once!"

"Lauren, please, Mirela is—be careful—"

"I chose it, and I *liked* it."

"Lauren, my God, stop it, please stop—"

"I was inside you. Me. It was always me. I was there. I was there all the time. I was waiting. From the very first second."

"Lauren, we're not—"

"I was there! It was me!" Lauren was really crying now, sobbing, one fist pounding her own knee, and Mirela's humming abruptly halted. "You can say all you want that we're not talking about your situation, but that doesn't change anything. It's still a person, no matter who it is. You say I made a mistake—well, that makes sense, right? Because *I'm* a mistake?"

"No. Never."

"It's one of the few things Mirela and I have in common, right? We are your two big fat fuckups!"

Mom turned around in her seat, wrenching her head to meet Lauren's eyes over the headrest. "Lauren, don't you dare."

Lauren pressed her head against her window, unable to speak. Mirela began *hmm*ing and kicking again, arching her back.

"I just wish . . ." Lauren inhaled. "I wish we could have an honest conversation about this."

"Honest?" Mom turned back and stared at the dashboard. "Okay. I can be honest with you, Lauren. Do you know what I honestly wish? You said you were waiting for me? I wish I had waited for you. You were worth the wait."

Lauren exhaled.

"You were worth the wait," Mom repeated.

Mom thought it was over.

"But," Lauren said, "I wouldn't have been me." She was newly in control of herself. "If you'd waited." She paused. Slowly, slowly. "You would have waited for me all your sorry life, because I would have been dead before I was born. Your precious baby girl."

"Baby!" Mirela said.

"Only God knows such things," Mom said.

"And you think God—"

"Baby, baby, baby," Mirela said. Each *baby* paired off with a kick to the back of the front passenger seat.

"I don't think anything about what God thinks," Mom said. "I don't presume to know. Why do you?"

"Bay-bee! Bay-bee!" Mirela sang.

"All you do is think about God," Lauren said. "You don't do anything without thinking about God. You got Mirela because you thought it would make God happy."

"Having faith in God is not the same as having understanding in all of his ways. I do know he loves you, and me, and Mirela."

"He loved Mirela so much he dumped her in some shithole and fucked her up."

"Lauren, you can't—"

"Some shithole you can't even bring yourself to talk about."

"You can't say something like that about God. You—you place your soul in such danger when you talk like that. Do you understand?"

"Mom?" Lauren asked.

"Lauren."

"When I was a baby, didn't you love me? Didn't you? *Didn't* you?"

"God in heaven, Lauren, what a question—"

"When I was baby?" Mirela asked. The kick to the back of the seat was punctuation, a question mark.

"Didn't you love me, Mommy?" Lauren asked. "You will love this baby, too. You will, Mommy. You will. You *will*."

"Lauren, Lauren, my sweet girl, listen to me: I found Mirela too late, and I found you too soon."

Mom bit down on the words like shards of glass.

"I'm so sorry," Mom said. "Please, girls, I am sorry."

Lauren listened as her mother gripped the car wheel and bumped her forehead against it—*mumph-mumph-mumph.*

"Oh God, forgive me," Mom said, as if to herself. "God, please forgive me."

"When I was baby!" Mirela said. Her voice was gaining in volume. She kicked harder and more. "When I was baby! When I was baby!"

Lauren felt the violence of what she had done, and a quickness and agility in herself—in the violence—that had otherwise completely abandoned her. Her pain was deep and honest and alive, and that meant she could sharpen it into the curve of a blade. She could make her pain into other people's pain. There was a heinous beauty in it. It glinted in her eye. It was the violence of it that held her in place in the back seat, hidden from Mom's eyes. It kept her from saying a gentle word to Mom, placing a hand on her shoulder. The slightest little thing. She had won, but one false move you lose.

"DON'T WORRY, YOU'LL get there eventually," Rajiv said over his shoulder as he passed Lauren in the hallway between classes. Giggles from whoever was walking with him. It wasn't worth the effort to register who they were. She could sit down right there in the stream between class periods without caring who saw her or what they thought. She was fumbling through a sandstorm.

"Can't we all get *alloooonng*?" Rajiv was keening down the hallways. Mocking sobs. Even Stitch had told him how crazy-making it was.

She was encased in a suit of armor. Lifting and maneuvering her limbs took a great, crushing, cranking effort. All the passageways of her body constricting, her blood flow slowing, rerouting itself, turning on itself, jellifying. Hands and feet gone blue and cold. Her skull screwed on too tight—her bones had thickened, too, and they were expanding and contracting, and her brain jangled around inside. Sirening white streaks at the corners of her sight. She rattled and *chank*ed around, most people too polite or dismayed to ask her what was wrong, her steel boots sliding deeper into the sand.

She could drop out of the musical. Even now. The day of. It could be done. Lauren's understudy, Leslie Cochrane, attended every rehearsal, whether she was required to or not. Lauren's stupid Pink Ladies jacket would fit Leslie just fine, even if her saddle shoes were a half size too small—Leslie would accept any hardship for the sake of the role. But dropping out meant drawing on empty reserves of energy. Finding an acceptable excuse for dropping out, finding the right time and words for telling Mr. Smith, finding the courage to say the words and deflect his reaction, having to tell Mom and her classmates and her teachers, having to tell Paula and Stitch, and the whispers and scoldings to follow, and worse, the clucks and warbles of sympathy—it was too much to bear, too much to think about, far more trouble than the drudgery of *chank-chank*ing through her paces in the company renditions of "Shakin' at the High School Hop," dimly aware of the laughing boys and the squinting girls and Mr. Smith in the middle distance, arms crossed. If she dropped out, then there was officially, formally, *something wrong*.

She could not disappear completely, but oddly she could come closer to disappearing onstage than if she refused to go on it. Mindy had decided to turn "Look at Me, I'm Sandra Dee" into an ensemble number for all the Pink Ladies, "addressing their shared insecurities as young women," she explained, patting Lauren's arm. They would sing and dance in unison, no solos. They'd gone to all that trouble just for her.

"Lauren can't do anything by herself," Brendan said. "Can't sing by herself, can't dance by herself, can't *sleep* by herself . . ."

"You are *so fucking stupid*," Deepa told him.

"Can't we all get *alloooonng*?" Andy brayed at her. Rajiv's disease was catching.

Leslie kept telling Lauren she could take over for her. "You know, if that works for you," Leslie said. "Don't think twice about it." Like stealing from her would be doing her a favor, like Leslie's greedy pity was a gift.

"Honestly, Lauren, Ted wouldn't be so hard on you if you didn't have such an attitude," Claire said on the afternoon of opening night, during pizza break in Tedquarters. Lauren sat in the saggy center of one of the sad couches, a paper plate of pizza on her lap, Claire on one side of her and Stitch on the other. Lauren shifted positions constantly and winced as she did it. She didn't try not to wince; perhaps she winced more than was strictly necessary. Her hip touched Claire's hip, her knee touched Stitch's knee, and she felt the space she took up in their imaginations. They wondered what was going on with her but wouldn't ask, not directly. Or they knew and didn't need to ask. She would remain in the room with them after she'd left it. Maybe they talked about her the way Paula talked about her rock stars.

Abby drew up a chair to the couch. She had a Pyrex full of salad. "Do you want some, Lauren?" she asked. The voice of a cool cloth on a feverish forehead. Abby crammed a lettuce leaf into her mouth, as if to demonstrate. Lauren shook her head and lifted her slice of pizza off the paper plate almost to her lips. Her stomach hitched forward, and she put the slice down again. The cheese was congealing; the oil dotting the pepperoni slices was changing from translucent to a lurid orange. The paper plate was starting to sweat into her jeans.

"Here, Lauren, I can hold that for you," Stitch said, and Lauren nodded. He took the plate and set it down on the table.

The object with pizza break, as with any other unit of time—a class, a rehearsal, the gap between class periods—was to wait it out. Not only make it to the end but stretch it out long enough to delay the transition to the next task, and perhaps through this delay she could eliminate a few of the other tasks that the day demanded of her, like when she would be so late to class that it would be disruptive and quite frankly unfair to the teacher and other students to show up at all, like if she lay on the bathroom floor with her face on the cool tile long enough it would be too late for Mom to bother kicking up much of a fuss about whether or not Lauren came to dinner, that is, assuming Mom had noticed whether or not Lauren came to dinner and was not instead focused on the proven fact that Mirela had dumped her own dinner into a basket of freshly folded linens.

"Save it for later," Mirela would say. One of her first sentences in English. That's right, Mirela. There would always be a better time than now.

"Lauren," Abby was saying. "Honey. What's wrong? What's the matter?"

Lauren tried for what felt like a long time to respond, staring at the slice on the table as it succumbed to a yeasty rigor mortis, the greasy edges of the paper plate starting to curl around it like a carnivorous flower, her lips opening and closing around the thing she couldn't say.

A voice was calling in the distance. They were needed onstage. Claire and Stitch got up from the couch but Abby stayed in her chair beside Lauren. Someone standing behind Abby asked her to come, or told her—a surprise and affront in the request—and still Abby stayed. She sat there with her hands folded in her lap.

Abby never did things like this. She was orderly, rational. She didn't keep other people waiting.

"Lauren," Abby said. "Please. Tell me what is going on."

Abby stayed there so long the light started to change. When she finally got up and left the room, with a parting squeeze of Lauren's shoulder, Abby crossed in front of one of the halogen lamps and Lauren felt her friend's shadow alight briefly on her skin and lift again, and she closed her eyes against this bleak triumph, that she had not only outlasted her friend, exhausted her sympathy, but she had outlasted the whole day, she had starved and killed it, she had forced the earth to turn away from the sun. She didn't feel happy, but she did feel like she'd won.

WHEN SHE THINKS back to that night, her skin ripples and hardens into scales, ticklish and tender. Moths and dragonflies beating their wings inside her rib cage. Open her mouth and a wasp would fly out. She felt a queasy excitement, an exhilaration in destruction, to realize again the earthquake that swallows up and spits out your whole life could be *ecstatic*, could have ever been anything other than ecstatic. Like seeing the blood on the floor and realizing the blood was her. As if the four walls of the redbrick house had fallen down to reveal a theater-in-the-round, an audience in semi-darkness, and Lauren in her tight skirt and satin Pink Ladies windbreaker and hair that Abby had teased big with hot irons and hairspray, standing head-to-head with Stitch, in his painted-on jeans and black leather jacket and sparkling-wet swirly pompadour, and he snapped his next line through a big wad of gum—"Whaddya tryin' to do, Rizzo?"—and she couldn't remember what she was supposed to say.

Stitch snapped his fingers. "Whaddya tryin' to do, there, Rizzo?" he asked again.

She could only remember what she wasn't supposed to say, so she said it.

"I feel like a broken typewriter," she said.

Stitch's mouth dropped open. He might have been startled, or letting himself in on Lauren's joke, or preparing to speak his next line. Lauren would never know. Such was the charisma of Stitch.

"You know, like a broken typewriter—because *I skipped a period*," Lauren said, enunciating, smacking the *pee*, eyes sliding meaningfully toward the audience, and then Stitch said something about Rizzo always flapping her gums and Andy said his next line and Lauren felt herself altered, bewitched, the abracadabra of the forbidden line unlocking all her dialogue and marks and dance steps, which she could perform as if remote-controlled.

When she came offstage, she felt him before she could see him. Not physical touch but the weight and pressure of his body shifting the air near her. Grunting through gritted teeth. Then he grabbed her roughly by the arm, and she wanted to laugh it felt so good.

"Lauren, *how* could you do this. How could you do this *to me*."

Matter changing states in the wrong space. The person from the wood-paneled living room colliding with the person from school. Ardor then anger, anger substituted for ardor.

Andy stepping forward, his body poised to come between them, ready to launch into gangly action. *Andy Figueroa*, Lauren's mind typed out, *not so bad after all*. Claire and Stitch round-eyed, staring, but not at Lauren.

Changing states into an animal. What kind? Barking, snarling, foaming. All instincts and reflexes and endocrine receptors. Nothing to argue with. She wasn't an animal, and so she must have been the one who made him do it. She decided to. And she was glad. When she smiled, she bared her teeth, too.

"Ted," Andy was saying, "let go of her."

"Let go of her!" everyone was shouting, and still Lauren bared her teeth.

THE FUNNY THING was that nobody in the audience seemed to have caught on. Even a few people in the play, like Brendan, had no idea, although Brendan was an idiot. Mr. Smith left during curtain call, and after the players left the stage, some of them changing out of their costumes and storing them for the next night's performance, none of them gathered in Tedquarters as they normally would. As if by mutual unspoken agreement, they filtered out down the hall from the auditorium toward the front entryway, their parents and siblings gathering in the sunken cafeteria. The faces of their families were shining and unconflicted; their arms were open. Mrs. Figueroa scooped Andy off his feet and swung him around, and he looked so happy. They spoke to each other in Spanish. *Qué maravilloso, qué estupendo.*

"Vee yo so!" Mirela told Stitch, then wrapped her arms around Mrs. Kornbluth's legs.

The families mingled in one loose embrace among the long tables with the chairs stacked atop them. The overhead fluorescent lights took on a fireside warmth.

Stitch in his pompadour moved beside Lauren, close enough that their arms were touching.

"If someone asks me," Stitch mumbled, "what do you want me to say?"

"Nothing," Lauren said.

"I'll have to say something."

"No, I mean there's nothing I *want* you to say—say what *you* want."

"I don't want you to get in trouble."

Lauren laughed. "Too late. Probably."

"I think it will be okay."

"Thank you for being nice," she said. "Thank you for making me tapes."

The warm pooling feeling in her chest, the pleasurable sadness. Stitch was standing close enough to her that she could smell his pomade and hairspray but also his twigs-and-burlap Stitch smell, the smell of a kid air-guitaring in a big cold pile of autumn leaves.

"No one seems to have noticed," Stitch said, scanning the crowd. "Everyone looks happy."

"He totally blew up at me," Lauren said.

"Well, but I think that was a good thing," said Andy, all at once in front of them.

"What do I *care* what you think?" she said to Andy.

"No—listen—" Andy said.

"We all saw what happened, right?" Stitch said to Andy, nodding, eyes big and meaningful.

"He can't do that," Andy said, nodding back. "He can't act like that, no matter what."

"Andy just means it's good that everyone saw what he did," Stitch said.

"Oh," Lauren said. "I'm sorry. I misunderstood."

"It's okay," Andy said.

"Just say you were confused," Abby was saying.

"You didn't know what you were supposed to say," Stitch said.

"You were nervous—" Abby was saying.

"—because Mr. Smith was acting so weird," Andy finished.

"Everyone knows how weird he is," Claire was saying.

"You did what he wanted," Andy said.

"He made you do it," Abby said. "It was his stupid joke and he should have known better. He's the adult. Okay?"

Lauren felt conscious of herself as part of a branching, respiring system of affinities, loyalties, tribal urges. Breathing in time with it, assimilated. And she felt conscious, too, that she had been part of this system all along, although she struggled to dance in its formation or sing in its same key. An opinion or a set of beliefs could shape itself around the tiniest gesture of a single figure, the leading bird of an echelon nudging the vortex this way or that, according to the particular aerodynamics of that moment, the direction and speed of the wind. One arm swung forward and the other swung back, one voice began a sentence and another ended it, not out of coercion or conscious choice or preference, but because all the parts of the body needed to work together, according to their present circumstances.

"Okay," Lauren said.

Her mother was standing in front of her. Mom looked stricken, stunned. Just like her to overcompensate, just like Mom to watch a crappy high school play and fake it afterward like everyone was about to win Oscars.

Mom's arms were wrapped around her. Mom's face was in her neck, breathing her in.

"I love you so much, baby," Mom said.

Lauren was onstage again. She thought she could feel everybody watching, or trying not to watch. Crazy Mom again. This embrace was too somber and melodramatic for a high school play. Lauren waited for Mirela to pop up beside them, pressing her skinny arms together in a sword to cleave them apart. "Cut da cheese!" she'd always say. Mirela hated it when they hugged or got anywhere near each other. Or maybe Mirela didn't mind so much now—maybe the trip to Colorado had done some good. Lauren had meant to ask Mom how it went, but she hadn't gotten around to it yet.

"Mom?" Lauren said.

"That's me," Mom said, her voice wet and snagged.

"Mom, where's Mirela?"

OF COURSE SHE'D run away. Running away had become Mirela's job. She had played a runaway on local TV. Lauren understood why she did it. Mirela could find the aloneness she craved and at the same time remain the center of attention; she could have her cake and hoard it, too. Lauren found a bitter entertainment in watching a search party form on the spot in the cafeteria and fan out into all points of the radius: front lawn, soccer and football fields, auditorium, second floor. She'd seen it all before. She'd seen it on the news. It was as horrifying and tedious as those buffalo galloping off the cliff.

She walked out the side entrance of Bethune, still in her Pink Ladies jacket and saddle shoes. The moon was full, clouded over by the lakes. It had been drizzling on and off all day, and now the air was misty and raindrops clung to the grass. She half expected to hear Stitch's skateboard on the asphalt. She spotted him then, with his dad, already halfway across the football field in search of Mirela, Dr. Rosen's hand on Stitch's back.

Lauren's eyes fell on the opening in the chain-link fence. It occurred to her, in an impossible flash, that Mirela had seen her go through the gap every day, had learned it from her. The gap in the fence was about as tall as Mirela. Lauren crouched to get her sight lines level with Mirela's. If you were the size of a high school student, you had to squint at the overgrown grass and weeds that grew just past the school's property line to find the gap in the fence. But at Mirela's height, it would more likely present itself as a ragged doorway cut just for her.

Lauren walked toward the fence, her shoes *squelch-squelch*ing in the wet grass. She squeezed through the gap, the split end of one link catching on the pink satin of her jacket, and stood at the edge of the open lot on Fox Hollow. "Mirela?" she called.

A rustle of a squirrel, a bird. The crackle of twigs and branches beneath her shoes in the open lot. She reached the sidewalk and stood beneath a streetlight, looking up and down. Fox Hollow was so narrow, more like a wood path than a street. "Mirela?"

She crossed Fox Hollow and walked onto the Reillys' property, compelled by some dream logic that Mirela had taken Lauren's usual route home. Trying to be like her big sister. Lauren walked around the Reillys' house into their backyard. "Mirela!" It was abruptly darker now, under the maples and pines.

She had done this. Lauren. She hadn't thought enough about Mom. She was never home to help. She didn't pay attention. Her stupid plays that she made them come to. Her stupid birthday party. "Mirela!" she screamed. "Mirela, please!"

"I've got her," she could hear a man's voice calling.

"Mirela! Someone please help me!"

"I've got her—follow the sound of my voice. We're here. I'll keep talking. Follow the sound."

Lights were flicking on in the surrounding houses. Mr. and Mrs. Reilly appeared on their deck. Another figure, a tall redheaded woman, approaching from the other side of the Reillys'.

"Mirela! Help! Mirela, where are you!"

"Keep following my voice. Lauren, is that you?"

A large seated figure in the grass emerged from the darkness in its outlines and then its contours. It resolved into two distinct figures, one seated on top of the other, as Lauren grew closer.

"Lauren, it's you. Don't worry, I've got her."

Measurements she had taken with her own hands now slotted into place. The dimensions of his silhouette, softened and imprecise beneath the diffuse moonlight and tree shade, but unmistakable: the distance from nose to upper lip, the degrees of the angle of his jawline, the coordinates of the slope of the shoulders. He was sitting cross-legged on the unadorned back lawn. Mirela was silent in his lap, turned away from him. His hands were wrapped around her. They rocked back and forth.

"I'm doing the squeeze," Mr. Smith said, looking up at Lauren.

"Who's out there?" Mrs. Reilly called. She was off the deck now, coming closer. "Can anyone tell me what's going on?"

You could move your finger through the air and write a story.

"Does anyone need help?" the tall redheaded woman called out. "Is everyone okay?"

Yet another figure emerging now, from behind the hedgerow, someone from the fancier houses, the Rosens' next-door neighbor, maybe, hands in pockets, head craning.

She remembered what he said. That the audience wants to be told what to see.

What she did next wasn't a decision. It was the filling of the lungs, the contraction of the heart muscle. The wasp moved its stinger into the base of her throat. She could take no responsibility for what came next, could harbor no guilt, no second-guessing. Instinct, reflex, biological drive. One voice began a sentence and the other ended it. Maybe she was an animal after all.

"That's my little sister!" she screamed. "Let go of her!"

She looked through the audience's eyes. A man holding down a child in darkness and dirt. The child's older sister—though just a girl herself—rescuing her, saving her.

"Lauren, everything's okay. She's okay—" he said.

"Lauren, honey, are you all right?" Mrs. Reilly asked, her voice coming closer.

"What's going on?" the tall redheaded woman asked. "Whose child is this?"

The figure from behind the hedgerow was running toward Lauren now.

"Let go of her! What are you doing?! Let go of her!"

"Whose is she?"

"Joe, go back inside and call the police right now."

"Where is this child's mother?"

"Lauren, what are you doing—ma'am, no, please, this is a big misunderstanding—" he said.

"Whose is she?"

"SHE'S JUST A BABY!"

It was her. It was Lauren who was doing it. It was her voice she heard.

"LET GO OF HER! SHE'S JUST A BABY! SHE'S JUST A LITTLE GIRL!"

This must be what it's like to be Mirela. She was screaming like she could shatter the glass of herself, like she could scream away the world.

JANE

There were not many mothers who were saints. Jutta of Prussia packed her kids off to monasteries so that she would have no distractions in her service to the poor. Saint Monica cried endlessly over her reprobate son Augustine. The venerable Gianna, who would soon be a saint, was pregnant with her fourth child when a doctor discovered a tumor on her uterus. An abortion was out of the question, of course, but church officials deemed that a hysterectomy would be permissible. In catechism class, Sister Tabitha used Gianna's dilemma to illustrate the doctrine of double effect.

"'Nothing hinders one act from having two effects, only one of which is intended, while the other is beside the intention,'" the sister read from Thomas Aquinas. "'Accordingly, the act of self-defense may have two effects: one, the saving of one's life; the other, the slaying of the aggressor.'" A hysterectomy would be an act of self-defense, saving Gianna's life and slaying her aggressor—the aggressor being the diseased uterus, which happened to have a baby inside it. Gianna's case was a neat trade of cause and effect: substitute the cause of the baby's death, which performed a moral cleansing of the identical effect.

This was the stuff of the sort of philosophical debate Jane had once imagined herself having with Father Steve, but he stopped convening Respect Life meetings after the Spring of Life. Following Sunday mass, he demurred on all but the most perfunctory small talk with a cordial smile, a nod of businesslike blessedness.

Father Steve would never come out and say what was true, that the whole mental exercise with Gianna and the uterine substitution was Catholic gobbledygook—even Jane's mother would think so. Like how one of the Kennedy nephews sought to have his first marriage annulled so that he could remarry in the Church. "Would you imagine, pretending twenty years of marriage never happened, those beautiful boys, because Cousin Joe wants to take Communion!" Jane's mother said. "That poor woman—the mother of his children!" She crossed herself. "I'm not questioning the Church, mind you—I'm questioning those who would *take advantage*."

Gianna refused the hysterectomy. Of course she did. She knew double effect was a semantic shell game. She gave birth to a healthy girl and died a week later of sepsis, which was why the catechism students learned about her at all. No one would have sought out three documented miracles for a woman who decided to save her children's mother.

Perhaps the doctrine of double effect was at work the night of the skipped period. For justice to be served, a smaller injustice needed to be committed. One sister had been substituted for another in order to achieve the identical effect. For the real crime to be punished, another one had to be fabricated.

The parents of Catherine of Siena attempted to substitute her for her sister, and that's when she cut off all her hair and starved herself and broke into a rash. For the first time in her adult life, Jane had skipped going to mass on Catherine's feast day, April 29, because she was with Mirela in Colorado. April 29 was the day Los Angeles went up in flames, and Jane missed that, too—didn't even know about it until the fires were going out. She couldn't keep count of all she'd missed, all she'd never even looked at.

SHE WASN'T LOOKING for him when she saw him. Jane was mingling with the other parents in the Bethune cafeteria after the premiere of the musical, waiting for their performers to straggle out. She held Lauren's Bells bouquet, smiling and nodding vacantly. She exchanged excruciating *hello, how are you*s and *aren't our kids so great*s with the Rosens, one eye tracking Mirela as she clambered onto a table, not knowing if the Rosens knew who she was—or rather, there was no way they didn't know, yet they feigned as if they didn't, and so Jane could, too. And then over Mamie Figueroa's shoulder she saw him, emerging from the hallway that led out of the auditorium and into the front hall of Bethune, right in front of the cafeteria pit.

Her legs propelled her forward without her willing it. He was moving so fast toward the double front doors of the school, his eyebrows a dark slash, shoulders hunched. He was so young. He seemed younger than she had ever been. He was trying to be furtive; his frustration, or his anger, begged attention, but his anger might intensify if he was given attention. His movements like Pat's.

"Excuse me," she said, placing one foot on the step, "are you—"

He glanced over but didn't see her, moved past her, putting up an apologetic hand, a pained condescending smile.

She hopped up the steps out of the cafeteria pit and was standing almost in front of him, between him and the front doors. A hand on his sleeve. "Hi, I just wanted to—"

He stopped and gaped. "It's you," he said.

Jane smiled, puzzled. It was as if he were staring at his own face but not recognizing himself. Staring into the face of the moon.

"I don't think we've met before," Jane said. "I'm Lauren's mom."

"Oh, yes," he said, taking her outstretched hand. "It's nice to meet you."

"Lauren talks about you all the time," she said.

Jane had never sensed before that a man was afraid of her, and it occurred to her to apologize before it occurred to her why he was afraid.

"Anyway, I'm sorry to keep you—or would you like to stay with us a bit?" she asked.

She could hear it in her voice that she knew. But he was the one who told her.

Mr. Smith looked at the flowers in the crook of her arm. "You haven't seen the kids yet?" he asked.

"They're coming out now," Jane said, gesturing behind him to the first stream of performers skipping and singing as they approached the pit. He didn't turn around to see them. Her hands felt gray and frozen, dead on the dying flowers. The chatter echoing off the walls seemed both louder and more distant.

"I'm sorry, but I need to go," he said.

"Are you all right?" she asked. "You look sick."

"I think I am, a bit, forgive me. I have to run—have a wonderful night."

"You too," she said, and he turned and pushed through the front doors of Bethune.

"Bye-bye," she said, as she followed him outside. She watched him under the moonlight, walking toward the chain-link fence. The start of the same route Lauren took home. He bent down and eased his body through the hole in the fence, and the corners of Jane's lips recoiled in a rancid smile. It was about to hit her with the entirety of its force, she only had a few seconds left before the impact, and she clenched her fists and closed her eyes and all she knew or felt was an incandescent contempt.

She picked up the flowers from where they'd fallen on the pavement and returned inside. She looked for Lauren. The novelty of searching a crowd for a child who was not Mirela. Lauren was with her friends, standing notably close to Stitch, ducking her head, merry and diffident in her pink satin jacket. You would never know. Jane was propelled forward again, back down the three steps into the cafeteria pit, racing toward Lauren, like she had left her on the stove, like she was chasing a girl who was standing still, as rooted as a tree.

THE REST OF the performances of *Grease* were canceled. Assistant Principal Shaughnessy interviewed all the main characters. Stitch, Claire, Abby, and Andy each corroborated Lauren's account of Mr. Smith grabbing Lauren and menacing her backstage. Each of them, plus Deepa, independently volunteered, without prompting, that they'd observed Mr. Smith behaving in an erratic way at the same rehearsal during which he said something about "a broken typewriter" or a "busted typewriter" or possibly "a busted computer," which corroborated, if not proved, the contention that Lauren speaking the forbidden line was Mr. Smith's mischievous idea, not Lauren's, and therefore that she should not be suspended for it, that it was Mr. Smith who should face some kind of consequence. Each of these witnesses reiterated that Mr. Smith had been seen by several residents of Bethune's surrounding neighborhood, including Lauren, holding down Lauren's sister by force, requiring the intervention of the Town of Amherst police department, although that episode, which ended in Mr. Smith's arrest and brief detention, was beyond Assistant Principal Shaughnessy's jurisdiction.

Other evidence entered into the record. Claire described a straight-cut, brown corduroy jumper that came to her ankles, which Mr. Smith referred to as her "sexy Mormon skirt." Abby stated that Mr. Smith often told her she "needed extra meat in her sandwich," and once opined that her "saddle needed padding." Deepa talked about hugs that lasted too long, about Mr. Smith's self-imposed rule that he "never be the first to break a hug." Rumors traveled, puddled, metastasized: marijuana and drinking and mild sexual activity in Tedquarters. A whispering suggestion about some incident at teachers' college—maybe this story didn't take shape because it wasn't true, or because it was too scurrilous to be uttered. Somebody started referring to Mr. Smith as Ted Bundy, and that caught on, and then one day everyone seemed to have agreed that Tedquarters was now called Bundytown. Mrs. Bonnano quietly took over his classes for the rest of the year. Mr. Treadwell took over the end-of-year workshops, dumping Mr. Smith's plans for a tribute to Edward Albee in favor of a Cole Porter revue.

"That boy may never teach again, not with an arrest on his record," Mamie Figueroa said to Jane one evening on the phone.

"Well, he was arrested, but not formally charged," said Jane, who could say the same of herself. "And a potential employer wouldn't necessarily know any of this. He wouldn't have to disclose it. He could just start over somewhere else."

Pat and the older kids were eating ravioli in front of the TV in the living room. Jane and Mirela were eating toast and jam at the kitchen table. Jane planned to eat all of hers, to set a good example for Mirela.

"Andy always said there was something strange about Mr. Smith," Mamie said.

"Even his choice of play last fall—it had two suicides, World War II, negligent homicide," Jane said. "Is this appropriate for children? I know they do a good impersonation of adults, but they are still children, after all."

"I didn't understand why high schoolers would be asked to perform *Grease*, either," Mamie said.

"Oh, we watched the movie!" Jane said. "I remember loving it when we were kids. But it's ridiculous trash. Whatever else Mr. Smith did, he had abysmal judgment."

"I wonder what will happen to him now," Mamie said.

"He has no one to blame but himself," Jane said.

"Although it would be a shame for his whole life to be ruined by all this," Mamie said.

The egg timer on the kitchen table pinged. "Mamie, I'm sorry, I need to go," Jane said. "It's time for Mirela's bath."

FOR A FEW days it seemed likely that the Arden Attachment Center would sue the Brennans for damages. What had happened was never in doubt: Jane had stood on a chair, fashioned a blowtorch out of Carolyn's hairspray and Lauren's lighter, and aimed it directly at a sprinkler head. The visual shock of the fire itself, and the subsequent triggering of the sprinklers, was undoubtedly frightening and disruptive to the Arden staffers fleeing the scene, but there was little damage to speak of, and Arden was insured. Jane appreciated that Pat didn't take the incident and legal threats all that seriously, at least not in front of her. He called his dad, his dad called his lawyer, letters were written, counterthreats were issued. The guiding idea was that Arden wouldn't want anyone taking a close look at what went on inside their facilities. Pat listened carefully to Jane's account of the events, and he blamed her for nothing. He hadn't seen what happened, and so he took her at her word—she was his only witness. He believed in what he couldn't see. When he was sweet, he was so sweet.

And Jane was grateful to Arden, because if nothing else, Arden had given them a regimen. How long the regimen would last was open-ended. Every day, Jane and Mirela did the same things at the same time, together. Breakfast, lunch, and dinner were always the same, according to the day of the week. Mirela went to bed at the same time every night, behind a locked door. The egg timer went with them everywhere. Mirela could argue anything with Jane, but she rarely argued with the egg timer. Jane did not hold herself to any standard of cheerfulness or even equanimity; she aspired only to an inexorable thereness. All she wished for Mirela was the knowledge that her mother was there and there and still there. A basket hold of rigid, unending routine. Jane was a wall, a building, at times an impediment. They began each day by tuning in to the weather report, on both the radio and the television. Mirela could not control what the weather could be, and she could not, to her immense pique, control how accurate the forecasts proved to be, but she could control how many weather reports she consumed and how she synthesized their often subtly conflicting assessments of the day to come. Jane set the egg timer, and when it went off, there was no more weather.

Jane had to present her with something immovable and inarguable to attach to. Jane's inescapableness would at first seem negotiable, then perhaps dreadful, and then—if they were very lucky—something that Mirela could resign herself to. A structure wall for a future home, but first Mirela would try to climb over the wall, and then she would bash her head against it. Other concrete goals—starting a half-day kindergarten program, joining a soccer club, a playdate here and there—could wait. First they had to construct the wall and test its strength, its safety.

AFTER RESPECT LIFE petered out, Summer and Charity Huebler joined Witness for the Innocents. They did sidewalk counseling in front of Dr. Rosen's clinic every Wednesday morning and at WellWomen every Saturday morning. Jane begged off when they asked her to join them, using Mirela as an excuse, but they kept calling to ask.

"Charity," Jane said on the phone, "I had an idea. I wondered if, this Wednesday, you and Summer might be willing to swap places with me and my daughter—my older daughter. Lauren. She wants to see what sidewalk counseling is all about."

"Are you sure?" Charity asked. Jane could hear her flipping pages. "I think it would just be—let me check—yes, it's only the two of us that morning. LifeForce doesn't show up until the afternoon at Rosen's. Why don't we all go, the four of us? Strength in numbers."

"That's such a nice idea, but the thing is, my daughter is quite shy," Jane said. "It might be better for her first time just to come with her mom, see how it goes. Who knows, maybe we'll turn her into a regular."

"Or what if you went on Saturday? Saturday's our busiest day, of course—many more opportunities to engage."

"Well, I was thinking a quieter Wednesday would be better for my daughter, actually," Jane said. "For her first time. The proborts may not even bother with escorts on a weekday morning, right? Saturdays can get hectic."

A pause as Charity considered. "You know, I think this could be very powerful for the patients," Charity said. "There's the whole teen-mom thing that the two of you have—I mean, if you feel comfortable going into that, but also, just that picture of a mother and her daughter out there on their own, trying to make that connection."

"Mmm," Jane said. "Thank you."

"Although I think sometimes people think you're sisters!"

"Sometimes!" Jane said.

Wednesday morning. A rare, regrettable break in Mirela's regimen. Pat would be in charge of the egg timer during Lauren's "doctor's appointment." Pat would be responsible for adding the right amount of milk to Mirela's oatmeal—not too stodgy, not too runny—so as to keep it from splattering on the kitchen walls. Jane felt both anger and relief that he didn't ask why Lauren needed to go to the doctor, what type of doctor.

"YOU WANT ME to be ashamed," Lauren said to her mother. They were sitting in the dragon wagon in front of Judy's Hair Cutz. Mrs. Rosen, who worked as her husband's receptionist, had told Jane to park at the post office on one side or at Judy's Hair Cutz on the other and go through the back entrance, even on a slow day, just in case. But Jane already knew all that.

"Ashamed of what?"

"Of what I did. Of what I'm making you do."

"No."

"What *you* are making me do."

"Lauren, I'm not making you do anything. It's up to you. You can get out of the car and go in there, and I'll come with you, or we can go home. Or you don't have to go home if you don't want to— you could go to Paula's house if she's around, whatever. It is what you want. It is your decision."

Lauren's eyes bored holes in the glove compartment. "Don't you want to know who it was?"

"It's none of my business," Jane said.

"It's not?"

"Lauren," Jane said. "I know who it was."

Lauren's hands twisted in her lap. "How do you know?"

"I just do."

"Are you going to tell?"

"I will not tell a soul unless you ask me to."

"Well, I wanted it. I wanted it to happen. I don't care what you think."

"Lauren, I don't know if this is going to make sense," Jane said, "but in this case, it doesn't matter what you wanted."

Lauren snorted. Like somebody hit her and she was trying to laugh it off. "Does it *ever* matter to you what I want?"

"It matters deeply to me what you want. But in this case, no, it doesn't."

Lauren opened the car door. Even in June, the mornings took a while to warm up. The light was still low. They approached a line of scrubby trees that marked the border of the small back lot, enough for a half-dozen cars. Jane was mildly surprised to see two escorts chatting at the back entrance—a skittish aftereffect of the Spring of Life, perhaps.

Jane held Lauren's arm to halt her walking. It was Bridie and Jill. They hadn't seen Jane and Lauren approaching yet. It wasn't too late. They could turn back now. Jane squeezed Lauren's hand.

"Mom, I'm fine," Lauren said, tugging her forward.

"What's your first and last name, honey?" Bridie was already asking.

"Lauren Brennan," she said.

Bridie smiled. "That's the name we were after. Welcome, Lauren." Bridie pushed a ringer on the back door and looked up at a camera mounted overhead, waving and giving the okay sign.

"I know you," Jill said. "Jane. We've met before. Remember Jane, Bridie?"

"Sure do," Bridie said, smiling. "Big part of my job, Jane, is to never forget a face."

"Yes?" a scratchy voice on the intercom bleated.

"We have our eight thirty patient here. You can let her in." The door buzzed, and Bridie opened it, still smiling.

From the scrubby trees, a robin peeped. "Everything is going to be okay," Bridie said to Lauren, pushing the door open wide for her and Jane to climb the stairs. "It's a nice, quiet day today."

In the waiting room, magazines were neatly stacked on racks and on low circular tables. Bouquets of wildflowers and sepia-colored brochures, arranged in fans. Floral-print sofa, throw pillows. Picasso and Degas posters from the Albright-Knox were taped onto the brick covering the windows. A television set with the volume down low, murmuring morning pleasantries. Janice Cortusa appeared with the weather report, and Jane imagined Mirela watching closely, Pat reminding her to keep an arm's length from the television set, taking hieroglyphic notes on her sketch pad on cloud coverage and expected highs, the egg timer ticking beside her. As Jane and Lauren took their seats, Jane mapped and measured in her head where she would have been standing during the Spring of Life, if her own voice might have penetrated the brick and reached the patients in this waiting room, and when, and what words she would have been saying.

A woman in blue scrubs pushed through the pair of swinging doors adjoining the receptionist's area. She looked down at her clipboard and called out Lauren's patient number. Lauren looked over at Jane, who smiled and patted her arm. Lauren got up, brushed past the nurse, and walked straight through the swinging doors.

At one time Jane had memorized Dr. Rosen's schedule, his comings and goings—everyone in Respect Life had, all the Oh-Rs had, too.

Jane imagined that the nurse in white linens waited on the other side of the swinging doors.

Lauren was stalking back into the waiting room. She stopped short in front of her mother, tipping forward slightly with fuming momentum. Her voice was barely audible.

"I just wanted to check that you don't want to be with me," Lauren said.

"Do you want me there, Lauren?" Jane asked.

Lauren stared at her mother. She looked dumbfounded. Her anger was beating back her sorrow.

"Why," Lauren said, "why do I always have to *ask*." It wasn't a question.

"Lauren? Honey, please, I don't understand."

"Why do I have to say it," Lauren whispered. "Why do you make me *say it*."

Lauren turned and left the waiting room again before Jane could respond. Jane stared at the doors swinging behind her, exchanging places back, forth, brushing past, again, past, again, and when the doors stood absolutely still, that was when she put her face in her hands and wept, although it was a sin—to pity oneself was despair in disguise; what it signaled was a loss of faith—and yet she wept, she abandoned herself to her weeping, and when Lauren was done, she came back softer, consoling, conciliatory, her hand rubbing her back, it's over now, Mommy, it's all over, and even then she could not stop herself weeping, and there was no comfort in her return.

LAUREN

The block capital letters on the tabloid stacked outside News Haven on Sunday morning didn't make sense, and that's why she stopped to stare. It wasn't because she thought it had anything to do with her.

ABORT DOC SLAIN. Her eyes completed *doc* as *documentary* because of her seminar on cinéma vérité. *Slain* translated to *Sláinte*, the Irish toast she'd picked up in her class on twentieth-century Irish literature. She once tried to explain to Gwen, her roommate for senior year of college, that her grades were what they were not because she worked so hard or was so smart but because her classes stood in for a well-developed inner life. "It's all just programmable circuitry," she explained. "There is brain but no mind." She intended it to be self-deprecating, but it came out as false modesty.

A broadsheet stacked next to the tabloid. ABORTION DOCTOR SHOT DEAD IN HIS HOME. *Sniper-style. Anti-abortion activists. Williamsville. Rosen.*

An older couple, silver and slender, brushing past Lauren apologetically. Picking up their Sunday papers to read over coffee and muffins down the block at Atticus Cafe, she thought. They looked like emeritus Yale professors, like they'd have a big rambling house in East Rock filled with hanging plants and folk art and first editions. *I know him*, Lauren wanted to tell them, jabbing a finger on the broadsheet headline. *My friend's dad. That's my town. That's where I'm from.*

Oh, how terrible, the woman would say. *I'm so sorry.* And that would be it. What could she say? What could these strangers do with this information? It was a useless story.

The morning before, Mom had left a message on the answering machine in Gwen and Lauren's apartment. "Hi, girls, it's Mom—Lauren's mom—Lauren, honey, can you please—"

That was all Lauren heard before she pressed the stop button, smiling at the urgency in Mom's voice, skipping over the nervous oddness of "Lauren's mom." Sunday mornings, not Saturdays, were Mom's official phone time; Lauren was strict about it. Whatever it was—Sean scored two touchdowns in Friday night's game, Mirela got through her new modern-dance class without a meltdown—could wait. Gwen and her newish boyfriend, Stu, had recently started having sex, and Stu still lived in the dorms, and so Saturday was a big day for the two of them, obviously, there in the apartment. Lauren could go to the gym, the library, Atticus Cafe. Plenty of reasons for her to be out of the house.

On Sunday mornings, somebody was always up in Harkness Tower trying to play the main theme from *The Piano*, fighting to gain mastery of its imperious whorl of arpeggios; this person never improved, and his or her clumsy Sunday tradition over many weeks had become endearing. The sky was an impossible cerulean, a blue that Buffalo never knew. Lauren let herself into the apartment and was relieved to see that the door to Gwen's room was open. In the kitchen, Stu was fixing pancakes, and Gwen, hair wet from the shower, wearing a too-big Choate sweatshirt that must have been Stu's, was sipping tea at the table, piles of newspapers and journals and textbooks fanned under her elbows. The answering machine was flashing *4*.

"Hi, sweetie, all of those messages are your mom," Gwen said.

"Yuh *killin'* yuh poor *muth*-a, Low-wren," Stu said. Some kind of Italian-mother shtick. Last weekend, Stu blurted out to a bunch of their friends that Lauren was "virginal, like a little white lamb"—he didn't mean it literally, but rather as a dumb compliment about her straight-arrow studiousness, her spotless transcript and impossible extracurriculars, and she didn't care, but Gwen got mad at him, and he'd been overcompensating with Lauren in the days since, trying to lather up a fraternal rapport.

"Did you know this guy who got killed, from Buffalo?" Gwen asked, pushing a section of the *New York Times* across the table. "Rosen?"

"I only really met him once," Lauren said. "Is it okay if I use the phone for a while?"

THEY KILLED STITCH'S dad on Friday night. He'd just come home from services. A single rifle shot through the kitchen window that faced onto their backyard. He was microwaving a bowl of soup, or a muffin—reports differed. Stitch's little brother, Joey, standing right there. Stitch's mom in the next room. He didn't die right away.

"Mom, please, enough," Lauren said over the phone. "You don't need to go into all of it."

The memorial was set for Monday morning. Mom always said that Jewish families dealt with their dead properly—they didn't paint the corpse and prop it up for show, they didn't leave the body to bloat in a parlor while middle-aged children fussed over the floral arrangements.

"Mom, okay, I get it," Lauren said. Mom liked to show how open she was to what she called "other cultures."

Lauren could fly out and back and still make her Reconstruction & Redemption lecture on Tuesday morning. Mom said it was okay to put the flight on Dad's credit card. She could finish the reading on the plane. Gwen and Stu would never notice. A friend of the family had died—that's all she had to say to anyone who asked. Yeah, that abortion doctor; yeah, it's crazy. No, not a close friend, just paying respects. Went to school with his kids. She didn't need to go into all of it.

"You've kept in touch with Stitch?" Mom asked on the phone. "He graduated?"

"He's in his first year of med school, in Boston. I see him on breaks and stuff," Lauren said. "We email once in a while." In truth, they had kept a cordial, loving distance after *Grease*. The distance was paradoxical and necessary: she now felt permanently connected to Stitch, and any greater proximity to him would have smothered her.

When she was off the phone with Mom, she planned to walk over to the computer cluster at Connecticut Hall. She wouldn't have to wait for a free computer this early on a Sunday morning.

"They were always such nice boys. A nice family," Mom said.

No subject heading, Lauren decided. *I'm so sorry, Stitch. My heart is breaking for you and your mother and brothers.*

"Mom," Lauren said, "you don't know anyone from before—from the protests—who could have done something like this, do you?" A ridiculous thought zoomed past, that Mom's phone was tapped by investigators.

"No," Mom said. "I mean, so far as I remember. It's been six years."

"Six and a half."

"There were people during the protests who liked to think they could be capable of it," Mom said. "I just wonder if all that drama stirred something up that wasn't there before. Planted a seed of some kind."

"It wasn't anything, Mom. It was just a circus."

"There is blood on all of their hands. Mine, too."

"Don't be so dramatic."

"We told ourselves that words were actions, like prayer," Mom said. "You dehumanize someone, you call them a monster—then look what happens."

"Do you want somebody to forgive you," Lauren said dully. It wasn't a question.

"I feel a responsibility," Mom said.

"You always want to feel responsible for everything," Lauren said.

"And that's so bad?"

"It's like—you want to feel guilty about it, like you're being selfless, but you're not, you're just making it all about you."

"You want making it all about you, talk to Margie Dale," Mom said. "Margie Dale was out power-walking with Ellie D'Amato on Friday night, and she's swearing up and down to anyone who will listen that she heard the shot, she heard the shot. She calls me up: 'Jane, I heard the shot.' Who cares?"

"She heard the shot—like it's a trophy. Her souvenir of death."

The shot had come from just behind the Rosens' weeping willow.

"'I heard the shot,'" Mom scoffed. "What are you, the FBI? Stick it up your ass."

Lauren closed her eyes. The phone hot and slick against her cheek.

"Such a nice man," Mom was saying. "Such a shame."

She was standing behind the sniper, gazing over his shoulder at Stitch's dad in the window.

"He was a nice man, Mom," Lauren affirmed. "He was good to me. Kind and gentle."

She caught the sniper off guard, buckled his knees. She peeled the rifle off his person with liturgical solemnity, a ceremony in reverse. The same grass breathed her feet off the ground. The same darkness was milky and changeable, like you could move your finger through the air and write a useless story, a story that never even happened.

THE SHIVA WAS at Stitch's uncle's place, somewhere in Tonawanda, because Stitch's house was still an active crime scene. PJ and Sean picked Lauren up from the airport in the dragon wagon, PJ's Gumby-long limbs pressing his knees against the wheel, Sean in the passenger seat covered in a road map, his head likewise brushing the roof. The surge of androgens in their midteens had yanked them both skyward with a whiplash force that left them absurdly tall but also mellowed and frequently drowsy, especially in the mornings; PJ had scheduled all his fall-semester classes at UB for the afternoon.

Lauren climbed into the back seat, overnight bag at her feet. Her brothers twisted awkwardly around in their places to kiss her hello without breaking the stream of their quarrel.

"You can't bring two-buck chuck to a *memorial service*," PJ was saying as he pulled away from Arrivals.

"It's what was in the pantry!" Sean said. "There's no accounting for Mom and Dad's taste!"

"You might as well show up with a sack of potatoes and make some rotgut in the backyard," PJ said. "Bring a personal touch to it."

"Wait," Sean said, "is it even okay to bring wine to a shiva?"

"Food is better. Mom and Dad aren't coming?" She pulled herself to the edge of the back seat, propping up her elbows on either of her brothers' headrests.

"Mom said something about 'out of respect for the family,'" Sean said, dropping the map to make air quotes with his fingers.

"Listen, when I want to respect a grieving family I boycott their funerals—" PJ said.

"It's not a *boycott*," Sean said. "It's more like she's covering her eyes with her hands and hoping that means nobody sees her."

"—and I don't send a card, either," PJ said. "And I bring moonshine in mason jars."

"Mom will send a card," Sean said, "but she'll leave it blank because she wouldn't want to be presumptuous."

"I mean, I get it," PJ said, sounding unconvinced. "Mom thinks that her whole history with the—you know—"

"A *moral residue*," Sean said, like he was picking the words out of his teeth. Lauren recognized the phrase as a favorite of Mrs. Bristol's. Sean had her for English now, in his senior year of high school.

"Mom just doesn't want to cause any trouble—" PJ was saying, his voice strained at one end by sympathy and the other by sarcasm.

"It's not like anyone would turn her away, or even know who she was," Lauren said. "What, because she went on a march six years ago?"

"I mean, we don't know—there could be people there who would be uncomfortable," PJ said.

"Nah," Lauren said. "She's just using that as an excuse not to go. But what about Dad?"

Sean laughed. "Nana Dee could drop dead at morning doubles tomorrow and Dad would decide to replace the rain gutters before he showed up at her wake."

"That's mean," Lauren said.

"That *is* mean," PJ said. "He wouldn't replace the rain gutters. He would build a little shed in the backyard to grieve in. Table for one."

"Dad's always been a troubled loner, but Mom should know better," Lauren said.

"She should show up."

"Well, she's got Mirela to think about, too," PJ said. He had momentarily exhausted his resources for ragging on their mother.

"Mirela can handle a shiva," Lauren said.

Sean puffed out his lips in a daunted way. "*Sure* she can."

"Mom shouldn't hide behind a little kid," Lauren said. She disliked the hectoring tone in her voice and sat back in the seat.

"Man, do you guys remember all that time she used to spend at Dead Babies Club?" Sean asked after a moment. "Whatever happened to all those people?"

"She told me that she knew people in Dead Babies Club who were capable of something like—like this," Lauren said.

"*What?!*" Sean exclaimed. "Like who?"

Lauren felt an immediate, panicked remorse. "Or she said—she said they would have *liked to think* they could—"

"Jesus Christ," PJ said.

"I mean, I doubt it," Lauren said.

They drove in silence, the air inside the dragon wagon clearer and thinner.

"I think there's a Tops coming up on Transit, on the left, before you get to North French," Lauren said when the time came. "We can pick up a deli platter there."

THE FIRST FAMILIAR face inside the crowded foyer was Rajiv, who swept Lauren up in a silent, swaying hug. He'd developed an amnesiac courtliness toward her immediately after *Grease* that held firm throughout high school and beyond, and that now reminded her of Stu. Deeper into the house, still clutching the deli platter, the cling film starting to slip underneath her fingers, Lauren found Abby, who had a junior reporting gig at the *Buffalo News* and an internship at WGRZ.

"We've got hundreds of hours of footage of the Spring of Life, both professional and amateur," Abby was telling Lauren and Sean. "We've been watching all of it in shifts, trying to find even a single frame of a guy who might match the suspect's description, the police sketch—they think it's the same guy who's been killing doctors in Canada."

"Right, yeah, we read about that," Lauren said, Sean nodding beside her.

"They're really all over this. I don't think it's going to take long to nail somebody. But I was wondering, like—sorry if this is awkward—but if we found anything—it might be helpful for your mom to take a look? See if it jogs her memory?" Abby asked.

Lauren and Sean murmured *yeah*s and *of course*s and *definitely*s.

It's Paula you should ask, Lauren thought, waving across the room at Paula as she came through the front door. It was Paula who told her that Mr. Smith enrolled in law school; it was Paula who found out he was in the Bay Area, doing something low-paid and virtuous—indigent defendants, maybe, or civil liberties. Lauren told her she didn't want to know more, not to mention him again.

"I'll give you my number," Abby was saying. "It's a cell phone—I know it's obnoxious, I just need it for work." Abby handed Sean her business card, eased the deli plate out of Lauren's hands, and turned to carry it into the kitchen.

"Excuse me—is your name Lauren?" another woman asked. She had a baby on her hip and was somehow unplaceable, older than Stitch's friends but younger than their parents and teachers.

"Yes, I'm Lauren, how do you do."

The woman beamed. "My goodness, you look exactly like your mother. I'm sorry—I'm Elise. I'm a friend of your mom's from long ago." She offered Lauren her left hand because her right was slung around the baby. "God, I—I knew you when you were tiny, brand-new. Before you were born, even."

"Oh, how about that," Lauren said, smiling as they shook hands. "It's nice to meet you." She struggled to register Mom and Elise as peers. She couldn't picture Mom with a baby now, or wearing this black suit, anonymous yet ineffably fancy, its supple lines and textures foreign to the T.J.Maxx racks that Mom relied on.

"Your mom and I went to school together, kindergarten straight through high school. Is she here?"

"It's just me and my little brothers here today," Lauren said. She gestured across the room at them. "Or not so little. My mom would have liked to come, but she's got her hands full with my little sister."

"Oh, I see, too bad," Elise said. "Wow, Jane has four kids now?"

"You should give her a call," Lauren said. "I bet she'd love to see an old friend. Same phone number we've had since I was a baby," she added.

"I will—I'm in town for a few days," Elise said. An awkward, smiling lull. They broke the silence at the same time.

"I'm just gonna go get a—" Lauren started.

"Did you know the—oh, sorry, I was just going to ask how you knew Dr. Rosen." Elise shook her head. "So awful. No words."

"Oh—" Lauren started.

We used to wave through the window, she thought.

This wasn't the right answer, because it cast her as an ogler, an owl, a stickup artist. Placed her behind the scope of a rifle. And besides, back then she'd been waving from common land—backyards were more akin to trails than enclosures. The fences had started to go up her last year of high school, in the spring. The news had been dominated, perhaps more than usual, by men with violent grievances. The O. J. Simpson case had been going almost a year. (Dad was fixated for a while with the missing pockets of time surrounding the murders, as O.J. dashed through yards and alleys in his prowler's knit cap. Dad even drew a map of the ground O.J. had had to cover and in how much time, hypothesizing different routes, tracking them in corresponding shades of Sharpie.) A Gulf War veteran used fertilizer and race-car fluid to blow up a building with a day care in it, in Oklahoma City, and the *Buffalo News* spent several days trying to determine what it meant, precisely, that the terrorist was from Lockport. Rajiv got a week's detention for using the then-ubiquitous police sketch of the Unabomber on posters promoting his band's upcoming show at Mohawk Place. Gary Wisniak's dad accidentally shot him in the head in their living room—there was some scuffle; it was alleged that Gary had threatened his mom—and, shattered with remorse over his dead son, Mr. Wisniak immediately turned the gun on himself, fatally. But Gary was fine: the bullet only grazed him, enough to knock him cold and produce some blood, and he was back at school within two weeks, the white rectangle shaved into his hair crossed diagonally with a row of inflamed, bulging sutures. Gary came to Rajiv's show at Mohawk Place, did a full hour in the mosh pit despite his head. A few weeks into summer break, he was arrested for burglarizing houses on Sycamore Run.

The O'Tooles were the first with a fence—curtain-twitching Mrs. O'Toole and her hysterical dog were the vanguard of the neighborhood. An eight-foot vinyl number in a damp, fungal shade of gray. Lauren thought Dad might cry. But you saw more of the gray vinyl fences after the burglaries, as well as the cloying white-picket varieties, along with more security-system signs on front lawns. The Reillys, true to their rustic aesthetic, put up a low-slung row of farm fencing—you could imagine a heifer daintily slinging her legs over it to take her nighttime constitutional. Even where fencing did not consume physical space, the idea of it invisibly inscribed the neighborhood, which became less of a commons and more of a grid. One bee-buzzing August afternoon, Lauren was cutting through the yard with the overground pool, nodding hello at the house's new owner as he fiddled with the pool's cover, when the man put up a preemptive hand, asking what are you doing, why are you here. She started to reply—that she was walking to her friend Paula's house to ask if she wanted to go to a movie, and that ordinarily she would have called first, but Paula's phone kept ringing busy, which meant she was using the modem, parsing the latest on rec.arts.x-files or alt.music.nirvana—but instead she ducked her head and retreated wordlessly into the as-yet-fenceless yard next door.

Lauren smiled apologetically at Elise.

Dr. Rosen was my doctor once, she thought.

This wasn't the right answer, either, because the story was quotidian, forgettable. A single, uncomplicated appointment, less than thirty minutes of an ordinary day for him. A sting, a surprising pressure, some cramping. Nothing that could be described as pain. A couple of Tylenol, an okay to go to school the next day. He was tall, politely stooped, dark barrel-vault eyes under drugstore glasses, a glossy dark beard. A voice that traveled from somewhere near his sternum, as if the striated muscles within his chest curved around themselves in the manner of a contrabassoon, the grave quiet effort at speech producing a sub-bass frequency that Lauren could feel through her feet even as she leaned in to hear him better. Lanky like Stitch, nothing of Stitch in his face. But in the first of those thirty minutes, the stage of introductions and pleasantries, Lauren grasped where Stitch had derived his glassy stoicism, his somehow coexisting openness and impenetrability: permeable as the yards had once been, unselfconscious as the children who once walked through them. Stitch had been accustomed all his life to being gazed at like this, by this man, with unembarrassed and profound intellectual curiosity, like Stitch was a living text: open to interpretation, and even gentle molding, but belonging wholly to itself. Himself, herself. To be looked at like this was to reflect back the light that beckoned the world closer, and also to absorb the light that acted as a sealant on the self. After the appointment was done, he murmured something in subwoofer Hebrew to the receptionist, whom Lauren dully recognized as Stitch's mother, and she felt the same stupid recognition that she did that autumn morning coming home from the sleepover at Abby's: that hers was a half life, that she apprehended the world with a half mind.

This was the gift of an English major at an elite university, Lauren supposed, the ability to generate endless pages of close-reading on misremembered lines, to whip up a false and sentimental frenzy of meaning through sleight of hand and punny metaphor—a woodwind instrument, the woods of her youth—for the delectation of her mother's friends, on the subject of a now famously dead man to whom she could claim some tenuous connection. She could inhabit the spirit of Margie Dale, power-walking into this hushed house of grief to pluck a few shares of sorrow off the Tops deli plate, maybe wrap a couple more in a napkin to take home for later.

We used to wave through the window.

"I only really met him one time," Lauren finally told Elise. "Could you excuse me? I need to say hello to my friend."

Elise smiled and switched the baby from one hip to the other. "Of course. It was so nice to see you, Lauren."

"If I don't catch you again—do call my mom," Lauren said. "I bet it would mean a lot to her."

"Lauren, hey," Stitch was saying, and her face was in his starched white collar. He didn't smell like the woods at all.

This embracing joy of belonging. This branching, respiring system of affinities, loyalties. She'd wanted to tell the older couple at the newsstand that this was her town, this was where she was from, but she wasn't from anywhere.

"Lauren, do you remember my mom?" Stitch was asking.

She remembered how smug she used to feel in all they didn't know about her, what they wanted to know. How she would stay in the room with them after her body had left it. But there was so little to leave behind, really. A man who disappeared. A child who never was. Nothing of herself.

"I'm sorry," Lauren was saying. "I'm so sorry."

Six years ago, six and a half. She had made nothing, shared nothing, given nothing. The only power she'd ever wielded was in what she had withheld.

She was in his mother's arms. Someday she would tell her. She would be the mother you could tell these things to. Everything she never said would then be put to use.

MIRELA

Dad was upset. At breakfast he kept saying, "Well, he finally did it," again and again. Mr. O'Toole, the neighbor who Dad hated, cut down the beech tree, the last tree left in the yard from back when the lots were still forest, no houses. Mr. O'Toole said it was on his property line—it was his as much as Dad's. The stump he left behind was cracked and mangled. When Mr. O'Toole killed the tree he must have been angry, as angry as Dad was now.

"Bastard did the same thing—"

"Pat, watch your language," Mom said.

"—he did the same thing with the last chestnut," Dad said, "on the other side of his property, on the line with the Stedmores. The very last chestnut tree for miles and miles. You know, a long time ago, Mirela, there were chestnut trees all over the place. Their flowers were white, and when they fell in the spring it was like a second snow. Now it's just the cottonwoods, with the cobwebby kind of snow. You know those? Anyway, that imbecile went ahead and cut down that chestnut one day, needled and needled Bill Stedmore about it day after day, week after week, and Bill held firm, and even still, one day O'Toole went and goddamn did it."

"Pat, come *on* with the *language*," Mom said.

"He just went and did it. And then I guess it was my turn with the beech."

Mirela told Dad that he should call the police on Mr. O'Toole. Mom and Dad laughed quietly like it was a funny secret.

"I *should* call the police, Mirela," Dad said, "but I want to go easy on the guy."

"You should call the police," Mirela said, "and then they'll send Mr. O'Toole to Colorado."

And then Dad was looking at Mom like the light from his eyes could explode her and Mom was talking in a high, pulling voice about how heavy the cottonwood snow had been this past year and Mirela started laughing like they had been just a moment before, making noise to fill the dizzy space that had opened up between them.

She doesn't remember much of Colorado anymore. Maybe she dreamed it. In the memory or the dream, they hold her down. The good thing about being held down was that it meant the day was close to finished—it was what they did when they were almost done with her. The last day of all was different because they started with holding her down. That was how she knew it would be a short day.

Now the beech was something that was destroyed and still lived. A beech needs a lot of space to grow, and maybe this one did not have enough space to die. The tree had ended, and then there were the beginnings of the same tree. Splinters and shards from the top of the stump had scattered, pushing outward into a crooked semicircle, like voles or stoats had begun stacking the fragments as cords of firewood. One corner of the stump was hollowed out like a cave, with crags of bark hanging down like stalactites and strung with lichens. Moss bloomed on the bark, and toadstools lined the entrances to a pair of rabbit warrens, dug in the soft earth. A teetering mushroom stalk shot up nearly to Mirela's knee. A half-dozen green vertical shoots grew even taller, fanned with wide green leaves. These were the root suckers, like baby versions of the tree, copies, made out of a knot of tissue from the base of what had been the tree. You could almost kill the tree—basically kill it—and it would start itself over from almost nothing. You didn't need a seed or a flower.

. . .

IT WAS DAD who explained all of these things to her. His company was clearing some woods near Klein Road to build new houses, and some mornings, Mirela drove with him to the site in the red pickup truck. If they got up before anyone else in the house, arrived at the site by sunrise, they could usually see deer. Where their house is now used to be woods, too. You can tell which trees are the oldest because they are taller than the rest, and their branches start higher up, because they had to compete with so many other trees for space, reaching toward the sunlight and rain.

Dad knows all the names of the trees and plants and flowers and tells them to Mirela. She only has to hear each name twice, maybe three times, and then she remembers it always. You can learn all the trees, and you can also look at a leaf on its own, and then look up around you, and you'll know which tree the leaf belongs to, because this one has round, heart-shaped leaves, or that one has slender leaves edged with little spikes, like teeth.

She likes kneeling in the soil in the morning, when it's still dewy and her knees go cold. From the ground beneath the eastern white pine, Mirela gathers the pine cones and brings them home and glues them to construction paper, and she decorates them with paint and glitter. She gathers chestnuts and paints faces on them: smiling, sad, mad. Hickory trees have catkins, long droopy green flowers that look like caterpillars, and she brings those home, too. Same with the twigs of the eastern hemlock, which sprout blades of grass and look like tiny, doll-sized fans. They go in the big shoebox, the one that Mom's winter boots came in, with the caterpillars and the pine cones.

Mirela wanted the red buds from the dogwood, but none had fallen yet. You can't just take what you want off a tree—the tree has to decide to shed it first. The female cottonwood trees first make red flowers, like a dogwood, and then seeds with a cotton covering. She didn't mind the cobwebs of cotton that blew around in May and June—Mom and Dad didn't like how the cotton clogs the drains and gets in between the bricks on the patio. Mirela uses handfuls of cotton to keep her caterpillars cozy at night.

If you climb a tree, it will move with you—it shifts with your weight. If you slip on a tree, the branch will suddenly feel wider and denser than before; it will seem to sprout little knots and ridges, giving you more traction. It breathes with you and makes up for your mistakes. Your arms and legs start to feel a little harder, thicker, like you're becoming a part of it. Sometimes she scrapes her hands and arms on the bark of trees, but it doesn't hurt. The bark scrapes off like skin, and she doesn't think it hurts the tree, either.

You can call a tree all different things. A canoe birch is also called a paper birch and a white birch. You can also call a tree by its scientific name, which is in Latin, a language for trees and animals. She could say the names as many times as she wanted, as loud as she wanted, and usually Dad didn't mind. The American beech is *Fagus grandifolia*. The American chestnut is *Castanea dentata*. The eastern hemlock is *Tsuga canadensis*. The eastern cottonwood is *Populus deltoides*. Nobody else in her family knew Latin. No one can take it from her or tell her she's doing it wrong.

WHEN SHE WAS first learning her Latin tree names, PJ and Sean teased her about being a vampire from Transylvania. The names sounded to them like a curse in the Dracula movie they had on tape. There was a big orphanage in Transylvania, in Sighet, but that wasn't where she came from—hers was Cighid, in Ghiorac, near the Hungarian border. Not Transylvania. She could prove it because she had it all on a map. And then there was another orphanage in Siret, in the northwest. Cighid, Sighet, Siret—in the ear of a silly American boy who had never been anywhere in the world, who never knew another language, maybe it all sounded the same. PJ and Sean had never even been to Colorado, and that's in the same country. Mom sent away for the maps of Romania.

Mirela learned the maps and tried to show them to PJ and Sean. "Cighid, not Sighet!" she said, but they didn't know what she was talking about.

The bitternut hickory is *Carya cordiformis*. Bitternut gets its name because it produces nuts that nobody will eat, not even a starving squirrel.

Once, when they were looking at the maps together, Mom asked if she wanted to go back to Romania. A tantrum came over her because she thought Mom wanted to send her back to Cighid. And then Mom said she only meant to visit, but the only place they'd ever visited was Colorado, and she didn't want to go back there, either. Finally she understood that Mom was asking if she wanted to go to Romania just for a few days—not now, and not to stay. She was still angry at Mom because she should have known how to ask this question right. When she was little, she had to look for words in two languages. Mom never had to do that, and so she doesn't think as carefully as Mirela does about the right way to say things.

Mom didn't want her to watch PJ and Sean's Dracula movie because it was too grown-up, which didn't make sense because PJ and Sean weren't grown-up back then. They liked the bloody scenes and hated the kissing scenes, although some of the bloodiest scenes had kissing. Mirela did see a few minutes of the movie here and there. In one scene, hands in black gloves move over the fur of a white wolf. The thick white fur and the soft dark leather filled the whole screen, and a warm, deep cello played. She could feel herself going inside the fur, becoming another person, a movie-person. This other person could fall asleep in the dog's fur, curl up inside a finger of the gloves, the cello making the sound that the gloves felt like, and no one could see her—she couldn't see herself.

She asked Mom for a dog that looked like a white wolf, like in the movie. Mom asked if she wanted to do research on dogs first, like the research she does with the weather and the trees and the maps of Romania. She does want to visit Romania someday, but she needs to learn everything about it before she goes. She remembers some words: *elefante, girafa, tigru, urs.* In Romania there is only *urs.* Not the *tigru*—the lynx. The chamois, which is a cross between a goat and an antelope. And lots of wolves, like in the Dracula movie. The movie did get that right. When a grown-up mother wolf goes out to find food and comes back with a full belly, the baby wolves stick their snouts inside her mouth, trying to make her throw up into them. The wolves live in the Carpathians, the mountains where Dracula built his castle. She wishes she was from there but she's not.

Lauren, PJ, and Sean are all from Buffalo, born at Children's Hospital. There's a picture of them in a fancy carved frame hanging in the den, of the last summer before Mirela came. They're standing on green grass beneath a big blue sky, arms locked together, smiling into the sun. Long tan legs. They didn't know anyone named Mirela. There are no pictures of her before age three. She watched herself mirrored in the glass, there beside her family.

IT'S HARD TO fall asleep at night because you're waiting in the darkness until you fall inside it, and you don't know what will happen to you in there. Mirela rocks at night to tire herself out, so she can forget what she's waiting for. She sits up cross-legged, wraps her arms around herself, and goes forward and back, forward and back. The bedsprings squeak and the bed moves around on the floor. She bumps her head against the headboard—not enough to hurt herself, no matter what Mom thinks. It crowds out the thoughts, the turning in her head, nothing else coming in, no memories no pictures no shapes no shadows no-Mirela in the room alone *thump thump thump* no room for anything but *thump thump thump.*

One morning at breakfast PJ said something bad about the sound of the rocking of the bed, something very grown-up, and Sean gasped and Mom went scary-quiet, and Dad raised his hand and Mom jumped up and caught Dad's arm and PJ ran away, upstairs to his room. Then Dad threw his fork across the kitchen and it clanged against the dishwasher and he walked outside to his truck and Mirela went under the table. Ears ringing, room spinning, everything going fast fast fast too fast like she would break apart, and she wrapped her arms around her head to keep from flying off the floor. She rocked and hummed. She recited her tree names and the trees surrounded her. The alphabet letters in the names circled around her and she was safe inside them. The butternut tree is *Juglans cinereal*. The eastern white pine is *Pinus strobus*. The sweet birch is *Betula lenta*. Its caterpillar catkins are yellow, not green.

Everyone was gone except Mom, under the table with Mirela, not touching her, just there.

"I remember someone hit me," she told Mom.

"Who?" Mom asked. "Who hit you, my love?"

"I don't know. I can't remember."

Mom's voice was wobbly. "I'm sorry, Mirela. No one should hit anyone. No one will ever hit you."

"Dad was going to hit PJ."

"That was wrong. Dad should not have acted like that. Dad has never hit anyone in his life, and he never will."

"Why did Dad want to hit PJ?"

"He didn't want to—something came over him."

"Why did something come over him?"

"PJ said bad words. It was mean, and PJ shouldn't have said it. It made Dad angry. But it was no reason for Dad to act like that. Hitting is always wrong. Even *wanting* to hit is wrong."

"I hit you."

"No—you used to. You don't anymore."

"Sometimes I want to hit you."

"I know. Something comes over you, like it came over Dad. But you fight it. You fight it and it makes you stronger until you're so strong that you don't ever feel that way anymore."

What did Mom know? How could she say that she knew? She wasn't inside.

"Can I give you a hug, Mirela?" Mom asks, and she knows she's always supposed to say yes.

And then she says, "Are you ready to look at Mommy, Mirela?"

IT WAS LATE October. Mom and Mirela were going to the Saint Mary's playground to meet Mom's friend and her new baby. Lauren was home from college even though she wasn't supposed to be.

"Can I come, too?" Lauren asked. She wasn't really asking. When Mom and Mirela came into the garage, Lauren was already curled up in the front passenger seat of the Jeep, knees drawn to her chest.

Mom asked Lauren how she was feeling, and Lauren didn't answer. She was pretending to be sad and lonely. She'd been following Mom around all afternoon like she was on a leash.

"Stop stop stop stop *don't be mean*," Mirela murmured to herself as Mom was backing the car out of the garage.

"Whatever it is, Mirela, stop beating yourself up about it," Mom said, smiling at Mirela in the rearview. Like she could let herself inside Mirela's head when she felt like it, poke around at her stuff, act like she knew where everything went.

"No, *you* stop!" Mirela screamed, kicking the back of Mom's seat, and Mom halted the car in the driveway and folded her hands in her lap and counted aloud to ten, and Lauren turned in her seat away from Mom.

"It's okay to get mad sometimes, Mirela," Lauren said quietly.

Lauren was being fake—she was annoyed with Mirela, but she was fighting how she felt, pretending to be understanding. Mirela fought how she felt all the time, so maybe Lauren thought Mirela was fake, too. The one who didn't fight was Dad. Dad felt how he seemed.

They got to Saint Mary's as the sun was getting low in the sky. Mom's friend was taking her baby out of a bucket swing. Mom's voice went all high-pitched as she hugged her friend and asked to hold the baby. "Elise, she's *gorgeous*!" Mom said. Lauren smiled at the baby and held her tiny foot in its pink sock.

"Hello, Mirela, it's nice to meet you," Mom's friend said.

"Yes, thank you," Mirela said.

"Ah, she wants your necklace." Mom's friend laughed as the baby pawed at Mom's collarbone. But they didn't really know what the baby wanted. Babies can't say. Lauren held the baby while Mom and her friend stood around talking about what time the baby goes to bed and how the baby was learning to use a spoon. Mirela was angry because Mom was pretending to care about someone else's baby—being fake, with her hooting laugh. When Mirela was a baby, no one ever showed her off to their friends, no one ever thought about her like they were thinking about this baby—it was like she was never a baby at all. None of it was fair.

She closed her eyes and breathed in through her nose and out through her mouth like Dr. Delia showed her. From inside she asked to hold the baby, because that was fair. She wasn't sure if they could hear her, but they did. She opened her eyes, and Mom and her friend were looking at her.

"Would that be okay, Elise?" Mom asked her friend, who nodded. The nod was a lie. It wasn't okay with her. Mom's friend was fighting how she felt. And Mom was anxious about it, too. Mirela smiled to reassure them, and also because she was glad they were anxious—they were wrong to feel the way they did, so it was right for them to be uncomfortable. It was fair. Mom asked Mirela to sit down on a bench, and then Lauren carefully laid the baby down on her lap, the back of the baby's head nestled in the crook of Mirela's arm. She concentrated. She smoothed the baby's romper, which had pink and white checks. She adjusted the brim of the baby's hat to make sure her face was in shadow. She nudged one finger under the strap of the hat to check that it wasn't too snug beneath the baby's chin.

The baby had big brown eyes and shiny black hair. If she had ever been a baby, she would have looked like this.

She held the baby and they looked at each other's eyes and it didn't hurt. She didn't want to look away. She did look away to check on Mom's friend. Her eyes were wide and her body was stiff. Mirela noticed this and she felt the twin pinpricks, the heat of the anger and the satisfaction at the same time—to know how others see her. She looked back into the baby's eyes. Her thumb was in the baby's hand. The baby furrowed her brow, pursed her lips in an interested way. She cooed and the sound curled up at the end. The baby was thinking hard about Mirela. Lauren and Mom and Mom's friend faded, and now it was just Mirela and the baby, a robin peeping in the distance, a breeze petting the grass and tickling the hair on the back of Mirela's neck and making the baby blink. She took the baby into her quiet place. They were alone in there. Like inside a tree. Or Mirela was the tree moving with the baby, shifting under her weight. She lifted the baby closer so she could smell her, pressing her nose to her neck. Honey and almonds. The baby smiled and kicked her legs. She reached up to touch Mirela's face. Her fingers pressing on her cheek, her lips.

Alphabet letters circle around her, linking together. She is not afraid. She closes her eyes. She breathes in the baby and she hears the words.

You are safe from me.
I am safe from me.
The baby is me.

ACKNOWLEDGMENTS

In researching this book, I drew upon sources including Eyal Press's *Absolute Convictions: My Father, a City, and the Conflict that Divided America*; Izidor Ruckel's *Abandoned for Life*; Rachael Stryker's *The Road to Evergreen: Adoption, Attachment Therapy, and the Promise of Family*; the work of the Bucharest Early Intervention Project; and episode 521 of *This American Life*, "Bad Baby." *All My Sons* was written by Arthur Miller and first performed at the Coronet Theatre in New York City in 1947. *Grease* was written by Jim Jacobs and Warren Casey and first performed at Kingston Mines in Chicago in 1971. The quotations by D.W. Winnicott are taken from *The Child, the Family, and the Outside World*, published in 1964. The strange situation was devised and described by Mary Ainsworth in 1970. The photograph that Lauren sees on television is "Untitled (Buffalo)" (1988–89), by David Wojnarowicz.

Thanks to Sarah Stein, Alicia Tan, Claudia Ballard, and Jessie Chasan-Taber for their faith in this project; Jynne Dilling and Louie Saletan for providing me with a place to write in the woods; Andrea Lynch, who helped me to broaden and deepen my own ideas about reproductive justice in conversations that spanned twenty years; Oana Marian for her translation work; Julia Turner and David Remnick for their encouragement and patience.

I am grateful to all of those who read this manuscript—in sections or in full, and in wildly varying stages of its progress—for their candor and expertise: Rumaan Alam, Thayer Anderson,

Katherine Bonson, Callie Collins, Cris Cruz, Jesse Dorris, Liz Maynes-Aminzade, Siobhan Phillips, Darby Saxbe, Clare Sestanovich, and Katy Waldman. Ed Park made an exceedingly crucial suggestion for improving the book, and I owe him a great debt. I am likewise indebted to Carrie Frye, the most creative, thoughtful, and lucid reader a writer could ask for. Whatever may be worthwhile in this text, it is most likely due to Carrie.

This book is dedicated to the memories of two physicians who served the women and children of Western New York, Dr. Barnett A. Slepian (1946–1998) and Dr. Robert J. Patterson (1923–2016).

ABOUT THE AUTHOR

JESSICA WINTER is an editor at *The New Yorker* and the author of the novel *Break in Case of Emergency*. Her writing has appeared in *The New York Times*, *Slate*, *Bookforum*, and other publications. She lives in Flatbush, Brooklyn, with her family.